LEGACY

—

DAWN

by Rukis

Legacy — Dawn

Production copyright FurPlanet Productions © 2016

Published by FurPlanet Productions
Dallas, Texas
www.FurPlanet.com

Softcover ISBN 978-1-61450-307-1
Hardcover ISBN 978-1-61450-322-4
eBook ISBN 978-1-61450-321-7

Printed in the United States of America
First Edition Trade Paperback 2016

Table of Contents

Chapter 1

Staking a Claim

I was born in a small village near the Hyronses river, to a family of laborers working in the brick kilns. My family, as many generations back as the walls of my home and the scrawlings of previous dead relatives could trace back, have always been laborers on the clay flats, working the brick kilns. We have little choice. There is no elevation from the labor caste. If you are born a laborer, and you live long enough to have children of your own, they too will be laborers. That's simply how it is. How it has always been. How it will always be.

At least, that's what I was raised to believe.

I am not ashamed of my birth or my upbringing, or even what was to be my profession in life. My father used to tell me—and I'll never forget—working hard for a living is nothing to be ashamed of. Working the kilns is taxing, endless toiling, but it is respectable. Some days it was harder to swallow his words, to understand what he was trying to tell me. The hardest day's work may still not yield enough pay to fill your belly at the end of the night, and hunger turns your stomach bitter. That bitterness inevitably spreads, and some days it's hard not to let it take hold. Look to the people who were born better than us, and want what they had.

During those times, my father would simply take me to the square, to the posts the Hyenas had dug into the center of town. I remember the smell of the dead and dying to this day. It's a smell so primal, it sticks on the inside of your nose for the rest of your life. The luckiest souls who stood against their betters were simply beheaded and strung up. The most unfortunate, those who had truly earned the Hyena clans' ire, were strapped to the posts alive, to starve and cook in the sun.

My father would show me, and remind me of the futility in wanting more. I didn't think he was a coward for curtailing my hopes. Not then, not even now. It wasn't that he was afraid, he just knew the reality of our world far better than I did at the time.

The Caste System reduces us to grains of sand on the dunes, knowing no matter how much we strive to shift our place, what lies beyond is only another dune. Some who are lucky may stumble upon an oasis, but even there, we are still grains of sand. We can stare in wonder and tremble at the sight of the sparkling waters, but we cannot dip our heads to drink. But that is a sense of humility much of the rest of the world lacks, so in a way, it creates stronger people at the bottom.

Some cannot ever come to appreciate the life of a laborer for what it is. It is a hopeless life, but it is a noble one. The merchant who grows fat on the meager pay of starving families, the crime lord who builds her power upon the backs of slaves… those are shameful lives. An honest day's work may yield little reward in material comforts, but it leaves the spirit free and the mind aware of its own worth. I don't feel regret, as some of my caste might, for the life I was born into. If it was something I had done to myself, perhaps. But none of us can in any way affect the circumstances we're born into. I am a proud man, and I know I have good reason to be. I live without doubt that I have earned the right to wake and breathe every day. I am alive because I have worked for it.

Hauling and baking clay into bricks is the sort of labor only reserved for the most durable. Not many jackals choose the profession. What labor we pursue in our lives is one of the few choices we have, and there is other, less grueling work close to the Hyronses. Plenty of it. More than once I or my family members were mocked on the flats by the larger, more stocky sorts of creatures who are better suited to the work. Boar and big cats are the favorites of flat-owners.

But my family was strong, and they taught me to be strong. To value food, and the health of my body, over all else. To grow as large and as powerful as I could, and prove that our kind can be just as strong as any lion or boar. Our bodies were our tools, and like any other tradesman, I worked best if I kept mine honed.

I grew tall and hard as I worked my way through childhood. I knew schooling was a distant dream, and earnestly, I'd never had any desire for it. Some laborers have struggled to learn the written word, or how to manage numbers like the merchants do, but my father had never seen the point in my aspiring towards something so far removed from my everyday life, and because he didn't, I also never saw the value in education. I suppose most laborers don't.

Knowing what I know now, I believe this is a mindset the upper castes wish to maintain. Just another time-honored tradition that keeps us perpetually at their feet.

But I don't know why I'm talking about that now. That's what my father used to refer to as 'big thinking', and it wasn't for us. Regardless of what I eventually began to believe in my later years, when I was young I was actually very satisfied to be who I was. I accompanied my father to the flats on my sixth birthday, as soon as I was old enough to haul the cooked bricks near the ovens. I watched my father carry the clay drums from the flats over his broad shoulders, and I thought he looked like how a god must be. He and my mother worked like they were one, her digging, him hauling, and then I carried the bricks. Work made me feel like a true part of my family. When I ate at night, I was proud, because now I was earning it. And I think my parents were proud of me, as well. They never told me so, but that's just how they were. Reserved, as laborers should be.

There is one caste beneath us. One. The owned. The non-persons. The indentured. As a child, I would rarely see them. They are generally kept on plantations, or in estates in the cities. But as I grew older and I began to venture to the nearest city with my parents whenever we needed to trade, I would catch sight of one every now and then. I would always know them, and not just because of the glinting metal collars.

It was something about their eyes. I'd seen bodies before. People died working at the kilns, and hauling clay. We lost at least one soul a season, and often times it would be one a shift. There weren't many disastrous ways to die making bricks—save being kicked by a mule—so it was usually the heat. The elderly, sickly, or sometimes just the youngest workers were always at risk. We'd find someone we'd known, sunken into the clay fields or slumped near the baking bricks.

The indentured servants I saw when I went to the cities had the same eyes as the dead. Glassy, cold and lifeless. I'd asked my mother once whether or not they were truly alive at all, and she'd told me the indentured life was not life. It was a nightmare those people were having while they waited to die. To a child, you have to understand, that statement sounds like a riddle. Or poetry. Neither of which I was well-acquainted with.

I hadn't realized she meant it literally.

For the tenth time this hour, I work the now-chafed, cracking paw pad on my right index finger beneath the newly-adjusted snug fit of my collar. The guard reminds me again that my discomfort was entirely of my own doing, saying so in a paternal tone this time, as though he's honestly concerned for my well-being. It doesn't make the statement any less disgusting to me.

"Nothing in my contract said I had to work on a broken ankle," I snarl, curling my lip back against dirty teeth. They haven't let me have any kind of meat in weeks, let alone bones to clean my teeth on. I've lost more weight in this stretch than I ever have before in my life and I know my strength is beginning to fade.

But not so much that I couldn't take the brown, striped hyena escorting me, if I had the chance at it, I tell myself. If he weren't armed. And I wasn't in manacles, with a freshly-adjusted metal collar singeing the side of my neck where the hinge is still hot with solder. Apparently one of the favored punishments for people like me is to adjust our collars past the point of comfortably resting on our collarbones, to digging into our fur. In time, it will create a permanent part in my fur that will remain even when I work the collar around. A constant reminder, the blacksmith told me. For servants who need to be reminded.

It doesn't matter. The fact is, I'm not going to try to take the man down. For various reasons. But the most important reason is that attempting to kill a plantation guard was the reason for the aforementioned broken ankle. The bitch was good with a man-catcher, unfortunately.

He doesn't hesitate to bring that up. "Your contract requires that you *work*," the hyena sniffs, "you can't very well do that if you're on the run. We're legally obliged by our employers to keep you sedate and dutifully paying off your debt. By any means. Any injuries you sustain during an escape attempt are your cross to bear during the workday. The harvest doesn't stop just because you went and got yourself damaged."

I'm snarling again, so I make sure he sees it. He looks less than impressed. This time they gave me one of the seniors, an older hyena who's greying along his muzzle and heavier-set than most of the younger, leaner guards I've dealt with in the past. I don't recognize him from around the plantation, so he must work specifically here in this prison. The fact that he's well-fed likely means he's strong, and he hasn't made a single mistake since he came to get me out of my cell. Nothing I could take advantage of. He's kept a lazy but constant gaze on me the whole while, he keeps me in front of him when we walk, and he's got my manacles on a short lead. The woman they had on me last time was less experienced and I got that chain around her neck for a few seconds before some of her peers heard her screaming and got to us.

"Besides," the man chuckles, "what do you honestly know about your contract? You can't read it. It could say you have to fuck cattle for your betters' amusement. You don't know."

"They have to read it to us," I mutter, because both he and I know how pointless that statement is. It's more just a mantra we tell ourselves, because it's comforting. And I must be delirious if I'm believing it now.

"Right," the man snorts, "as if you'd even listen if I did." He pulls me to a stop at the end of the dusty corridor we're walking. I don't recognize the hallway, haven't recognized this place since they put me in it what felt like weeks ago. I'm realizing now as we walk it that it's not as large as I'd assumed it was. I'd thought for certain I was locked away in the Yari Hyronses Prison, a sort of warehouse I'd always known about growing up, but never seen. It's a notorious dumping ground for unwanted persons, where the majority of 'unmanageable' servants ended up. I would have been content to rot away there in my cell for what remained of my life, rather than return to the fields.

But now that I think about it, the small cell I'd been kept in while I'd been starved, fed stale bread and stagnant water and, (almost against my own wishes) had begun to recover from my ankle wound, was far too quiet to be in any part of that crowded hell-hole. I would have had to share it with someone, I doubt they would have fed an ailing man anything whatsoever, and I distinctly smell pollen drifting through the air. In fact, I can see it, filtered through the dim light that penetrates the small building I'm in, dancing specks in sunlight. It's unfamiliar pollen, too. Nothing like the meager flowers that managed to grow on the sandy banks of the Hyronses. This is thicker, richer, more potent.

I'm not in the desert anymore. This smells like the country. Somewhere with monsoon weather. Now that I'm paying attention, I can even tell the air's more humid.

The hyena must see me dragging the new scents through my nose, because he gives a smirk. "You don't even know where you are, do you?" he echoes my thoughts.

I give him no reply, but then, he doesn't need one. "It's on your contract," he says. "Although an unruly son-of-a-bitch such as yourself probably doesn't give a damn what that thing says, do you? Afraid you'll find out how much your miserable ass is actually worth?"

I don't want to confirm his statement, and I definitely don't have the energy to fight it, especially when it feels so true. So I continue to say nothing. He seems plenty fond of talking on his own.

"You're in Charic Pradesh," he says, and now I'm catching the subtleties in his accent. The deep, throaty way he emphasizes the 'Hah' in 'Charic'.

My eyes widen marginally. "Near the sea?"

"Ocean," he corrects me. "The Somanta is no mere 'sea'. You're in Tavesi, boy. Came quite a long way."

"How—when?" I stammer. I don't remember any of this. After

13

the incident with my last escape attempt and the injury from the man-catcher, I'd remembered little other than refusing to work, getting beat into unconsciousness, then going to sleep slumped in a shed at the plantation I was working on, and then...

I had woken up in that room. There'd been feverish dreams, but I thought those had been brought on by the wound and the starvation.

"You were sold," he states simply, then grins. One of his canines is missing. "Or rather, given away. Our Matron shares relation with the Sura, the clan that owned you last. She is a pragmatic woman," he says with an air of earnest respect, or else he fakes it well. "Not too proud to take unwanted refuse, if it comes free or at a bargain. Here near the ports, strong servants are at a premium. The merchants are well aware they can simply ship them to the Shanivaar for better rates than compete and undercut their worth."

He hefts me by my bicep, tugging me along towards the door, but still irritatingly vigilant about keeping me in *front* of him. He has experience. Unlike the guards at the last plantation, and the one before that.

"Most of the workers here had their contracts bought from the interior. Desert refuse. Like you," he says in a remarkably jovial tone. "So you'll be amongst the dirt you're accustomed to."

"Why can't I remember the trip?" I demand. It's the one question he hasn't answered on his own, and the question that haunts me the most. I've never before had so much time in my life simply slip away like this. I've been drunk, I've lost track of a night, I've had days of work blend together. But nothing like this. It honestly frightens me.

And not much does that anymore.

He's silent as he pulls out his keys, reaches past me and begins turning them in the lock. Sunlight streams in from outside and that pungent scent has grown stronger. I'm fairly certain he's not going to answer me at all, but then he does, and his hesitant, uncertain tone tells me something I didn't expect. It's not that he doesn't want to tell me. He honestly might not know.

"My guess would be they smeared Divine in your wounds," he says, and there's a heavy creak of metal as the lock slides free inside the door. Metal locks. This place would have been nigh on impossible to break out of, if I'd tried. It was remarkably secure for such a small building.

"'Divine'?" I parrot. I know the word, but not in the context.

"The extract from the flowers we grow here," he states. "You'll learn all about it soon enough."

"Wait—you mean the drug the holy men smoke?" I demand. "They *poisoned* me!"

"Market value for that poison is higher than gold, by weight," he snuffs. "'Course whatever they gave you was probably old, weak product. But still," he gives a feral smile down at me, as he pushes the door open and piercing light streams in, "did the trick, didn't it?"

I'm blinded by my first glimpse of sunlight in weeks. It bores into me, staggers me back. The dampness that's sunk into my fur in the small, dank cell seems to be lifting from me already, my skin prickles with warmth beneath, and slowly my pupils constrict, taking in the sight before me.

I knew there would be flowers. I didn't think that was *all* there would be. But it is. It's all I can see for what seems like miles.

A tapestry of red and green in patches. Poppy fields, as far as I can see, save a few long buildings half-obscured by a dip in the terrain in the distance. Dusty dirt roads thread between the fields and speckled amongst the mostly green patches I can see the hunched figures of plantation workers, doing I know not what.

Poppy fields are illegal near the Hyronses. For centuries, rival clans fought and spilled blood over the scarce few patches of good land to grow the flowers on, until the increase in trade from Tavesi, the large delta to the southwest where the growing season was longer and water was more plentiful, made scratching out a living from farming in the desert a pointless venture. The most prominent clans of the Hyronses made production farms like this illegal to assure that whatever land they had available that could be irrigated was used to grow food, not drug.

That doesn't mean I've never seen a field before, though. People still grew the flowers illegally, just not on this… scale.

"This *is* Tavesi," I say quietly, more to myself than the hyena.

My head rocks back as the hyena slaps me hard in the back of my skull. "Were you not listening, boy?" He chuckles gruffly, then shoves me hard enough that my weakened legs nearly give out. "You're in Matron Sura's fields, now. But that's of no matter to you. All that you need to know, all that should fill your dense little head now, is me."

I don't bother to look back at him and show my teeth, much as I'm tempted. I'm too tired, too thirsty, too hurting to be disobedient for the sheer sake of it, right now. We begin to walk and he continues to talk at my back.

"I'm your entire world now, dust dog. Me and these fields," he gestures. "You do as I say, you work like I tell you to work, you'll do fine here. I know you got one over on a few of your previous employers, but let's be clear right at the start," he shoves me again, but this time it isn't idle, this time it's straight in the small of my back, with enough force to make my vision go white for a second or so. I know I'm going to fall, but I grit my teeth and ensure at least that I don't fall face-down. My knees strike the dirt hard, pain courses through my bones at the joint, and I'm nauseated for a few moments, but I'm not fully down, and that's what matters.

"That's not going to happen with me," he declares, stone-faced. "Not a soul on my watch acts up without consequences." His claws scrape in the dirt as he paces around in front of me, gray-blue eyes staring down imperiously. I stare right back. I may be tired, but this man won't see me prostrate myself before him. He'll have to take every inch by force.

I've been through this before, many times now. He wants me to know he has the power here. I want him to know that he'll have to earn it. I'm a proud man, but even I'm not so arrogant as to say I haven't been beaten down before. No man is impossible to conquer when you've got weapons, money and strength of numbers to keep him subdued.

That doesn't mean I'll make it easy on him.

"Keep on top of me, then," I warn, forcing a rough laugh through my teeth. "I'm told I'm troublesome."

He grins, that one missing canine a black hole in his smile. "Oh, you're not my type, boy. I prefer my meat lean," he gestures to the road a ways down, where out of the corner of my eye I think I see a lion, escorting a ragged bunch that have to be other workers. "But Vikram there, he'll take just about any mongrel he can get bent. He doesn't mind the thicker boys."

I've been through this before, too. The guards always let you know who you can fuck for extra privileges, or food. My pride won't allow it, of course. Or maybe I've just never been that desperate.

"That's alright," I snort, "I'd rather die than let a hyena fuck me."

Finally, I get a reaction from the man that isn't mirth. His muzzle twists down into a frown, and he reaches down to grab me by my collar, yanking me to my feet. I stumble as I find my bearing again, and briefly note that he had me off the ground for a moment. That's no mean feat, considering I'm at least six inches taller than him.

"Aardwolf," he snaps. "*Not* a hyena. And if I ever hear you call me one again, I'll put solder in your eyes. We understood?"

I mentally note his intensely antagonistic reaction to the common misconception, but only nod mutely for now. Could mean something, could mean he's just tired of people mistaking his species. Either way it's interesting.

He shoves me again, something he's clearly fond of. The man's strong, there's no mistaking that. This time I manage not to fall, and we begin walking again. It looks like we're heading towards the long rows of shanty buildings in the distance. Servant lodging, I can only imagine. Servants are the only people who'd willingly live in hovels like that.

"What's your name, boy?" the man I now know is an Aardwolf asks.

"Why do you care?" I mutter.

"I like to put a name to my daily frustrations," he quips back, and just like that, the jovial tone is back.

"Kadar," I say, finally.

"Lochan," the man replies in return. "But to you, Master Lochan. Or just Master."

"Or we can simply never speak again," I offer.

He laughs. "See? You're understanding. Listen. That's all you need to do, so long as you're here. Listen, and obey, and pay off your contract debts."

"What's the boarding cost here?" I ask idly. As though it matters.

"What do you care?" Lochan chuckles. "You can't manage numbers, can you?"

I'm silent.

"None of you can," he says. "The clan will handle your day-to-day expenses and deduct them from your total earned each day. Your debt is paid when we tell you it's paid. Now move your legs," he kicks at them. "We need to get you cleaned off. You smell like death."

The lodging for the servants is exactly what I expected it to be, and exactly what every other lodging house has been like at all of my previous plantations. When I arrive, the houses are already filling with people coming in from the fields. The few straw mats in each building are at a premium, and men are claiming their ground when we arrive, but I have to be taken to the baths first. I watch a painted dog shoving a boar away from one of the last sleeping mats as we pass, knowing with a yearning in the pit of my stomach that by the time we return, all that will remain are bare patches of earth to sleep on. I've been sleeping on the dirt floor of the small prison cell I was being kept in for weeks now. My body aches from the cold that seeps up through the ground when the night falls. I'd give anything for one of those straw mats.

Eyes follow me as I'm led towards the baths, sizing me up. I see quite a few men here that are larger, and most definitely stronger than I am at the moment. In my prime I might not have worried so much, but there are at least four lions, a pair of warthogs that look related and have some significant bulk to them, and a cheetah who leans more towards my end of the spectrum. Tall, not as broad, but strong.

At the very least, I have nothing they want. Still, this is a bad way to start off my entrance to a new workers' circle. Malnourished, sickly and still nursing a slight limp. My fur stands on end, but I resist showing my fangs, for now. No need to antagonize until it becomes necessary.

I know I'll have to make a reputation for myself, and fast. Make it clear I'm not worth the trouble for most of them to mess with. Even injured and exhausted, I can manage that, I tell myself.

The bath is little more than three cold buckets of water poured over my body, and camel fat soap to rinse the filth out of my fur. Lochan clearly doesn't want to waste much time doing this, because he hurries me through it with an air of indifference. The icy water, pulled up from their well I'm certain, saps what little remaining strength I had in my body straight out of me, and the cloying cold sinks into my bones. I try to shake as much of it as I can from my fur, but the light is dying fast, and I know I'll still be wet when I try to sleep. What's more, Lochan takes my tattered clothing and returns with only a long loin cloth.

When I examine the meager scrap of clothing, he merely shrugs. "If you want a dhoti or a sarong, you'll have to buy one from your earnings. Be thankful we've given you anything at all."

"I'm going to freeze in this, tonight," I point out, my ears flattened to my skull.

There's that grin again. "Make a friend?" he offers.

My intention, actually, is to do quite the opposite. He escorts me back to one of the sleeping lodges, thrusts me through the door and points me towards an older Dhole, the only woman I've seen since I came here. A gruff, "Eat," is the last command I get from the Aardwolf before he heads off.

My fur is still sticky with water and some unrinsed soap, but the promise of food is strong. I head towards the elderly, stooped woman, collared like the rest of us. Normally women don't work on plantations, female servants are more desirable as house workers and, of course, in the sex trade. But this woman is too elderly to be of much use even in a house, and probably too unwanted even amongst forty head of male workers to be at physical risk. Or she simply doesn't have a choice.

I feel for her, of course. But mostly, I'm disappointed when I make my way to her, because all that remains on the tray she holds in her slightly shaking paws is stone-cooked flat bread. The same bread I've been eating for weeks now. I can smell cooked meat in the air, I know there must have been some available, but of course it's all gone now.

The woman barely regards me as I take a few portions of bread, except to say, "Just two." I take three, and she doesn't notice. She's probably half-blind.

The water in the bucket near the door that I collect in one of the chipped clay cups available is at least clean, unlike the water they were bringing me in that damned cell. It's as cold as the bath water, and probably from the same well, but I drink all of it and go back for a second cup without thinking, while forcing the bread down my throat. It's at least not stale here, and I have to eat.

I'm getting little more than a few curious stares, because most everyone is settled in for the night by now and no one wants to move and give up their purchase. Tomorrow, I'm sure, will come the testing. I need to somehow rest my body tonight, so I can stand my ground then. But the chill in the air is already getting to me, and there isn't a straw mat available. In fact, several of the men here are already sleeping on the ground, suggesting this is a common problem.

I'm sure the house will still charge me as if I've been given a mat, though.

I finish the last piece of bread I took, swallowing dryly and taking another cup of water to wash it all down. It's not meat, but it's more food than I've had in one single helping in a long time, and it feels good to be so close to having a full stomach. I sweep the room with my eyes, finally taking a good long look at the men I'll be bunking with in the dimming light. Only one of the lions is in this building, but so is a tiger I didn't see before. And that painted dog. I dismiss the mere thought of targeting them outright. I can't run the risk of being seriously hurt again right now.

But I also can't shoot too low, or I'll be seen as a coward.

Stripes catch my eye, black against grayish white in the fading light. That could only be...

A hyena?

I Iere?

I size the man up. For the moment his back is to me, and he's either asleep or not perceptive enough to notice he's been targeted. A few of the men near him notice though, and a meerkat quickly scuffs his mat a good foot or so away from the hyena, clear of my path.

The hyena's ears flick, and I know by their distinct shape that my suspicions were correct. Definitely a striped hyena. He's tall, broad-shouldered and has a fairly strong frame on him. Possibly even as tall as me. But he's thin. Almost to the point of looking malnourished. And unlike me, he hasn't got much muscle to back it up. He looks almost... soft. Not like a worker. More like a house servant, or one of the clan hyenas themselves.

But he's got a collar, and he's here in the workhouse. So it's not his lucky day.

The corner of my muzzle twitches up as I make my way across the crowded room towards him. I'm not too embarrassed to admit that the thought of beating on a hyena has me a little thrilled. It's rare they get contracted out, let alone sold to their own kind. The clan heads might be unreachable up on high, but this one, he can't get away from me.

And I know no one here is going to help a hyena.

I pass the cheetah on my way, and I'm fairly certain he shakes his head at me, as if to warn me away. I ignore him, but then I hear a "Don't," from behind me, and when I turn to regard him, he shakes his head again.

He doesn't give me much reasoning to back up the warning, so I only pause a few moments. Maybe the hyena's a little tougher than he looks. Maybe he's got friends after all. I can't really be certain. But I'm fairly well committed to this now.

I am *not* spending another night in the dirt.

By the time I'm five feet or so away from him, his ears twist and he finally notices me, turning to regard me. So he wasn't asleep, after all.

I soon see what had him so occupied though, and it only fuels the fire in me more. He has a chopped shank of some kind of meat, and there's actually a decent amount of flesh left on it.

I drop to a crouch beside him and thrust my paw out, my voice coming out in a hoarse snarl. "Give it over," I demand, and hope the sick still stuck in my throat comes off sounding menacing, not weak.

"I—what?" he blinks up at me, dark eyes dropping to my paw in apparent confusion.

"The meat," I snap. And then for emphasis, because he mostly looks confused right now and I want to make myself clear, "*Now!*"

This is the part where you find out what kind of fight you really picked. It's a risk you run any time you try to take on a complete stranger in a strange work group, but I had to take the first step here and now, tonight. Now it's really only a question of how much he's willing to get hurt, and how much he can hurt me in return.

The rest of the house is silent. Doesn't seem like anyone's going to try and help him, after all.

Hyenas can be brutal. Even the lean ones. There's a reason they're at the top of the caste hierarchy, more often than not. Even lion prides lose ground to them in most clan wars. They're tough. Resilient. Enduring. And vicious.

I ready myself for a fight. It was enough when it was just the straw mat. But he has meat.

… and he's holding it out to me.

I blink down at the man. I thought, of course, there was a chance he would just give in. Albeit a very small one. But I expected at least in that case that he'd have the decency to look crestfallen. Belligerant. Something.

Instead, he simply looks resigned. Not even resigned and visibly upset. There's no fight in his eyes at all.

I snap the shank of meat away from his hand and wait a few

seconds, curious how far I can push this. Even more curious why I was warned away by one of the other workers. Clearly they know something I don't. I'm waiting to find out what that is.

But all he does is stare up at me. Now that his face is closer to mine, I can get a better look at him. He definitely lacks the muscle tone to be a plantation worker, or at least not employed for long. But he's also not unmarred. There are faint black lines beneath the fur along his muzzle that I recognize as old scars. Not from insects like on the battered lion's muzzle, the big male already asleep in the corner. Not from kiln embers, like the occasional dark marks on mine. Just scratches, and the occasional chip in his large ears. He's also got a few large holes in his ears that have to have been piercings at one time or another, and one remaining in his nose. It doesn't look valuable, or it would have been stolen long ago, I'm certain.

His fur is better kept than most of the men here, and he certainly smells a lot better than most of them. Which is saying something, because I've always personally loathed the scent of his kind.

I shove him by the shoulder and find I don't have to put much force into it to get him to give. But he doesn't seem to know what I want, so I clarify, "Your mat, too," I grunt, moving onto it on my knees and stabbing a finger past him. "Get off."

That, finally, seems to get a reaction out of him. His ears flatten and he stiffens up a little, clutching the sarong he has bunched at his waist. "But, I sleep here."

"Not tonight you don't," I snuff, shoving him again. I put more force into it this time and he catches himself on outstretched paws as he falls backwards. From there on out it's fairly easy to shove the rest of him off the mat with a kick or two, and soon he's skittering away.

I'm almost disappointed, honestly.

But I'm tired, I'm worn out, and even if the hyena wasn't much of a challenge, he was apparently enough of a risk around here to the

other men that they weren't willing to push him around. So if that got me some ground, so be it. All I care about right now is that it got me a place to sleep.

I chew on the bone for a while after easily picking off what remains of the meat. It's so damned satisfying to feel the scrape of bone against my teeth again, I almost don't notice the hyena making his way back towards my side, tentatively.

My eyes flick to him and I toss the bone his way, letting him know I still have my wits about me. It plunks into his shoulder and clatters to the hard, dirt floor, but all he does is flinch.

"You don't offend easy," I mutter.

"I'm sorry," he says in a quiet, subdued tone.

I arch an eyebrow at him, pushing myself up onto my elbows. I search his features for anything mocking, but the apology seems to have been earnest. I cast one more perplexed expression his way, and

25

he averts his eyes to the ground, unable to hold my gaze.

I sigh, leaning back down on my back and threading my fingers together behind my head. The room's begun to grow dark and there isn't much sound other than the occasional low murmuring in some other corner of the room, and the thrum of the night insects beginning their chorus.

It sounds so much different than in the Hyronses, and yet somehow, everything still feels the same. No matter where I go in the world, the work is the same. This life is the same.

I try not to think about it, for now. I need to sleep.

Shifting to the left of me catches my attention. I realize with a start that the hyena has wormed his way up near a corner of my mat, and he's resting his head on the edge of the straw, staring at me in the darkness. It's unnerving.

Maybe people avoid this man simply because he's strange.

I plant a foot on the top of his skull and shove, and he gets the point, backing away from the mat by at least a few inches. Still, he seems intent on sleeping close.

I really don't care, so I let him.

Chapter 2

Untouchable

I had my first real experience with hyenas when I was eight years old. I was injured for the first time working at the kilns. I'd been scraped and bruised many times prior, of course, but this was my first broken bone. I'd been carrying a load of clay that had turned out to be far more than I could handle, and I'd dropped the basket on my right foot. It wouldn't be the last time in my life I made the very same mistake, but it had certainly seemed far worse as a child than it had when I'd done it five years later.

When you were injured working at the kilns, one of two things happened. Well... three. If you died, your troubles were over.

Either you were asked to leave employment until you recovered—in which case of course, you were not paid for the time you couldn't work—or more rarely, the kiln owner would pay for you to see a healer. You still wouldn't be paid for the time you couldn't work, but at the very least you'd be back working again sooner and you wouldn't have to pay a healer yourself, which could cost a week's worth of wages for an entire family, depending on the injury.

Our kilns were rare in that they were owned and run by a man. Most everything owned by the Hyena clans was supervised by a female, whether it be a brothel or a brick kiln. But the man who owned our kilns had been married to a Clan Matron's sister, and she apparently felt it was beneath her to work at the site.

The man who owned our kiln was a spotted hyena, graying along the edge of his muzzle, but otherwise sporting his age well. He was a severe man and not shy about letting us know when we'd done something wrong or our production for the day was slower than expected. But my father insisted he was kinder than many foremen we'd find and that he would take care of us if something happened while we were working. That was a very big concern for the men in our family especially, since we doubled as mules throughout much of the work day.

I'd asked once why they didn't simply buy more mules. Apparently, actual mules were expensive. It was less expensive to pay us than to buy them, feed them, and care for them.

When I'd broken two of my toes, we'd counted on that help. My father assured me, while I sat there trying not to get sick from the pain, that the hyena would call a medicine man for me. That he had done so many times in the past for my father and my mother when they'd been injured. And then I would just have to rest and wait to come back to work.

But when the hyena finally showed, he'd only brought a man who worked for him at the kilns. The black-footed ferret at his side had given my foot a cursory once-over that involved squeezing my toes, and I'd nearly blacked out from the pain. When afterwards the ferret had declared the injury to be 'minor', which I contest to this day was an uneducated guess, the hyena had simply frowned down at me like he would have a cracked brick, and casually told my father I was to leave the kilns until I could walk again. When my father inquired where the medicine man was, the hyena had simply explained that the ferret *was* a medicine man, and that he'd said I could go home to heal, and if my father felt the need to bother him with the matter any longer that the rest of my family could leave as well.

I found out afterwards, when I was resting at home with a freshly-wrapped foot we'd had to pay an actual medicine man to treat, that the hyena's interest in his workers' well-being was primarily tied to how productive they were at the kiln. The man was shrewd, not charitable. And I was eight years old, so in his estimation, not worth the investment for an actual healer.

What bothered me about the whole incident wasn't even that we'd been screwed. It was that my father, the man I worshipped, the man I was proud of each and every single day, had accepted it without so much as one word of argument. He'd not even insulted the man or spoken one ill word about what he'd done when we were at home. Not even when we were forced to live on barley water for a week to pay for my treatment.

Eventually, it had gotten to me, and I'd done something I rarely did. I'd raised my voice to my father. I'd demanded to know why the hyena hadn't helped us, when my father had always told me he would. Wasn't he supposed to be a good man? Wasn't that why we chose to work for him? Why hadn't my dad *made* him do what he'd promised?

My father had backhanded me.

Looking back on it, it's still hard to think he was wrong. I couldn't understand at the time what kind of pressure my father was under. How thoroughly dependent we were on the steady work from the kilns. Losing my income for a short while, we could and did survive. If my father and mother had been asked to leave, we would have had absolutely nothing to live on while they sought out new work, and we very well could have starved before we'd found anything steady again. My father understood that. All I could understand at the time was that I was hurt, hungry, and the employer I'd thought I could trust hadn't kept his promise to my family. The pain from my injury, and the sense of betrayal I felt at being let down by the hyena had been echoed and reinforced all that night as I nursed the bloodied nose my father had given me. It all sunk deep into me and festered, and became one experience.

But I never blamed my father. I blamed the hyena.

Even though I eventually realized how immature I'd been at the time, that day had left an indelible mark. I never trusted his kind again. They'd done more than just neglect my family. They'd turned my father against me.

I don't sleep well that night. The lodging's new, the sounds are new, and even on the straw mat, I'm cold. I wake countless times, startled by something that isn't there, a shadow I think I see, the scent of a memory. I dream, but only in flashes.

I'm all nerves by the time the morning comes around, and I've been awake for an hour when the bell rings out. The backs of my eyes feel heavy, my body feels leaden and sluggish, and I'm still shivering when I stiffly pull myself up into a sitting position. The men all around me are beginning to stir and wake to various degrees, including the hyena, who apparently managed to inch his way closer to me throughout the night. He's curled into an impossibly small ball for a man so tall. He's all limbs when he unfolds himself from the sarong he was using as a makeshift blanket, and a mouth full of clean white teeth flashes as he yawns.

I don't have time to concern myself with him anymore. A guard is at the door, not Lochan but that lion I saw the other day. His voice is rough and demanding as he calls for us to wake, and he starts pacing the lodging house, digging his foot into people who aren't stirring fast enough for his liking. He's leaner than the Aardwolf but no less threatening-looking, and judging by the various scars I see criss-crossing his arms, legs and muzzle, and the deep umber brown color of his mane, he's also a veteran. I don't need trouble with him or anyone else right now, so I force myself unsteadily to my feet and take as little time as I can to wipe the exhaustion from my eyes.

He notices me, of course. Likely just because I'm new. He regards me from several mats away for a moment or more, then gives an odd, twisted kind of smile, only one corner of his muzzle twitching up. The other side of his face has a deep scar running from one cheek down to his mouth, and he might honestly not be able to move that side of his face.

He doesn't spare much more time for me, though. There's a thin, old squirrel at his feet still asleep, and he levels a kick at the man at about the same time I decide to look anywhere else. I'm concerned if I hold his gaze much longer, it will be an invitation.

I move off towards where the men are massing in the gathering area between all the lodges. A doused fire pit and a few rocks drug in to scattered positions around it likely make up the area for social-izing at the end of the day. The workers have begun to mass in and around the pit from the various lodging houses, and I try to fall in amongst the crowd departing mine, but most of the men are giving me a wide berth. I'm not certain if that's a good thing or a bad thing just yet, but at least no one's messing with me.

My peace is short-lived.

I'm watching a small gang of canines gathering, mostly dholes, other jackals and a few wolves with thinned-out coats that were chopped down by the least precise of groomers, when I'm sud-denly pitched forward into the dirt. The double-blow catches me completely by surprise and had to have come from a powerful set of paws, because I have absolutely no chance to catch myself.

I fall mostly on my knees, then my right shoulder, skidding hard enough against the coarse, exhausted soil that I know I'll be pick-

ing fragments out of my scraped skin for the rest of the day. I roll to my back with a groan as I finally let the wind out of my lungs. Whoever hit me had caught me in the small of my back with a good hook, before shoving me into the dirt. Something around my kidney hurts… it might actually be my kidney. But I don't have much time to reflect on it, because just then the figure behind me makes his way into my line of view, blocking out the dim morning sunlight, and he's leveling a kick at me while I'm down.

I get my wits about me, finally, and roll back on my spine, snapping my own legs out at the man and catching him first. My foot-paw connects with his shin and I hear him grunt and stumble back. Unfortunately he *does* manage to catch himself, unlike me. But at least it gives me the time I need to struggle back to my feet, too proud to clutch at my side, but gods how I want to.

It's the cheetah. I was right to be concerned about him the night before, as it turns out. I don't know why he waited this long, he could have easily come after me in my sleep, but I've heard stories about their kind and their odd behavior. Something about their lone lifestyle makes for a strange kind of people, with a religion all their own that most other peoples consider wildly insane. Or, as my mother once tried to explain, 'respectable but strange'. I've never known a cheetah well, they don't tend to work manual labor or stay in one place for long. And I've rarely seen them indentured, either.

I've seen enough of them to know this one looks odd, though. He's like most of the ones I'd seen along the Hyronses, tall and lean, but he has a bit more bulk on him, just like I would have said about myself compared to most jackals. At least, before the last month of malnourishment and imprisonment.

His collar is tighter to his neck than mine, suggesting he's had disciplinary problems in the past too, and he's got blue eyes. But most strikingly, his spots don't look right. He's turning around and straightening when I catch sight of him first, and I can tell the normally small, black points along his fur are far too large, melting together in places, and forming three near-perfect lines down his back, following his spine.

He narrows his eyes at me, and I snuff out a nose-full of dirt as the crowd parts around us. I can tell by the scattered looks of fear and the fact that absolutely no one seems to want to be a part of this that he must command a certain reputation here. So either he's laying down the law right now as part of some rite of passage, or I pissed him off somehow.

A dim memory from the night before prickles at the back of my mind, and I curse under my breath. Right. He'd been the one to warn me about the hyena.

But, he hadn't exactly stopped me last night. So I'm left wondering if that really has anything at all to do with this sudden attack. It's damn confusing.

"What the hell is your problem?" I demand, peeling back my lip to flash my canines. I straighten my hips and cock an arm out in front of me, guarding my head, and drawing the other back and balling a fist. I know how to scrap, and I'm not afraid to give the man a fight, whether or not I have a chance at winning it. I'm not at my prime right now, but that doesn't mean I'm going to let myself appear weak. Men like this will target you from the day you start working until the end of time if you let them think you're an easy meal. I've got to shake him now while I have the chance, let him know I won't allow it without getting in a few good knocks, myself.

"Raja!"

I twist an ear to the side at the sound of someone shouting. Mostly because it's the first voice to pierce the silence since the crowd formed up around us, but also because it seems to have caught the cheetah's attention, too. He stares past me, his expression hard to read, but something in it shifts and suddenly he looks less confident. Not scared, not intimidated exactly, more… concerned?

I wait for him to come at me again. There's a shuffling in the crowd behind me, but I can't turn to look at it without taking my eyes off the man, which I'm not going to do.

"Raja, please," a voice—a voice I am now beginning to recognize—pleads from behind me, "don't hurt him anymore."

"Fuck off!" I snap at the hyena behind me, without turning anything other than an ear towards him. "This isn't your fight!"

The cheetah seems to be relaxing though, and for some reason that infuriates me. The last thing, and I mean the *last* thing I wanted right now, was for the damn hyena to stand up for me. The scrawny shit is demeaning me, and I can't even stop him without taking my eyes off the cheetah long enough that he might floor me.

The lean cat stares over my shoulder and sniffs the wind suddenly, his tail thrashing behind him once, in that way big cats' tails do when they've noticed something. His eyes shift back to mine, and he speaks in a deep voice that honestly might be more fitting coming from a lion.

"We will speak later," he promises, and heads back off into the crowd.

I'm tempted to follow him, but hitting him with his back turned to me would only cement my reputation as a coward, and that's not going to help me. Instead, I turn and direct my ire towards the only other available target. The striped hyena. He literally back-steps when I level my gaze at him, and his ears wilt back, his hands knitted nervously in front of him. He's stooped and cowering, just like he was last night, and the posture looks especially pathetic on him when he's standing.

"Who said I needed your help?" I demand fiercely, advancing on him. For every step I take towards him, he takes another back, somehow lowering himself with each one until he's literally about half his height.

He holds a dark paw up, as if to shield himself. He's stammering something that was probably meant to be words, but he's not fitting any of them together properly and it's all coming out in a jumble of near-whispers.

Despite all of that, he's got the oddest expression on his face. His eyes are wide and I'm fairly certain he's afraid of me, but he also looks somehow… hopeful? The best I can compare it to is the dim look you get from animals when you're trying to discipline them and they're too stupid to understand that they've done something wrong.

"Jackal, fall in!" A gruff shout echoes across the camp, and I know immediately that it's Lochan. He and the lion, as well as two other guards, apparently made an appearance at some point in the last few minutes, and they've begun collecting groups of men. That was likely what the cheetah heard.

I cast one more glare down at the piteous creature, but I was never going to attack him in the first place. In fact at this point, I want nothing more to do with him.

"Don't you get between me and that cat again," I snarl. "It's not your business!"

I leave him at that point, pushing through the crowd towards the guards. At this point, a day of hard manual labor is actually sounding better than it has in a long time. I might be sore and tired, but I'm also angry, and work has always helped me burn off unwanted feelings.

Lochan begins to go over the day's work, and I'm finding it sounds a lot less familiar than I was hoping. I've never worked in poppy fields before. He's talking about 'scoring' duties, and 'collecting' teams, and I have no idea what either of those two words mean in the context of plantation work. When he mentions they need carriers for the weeders in one of the fields though, and it seems an unpopular job, I instantly raise my hand to volunteer. I can carry whatever they need me to carry. I can do that all day long.

Lochan gives me an 'aye' when I raise my hand, and gestures for me to join a team of men gathering to his left, and I do just that. The cheetah isn't amongst them, thankfully. In fact most of the men on this team seem comprised of the smaller races. A ferret, a weasel, that old squirrel I saw earlier, and one other large man, the painted dog. He'd also volunteered to be a carrier.

I readjust the collar around my neck, still not used to its tighter fit, and consider asking the painted dog about the work, when he speaks up first.

"Leave the hyena alone," he says, in a quiet, civil tone. "And Raja will leave you alone."

I sigh. "Is that really what that was about?"

"He won't beat on you so long as you follow the lodge rules," the painted dog explains. He's got a patient, calm tone that sets me at ease, somehow. Everything's been absolutely mad since I came here, but I'm instantly comfortable with him after just a few words.

"I just came in last night," I explain to him raggedly. "I don't *know* the lodge rules."

He gives me a sympathetic look. "I'm sorry you had to learn the hard way," he says, sounding honestly apologetic. "But Raja deals in absolutes. He warned you once, and you didn't listen. That means punishment, as far as he's concerned. I think he feels he made his point, though. Just leave the hyena be and you won't have to worry about going through that again."

"Until I break another rule I'm not aware of," I point out.

"I can tell you all the rules while we're in the field," he offers. "There really aren't many. Don't take anything from Raja. Don't beat on too many people who don't deserve it. Don't leave the lodge at night, and *don't* mess with the hyena."

"Why?" I ask, perplexed.

"We're not really supposed to talk about it," the painted dog says with an air of discomfort. "Just..." he pauses, "...just leave him be. Don't even talk to him. He's untouchable."

What he actually uses is the word 'Harijan', which up until I became one, I'd heard used to describe indentured people. 'Servants' like everyone here, and myself, unfortunately. When I'd been a pup, my mother had explained it meant people that were so low below us, touching them could bring whatever curse or disease afflicted them on us and our family.

But we were *all* indentured servants here, so what the hell did he mean? What was lower than us?

The painted dog seems really uncomfortable now, and I feel a distance growing between us, which I definitely don't want. For many reasons. For one, he's the first person to honestly reach out to me here, *and* he's canine. I'm an independent man, but you always want to have friends amongst your work force. Especially when you're indentured and you literally can't have friends or confidantes with anyone else in the world.

So I drop the subject for now. "What's your name?" I ask instead.

"Chandan," he replies, his wide ears perking in my direction. I get a polite smile out of him, and just as soon as it had come on, that distance is gone.

I extend a hand to clasp his, and he takes it, and then I'm smiling a little as well. "Kadar. Well met," I say, and he nods back.

"I'm sorry again about Raja," he says. "He's not a bad man. A bit of a bully, but someone's always cock of the roost out here."

I wave his comment off, even though my kidney still hurts and I'm honestly not done nursing a grudge towards the cheetah. Obviously, he and the painted dog are friends, or he's at least earned the man's respect, and even if I can't understand why at the moment, I'm determined not to make an enemy of *every* man here. We'll see how things shape up with the cheetah. Hopefully he and I can just avoid one another from this point on.

Besides, everything, all of it, was ultimately the hyena's fault. They want me to avoid him? I have no issue doing *exactly* that.

A lioness guard comes to escort us to the field we'll be working on that day. I fall in line with the others, trying to ignore the pain in my side and the fact that my stomach's begun to twist with hunger again. They'll bring us our midday meal out in the fields after a few hours of work, and I can wait that long. Maybe there will even be meat, I think. Probably not. But one can hope.

Just because I hate the life I've fallen into, hate everything about it and every circumstance that led me to this point, doesn't mean I fight it every second of every day. More often than not in fact, my baser need for survival wins out over my pride. There's only so much hunger and pain a man can endure before you start to think that maybe falling in line might just be your best option for the day.

Of course, that's what they rely upon. The people who own us.

The march out to the field is long, so I take the time to ask Chandan a few questions. Most of them he answers patiently and, it seems, as honestly and directly as he can. But when I get to questions about our contracts, he's a bit more hesitant.

"Didn't they go over everything about your contract to the Sura clan when you were first sold here?" he asks. "That's personal. I can't know the details of your contract, they're unique for all of us."

I snort. "They didn't even tell me they were moving me here. They drugged me, I think. I woke up in that stone building up on the hill, in a cell. I didn't even know I was in Tavesi until Lochan told me last night."

His ears fall back. "I'm sorry," he says quietly. "That's hard."

"And illegal," I point out, "not that that matters."

He nods. "They would have sold your contract whether you objected or not, but… yes, the people who sold you should have gone over it with you. They're supposed to. But that's how it was for many of us. Raja doesn't talk about it much, but I think it was the same for him."

"Oh?" I ask, idly. I don't want to prod the man about the cheetah too much, but I *am* curious.

"Well he was pretty much starving and injured when he first arrived," he explains, "much like you." He drops his eyes to my limp. I thought I'd been covering it well. "Are you certain you'll be alright to carry?" he asks. "The bundles are heavy."

"I'm on the mend," I assure him, with a firm tone. I don't need anyone questioning my physical capability right now.

He seems to get the point and just nods, changing the subject. "We'll be weeding in a field that hasn't reached maturity yet," he says, "and that's probably where you should stay, for now. Keep away from the scored fields. If they drugged you, the allure of the Divine will be strong. The last thing you need in this line of work is to be caught stealing product. You'll be hung. And an addiction you have to pay for is just a slower form of death."

"I have no interest in taking their drug," I snarl, dismissively. "What the hell would make you think I would?"

He shrugs. "If you can't remember your time under its influence, or it simply didn't agree with you, so much the better. For some the Divine takes well, for others it's not nearly so pleasant."

"I mostly remember nightmares," I murmur.

"That's for the best," he repeats solemnly. "It is a crutch you don't need."

When we at last reach the field, the sun's begun to creep its way further into the sky and the morning chill has worn off. I can tell it's going to be a hot, humid day, and I actually am glad that all I'm wearing is the loin cloth. For now. By tonight I'm certain I'll be cold again and wanting my old, ratty clothing back. But they've probably burnt it by now.

As it turns out, weeding a poppy field isn't much different than weeding a grain field, or anything else. The weeders set to work immediately, moving along the rows removing unwanted growth, and Chandan gives me basic instructions. Follow, collect, bundle and carry. Once you reach the end of a row, bring your bundle to one of the wagons then start on the next row.

It's usually the smaller types of people who weed, especially those who are most comfortable being on all-fours for most of the day. If I did work like that, I'd end up stooped and crooked over like a hook in a few years. But for the rodents and the weasels, it's more suitable work.

It takes me a row or so to figure out how to bundle the long grasses and various weeds, but eventually I get the hang of how to knot and undo the rope without losing the whole bundle. Chandan has to show me more than once, but he doesn't seem frustrated with me, so I guess I caught on pretty fast compared to most. That or he's eternally patient.

I'm still tired and sore, but work helps me forget. And it feels good to use my body again. The last few weeks in the prison weakened me, and I don't like feeling weak. A few weeks of work like this and some decent food, and I'll be able to regain my strength. For right now, that's a goal, at least.

I'm honestly enjoying the heat when it comes, (not so much the humidity, we don't get a lot of that near the Hyronses) and by the time our midday meal arrives on a donkey cart, I'm feeling better than I have in all the time since I came here. I sit down with Chandan near the meal cart, drinking the bowl of soup they brought us. No meat, but I taste weak chicken broth mixed into the barley water, and there's some hearty root vegetables of some sort that aren't all that bad. And of course, more of that stone-cooked bread. I get the feeling I'll be eating a lot of that.

And then the day goes downhill, all at once. Because cresting the road in the distance I see the person I least want to see in the world right now, followed closely by the second person I least want to see in the world. Chandan notices me stiffen beside him and his large ears twist towards the horizon, where two tall silhouettes are making their way towards us.

"I thought you said he'd leave me the hell alone," I snap, not intending to take my irritation out on Chandan, but I want answers.

He looks nervously towards the cheetah approaching us and slowly stands, dropping his empty bowl in the dirt and wiping a paw down his chest fur to shake off any crumbs from the flat bread. "I don't know why he's here," he admits.

I stand rigidly, straightening my posture and putting weight on my foot, even though a pang of pain reminds me I should be showing more care with it. I am *not* feeling up to another fight, especially right after a meal, but—

Chandan calls out to the cheetah as he approaches, cutting off my train of thought. "Raja!" he takes a step past me, putting an arm back in an obvious gesture to me to stay where I am. Picking up on my tension, I'm sure. "What's wrong?" he asks as he approaches the spotted cat.

And why is the hyena with him? I want to ask. The creature's eyes are downcast and he's barely shuffling behind Raja. He looks guilty for some reason, but every now and then he looks up at me in an altogether different way.

I curl back my muzzle when he catches my eyes, but I'm caught in the man's dark-eyed gaze just long enough that recognition finally strikes.

He's *hopeful*. That's the emotion I've been unable to pinpoint all this time. Hope isn't a feeling you have, let alone see a whole lot of, in this life. The sheer fact that those thoughts just went through my head makes me feel melodramatic, but there's no denying it's true. That's why I couldn't read it until now.

Raja and Chandan are speaking lowly, and I haven't really been paying attention, but when the painted dog turns to regard me for a moment with a questioning expression, I avert my gaze from the hyena, finally. But Chandan doesn't say anything to me yet, he just turns back towards Raja and mutters something. If my ears weren't still so full of dirt and grime from the weeks I spent in the cell, I'd probably be able to make out what they're saying.

I need to take a more thorough bath.

I'm getting tired of all this clandestine shit though, and I finally work up the nerve to tell them so.

"If this concerns me," I say, annoyed, "then I damn well have a right to know what you're saying. If not, I'm going back to the fields." I turn to go, hoping that the cheetah did in fact come to speak to Chandan and not me, but at that point the cat finally raises his voice.

"Jackal," he calls out, "come here."

I'm half-tempted to disobey, but my side still hurts, and honestly I'm curious. So I take a few moments to hesitate like I'm thinking about it, let him know I'm not going to fall in like a good little lap-dog, then I make my way over there, again being careful not to show my limp. When I make it to them, he reaches out for me and I nearly pull away from him when he puts a paw on my shoulder. But even though his eyes are boring into me and he's got a very no-nonsense look about him, I don't sense the same aggression from him he was displaying the last time we met. And you can always tell with cheetahs, with the ragged scruff of fur down their necks and backs. He's relaxed, now.

"He is your responsibility, now," he says, stone-faced. For a moment I have absolutely no clue what he means. At all. Then he jerks his thumb back towards the hyena behind him, and answers at least one of the ten questions I might have asked.

I blink, then snuff derisively. "Excuse me?"

"The hyena," the cat states. "He is yours now."

"I heard you," I snap. "What the hell do you *mean* by that? Make sense."

"He must remain safe," the cheetah explains, as he explains everything. In the least amount of words possible. I'm getting the feeling this isn't a particularly deep man. "Or the entire lodging house will suffer. I have taken care of him until now. I am giving him to you. You are to look after him now."

"Like hell!" I growl, outraged. "What the fuck makes you think I want that responsibility?"

"I don't give a shit what you want," the cheetah states plainly. "*He* prefers you. I prefer not to have the burden any longer." He drops his grip on my shoulder, and turns on one foot-paw, speaking over his shoulder. "Make sure no harm comes to him."

"We aren't done talking!" I take a step forward after him, and feel Chandan's hand replace the cheetah's on my shoulder, trying to hold me back. "I don't want him! I don't want anything to do with this, *whatever* the hell is going on here!"

"No one said you had a choice," Raja says as he passes the hyena. For his part, the striped, thin man mostly looks frightened now. Of me.

Good.

"I won't do it!" I threaten. "I'll let the little bastard get beaten on day and night—"

"The only one stupid enough to do that was you," Raja replies coolly, levelling one last stare at me just long enough that my next words catch in my throat. His fur is raised, and there's a low growl in his voice. The threat is there, and obvious.

"Kadar," I hear Chandan behind me, his calm voice easing me back into a state of clarity. "Don't. Not right now. We'll work this out at the end of the day."

I yank my shoulder out of Chandan's hand, snarl pretty well plastered on my muzzle now. The cheetah is leaving, as though he has absolutely no reason to question that his commands will be followed. He probably doesn't, when it comes to most people around here. If he'd asked me *anything* else, I might have honestly decided it wasn't worth my time or effort to say no. But this…

The hyena is looking at me again, his dark eyes mostly on the ground, but occasionally flicking up to mine then down again, as if he's hoping I might somehow warm to him. He's clutching his own bicep with one hand, and his paw looks to be shaking where it's gripping his fur. The way he's stooped over bothers me.

"Stand up straight!" I finally snap at him. "The way you skulk and slink around is making me fucking uncomfortable."

"I—I'm sorry," he says, his ears perking up just a bit. He *does* stand a little taller, if only for a second, before I raise my voice at him again.

"What the hell is wrong with you, anyway?" I demand. "Why does everyone here treat you like you've got the goddamn plague? And why are you here?"

"I'm indentured," he murmurs.

"I meant why are you *here*, you little shit?" I growl. "Here! With me! Right now!"

The man is quiet for far longer, this time. At this point I'm starting to think he might be simple, or far younger than he appears. He has the bearing and many of the expressions of a pup. When he does speak, at length, he does so in a near-mumble, and I have to crane my ear to hear him.

"You talked to me," he states simply. I wait for more, but apparently there isn't any.

"I'm regretting that," I say, still perplexed and increasingly annoyed. "Honestly, if I'd known you were such a pushover, I wouldn't have targeted you. I thought you'd put up a bit more of a fight."

But not so much of one that I couldn't handle him. That had been the plan, anyway. I'm starting to think I made an enormous mistake. A niggling voice at the back of my mind tells me exactly what I don't want to acknowledge, but can't deny. *You brought this on yourself.*

I shove those thoughts aside for now. How was I to know there was something wrong with this hyena? This particular hyena? I couldn't know there was some lodging house conspiracy surrounding him. Couldn't know that stealing his mat would lead to all of this. I'd literally just arrived here yesterday. I didn't know the goings-on of this place, yet.

And I'm getting tired of being in the dark.

"No one talks to me," the hyena says, his first un-prompted words since I've met him. "Ever," he finishes in a quiet, defeated whisper.

"The people here are afraid of being near you," I state, making it clear with a step forward and some heat behind my words that *I* am not. Chandan is still somewhere behind me, I can all but feel him hovering there, probably afraid I'll hurt the kid.

When I advance another step, the hyena looks like he wants to bolt. This time though, this time he doesn't. The leg he has tilted back is shaking slightly, but he's not moving. And he's slightly less hunched. That's something of an improvement. I'm close to him now, and this is the first time I've been so close to him and he's been standing even remotely up to his full height. He and I are actually pretty well matched if he would just stand like a man.

"Why?" I demand, sick of the games. "Why are you untouchable?"

"Kadar," Chandan warns from behind me. "Listen, I'll explain it—"

"Shut up," I say without looking behind me. "I want to hear it from him. If Raja wants me to watch his ass, I want to know why. And he needs to stop being a fucking child, and speak for himself. You hear that?" I demand of the hyena, taking the final step to cross the distance between us. His ears are flat against the thick fur down the back of his neck, and he's beginning to hunker down away from me again, so this time I reach down and hook three fingers under the edge of his collar, yanking him back up.

"I said *stand up straight!*" I bellow, and he gives a breathless yelp as I yank him up. "Have some rutting self-respect, would you? Address me like a man!"

He's still not saying anything intelligible, and my blood is hot, the midday sun is hot, I'm still hurting from this morning and it's his fault, and I feel my anger at the entire situation starting to bubble and burn in my chest. A familiar feeling takes hold, and though usually I'd repress it, right now I'm frustrated and hurt and *still* tired, and I don't have the patience for any of this.

I guess I hadn't even realized I'd raised my fist, until he cringes and closes his eyes. He doesn't fight me, doesn't even try to get away. He just waits. And my vision seems to blur, to snap back to a memory. A lifetime ago, a different pair of eyes staring up at me.

I pull my hand free of his collar like it's molten to the touch and take a few steps away from him, lowering my fist. He slowly opens his eyes, staring after me as I back away, and mostly, he seems confused. He's still hunkered down and looks like he's anticipating I might change my mind, but I'm forcing myself to calm down, willing away that heat in my chest.

I hate that feeling. I hate it more than anything. Even the collar around my neck. And I'm privately horrified that I nearly let it take hold again.

I have to force myself to recognize that I might have been letting my frustration weigh on my decisions too much, and I'm not myself right now. Those aren't my words, of course. They came from a far wiser mind than mine. My mother used to say them.

Anger isn't an excuse, I remind myself, like a mantra.

A shout from our supervisor is exactly the sort of interruption I want right now. His voice cuts through the silent, tense moment passing between the three of us, sharply commanding us to get back to work in the field. I give myself a few seconds to cool my blood, gather my thoughts and re-focus. Work. Work always calms me down.

I turn from the hyena and try to put him out of my mind for now, passing Chandan as I make my way back towards my row. The painted dog follows me a step or two, speaking at my back as I go.

"Kadar," he calls out, "are you—"

"I'm fine," I insist, quiet but firm. "Let's get back to the fields."

Chandan can only follow me so far, since only one carrier works per row. But he isn't the only one who's following me. At least twenty paces back, the hyena is hesitantly tailing me. He has to work too, I tell myself. I'm going to have to get used to being in the fields with him.

When he joins me in my row as a weeder though, I have to bite back on a growl. I thought for sure he'd be here as a carrier, considering his size. At least then we'd have a good distance between us all day. He falls in silently to do his work and it soon becomes clear he's probably been a weeder before. He's fairly good at it, despite being so tall. Probably comes natural to someone who stoops so much, anyway.

My thoughts are a tangled mess of continued frustration and encroaching guilt over what I'd nearly done. It's confusing, and I don't like being confused. But I definitely don't feel like beating on the kid any more, and that's probably for the best, for obvious reasons and others that have yet to be explained to me.

It's like he's in my head. Or maybe, it's just that it takes him an hour to answer the last question I asked him. Because midway through our second row, he speaks un-prompted, again.

"I belong to Matron Sura," he says, as he plucks a long stalk of grass, and instead of depositing it on the ground, hesitantly holds it out to me.

I take it. One less time I have to bend over to retrieve something. I don't hide the ire still in my eyes when I reply. "We all do," I mutter.

"I belong to her... directly," he explains quietly.

I digest that for a few moments before it begins to make sense. "You're from the house?" I clarify. "One of the ruling Matron's personal servants?" He nods after that, and then I'm shaking my head. "*That's* why no one wants anything to do with you?"

"I believe," he says, still speaking so softly I'd not hear him if I wasn't a jackal, "they are afraid that damaging me or upsetting me in some way may bring down the ire of my Matron."

That actually makes some degree of sense to me, but then I have to wonder, "Then why are you here?" I demand. "At all? Why did she send one of her personal servants to the fields to work?"

He clearly wasn't suited for the work physically. It explained everything, really. Why he seemed so well-maintained. Why he didn't look like he'd done a day of hard labor in his life. The holes in his ears, where he'd likely once had jewelry. Not to mention his sickening demeanor. House servants have to be especially obedient, especially trustworthy, for the Matrons and their families to allow them to live in their personal space.

Some servants get strange like that when they've been indentured for too long. Or indentured young. I've seen it before. It's disgusting to me, but I have to admit, to myself if not out loud, it's probably not his fault. But you don't see it in field workers, often. And I've never really met many house servants, except in passing. Are they all like this, I wonder?

"So what did you do?" I ask as I set back to work, once it becomes clear he's not going to answer my previous question. I scoop up the remainder of the weeds ahead of me that he'd pulled prior to starting this conversation. He hesitates, but then gets back to work as well. "To get kicked out of the house, I mean," I speak up, so he can hear me over the shuffling of my bundle. If the hyena is secretly some kind of hell-raiser, it might honestly improve my opinion of him somewhat.

"I asked to leave," he says, his tone hard to read. But then that's no real change. Everything about the way the man talks and acts is sort of strange and foreign to me. At least now I have some idea why.

"Seems like an odd choice," I snort, "for someone like you, anyway."

He pauses, turning to regard me, and I nearly bump into him. He looks up at me, (something he wouldn't have to do if he'd just correct his damn posture) and flicks an ear, his expression inquisitive. "What do you mean?" he asks.

"I mean you're a soft, pampered, cowardly thing," I state plainly. "You can't possibly prefer it out here. Wouldn't you rather be back where you belong?"

He looks down for a moment, like he's honestly considering my words. When he looks back up at me, his voice sounds the least hesitant, least uncertain it has since I met him. There is almost a grain of strength behind it. "I do not belong there anymore," he says decidedly.

I give him a long stare, trying to see past the fact that he's a hyena, to look at him like I might another jackal, or really *any* other species. It's hard. I hate their kind. I see every one of the guards, clan members and swindlers who's locked me into the life I'm trapped in now when I look at a hyena. *Any* hyena.

I picture, without wanting to, what it would have been like to hit him. And even the imagined sight sinks into me like a hot blade. My stomach cramps, and I feel vaguely sick. It would have been like striking a child.

The guilt gnaws at me enough that I manage to let the anger go, at least for the moment. My voice comes out with less of a growl this time when I speak, and he notices, his ears lifting up just a fraction. "Why didn't you just stay with Raja?" I ask, with a sigh. "I didn't... I wasn't trying to... I don't know what you thought I was trying to do." I wasn't trying to reach out to him, that's for damn sure. And that's the way he seems to have taken this. "I just wanted your straw mat," I explain raggedly. "I didn't know any of this about you. I didn't want to."

I still don't, really.

"You can have my mat," he says quickly, so quickly I feel like a bully, now. And considering the issues I've already had today with the local bully, that just makes me feel like shit even more.

"That's a given," I mutter. If he's going to fold this easily, I'm hardly going to have to try as hard in the future. "I just don't see why I have to be the one to watch you now," I try to explain.

"You don't," he says quietly. "I just hoped you would."

"Why?" I ask, confused. I'm about to say *what's so wrong with Raja?* But the words seem stupid even as I'm forming them in my head. Raja, the cheetah who'd just beaten the hell out of me in the yard earlier that day. The man who spoke about three words at a time, whose only discernable inflection was growling.

"Raja doesn't really…" he pauses, "…talk… to me much. He just decided I needed to be protected, and he does that. He makes sure I work in the same field with him, but he treats me like everyone else does." His ears drop. "Like I don't exist."

"Listen," I open my mouth, then pause.

"Ahsan," he fills in for me. And then finally, I have a name other than 'hyena.'

"Ahsan," I say, measuring my tone and still somehow managing to keep my frustration out of it. I'm not calm exactly, but my remorse for my previous outburst is helping me retain a bit more self-control. "You don't really need anyone to protect you," I insist. "Everyone knows you're off-limits. You'll be fine. You don't need to barter your straw mat for some kind of guard. In fact, you're a…" I pause, "…well you're no rodent, or even a fox. You're bigger than half the men we work with. You can probably take care of yourself, even *if* you think someone's going to mess with you."

"I can't fight," he says, almost amused at the concept. The slightest hint of a smile on him strikes me as looking far more fitting on his dark muzzle than the terrified, despondent look he's worn up until now. I dismiss that thought almost as soon as it comes, because why the hell would I care?

"Would you really be happier being dependent on someone else?" I try to reason. "If you want to work in the fields, you're going to have to learn to take care of yourself eventually. You can't live this life and stay docile. Trust me. I've been doing this for a long time. Even a reputation only gets you so far."

"I can't be like Raja. Or you," he says, knitting his hands in front of him, nervously. "I'm just not like that."

"Like what?" I prickle.

"There are those who command, and those who listen," he says in words that don't sound like they were ever his own. "I am one who listens. I am meant to be kept, not a keeper."

"*No one* is meant to be kept," I say, pushing the words out with all the emphasis I can. His eyes widen somewhat at my change in tone, but he doesn't look scared. Instead he's staring at me even more intensely now, enrapt. His paws are still wringing at one another near his waist, tail tucked, but at least now I have his full attention. He waits expectantly for me to continue.

I get the sickening feeling this was what he wanted. It makes me feel dirty, taking advantage of the spineless obedience that was clearly ground down into this poor creature.

"Please," he pleads, after I've made it clear I have no more to say, "tell me what I can do to change your mind."

"Nothing," I say flatly. "Stand on your own two feet. Or go back to Raja. I'm bad at taking care of people, trust me." I begin to heft my bundle, so we can get back to work.

"I can get you meat at meal times," he offers quietly.

My ears perk. "Say what?"

That night, Ahsan comes through on his promise. I'm sitting on his straw mat, starting off with my bread for the night, when I see him appear in the doorway of the slowly-filling lodging house, a steaming bowl in his hand. The bowl in and of itself isn't odd, I have one just like it, full of rice and some kind of vegetable curry, but when he makes his way over towards me and sits down, I smell lamb.

I take it from his offered paw, staring down at its contents almost disbelievingly. Last night I'd simply assumed there'd been meat available to everyone in the house, and I'd just missed it. But tonight disproves that. I got to the chow line early and got all there was available. Bread, rice and vegetables. When I asked some of the other men working here, they informed me they only ever include meat in the soups they give out at midday. If you want anything other than weak broth, you have to pay for it. I'm starting my work here with a zero balance on my contract, so that isn't exactly an option for me.

"How?" I ask, mystified. The corners of his muzzle turn up a little, and he sits cross-legged beside me. I'm fairly well-inclined towards him as I dig in to the food, so I let him.

"Master Lochan always saves me some of the guards' meal," he says, reaching down into the sandy dirt beside the straw mat to idly trace curling patterns in the earth with a claw. As he does so, I can't help but note the diameter of his arms, the ridges on his spine that are visible, the way his waist barely even bunches when he leans over…

I pause, glancing down at my bowl and spooning out a handful with my paw, before handing what remains back to him. "Here. You haven't eaten, right?"

"It's for you," he insists quietly.

"Have you eaten or not?" I demand.

"I'm not hungry," he murmurs.

I knit my brow, and shove the food in my palm into my muzzle, chewing it and savoring it less than I'd prefer to right now. Then I reach forward with the same hand and grab him by the wrist, forcing the bowl with the remaining food into his palm.

"You want someone to tell you what to do?" I say, putting some authority behind my words. As expected, that gets his attention. "Eat, you fool. You don't have a day of lazing around an estate ahead of you. I don't know what you did for the Matron, but it sure as hell wasn't manual labor. Your body will break if you don't feed it, and your body is your tool. *Eat*, or you won't be able to work."

The speech gets the desired result. Hesitantly at first, but eventually with enough interest that I know he must have been lying about being hungry, he eats what remains in the bowl.

I sit there and finish my bread while he eats, idly taking in the sights of the house while we finish our meal. For the most part, the people here are still giving me a lot of space, which earnestly, I'm fine with. It's actually been the easiest first day I've had at a new lodging house in several years. I see Chandan with a group of other canines, laughing and talking about something while they finish their own meals, and I have a brief pang of longing to be amongst some of my own kind again. But forcing my way in won't work. At the very least, I know Chandan, and he strikes me as the type of man with a lot of friends here. Maybe eventually, I'll gain acceptance through him.

My gaze catches on an intense, blue-eyed stare from across the room. I glare at the cheetah to let him know I noticed him looking at me, but he doesn't seem to care. He keeps his vigil of me steadily, without flinching. Ensuring I'm following his command, apparently.

I don't care what Raja thinks. In fact I don't really care what anyone here thinks of me right now. At least, that's what I try to tell myself.

The fact is, I'm eating meat right now and they're not. And even if that means I had to take on a disease no one wants, to become untouchable too, at least for the moment, I'm eating better. Things like this get forgotten eventually. I might not even be at this plantation long, let alone in this specific lodging house.

"Do you want my sarong?" Ahsan asks, breaking me out of my reverie. I glance back over at him as he unwraps it from around his waist, where it's bunched and tied around the hem of his loose pants. "It's thin, but it keeps some of the cold away if you wrap it around yourself."

"The last place I worked at had blankets," I mutter. "They were ragged and flea-infested, but they were free."

"The merchants come here sometimes with blankets and clothing for sale," Ahsan says. "But it's expensive. Especially the blankets." He holds out the bunched-up sarong to me. "Here."

I consider taking it for a few moments. "You've got a lot less meat on your bones than I do," I finally say with a sigh. "Keep it."

His ears droop, and he looks down at the bundled cloth. He's silent for a little while, then his muzzle twitches nervously and he takes in a breath. He looks like he's about to suggest something stupid.

"We could sha—"

"No," I say firmly, regarding him with a sour look. "Don't push your luck." I turn away from him and lie down on the mat, rolling over onto my side so I don't have to face him anymore.

I hear him shifting eventually, wrapping the sarong around himself, and then he's settling down beside the straw mat just like he was last night. I'm vaguely relieved he didn't move off somewhere else to sleep tonight. Because... because I would have felt guilty for taking the meat, if I wasn't actually playing guardian for him.

Of course it's pretty hard to guard someone while you're facing away from them. Even though that thought is ridiculous, even though, I rationalize, I'll be asleep soon and it's equally hard to guard someone while you're asleep, I eventually convince myself I should at least roll over. Make something of an effort to fulfill my end of this deal.

I turn slowly, hoping he's asleep and I won't have to tolerate the awkwardness of staring at him in the dimming light. I find that he is, or he's at least got his eyes closed. But, no, his breathing seems even. He fell asleep fairly fast. I only wish it were so easy for me. Last night was absolutely awful. It took me what felt like hours to really, fully fall asleep, and then I woke constantly throughout the night, stirred by the cold.

But he's sleeping a little closer tonight and his breath's coming out in soft, warm puffs that I imagine I can almost feel on my chest fur. I'm not really certain if I'm warmer at all just because he's a few inches closer than he was last night, or if I'm just imagining it. For a few fleeting moments, as I take stock of how many other men here share straw mats, I entertain the thought of dragging him up next to me. Because really, that was a pretty obvious, smart thing to do, and when you're half asleep, some things that are really, really bad ideas seem like very obviously good ideas.

But amidst that train of thought, I fall asleep, and thankfully don't act on any of that nonsense.

Chapter 3

Riches

Money was never something I had a lot of experience with growing up, or even throughout most of my young adult life. As a child, I rarely saw my parents use actual coin. We made our living primarily on trade, whatever was paid to my father at the end of each of our working days was used at the market almost immediately, and I never even saw how many of the small metal discs we'd actually earned. I just knew that however many we'd been given, it was never enough to feed us. So, every morning, we'd trade some of our possessions for food. Usually a few tools, a blanket, even clothing. We worked for most of the day, from sunrise to sunset, so we had to eat in the mornings or we'd be too tired to get through our workday.

Inevitably, by the end of the day, we'd use the money we earned to both buy dinner and buy back the possessions we'd sold at the beginning of the day. Every day, it was the same. There was never anything left over. Sometimes we'd forage food when the rains came, or we'd fish. On good days we might be able to catch a snake or a sand lizard, and then we'd be able to buy back our possessions as well as something extra. A replacement for something we owned that had broken, new cloth for my mother to turn into clothing, even extra food sometimes. But even those days, I never really saw the coin we earned. And there was certainly never any left by the time the sun set.

The only exception to this pattern was when we had to pay our landowner at the end of every month. For those three days, we couldn't buy food. My mother usually tried to save bones for broth throughout the month, and my father would try to hunt or fish, but those last few days were always difficult. Hungry days, I used to call them. But the landowner had to be paid, or we'd lose the roof over our head.

During those days, my father would have coin. I knew it, but still, he never allowed me to see it. He never even allowed my mother to see it. When I grew older and he began to regard me more as a man and less as a child, he admitted to me once that my mother could not be trusted with coin. She would buy things, he'd say. She wanted more for our family. More than we could afford. She wanted me to eat better food. She wanted us to have thicker blankets. Clay jugs to keep water in, so we didn't have to always walk the mile to the Hyronses when we needed it. But we couldn't have those things and still eat and pay the landowner. That's how he explained it to me, and it made sense. I remembered being angry at my mother for not being able to understand something so simple. We could only afford what we could afford, and that's why he couldn't ever give her the coin. She wasn't responsible enough to know what we could buy, what we could trade for, and what we couldn't.

There was something else father would buy at the market, I'd learn one day. Something he didn't bring back to the family. But the man of a house bore the weight of a family on his shoulders at all times. He worked for my mother when she was carrying me. He worked harder when they had to feed me as a young pup, before I could earn my own keep. The weight of that responsibility was always on him.

Men drink because their lives are harder. That's also why they are more prone to anger. The weight of all that responsibility. The back-breaking days. At least, that's what he told me. I remember thinking then that it had sounded right. But at the same time, it always seemed like my mother worked very hard, too.

A dozen turns of the sun and meat with every meal at night, and I'm beginning to feel more like myself again. I can't honestly deny the fact that there are definitely some benefits to having Ahsan around. The hyena is bizarrely loyal to me. Probably more so than I've earned.

I'd have felt like I was exploiting him if he wasn't in such high spirits about it. In the two weeks or so since I'd agreed to play his bodyguard, or whatever the hell it was he wanted me for, he's seemed more content with each passing day. His mood is subdued as ever, but he's less obviously frightened around me now, less hesitant. And considering the man practically flinches from his own shadow, I can only assume that means he's happy with our situation.

I'm ambivalent. I like the perks, and I can't feel guilty about it when it's clearly what he wants. So why fight it? I guess ultimately, even with as little regard or concern as I have for him, I'm a better option than Raja.

We don't talk much. Not at night, not even in the fields while we work. Passing comments now and then, it's not like we're ignoring one another exactly, I just don't have much to say to him and he rarely speaks unless spoken to. Really, the main thing I'd want to talk to him about, he very obviously doesn't want to speak on, and that's his time at the Matron's manor. It's not exactly that I want to know more about *him*, I'm just morbidly curious about the woman who owns us and the lifestyle she leads. Workers like me rarely interact with our actual contract owners, and I've literally never set foot inside a manor. I've always wondered how the upper castes live.

But maybe it's for the best. Because I'm certain if I knew the extent of her frivolity, of how easy the rich live, it would only serve to enrage me. And right now I'm actually walking the line here, getting up every day and doing my job. I'm not certain how long I'll be able to bear it, I always inevitably grow restless at each plantation I've been sold to, but right now I'm still recovering and I don't need to be making trouble just yet. Inevitably, I know I will. Things never go smoothly for me.

It's not that I mind the work, even. In fact, plantation work is actually easier on my body than brick kiln work, and they don't even feed us poorly here. I could live this way the rest of my life and probably live about as well as I had a kiln worker.

It's the fact that I'm owned.

I was born free, to a family of workers who had proudly remained free for as many generations back as we could trace. Becoming a servant—becoming indentured—was never supposed to happen to me. I steered clear of the hyena clans and their gambling dens, their drugs, their women. I owned no land that could be taxed. I never took coin from loan men, never rung up a debt with any man, woman or Syndicate. I worked day in and day out, lived honestly, lived hard, and tried to provide for my family as well as I could.

That's always what drives me to madness, to restless anger, pushes me to lash out against the people who own me. It's why I've attempted to escape so many places, why I've refused time and again to accept this life. Because this wasn't supposed to happen to me. I shouldn't be here, shouldn't be owned, shouldn't be collared.

I should be free, out in the world, trying to find my family. Reclaiming the life I once had. Reclaiming that life for *them*.

I feel that familiar burning in my chest, and throw the bundle I'm carrying to the ground with more force than necessary, panting in the wake of the effort. I stand there for some time, staring down at the tangled spool of weeds, dragging the hot midday air through my teeth and balling my fists until my claws are digging into my paw pads. I've let my thoughts wander too much. I'm beginning down that road again, only moments after reflecting on what a good idea it's been to stay docile for the last few weeks. I need this time to rest, I tell myself again. To regain strength, physically and mentally. Then. Then...

My mind goes blank at that, because of course I don't have any plans after that point. In fact, I have even less idea what to do now than I did at the last plantation, because they've taken me farther away from the Hyronses. From everything and everyone I once knew, and any contacts I might have had on the outside.

But I am closer to the ocean. And that's something.

"Kadar?"

Ahsan's voice interrupts my thoughts, and I don't bother turning to regard him, because I can hear his quiet footsteps barely a few feet behind me.

"Are you alright?" he asks timidly, and I feel his paw settling gently on my shoulder. I shrug it off, and he lets go without any resistance. He likes to touch, I've learned by now. Some people are just like that, tactile, I guess you'd call it. I'm not.

"I'm fine," I mutter, shoving the bundle with my foot onto the dusty walkway between the two fields we're working on today, so the mule cart can come along and collect it. "Come on," I say as I turn, "let's start on the next row."

"Alright," he acquiesces, even though I can tell by his eyes that he's still concerned. But he never questions me. It's still a little frustrating for me to see someone like him, stripped of everything that once made them a man, reduced to such a timid, complacent, child-like creature. People shouldn't have their independence wrung out of them. It's sad.

He's still looking to me, dark eyes wide, waiting expectantly for me to lead him to the next row. This is what we do now. I lead, he follows. He's with me nearly every second of the day, and I honestly thought for the first few days it might bother me more, but he's so inoffensive and so careful not to get in my way, it's hard to really see it as an imposition.

"Stand up straight," I remind him for only the third time today, in a hard tone. I've tried to stop snapping at him, though. It bothers me to see him flinch, especially when he's finally started to act almost normal around me.

He straightens up from his slight hunch, obediently. He tends to settle back into slinking around naturally, like he's deliberately trying to be shorter, to be beneath notice. For some species, like a weasel or a ferret or something, I suppose that would look natural, but on him it just looks wrong.

"Walk tall," I grouse at him as we head towards another row. "You're a strong young man, not a little old woman. You don't want to end up bent over like a vulture before you're thirty, do you?"

"I don't like being tall," he says in a distinctly morose mumble.

I snort. "Why? When I was young I couldn't *wait* until I was taller than most of the people I had to work with. You're literally letting people look down on you, when you don't have to. You're at least as tall as me. Use that to your advantage."

"I'm not..." he pauses a moment, "...strong like you," He eventually settles on. "It doesn't work as well for me as it does for you."

"You could be," I say over my shoulder. "Hyenas aren't a weak lot. Not naturally, anyway. You're no clan member, you're a servant. You can't afford to be delicate or soft. You should feed your body better. Start doing something other than weeding. Build up your strength."

"I don't want to get bigger," he says. "I already grew too big. Much too big."

"How old are you?" I ask, turning to look at him and stopping in the middle of the row we've walked down. I'm aware suddenly that this is the most we've talked in nearly a week.

"Se—seventeen years," he mumbles, after a brief pause.

"You're an adult," I affirm. "You're exactly the size you should be. It's natural for young men to grow. I don't know what got your head twisted backwards, but you're supposed to be happy about it, not trying to cover it up."

"I'm not—" he begins, but even as he starts speaking, he's falling back into that hunch.

"Stand up straight!" This time I *do* snap, and he *does* flinch. But it's like with children. You have to be firm, or they won't correct their behavior.

No, I tell myself after a moment of silent thought. That's not the right way to think about it. The man's probably the way he is *because* he's been treated like a child his entire life. Or like a feral animal. A possession. I have to try—hard though it may be—to rise above the people who made him like this. Otherwise it won't make much sense for me to keep thinking myself above them. Morally, anyway. And that's literally the only superiority a servant can have over his owners. It's something I need to hold fast to, even when it concerns another hyena. I can't be like them, even when I'm dealing with them. Or in this case, their refuse.

I sigh, collecting the new length of twine I'll be using to bundle the next row around my palm and elbow. "I'm sorry I yelled," I edge out from between grit teeth.

He seems surprised, his ears slowly lifting. And with it his posture, I note. Maybe yelling really is the worst way to correct him, in this case. I suppose it makes sense, if you honestly think about it. Most people tend to hunch when they're scared.

A sudden thought occurs to me, and I can't hold myself back from asking it. "Ahsan," I say, taking a step forward towards him, "did they beat on you, at th—"

The sound of hoof beats—not the slow amble of a mule, but of horses—breaks through the quiet of the fields, catching both of our attention. It's not just unusual out here in the middle of the day, it's unheard of. The only horse I've seen since I came here belonged to, or at least was being used by, one of the guards. The big scarred lion, specifically. They rode them on their patrols around the workhouse at night, and sometimes, albeit rarely, through the fields when they were dealing with troublesome workers. And that last bit I only knew from previous experiences and my own attempts at escape at previous plantations. I'd yet to see anyone being disciplined or brought down by a guard here, yet.

Still, this couldn't be anything but trouble. I stand up from the row and brace myself for whatever's to come, thinking back on my time here. Wondering what I might have done wrong. There's no one else in this field but Ahsan and I today, they couldn't be here for anyone but us.

I'm somewhat relieved when the rider comes into sight and it's Lochan. Not that I'm particularly fond of the prick, obviously, but the lion would be a lot more worrisome. He's never so much as said a word to me, but I know a predator when I see one. It's in their walk, and the hungry way they look at you. Like they'd eat you alive if you gave them the chance.

Lochan at least just seems like your standard guard who's fond of being in a position of power, and from what little I've seen of him interacting with the workers here, he doesn't appear to take pleasure in being abusive. He does, however, take his job seriously. That means keeping us in line, and he's not afraid to be a brute about it, but men like him you can anticipate. Honestly, if he was a little less experienced, a little less sure in the way he carried the scimitar at his side, I'd say he'd be like most other guards I've dealt with.

He slows as he approaches us atop a white, warm-blooded desert horse. He's got a second he's trailing by the reins, which is curious. But whenever a guard makes an appearance in the fields, we're supposed to leave our row and come to stand at the dirt road so we can hear them, so I'm expecting whatever's going on, he's about to tell us.

"I don't need you, Jackal," he says with a dismissive wave of a paw still holding his reins, "so you can get back to work."

"Not without my weeder I can't," I state pointedly. Also, Ahsan is suddenly looking incredibly nervous and I'm supposed to be watching him, so I'm not about to leave him to the Aardwolf.

"We'll be sending the meerkat over," Lochan says with a snort, spitting on the ground at the horse's feet. "We're relieving Ahsan for the day."

"Why?" He speaks up from behind me. I can feel his presence just at my shoulder, uncomfortably close within my personal space for my tastes, but right now, I don't plan to admonish him.

Lochan hesitates for just a moment, which makes my fur prickle. "You're wanted at the manor," he finally says. "Matron Sura has requested your presence."

I can't see him, but I can feel Ahsan stiffen. He stammers, like he's trying to ask something. I'm fairly certain I know what it is, so I ask instead. "Why?"

Lochan actually rolls his eyes. "As if I should know what's in that fucking woman's head. Come and find out for yourself. All I know is what I needed to know. She requested I bring you, so that's what I've come to do. Are we going to have a problem here?"

I finally turn to look at the hyena. He's strangely still, and very quiet. And he remains that way for quite some time. Lochan seems to be getting impatient, when Ahsan finally straightens up and speaks.

"Can Kadar come?" he asks.

"No," both Lochan and I say in unison. I follow with, "What the hell are you thinking? They don't let workers on the manor estate." I've barely ever been within eyesight of one, in fact.

"Please," Ahsan begs, uncharacteristically not backing down immediately, for once. He looks to Lochan then, as if he could possibly appeal to the Aardwolf. "I don't want to go there alone, Lochan. Please."

"You won't be alone," the Aardwolf reminds him. "I'll be there with you."

"You have to do what she says... what they all say," he murmurs.

"So does he," the Aardwolf points out, and I'm forced to inwardly agree with him, even though it grates at me. Wait, no. Hang that. Since when have I given a damn about following orders? Especially from a hyena.

"Don't speak for me," I growl at the Aardwolf. "I haven't met many soft-bellied clan members who could push me around."

"They don't have to," Lochan snaps. "All they have to do is tell someone else to push for them."

"Like you?" I counter, snarling through a smile. "Go on, Lochan. Push me."

He doesn't seem amused. "We're not arguing about this," he addresses Ahsan, ignoring me entirely. His tone is decidedly gentle with the hyena, a fact I make a mental note of for later. I've long suspected Lochan has a soft spot for, or at the very least is being forced to be kinder in handling the hyena than he would be with the other workers. Probably because of his Matron. "He couldn't even set foot inside the estate, Ahsan. You know that."

"Then just let him come with me as far as the yard," the hyena persists. "Please, sir. I—I would feel much better about going."

"You're going regardless," Lochan states, clearly trying to be firm. "She requested you. That means I bring you to her, one way or another. That's how this works."

"Would you really hurt me, Lochan?" Ahsan asks, and I find the inside of my muzzle's gone strangely dry. There's something altogether new and moreover very strange, about the sudden drop in pitch in the hyena's voice. It's low, gentle, like it normally is, but there's something else, an undercurrent in it that tugs at me. Makes me feel odd. I never knew a man could conjure a voice like that.

Whatever power he has, it apparently holds some sway over Lochan as well, because I see him wavering. "Ahsan—" he begins.

"You said I should make some friends," Ahsan insists, "amongst the workers, when I got here. I did." His eyes flit briefly towards me, then just as quickly, away again. Like he's afraid I won't confirm that he's a friend. Probably wise. "I just don't want to be seen leaving the fields alone. The other workers already suspect I'm afforded extra privileges. If Kadar comes it seems more like we're being called out for some general reason."

It's a good lie, but it doesn't look like Lochan buys it. If I can tell Ahsan is scared, so can he. The difference is, he probably knows why.

Another mental note. The hyena and I are going to talk when this is all over.

"Fine," the Aardwolf says at length with a ragged sigh. The fact that he folded surprises me, and suddenly the two of them are looking at me, and I'm not prepared.

"Kadar?" the hyena's ears drop, his eyes searching mine imploringly. "You'll come, right?"

Whatever this is, I'm not sure I want to get dragged into it. On the other hand, I'm a man of my word, and Ahsan seems earnestly scared. And I did promise I'd protect the little shit. And it's a chance to see the Manor.

"What the hell," I shrug. "I'll track mud inside their pretty gates.

Sure."

Ahsan gives an earnest smile that melts even some of my resolve to act like I don't give a damn about any of this. I think I catch a flash of relief in Lochan's expression as well, but it's gone as soon as it appeared. He hands the reins off to Ahsan, who looks to me.

"What?" I say dryly. "I can't ride."

"The Matron's estate is across another part of the plantation where we grow rice," Lochan states, tapping at his horse's sides with his ankles. "The land's flooded. You're not going on foot, you'll be a sodden mess."

"Sounds like fun," I snort. "It's hot out."

"I'm already regretting allowing this," the Aardwolf calls back to Ahsan as he begins ambling his horse down the row.

"You've never been on a horse?" Ahsan asks me shyly.

I tip my ears back. "Horses are expensive," I inform him. "My family never even owned a goat."

"Just, um," he pauses, "here… I'll help you up."

He puts two hands together, and it takes me a moment to figure out what he's doing. Luckily for him I used to use the same trick with a few friends of mine growing up to climb walls into the inner district when I was too hungry to care about my father's 'no stealing' rule. I put my footpaw in his palms and step up, pulling myself up onto the back of the large animal in a less-than-graceful manner. I'm feeling fairly unstable when he slides up behind me, entirely without assistance. I can feel his chest inches from my back, and the fur along my nape prickles when he reaches around me, but it's only for the reins.

"I probably should have sat behind you," I point out. I hadn't exactly been the one to make the choice, after all. He could have gotten up in front of me instead of how he chose to. I don't know why that bothers me, but it sort of does. I feel like it should have been reversed.

"It doesn't really make much of a difference, does it?" he asks.

"I guess not," I grouse, flicking my tail aside, since he was nearly sitting on it.

He clicks at the horse and does something with his legs, and we begin to move. I can't seem to get my balance on the damned thing as it is, but when we really get moving to catch up with Lochan it's not only a lot faster than I'd anticipated, but we... bounce... a lot. With a curse under my breath, I grab at the mane of the animal as my weight begins to shift, and I can't help but lean back. I feel like I might almost fall for a moment, but then my back hits Ahsan's chest and his elbows tighten around my sides.

I don't like how vulnerable all this makes me feel, how dependent I am on him at this very moment, but I'm not about to bring that up. Instead I try to focus on watching the fields move by. I can see why the people with money and power prefer to go everywhere on horseback. It's damned uncomfortable, but it does make you feel above the rest of the world. Literally as well as figuratively.

"Your paws are very large," Ahsan murmurs, rather out of nowhere.

"Excuse me?" I snuff.

"Just... when you were stepping up," his murmur becomes more of a mumble. "I noticed."

"I'm a large man," I say, confused and unsure whether or not I should be offended. "They're proportionate. Why? Are you trying to say something?"

"No!" He says rather quickly. "N—no. I'm sorry."

"You're stranger than I ever gave you credit for," I mutter. And that marks the end of our conversation for the rest of the ride. I see a few of the other workers I recognize as we move through the fields, although not Raja, thank the Gods. I don't even want to know what he'd think about all of this. I do see Chandan however, and I catch a questioning look from him as we ride past. I'll have to talk to him later, after I know what the hell this is all about. Right now I'm as clueless as him.

We near the rice paddies after about half an hour of travel, proving just how vast this plantation is. The rice is probably just for the clan family, because the flooded fields aren't that large, and I can already see what *must* be the Manor in the distance. It's enormous. It's hard to believe at first that it's a dwelling at all. I've seen large buildings in the city I grew up in, of course, but the largest there that I ever laid my eyes on was a temple. And this house is at least as big, and better maintained. The roof doesn't appear to be made of gold, like the Grand Temple in the Capital is famed to be, but it's covered in clay red shingles that shine in the sun, and a sandy brick exterior. Probably made entirely from bricks from the local clay flats. I wonder briefly if I'd ever made that many bricks in my entire working life.

It's hard to fathom anyone having this much wealth, when every coin you've ever chased has been so elusive. How do they make it all? Where do they *keep* it? How well must they eat, if they can afford to spend *so* much on bricks?

I can't see much other than the top two floors of the Manor, because there's a stone wall that surrounds most of the Estate. And it is not made of brick, but smooth, large, rectangular stones. Flat. Tall enough that even the largest workers couldn't grab at the top to pull themselves over. Incredibly difficult to climb, if it's possible at all. There's a gate, of course, but it's wrought iron and predictably sharp all along the top.

Lochan pulls his horse to a stop ahead of us and calls out past the gates. I just barely catch the back of an armored hyena as he moves to the side, then returns a few moments later with another man in matching armor. Hardened camel leather, by the look of it.

Well-fitted. Expensive. I had a neighbor back in the district I grew up near the Hyronses who was a tanner. Reeked like piss and sinew, but I could listen to him talk about his craft all day. What he did was artistry, not just labor. There's no artistry in making bricks.

With a heavy metallic clang, likely a lock being unhinged, the gates begin to swing open. I peer past the horse's neck and catch my first glimpse inside the estate. I can't help but notice the paved white stone that forms a path towards the house, bold white against the otherwise sandy, tan earth. If there are gates to the afterlife that truly do lead to enlightenment, to paradise, that must be what they look like, I decide. A pristine white walkway, cutting through the dirty earth.

Except this one's also flanked on all sides by a garden, spread out over the inside of the grounds. As we make our way inside, I sweep my eyes over the bounty before us and wonder how the hell there's enough water in the world for so much to grow. Many of the plants, I've never even seen before. Succulent, thorned bushes with flowers, trees that grow so straight and proud they'd have put my father's posture to shame. Fruit-bearing bushes, a whole row of fig trees, something with large orange globes dangling so heavily from its branches, it seems almost obscene to me.

The grounds themselves actually look larger from the inside than I imagined them to be from the gates. There isn't even just one dwelling. There are several smaller ones, spread out sporadically amongst the landscape of criss-crossing pathways and gardens. There are also several statues spread throughout, depicting gods and goddesses of the Hyena pantheon. I've seen their like before in the cities, but in the lower districts the lions had knocked several of the arms off the statue of Ishma long ago, and her body was carved with graffiti. It had even become a beloved local custom to festoon a jagged part of her lower abdomen with rotten, suggestive fruits and vegetables.

Actually, that was a myth I could settle right now, come to think about it.

"Hey, Ahsan," I ask casually, "do female hyenas really have penises?"

"What?" he exclaims, his whole body startling.

I shrug. "Poshka, a friend of mine growing up, claimed he'd seen one naked once. He said she had a penis. I thought that was just a myth the lions cooked up."

"I... wh..." he stammers.

I smirk. "They do, don't they?"

"I never said that!" he insists in a hushed, horrified whisper.

"Your lack of any denial speaks volumes."

"You two aren't being as quiet as you think you are, you know," Lochan calls back to the two of us as we begin down one of the paved white rows.

"I agreed to come, not to keep my muzzle shut," I remark cheerfully. "And you're not disagreeing either, Lochan."

"It's 'Master' Lochan," the Aardwolf mutters. "And what makes you think I'd know?"

"Well, you're—"

"*Not* a hyena!" he barks.

"...I was going to say in close with the clan. A man in your position?" I snort. "I know the guards don't just fuck the workers. Are you honestly saying you haven't ever?"

Lochan sighs. And then oddly, answers me. "It isn't a penis. It's just that their sex is larger than most females."

I arch my brow. "Women are a different shape entirely. I don't get your meaning."

"H—he means their..." Ahsan stumbles over his words, awkwardly, then clears his throat and gets it out. "Their 'bud."

"Their what?"

"Please don't make him define that," Lochan growls from just a few feet ahead of us now. We've slowed our horses so that we're nearly walking side by side. The Aardwolf gives me a sidelong, irritated look, which slowly morphs into one of earnest surprise as I continue to stare at him blankly, waiting for him to be more clear. Then he starts laughing.

"Please tell me you weren't ever married!" he guffaws.

My chest tightens, and the stiffness goes through my whole body. "I *was*," I grate out.

"That poor woman!" he cackles.

I curl up my lip, feeling the edge of my canines, balling a fist at my side. Whatever the hell the bastard finds funny about my lost life, I can't guess, but in my mind it's not something any man should be finding humor in. It's entirely possible he just gets off on stories of woe, and feeling superior over all the poor souls who work these fields. If he wasn't marked for a fierce beating in my mind before, he is now.

"Kadar?" Ahsan leans somewhat over my shoulder. "You had a wife?"

"Most men have had wives when they're my age," I respond icily.

"I just," he flicks an ear, averting his eyes, "never knew."

"How would you?" I reply, pushing the three words out with the same coldness, so he knows to stop. Right now.

He doesn't seem to catch on, though.

"What was she like?" He asks. "Did she—"

"Ahsan," I snap, not masking the growl beneath my voice. "I was married. I am no longer. That ought to suggest to you that something went south, right? So maybe I don't want to fucking talk about it."

"I'm sorry," he says, shrinking back. His arms inch away from my body, holding the reins wider.

"Boys," Lochan cuts into the following silence with a tone of authority. "Clan guards. Keep your muzzles shut for a bit, would you? Try and behave."

I spot what he's talking about a few seconds after he mentions it. There's a fairly large group of men and women in the distance, gathered around a granite basin, which I can only assume is used to keep water in. For what purpose I don't know, but they should really keep a better watch over their resources, because it's currently full of birds, which are probably ruining the water. There are five of them, (the guards, not the birds) the most amount of armored warriors I've seen in some time. At least since that unfortunate incident a few plantations back that saw me nursing a flayed back for several weeks, and ended my employment there.

These guards are even more heavily armed, with falchions that look both ceremonial and well-made. They're wearing that camel-hide like the gate guards, and two of the women are wearing something on their belt I've never seen before, but I'm all but certain by the amount of metal comprising it that it's some kind of weapon. It looks almost like a crossbow with the bow removed. Odd.

Lochan seems to spot where my eyes are wandering, and sniffs. "Amur weapons," he says distastefully. "Sloppy. Imprecise. Loud. Only a coward kills you from ten paces away."

"I don't like it when they practice with them," Ahsan murmurs. "It hurts my ears."

"They're all the rage for the clans that can afford them, these days," Lochan sighs. "I miss the age when 'exotics' meant rare pelts and pets. We gave those curs a good, hard shove in the last war, letting them inch their way back in now is only going to start another one down the line."

"I don't know much about the war," I mutter disinterestedly. Even people like me knew about it, of course. Everyone in Mataa did. The Amur, otherwise known as the 'Dog Lords' to most, share our northern border, and their ways are worlds apart from ours. I'd heard them called many things. Pretentious, arrogant, greedy... always looking to convert the world to their specist way of thinking. Honestly, they didn't sound too far off from the hyena clans. Except canine, so who knows, maybe I'd have had an easier life if I'd been born there.

In Mataa most canines were in unfortunate circumstances, not quite at the bottom since we could be fierce and hardy, but certainly very few were ever afforded the chances that a hyena, or even a lion, might have. Even the tigers fair better on the whole. Of course, they were enormous and tended towards isolated families, so really it was more a case of most people not wanting to bother them. I'd never really been close with a tiger. Jackals and tigers rarely mixed.

"The more we rely on them for trade, the more we let them in," Lochan growls. "That's how they want it. Get their claws in again."

"I met a, um..." Ahsan pauses, "...I don't know. Dog. There are many kinds, I'm told. This one was actually very small. Shorter than Matron Sura. He was the one who came to sell the pistols. He stayed for nearly a week, and I thought he was actually very nice."

"Don't let their manners fool you," Lochan snorts. "It's all fake niceties. They're all about appearance. Gotta cover up the stink somehow."

"I didn't think he smelled bad," Ahsan shrugs. "Different. More like you than me, Kadar."

"Then he reeked," I reply. Lochan laughs again.

"He walked with me in the garden," Ahsan recounts quietly, his ears tipped back. "He talked a lot about my collar. He said it was wrong."

"Yeah, that's what they fought the war over," Lochan says. "Or, at least, that's the excuse they used. They want all people to be free to know their place in their rutting hierarchy of holiness."

"I'll live with being unholy if it means you'd cut this fucking thing off me," I feel the desire to step in to the conversation.

"They're not your saviors, Jackal," Lochan bites back. "Stop talking ignorant shit. You don't know a damn thing about any of this. You want to know what that bloody war accomplished? The Hyronses choked with bodies, twenty-odd cities burned to the ground, and now we get to call you 'indentured servants' instead of 'slaves.'"

"Not much of a difference there."

"Exactly," he fixes his eyes on me. "The Amur aren't going to set you free. You know what will? Work. Do your damned job every day, keep your nose out of the Divine, and you'll pay off your contract and leave this place a free man."

"I don't believe that for a second," I say flatly.

"This place isn't like other plantations," the Aardwolf states. "Your board is low, that's why the lodgings are sparse and we don't buy much meat. It's so you sorry bastards don't rack up more debt than you make in a day. We don't run our place like that."

"Why?" I ask, unimpressed. If he thought I was buying this load of horse shit, he was wrong. I wasn't new to plantation work. Indentured servitude kept you indentured, for as long as possible. Usually until the worker broke down and was too useless to own any more. We were charged for lodging, for food, for the tools we used, practically for the air we breathed. And all of that came off our earnings each day. You could put in a year of back-breaking work and owe more than you'd begun with.

"Because an angry, frustrated worker is a pain in the ass to control?" he offers. "Because broken-down, old workers don't pull their weight? Take your pick. Work-forces like that only suffer in the long run. It's more cost efficient to keep a string of cheap, young, new workers coming in. That's why we take problem cases like you with low contracts. Reform you, get you off your lazy ass, get you working and paying off your debt. Everyone fares better in the end."

"Hyenas don't give a damn about how anyone 'fares' unless it's another hyena," I flick an ear back towards Ahsan, "and sometimes not even then."

"Hyenas don't run this work-force," Lochan growls. "I do."

I tip both of my ears up at that, surprised. I'd never pegged Lochan as anything more than a guard, but he sounded dead serious. And offended, which supported the idea that he might just actually be taking pride in what he was saying. He wouldn't be so defensive about the hyenas, he'd made it abundantly clear he didn't want to be lumped in with them by this point. So it was possible he was honestly telling the truth.

Was the clan here allowing a non-hyena as an Overseer? Granted, he was close enough, and maybe that was why it was a possibility at all.

"Both of you, shut up," Lochan suddenly snaps in a harsh whisper, and I soon see why. We're rounding a large row of thick bushes, and behind them, I can hear the sounds of many footsteps, many horses, and a lot of conversation. The occasional distinctive bark of laughter means hyenas. Many, many hyenas.

Lochan and Ahsan both slow their horses and we take the corner, coming out into the sun past the gardens. The Manor looms tall and shining before us, with a wide, paved courtyard surrounded on all sides by those imposing bushes that blocked our line of sight until now. There's a statue of a hyena in the center of the court, not a deity I recognize, so possibly just of a clan member. She's tall and thick-bodied, holding a spear in one hand and a large rolled scroll beneath her other arm, and she's staring outward at the main entranceway (not the one we walked our horses through of course, that one is more off to the side), as though defending the Manor.

Most importantly, however, are the throngs of hyenas filling the courtyard. There are at least a dozen horses about, either being led by servants or still mounted by their riders, and several ornate tangas pulled up in the courtyard lot. It's clear by the dust and sand caked on their wheels that some of them came particularly far. The place is crawling with spotted hyenas, all of which look to be either wealthy, or working for those who are. The bright array of expensive dyes and baubles festooning their clothing denote them from their various regions, but all of them are spotted.

"A clan gather?" Ahsan says worriedly. I can feel him stiffen behind me, as he turns to Lochan. "I'm… I'm just going to get in the way here, Lochan."

"The Matron requested you," Lochan says, dismounting. "Now that you're here you need to at least go speak to her."

I shift on the horse, ready to get off. I start by clumsily trying to jerk a leg over one side of its back, growling out a, "Not planning on helping me off, then?" back towards Ahsan. But when I turn to look at him, I'm struck by the fear in his eyes. Not only that. He's physically shaking.

This isn't like his usual nerves. Something's wrong. I turn as well as I can atop the horse and reach a hand out, jostling his shoulder. "Hey," I say, and he seems to snap out of it for a moment, blinking up at me, "let's get off this thing."

He nods mechanically and slides off the back of the horse, reaching a hand up and helping me down afterwards. I try not to embarrass myself. I have to dust off my inner thighs and adjust a thing or two after my feet touch the ground again, and it occurs to me that people who intentionally ride for long periods of time must either be crazy, or female.

"Kadar," Ahsan speaks, quietly but sort of rushed. "I don't want to be here."

I regard him silently for a moment. But looking at the way he's subtly shaking, at the nervous twitch of his whiskers and his now perpetually tipped-back ears, it doesn't take me long to come to a decision. Hyena or no, I know fear when I see it, and I don't need to know why right now.

"Alright," I say, reaching out to put a hand on his shoulder. "Hang this. Let's get the hell out of here."

"Ahsan," Lochan warns, from behind us. I'm about to tell him to shove off, when Ahsan's eyes widen, and I realize Lochan's warning was not meant idly.

"Ah! It's my little one!" a smooth, feminine voice speaks up from the courtyard beyond us. I don't miss how Ahsan's attention suddenly becomes fixated, and I can't help but look myself as the figure of a slender, hawk-like woman parts the crowd in her way as she makes a path towards us. She's a hyena of course, flanked on both sides by two enormous male guards with equally imposing arms and armor, and one female guard in less flashy attire, keeping a vigil behind her. The woman herself looks fragile, older and strangely malnourished for someone wearing so much wealth on her physical person. Her saree alone probably costs more than I've made in my working life, the color of the sea and trimmed with gold, with glistening patterns of small crystals over it that shine like waves shifting. She's wearing gold bracelets that come nearly to her elbow, her nose and ears are pierced with dangling gold jewelry and her fingers are covered in rings. She couldn't be more audacious if she tried.

The only female hyena in a position of power that I'd ever previously seen was part of a Syndicate, and she didn't look like this. She was thicker, armed and armored, missing part of an ear and looked tough as hell. Like she'd give me a run for my money in a scrap. There wasn't much that was what I'd call 'ornamental' about her. But I guess there's a big difference between the clans that run the drugs and sell them on the streets and in their parlors, and the clans that grow and supply them.

Ahsan actually pulls away from my hand, and bewildered, I let him. He slowly approaches the woman, her guards allowing him to do so without any sign of getting in his way, and I have to bite my tongue to stop myself from correcting his posture, because he's fallen back into that submissive hunch. This time though, it doesn't seem to be from fear. I think I catch the hint of a hopeful smile on his muzzle, as the woman smooths a hand over his head and pushes back some of his mane, threading her bejeweled fingers through it. The whole scene makes me incredibly uncomfortable, for some reason.

The woman clucks her tongue and sighs. "You're filthy," she admonishes in a soft, almost motherly tone. "Look at you." She curls a paw around one of his ears and cups it, rubbing a pawpad over a spot of dirt ground into his fur on the lobe of his ear, where he must have once had a piercing. I'd actually seen it that morning and considered pointing out to him that it might get an infection if he didn't wash it out, but I felt a bit guilty about doing so, since it had probably gotten that way from him sleeping in the dirt the last week or so, after I'd stolen his mat.

"Are you ready to come back home, now?" I hear her say, and that's the first time since she's arrived that Ahsan actually turns to look at me again. She follows his line of sight, and sets her green-eyed gaze at me, something sour in her expression, only vaguely disguised by her mask of indifference.

"Aard," she levels her stare at Lochan, "why is there a dust dog inside my estate?"

"Ahsan wouldn't come without him, Matron," Lochan explains in a subdued tone.

"He's my friend," Ahsan finally speaks up. I've never heard him sound so placating, so soft-spoken. I have to crane an ear to even hear his words.

"You made a friend?" The Matron turns back towards Ahsan. It's hard for even me to tell whether the question hid a threat, or was simply a question. Her tone is passive, hard to read. It's not hard to read the way Ahsan's ears tip back, though.

"Y—yes," he replies, at length. "In the fields. You said I should get to know the people there."

Her muzzle quirks up in half a smile, and there is nothing masking the edge of mockery in her tone, this time. "Oh, little one," she strokes his mane again, before removing her paw and flicking some of the dirt off of it, "I didn't think they'd give you much of a choice in getting to 'know' them better. They're field workers." Her gaze returns to mine for just a moment, before disregarding me again, and returning to Ahsan. "I just hope you haven't caught anything… unfortunate."

For some reason, Ahsan glances away guiltily at that, and for the life of me I can't understand why. I know what she's implying, and I also know for a fact that nothing of the sort has happened between Ahsan and I. The implication leaves me feeling pretty damn insulted, though.

Whatever. People like this are never going to see me as any more than a feral animal. I learned that long ago. May as well make the most of it.

"Hey," I speak up, and everyone, the Matron, her guards, Ahsan, and a startled-looking Lochan, all look my way. I scratch some of the dirt off the underside of my neck ruff, especially where it's embedded beneath my collar, making sure to pick a piece or two off with my claws and flick it on to her pristine walkway. "Anywhere I can take a piss? Ride here was *long*, and jostled my boys around something fierce. All the water around this place don't help, either."

The look of complete disgust I get from the woman is worth

whatever comes next, I decide immediately. I'm not terribly surprised when Lochan grabs me by the shoulders and shoves me down forcefully onto my knees. I make sure I don't make it easy on him, but he's a strong bastard.

"Please forgive his tongue, Matron," Lochan says through grit teeth. "He's not accustomed to being in the presence of a woman of station."

"Charming," the Matron says acridly. "Just get it out of my courtyard, please?"

"As you say, Matron," Lochan says, dutifully. "Shall I wait in the stables?"

"Wait?" She brushes the back of a paw over her glistening saree fabric, probably wiping off imagined dirt. "Whatever for?"

"To return Ahsan to the fields, Matron," Lochan gently reminds her.

She again quirks that odd, almost mocking smile. "That may not be necessary, Aard. But if you wish. If I've not sent for you by dusk, take the jackal and go." She begins to turn, then pauses. "Oh. And don't ever bring him, or any other field worker, within these gates again. You're forgiven this one time, but don't make this mistake again."

"Yes Matron," Lochan replies dutifully, bowing his head. I'm at eye level with him, within a foot from him at his side, which is about the closest I've ever been to the man side-by-side. So for just a moment, I feel oddly like I'm on the same level as him, standing beside him as a fellow worker, not as a servant and a guard. We are both bowing to the same woman, in the end.

Also, there's something prickling at the back of my mind. As if there's something my eyes caught that my mind has yet to register. I reflect on it for a few moments, trying to dig up what it might be... and then it occurs to me.

Aardwolves have a very thick mane that comes down their shoulders, and in Lochan's case, is partially pulled out and hangs messily braided down his back. But his neck ruff is oddly staggered where it should be flowing seamlessly into his mane. There's a crease there, where the fur grew wrong, probably over a long period of time.

I run a finger beneath the edge of my collar, where the metal has begun to create a groove in my own fur.

Well that's interesting.

"*Now*, Aard," the Matron emphasizes, and then he's pulling me back up onto my feet and dragging me away from the courtyard. I look back towards Ahsan, thinking I'm going to see another of those plaintive, frightened looks, and wondering what I'll do when I see it. But now that the Matron's here he doesn't even spare a glance back for me. I leave feeling irritated and vaguely betrayed. Why the hell was I even worried to begin with? He used to work here. He was well taken-care-of, even. In fact if that meeting was any indication, he was something of a favorite of the head Matron. Of course he'd be happy to return here, if even for a day. He'll be treated like a pampered pet. Spoiled.

There's that question lingering in the back of my mind, of course. If it was really as pleasant to work here as his serene smile seemed to denote, why would he have wanted to leave?

Maybe he was sent off as part of a punishment? Was that it? Was that at an end, now? Back to house work for him?

Good, I tell myself. More trouble than I needed.

"Ahsan seemed fine," I mutter as I follow Lochan towards the stables. He's re-taken the reins of our horses and is leading them. Still keeping an eye on me, though. Ever vigilant. As if there was anything I could do inside these walls, with all these guards around.

"Hm?" he rumbles.

"I'm just saying, we can probably leave," I sigh. I don't exactly want to go back to work on the fields, but I also don't feel like wasting my time here, watching rich hyenas cavort around their little oasis.

"We stay until he's ready to leave," Lochan says in a firm tone.

"That woman seemed to think he wouldn't be," I point out.

"Yes, well, she thought that the last three times."

I stop in my tracks. "He's been back before?" I ask, uncertain what that could mean.

Lochan regards me fully, turning his entire body to face me. Instead of answering my question, he asks instead, "Do you honestly care?"

"What?" I bristle.

He shrugs, almost casually. "It just seems to me like you're not all that interested in his welfare. Do you really care what happens to him? Because if you just want to leave, I can send you with another guard."

I pause, making sure not to stammer. Father ground into my head that only children stammer. If you're uncertain, stay silent. But Lochan is looking at me, expecting an answer, and I'm honestly having trouble finding one. *Do I care?* I think back on the food, the mat, the fact that he's actually an inoffensive person to work beside. I decide inwardly that that's enough of an excuse to care.

"Say I do," I say, trying to sound as casual as he does. I'm not as good at it as the older Aardwolf. "Do you? I have to assume you wouldn't have brought him here if he was in danger or something."

"I had orders," Lochan states. There's something hard beneath his tone, like saying that actually bothered him. Shit. That isn't good.

"What the hell did he do here?" I finally ask, outright. "His work, I mean. What sort of servant was he to the clan family?"

Lochan's muzzle twitches, and he glances aside. Again, shit. I'm liking this less and less by the second.

"I think you can imagine," he finally says, his gaze returning to mine. "Most people notice it in his manner. I know you're dense, jackal, but you can't be *that* dense."

My mouth's gone dry. I nod, because yeah, I'd noticed. I'd convinced myself until now it was something else, because you don't always think sex worker when you're dealing with a man. But the signs were all there. The placating, submissive demeanor. The way he's always touching me like it's second nature, his unflinching reactions to being manhandled and his quiet acceptance on the one occasion I almost hit him.

It makes disgust coil low in my belly, and I want to reserve all of that for the clan family, but some of it, I had to admit to myself, is also leveled at Ahsan. I know that's probably unfair… that he'd probably not chosen in what manner he was to pay off his contract… but I still can't shake it. I'd always had a lot of revulsion for the women in the city I grew up in who sold their bodies, and even for the servants in the Red Lantern district. Even though I knew they had less choice in the matter. It was hard not to see them as dirty, as tainted. Many of them were diseased, and even though I knew that likely wasn't the case with Ahsan or I would have smelled it, it didn't entirely alleviate the suspicion.

And somehow, it seems worse, because he's a man. He's stronger, at least physically. He could do other work that some of those women couldn't do. He doesn't have to sell his body.

But that's exactly what he'd been doing, I realize. Maybe that's why he'd ultimately gone to the fields. To escape that life. One person would know for sure.

"Was Ahsan sent to the fields as some kind of punishment?" I ask, as we move into the relative cool of the stables. I actually like it better here. The reek of animals and hay is more natural to me than the pristine courtyard and the overwhelming scents of pollen and fruit. "Or was it his choice to leave?"

Lochan leads the horses into two adjoining stables and begins hanging buckets for them. "It was his decision. Although I believe he felt he had little choice in the matter."

"Were they hurting him here?" I ask directly.

Lochan's eyes snap to mine, and for a moment he looks strangely defensive. He pours some water in one of the buckets, keeping his gaze leveled on mine. "That sounds dangerously close to you giving a damn," he states.

"I already told you I did," I reply. "We work together. Servants have to look out for one another."

Lochan snorts. "Someone should tell them that, then."

"What does it matter to you whether or not I care? I'm asking, aren't I?"

"Well," Lochan hefts the bucket with an exhale. "It's just that when he started giving his meat to someone other than Raja, I was a might concerned whoever it was might be taking advantage of him. The cheetah at least left him alone. I haven't missed you've claimed his sleeping mat, you know." He points between his eyes and mine. "You think I don't keep tabs on my workers?"

I'm getting the sneaking suspicion the Aardwolf and I are both dancing around the same issue, so I just say it. "Look, if you're worried, I'm worried," I say. "Alright? He's a simpering little shit, but I don't like watching the Clans abuse people. Problem is, I'm not exactly in any place to do anything about it. You are."

"I get him extra rations on the fields and look out for his well-being," Lochan says. "And I didn't steal his sleeping mat in exchange for that. Besides, I'm just as beholden to the Clan family as you are." He shrugs, but it's less casual this time. "If they want him here, I bring him here. I can't exactly hide the boy away, whether or not I think there's been ill treatment. I oversee the fields, not what happens here. If it was one of my guards abusing a worker, I'd have some say, but—"

"I'd just think you'd have a lot of sympathy for a servant being abused, is all," I say carefully, gauging his reaction.

I get one, but it's hard to read. He looks at me a moment, evenly but silently, then he just fills the second bucket. "Every servant is his own man, in the end," he says at length. "The boy's made his own choices in addition to the choices that were made for him. I'd think a fiery jackal like you would get that. Self-reliance, and all that. Boy needs to fight his own battles."

I want to agree with him, because what he just said sounds like something my own father would have said. Something I would have said, before the last two weeks. But this situation is complicated, and I don't know if that kind of logic works for someone like Ahsan. How can you ask someone to make their own choices, when they've been conditioned not to?

Lochan moves off to one corner of the stables and I to the other. At some point he must have grabbed a piece of fruit, because he begins eating it while we wait. I stand at the open doors, peering out into the sunlight and the courtyard beyond, arms crossed over my chest, my mind a tangle. I hate thinking like this. I prefer my decisions to be straightforward. Obvious. They usually are, in my mind. I can almost tell what seems right and what seems wrong. But this is… deep. Deeper than I like to go. Too many things to consider, and I'm not good at consideration.

Time passes slowly at first, then as most of the hyenas filter off into the Manor, I become engrossed watching all the birds around this place, and I lose myself in other thoughts. Thoughts far away from here, concerning the people in the world I *should* be worrying over. People I lost track of long ago, who might need me now. And I'm trapped here. I watch one of the small, fruit-fattened birds dancing around in the water in one of those basins, and a moment later, like it's the most natural thing in the world, it flits off and is gone. I can't help but be envious. Something so simple, so common, would solve every problem in my life. Collars mean nothing if you can fly.

The courtyard's been empty for at least an hour now, I'm certain. I'm considering sneaking back out there to steal some fruit myself, because my stomach's begun to growl, when I catch a voice on the wind. Or at least, I think I do. Whoever they are, they aren't speaking loudly. The only reason I thought I heard it at all was because it vaguely sounded like Ahsan. Gods, am I back to worrying about that wretch? I thought I'd put him from my mind.

But then I hear it again and no, it's definitely real. There's another voice too, louder, older. Neither of them is shouting or anything, but something about Ahsan's tone sets my nerves on edge. I can't help it. My feet are moving before the rest of me stops to think whether or not it's a good idea.

"Hey!" Lochan calls out to me from where he's seated. But he'd made the mistake this time of being at the opposite end of the barn, and I was leaning on the door, so all I have to do is duck around it, and I'm out of sight. I hear him curse behind me, and the shuffle of the larger man shifting his bulk, but by that point I know I'm finally out of sight of him, and I seize the moment, taking off across the courtyard. Maybe I'm running at this point just out of sheer glee from having slipped the Aardwolf, but despite that I'm still definitely heading in the direction I heard those voices from.

The Manor is shaped sort of like a sideways V, and it's around the lower prong that the voices sound louder. I haven't seen a guard yet, they must all be at the gates or inside, so I'm home free to wander. There isn't much more of interest behind the Manor than there was in front. More bushes. Another statue, although I only see one back here. Probably wanted to keep most of those in front, where they'd maximize the impression they made on people. Back here it seems sparser in general, and I see several open doors that lead down into the rooms beneath the Manor, where I hear voices of many different peoples, not just hyenas. I also smell food cooking. So, probably the kitchens and servant hallways.

The voices I heard actually weren't far around this corner. Outside, not close to the Manor. I smell Ahsan before I spot him, as well as the musky scent of an older male hyena. You can never mistake them. I catch the end of something Ahsan was saying, something about 'enjoying my work,' but at that point I'm getting close and I really don't want to be seen, either by them or Lochan, so I duck behind a hedge and crouch-crawl my way forward a bit, perking my ears just enough past the edge of the foliage that I'm fairly certain I'll be able to hear most of what they're saying now. I feel a bit ridiculous, acting like a pup like this, but at the same time it's sort of an immature thrill.

Until I hear what the hyena's been saying.

"—your Matron's given her permission, and accepted my offer. It's nearly double your contract."

"I don't feel I'm honestly worth that much, Lord," Ahsan's voice, now. Quiet, and with that edge of fear I've come to know so well, returned after so little time. Whatever happened inside in the last hour, it clearly wasn't what he'd hoped for. "I'm certain you could find a better... younger... smaller boy, for much less."

"Your mother's the one who prefers you slight," the man says in a deceptively soft, easy tone. It makes my skin crawl. "I'm very fond of the young man you grew into. I would never berate you for that."

"She doesn't—"

"Of course not," he eases, and I hear the shifting of cloth, and know without looking that he's got his hands on Ahsan. I can smell the sudden spike in fear from the striped hyena, like prey reacting to a predator. "Your mother loves you, Ahsan. But you're older now, and it's really time for you to move on. You know I'd provide for you."

A long pause, and a short inhalation of breath. "She really said... she wanted to sell me?" Ahsan asks, his voice trembling.

"I'm certain she'll miss you greatly," the older hyena says gently. "But you're an adult now. You're not her 'little one' any longer." A pregnant pause. "I think you know, it's what's right for her, as well. Having you here, it puts a lot of strain on her. You've seen that, haven't you? She has to run the clan. She really doesn't need the distraction."

My breath catches in my throat. By 'mother', does he mean the Matron? Is that just a term they use for her regarding all her servants? I've never heard it before. But it can't be literal. Ahsan is striped, Matron Sura is a spotted hyena. I'm no expert on hyena clans, but I know at least that the two can't have children together.

"It's what's right," the older hyena says again, and I hear Ahsan's paws on the cobbled walkway, stepping backwards. I know the sound of his footsteps by now. That scent of fear is strong in the air, and the mix of smells I'm getting off the older hyena are disturbing. He has bad teeth, I can tell that much right away. Also, he drank recently, and there's the definite reek of arousal mixed in there. We're in a very isolated area of the yard, but still, surely he wouldn't attempt anything in public like this?

"Please don't," Ahsan barely whispers, and I don't need to see what's going on to know he's being touched. It hardly even matters where, whether or not he's being violated or just got paws on him he doesn't want there. I don't need to remember meat with my meals and a sleeping mat to know I've got an obligation. This is an easy decision, simple right and wrong. I'm almost relieved, because it means I can think about all the complicated shit later.

I stand and round the hedge, seeing the two of them standing in the clearing obscured from sight by some of those same tall bushes. I wonder vaguely if that's the whole reason for them, so hyenas can have clandestine liaisons and do shit like this to their servants without running the risk of being seen.

As it turns out, the older hyena, whom I can now see is one of the men who was in the courtyard earlier, (a tall, lean man who still somehow manages to sport a potbelly) has only got a hand wrapped around Ahsan's forearm, and another on his hip. Still, the striped hyena seems none too happy about the fact, and is in the middle of saying, "Please don't—" again when he spots me, his eyes going wide and his ears perking. The hyena seems engrossed in another diatribe about his selling points, when I interrupt him.

"Hey," I growl. I get his attention real fast, and he turns to regard me.

However, when he spots my collar, he only scoffs. "Do you mind? Return to the kitchens, or wherever it is you came from, else I'll report you to the guards."

"Let go of him," I demand, not shouting, not even letting my fur get riled. I'm not intimidated by this man.

The hyena almost laughs, but mostly he seems offended. He's wearing rich man's clothing, but no weapons, I note. Probably keeps guards. Pity he didn't bring them with him. "You presume to order me about?" he snorts. "Go on now. I'm not a cruel man, I don't like to see servants disciplined unless they've earned it. Get on back to your work and no one needs to know you were neglecting it."

"He doesn't want you holding him like that," I state, looking past him to Ahsan. "Do you?"

Ahsan pauses for just a moment, then swallows and shakes his head, averting his gaze from the hyena. Who still hasn't let go of him. In fact if anything, his grip on his arm seems to have tightened, and he yanks at Ahsan, causing the striped hyena to yelp. That about does it for me.

"I won't say it again," the man says, showing yellowed fangs.

93

"No, you won't," I agree.

He leaves himself so open to the punch, it's almost unsatisfying. But then I hear the crack of a tooth as my fist slams into his muzzle and I decide, no, totally worth it. The force of the hit sends him spinning to the ground, and he lets go of Ahsan's arm in the process, grabbing at air as he falls. He doesn't manage to catch himself much, so he mostly ends up in a heap on the ground. Ahsan bolts to my side and slightly behind me.

When the man stares back up at me, he's clutching a paw to his muzzle and his eyes are tearing up. He's sputtering and I smell blood, but he can't seem to get a word in past the sobs. I resist the urge to laugh, just barely. I honestly haven't seen someone cry from a punch since I was a kid. It's almost nostalgic.

"Gods-be-damned!" A growl from behind me worries me slightly more, and I put an arm in front of Ahsan protectively, tucking him behind me as Lochan barrels around the corner, his blade out. He skids to a stop in the clearing and assesses the scene, his blade dropping slightly. Then he just glares at me, irritated.

"Kill him!" The hyena on the ground bawls, clutching at his muzzle, blood leaking from between his fingers. "He attacked me!"

"Lord Sachsen-Sura," Lochan sighs, sheathing his blade and moving past me with one last, angry look. He extends a paw to the fallen hyena, "Here, please. Let me help you up."

The man bats at the Aardwolf's hand, fiercely. "You—don't touch me! I want my guards! Get my guards!" He stumbles to his feet slowly, looking wary of me, but unwilling to go near the Aardwolf, either.

"We can do that, Lord," Lochan says, putting his hands out. "But first, I need to know what happened here. This is our territory, after all. Why were you in the garden alone with this servant?"

That gives the hyena pause. I stay silent, because Lochan has this look about him that makes me feel he has the situation in hand.

The Aardwolf exudes the same confidence whenever he's handling an unruly servant. Like he's got the upper hand, and he knows you won't get one over on him.

"That doesn't matter," the older hyena sputters. He stabs a finger in my direction. "I want him handled! Disciplined! Or I'll report this to the Matron!"

"I'll see to it, Lord," Lochan promises. And just like that, the hyena goes silent. I wonder at what point 'killed' turned into 'disciplined'. Probably around the time Lochan pointed out that he had something over the man.

It's probably a net win, considering what I did. I hadn't really considered the consequences of attacking a clan member. Because I never really do. But of all the things I've done in my time as a servant, this was actually a new offense. And probably a very serious one. Even if it had just been one punch… it's possible they *might* have seen it as enough to hang me. It's fortunate Lochan was here.

Gods, did that thought actually just go through my head?

Ahsan is quite literally touching my side almost the entire way out. Lochan herds us back towards the stables, after Lord… whomever… makes a hasty retreat. He didn't seem to want to spend any more time around Lochan than he had to. I saw him cast one last glance back at Ahsan as he left, but it was tinged with anger and loathing. The striped hyena deserved none of it, of course, but I'd be glad if this incident soured his opinion of Ahsan, honestly. The man had bad air around him.

"Ahsan?" I venture a glance down at the hyena hunkering at my side, as we walk back to the stables. His eyes find mine immediately, and I can see the gratitude there, but he's been very quiet ever since we picked him back up. I was going to ask him something about the man, but instead, I settle for, "Are you alright?"

"Yes," he says softly. "Thank you." His muzzle drops at that, and

I think for a moment that he's done, but then just a short while later, he breathes out a few quiet words. "He likes to hurt. Thank you for hurting him back."

I swallow back what tastes like bile in my throat. "No problem," I say, firmly. I don't put a hand on his shoulder or anything, because I feel like he probably doesn't want to be touched right now.

"I take it you're returning to the fields, Ahsan?" Lochan asks, from behind us. He hasn't spoken this whole while, but his voice sounds rough and angry.

"Yes, sir," Ahsan says quietly.

"Fine, then. Let's get going, before we attract any more fucking attention," the Aardwolf growls.

We leave, and honestly, Eden or no, I've never been so glad to leave a place in all my life. To hell with these people and their wasted water and pointless wealth. My fist still stings from where I cracked that bastard in the jaw, and that feeling is worth all the riches in the world right now. What's more, it seems like I might have gotten away with it.

That thought is shattered when we make it back to the servant barracks, though. Because Lochan doesn't take us straight to our sleeping quarters, where everyone else is getting their meals right now, and settling in for the night. Instead, we move past the lively area, and make our way back up a road I recognize. Towards the stone building. The place with the cell, where I've long suspected the guards also live.

I'm briefly afraid I'm going to be locked back up, when Lochan speaks, dispelling those fears. "What you did was incredibly stupid, Jackal," he says from behind us. Although the anger doesn't seem to be there, any more. He mostly sounds tired. "You're lucky that bastard's been on my bad side before, and you're even luckier he was getting handsy with some of the Matron's property in the garden. That's pretty well forbidden on that property, especially if she doesn't know about it. Ahsan. Did she know about it?"

"I... don't know," he admits in a depressive tone. "She just took me inside, talked with me for a little while, but then told me she had a meeting, and that someone else wanted to talk to me. But we were supposed to talk in the common room. It was Lord Sachsen who insisted we go outside."

That sounded very much to me like he'd been set up by the Matron, but it seemed to be enough for Lochan. "Fine," the Aardwolf states. "Don't be so trusting in the future, then. And jackal, don't look so satisfied. That man may not be able to take a punch, but he's dangerous. You picked the wrong hyena to anger."

"Why?" I have to ask.

"Because Lord Sachsen is Matron Sura's Spymaster," he informs me, and my fur goes rigid.

"That sounds bad." I guess.

"For you? Could be," Lochan snorts. "He's got men and women everywhere, and he's petty. He won't take this without some kind of retribution. So we're doing this by the letter of the law. If he thinks you honestly got what you had coming, you're probably in the clear."

I sigh. "How long are you going to lock me up?"

"Oh, that won't be enough for him," Lochan says darkly. "Hyenas like blood."

"What?" Ahsan gasps, "No! N—no, I... it was my fault."

"What kind of blood are we talking?" I ask, keeping my voice impassive.

"Bull whip. You can take it, can't you?"

"I have before," I say with a ragged sigh. I hate the whip. But then everyone does. Nothing worse than dealing with a flayed back in the sun for days. But I can deal with it. It's probably getting off light, considering what happened tonight.

Ahsan seems absolutely distraught, though. His arms have tightened protectively around me where he's holding the reins, and he starts to plead with Lochan. "He did it for me!" He insists. "Because I asked him to protect me. Please, you can't—"

"Ahsan," I say calmly. "I'll live. It's just broken flesh. Won't be the first time. I'll heal."

The hyena's breath is trembling, and I know he wants to say more, but Lochan speaks again before he can. "I'll do it myself," the Aardwolf says. "Clean and fast. You want it that way, trust me. I've got some old rice wine you can wash the wounds in afterwards. Don't need them getting maggots."

Ahsan's breath hitches in what almost sounds like a sob, but there's nothing I can say to him to make him feel any better about all of this. I *did* get myself in trouble on his account. Thing is, this is the kind of trouble I'm used to.

An hour later, I'm standing trembling in the empty, dark bath house, waiting for the striped hyena to bring us our water. My back hurts like hell, and I can feel rivulets of blood tracing their way down through my fur. With the searing pain comes that familiar, burning streak of energy. It makes me feel oddly alive, even if I'm in misery. That's one of the only good things about pain. It reminds you how strong you can be, and that you haven't been put in the ground. Not yet.

It's an odd thing to say, but Lochan really *was* good with the bull whip. He was precise, stayed away from the same areas, made sure to spread the strokes out so the marks wouldn't go deeper. And he did it fast, didn't drag it out like some guards I've dealt with. If I thought the man was a sadist before, I was wrong. That much at least was clear. He hadn't seemed to take *any* pleasure in the act.

Of course, now I have a suspicion why.

I hear Ahsan's pawpads on the wet, cold floor, hurrying back into the bath house. I give a pained whuff of a laugh, murmuring, "Don't drop it now. It's getting colder in here every second. Don't want to have to wait for you to pick up more."

"I'm sorry," he pants, depositing both buckets on the floor with a clatter. I feel his hands on my shoulders, trembling, steering clear of the wounds, but it's clear he's looking at them. His breath catches again and he forces out another, "I'm so sorry."

"Save your apologies for when you pour that wine over my back," I mutter with another mirthless laugh. "Speaking of, let's get that over with."

I hear him uncork the bottle, then pause, but I lash my tail to let him know I'm getting impatient and he begins to pour. I hiss as the first of the alcohol hits my wounds, and there is *nothing* satisfying about this kind of pain, but I know it's necessary, so I bear it.

"Slow," I remind him between grit teeth.

"But it's… hurting you," he says miserably.

"It has to, or it doesn't work," I insist. "You've got to get every wound. Alright?"

"Alright," he says softly, and continues pouring it, more slowly this time, over the marks on my back. I'm fairly certain by the pain alone that he's probably gotten them all, but he uses the whole bottle and I don't stop him.

I lean against the wall after he finishes, exhausted and not too proud to show it right now. I stand there for some time, catching my breath and waiting for the waves of pain and nausea to pass. At length, I hear Ahsan dipping something into one of the buckets, likely one of the rags they give us to wash with, and he rings it out slowly over my back. The water is cool but not cold, he probably heated it over the fire for a few minutes, and it feels pretty good in comparison to the alcohol as it trickles down my back.

"Are you going to be able to work?" he asks quietly.

"I'm a fast healer," I say. "Tomorrow will be rough, the day after a little less so. Give me a few days and I'll forget about them."

"That's very impressive," he says with no false reverence. "I'm not so good with pain."

"My family was full of tough bastards," I chuckle, still not bothering to push myself off the wall. Ahsan goes quiet for a time, gently pressing the washcloth over the wounds. I hadn't asked him to help clean them, but I suppose it's the least he can do.

I don't actually feel like this was all his fault, is the strange thing. I mean yeah, if he hadn't become a part of my life lately, hadn't begged and pressured Raja, and all but forced himself into my sphere, I wouldn't be here right now nursing these wounds. But on the other hand, how the hell do you blame someone for what happened to him at the Manor? And I don't even have most of the story. I haven't asked him why that man called the Matron his 'mother', and the answers that my imagination dredges up whenever I think on that are all pretty fucking horrible and twisted. I don't *really* know what he did at the manor estate, even though now, I have a pretty good idea. I don't know what ultimately made him feel as though he had to leave, to lower himself to field work instead of whatever awaited him in that house, although I strongly suspect it had to do with that hyena I punched.

He'd said the man 'liked to hurt', which I could only interpret meant he'd hurt him before. I'd seen the light scars on his muzzle and his ears, and there were probably others on his body, covered up by his thicker fur. They were all small and thin, not wounds you'd see sustained from a weapon, or even most labor accidents. Probably made by *someone*, not something. Claws. Teeth.

I don't want to think about it anymore. This is too much for one day.

"You stay close to me, for the next few days," I command him, leaning my brow against my arm, and shifting my shoulders as he runs the cloth down my lower back. "If that rotten-mouthed bastard wants more blood, he might want it from both of us. Just stay in sight, alright? Otherwise I can't protect you."

"I thought," he barely whispers, "I—I… thought you didn't want me around."

"We had an arrangement, didn't we?"

"Is all of this really worth a few pieces of meat and a mat to you?" he asks, his voice small and vulnerable.

I'm silent a moment, before replying honestly. "No." I can *feel* his shoulders droop. "But," I continue, "it's not really about that anymore, for me. When you first asked me, I didn't think you really needed the protection. Now I guess…" I pause, flicking an ear. "I just don't like watching people get abused, alright?"

I get a fragile smile from him at that, which I can see out of the corner of my eye, because he's very close against my shoulder. "But I'm not always going to be here," I continue. "You need to learn to stand up for yourself. Fight back. We'll work on that. Then in a while, you won't need me anymore."

I get a lot of silence at that, which worries me for a few moments, until I feel his forehead press to the back of one of my shoulders. He leans there for a long time, shaking slightly. I can't see him the way I'm facing, so I have no idea what he's doing. At length though, I hear a sniffle, and I have to sigh.

"Don't do that," I growl.

"There's nothing wrong with crying," he mumbles against my shoulder.

"If you're a woman, or a child," I grumble. "You're a man, for gods' sake. Act like it."

"Men can cry, too."

"That doesn't mean they should," I mutter, wiping a paw over my muzzle.

"Kadar?" he asks. "What do you do, then? When you're sad?"

I grind my teeth, and stare at the wall. Even recognizing sadness isn't a place I want to be at right now in my life. But there's no denying it's there, sometimes. "You put it away," I say, resolutely. "Like, your living space can be a mess, and so can your head. You just clear it away, so you can get on with life."

"How—"

"Being sad is pointless," I interrupt, "It's like trash. It's not doing you any good, so you just… put it away. Alright? Pretty damn simple."

"I guess so," he murmurs. His paws slowly run in circles over my shoulders. Most of my injuries are along my back, so that's a fairly safe area. And I have to admit, it feels good.

"No one's ever been this kind to me," he murmurs.

"Well, you've been surrounded by a lot of shitty people," I mutter. "Trust me, I'm not much better than most of them, you just lack perspective." I briefly consider pointing out that Lochan seems to worry about him, and probably violated a few of the plantation rules today, and put himself on the line doing what he did for us, but he's also the one responsible for the painful marks on my back, so I'm not really in the mood to talk him up right now. Even if it *was* all for my own good, somehow. "Besides," I sigh, "I'm sure you had a few good people in your life before you were contracted here. Just by averages, you'd have to."

"I don't remember a time before working here," he says as he wrings out the rag and returns to my fur with it.

That makes me pause. "You've been here since you were young?"

"I was sold when I was a very small cub."

I put a palm to my head, trying not to read too deeply into the implications there. There are a lot of questions, and a lot of answers—many of them worse than I'd even initially imagined—

that have suddenly opened up as possibilities, and I don't necessarily want to know them all right now. Ahsan's stopped crying at least, and seems very focused on cleaning my fur instead. I try to focus on that, as well. I've never had anyone else clean my fur before, except when I was little. But right now, I hurt and I don't mind being doted on. It spares me from having to continuously lean down and wring out the wash cloth myself, at least. Leaning in any direction is agony right now.

Ahsan is gentle, good with his hands, and I again have to force myself not to think about why that is. That question, I'm pretty certain I know the answer to, and thinking on it while I'm nude and he's got his hands on me makes me feel uncomfortable. But the bath is just a bath, and he's actually able to get a lot of the dirt out of my fur that I'd failed to, so it's useful, even. He bathes himself after he's done with me, and I rest in the frame of the door and hope this pain abates some, so I can sleep tonight.

By the time we tiredly make our way back to our sleeping quarters, most everyone else is asleep. Despite that, oddly, our sleeping mat has been left on its own. I'm curious why, until I spot Raja staring at us from across the darkened room, his eyes flickering in the dark. He watches us head to our spot, then begins to settle down himself, like that's what he was waiting on. The King keeping his kingdom orderly, I suppose. *Such* a strange man.

I sit down on the mat by reflex, considering how I'm going to sleep. Side seems safest, I don't sleep well belly-down, and keeping my muzzle twisted to the side like that all night is bound to result in a stiff neck. There's always the chance I roll onto my back from my side, but if I do that, presumably I'll wake up from the pain, so it won't be a problem for long.

Ahsan begins curling up in the dirt beside me, and I can't help but remember the spot of dirt on his ear that the Matron had scraped off. For some reason that stuck with me, and it bothers me even now.

"Ahsan," I say, after only a moment of hesitation. "You willing to share that sarong?"

His ears perk, and that melancholy expression just drops away, like it was never there. Hesitantly at first, then almost excitedly, he crawls onto the mat with me, offering me one corner of the sarong to pull my way. I take it and tug it over my shoulder, turning towards him on my side as he settles in. Probably best he not knee me in the back all night.

He manages to make himself very small when he sleeps, which I don't necessarily mind because it means I have more of the mat to myself. Having him close like this, especially sharing the same 'blanket', or what we're using as one anyway, actually does make the cold, worn mat seem a lot warmer. His breath's coming out in soft puffs before long, his dark eyes slipping slowly closed, but watching me until the last moment before he drifts off to unconsciousness.

Maybe the pain's dulling my head. Maybe it's because I want another reason to hate the people who own me. Or maybe it's just been a long time since I had something to protect. But until tonight, it was just an idle promise made for meat and a better place to sleep. Now, I'm decided.

I'm not letting these people who own us inflict any more suffering on him. It doesn't matter that he's a hyena. All that matters is that I remain a better person than them.

Chapter 4

Learning

Father always said that people like us that tried for education were lazy, and thought too highly of themselves. There were some mothers and older men in our community that knew how to read, and some families would send their children to them for an hour in the mornings to study. But that was an hour lost to idleness, as far as my father was concerned. Honestly, I think in some cases he was right. Most of the children I knew who started their learning, originally did so precisely for the reason my father said… because they were lazy. It was an hour they didn't need to work.

Apparently reading could be just as difficult as real work though, because most of the children I knew never finished their learning. They all inevitably ended up back at the kilns, except for one girl who learned enough to read signs in the city. She died from bad water before she ever got a chance to make use of her 'education', though.

I never thought it would be necessary for my life. But then, that was back when I thought I'd make bricks my entire life. Marry another worker. Have a family, and raise children who'd also make bricks. Just as my family had for generations.

Honestly. Was that too much to ask for?

When I'd first seen my contract, I'd let my pride overwhelm my common sense. I hadn't been willing to admit to the man who, at the time I'd thought was hiring on workers for a caravan, that I couldn't read. I'd thought that because I'd trusted the man who referred the work to me, that I could trust the man hiring me.

No, that's wrong. He was a hyena. And even if I didn't loathe them as much then as I do now, I still didn't trust him. The truth was, I even knew about those sorts of deceptions. I'd heard about people foolish enough, stupid enough, to get tricked into a contract. People who thought they were signing an agreement to rent land, or to work a job, or send their children to school, but instead signed their lives away without even realizing it. But the fact is, I'd always thought myself more clever than that.

Stupidity, I realized too late, wasn't always being too desperate or dim-minded that you didn't question what you were signing your name to. Stupidity could be pride, and the stubborn refusal to admit you were incapable of something. I'd lost my life to a collar because I hadn't been willing to accept a failing.

And partially out of desperation, as well. I was no better than any of the people I'd once snuffed at. All it had taken was the right set of circumstances, and I'd given my life up.

My limbs are stiff when I wake, and there's an odd pressure atop my left arm, my fingers gone partially numb. My eyelids feel tacky as they do most mornings in the dusty, dirty, moist warmth of the labor lodge. When I finally manage to open them and my surroundings come slowly into focus, I find my field of vision is mostly taken up by the hyena tucked against my side. He's fallen asleep on my arm and somehow managed to snake his own arm around me in the midst of the night, and he's wedged too far up in my personal space for my liking.

Just as he has been every morning for the past several weeks. Ever since I'd given him permission to sleep on the mat beside me, I've not been able to go a single night without inevitably dealing with a hyena blanket. The boy seems incapable of respecting my boundaries while we're asleep, even if he's completely polite when we're awake. At first I'd wake in the midst of the night when he'd shift his way slowly into me, and shove him back. But he sleeps like the dead, he always inevitably creeps his way back over towards me by the time the morning comes, and at this point I've honestly just been allowing it. Keeping close company with Ahsan has made me anathema to most of the other men here anyway, other than Chandan and a few brave souls who are willing to look past the hyena's origins, so I don't honestly care what any of the rest of them think.

The fact is, I've given up on hating the hyena. I've mostly let go of the idea of disliking him. And I'm trying hard not to pity him, not because I don't feel he's deserving of pity, but because I earnestly believe it's the last thing he needs. Ahsan's grown enough in my estimation, (primarily I'll admit because he's still bringing me food) that I want to do more than *pretend* to help him. He doesn't need protection from the men here. He doesn't need a bodyguard. What he needs is confidence, and to rise up from beneath the distant heel of the Matron. Even now after he chose to leave the estate, he still speaks of her and the Manor on a daily basis, wistfully. Perhaps he does so now more that I've seen it, been there, learned more than I wanted to know about the place he grew up in and the people he was beholden to there. He's always sparse on details, and I don't pry for them regardless.

But whenever he speaks on his previous life while we're in the fields, or lying on our mat at night, or just whenever I catch him staring off towards the west where the Manor lies, I talk to him about something else. Anything else. I tell him something new about myself, because that always catches his attention, enraptures him. I can't say why, my life has hardly been extraordinary. But whatever distracts him. He'll often follow by telling me something about himself. The conversations at least have been enlightening.

I've learned much of what I already knew, and some things I suspected. He has no memory of life before the Sura Estate, or this plantation. He seems to believe he was as important to Matron Sura as a son, and in fact calls her his mother more often than not. He loves her still, even if it seems to me that if she ever loved him in return, that is no longer true. Something clearly happened between him and the Matron. I hope he raised hell, made trouble for her. But I'm certain that's not it.

I think he must have lost his value to her somehow, in the way a laborer does when he hurts himself. Perhaps because he didn't wish to entertain men like the hyena I attacked in the garden. If that's what he'd been raised for, to be an entertainer and whore for her nearest relations and he refused to do that sort of work, that would explain why he's here in the fields now.

He insists he was treated well there, raised as part of her clan, but the hairline scars I can see etched into the shorter fur on his muzzle, ears and wrists suggest otherwise.

And he wears the same collar I do. I don't care what they made him believe over the years, your 'family' isn't supposed to own you.

I wake him the same as I do every morning, and we file in line for the flat bread we'll be taking out to the fields with us, our only meal until the midday cart comes. As usual, Ahsan tries to give me his, and I inform him forcefully that he'll be eating his own food whether he wants to or not. He's learned by now not to argue with me.

He seems overly concerned with his weight. It's the strangest thing I've ever seen, especially for a man. He seems to hate his bulk, his height, and he's terrified of growing bigger in any way. The boy's as narrow as a shadow, and it only inhibits him as a laborer, so I've done my best to talk some sense into him, but I fear the Sura clan's got a leg up on me. The hyena has some odd opinions about how he should act and look that were firmly nailed into him far before I got here.

Today ends up being a quiet day in the fields, mostly weeding, although we're near one of the fields being scored, and I'm oddly happy about that because Chandan is working there and I'm looking forward to having my midday meal with someone other than Ahsan for once. It isn't often we work near enough to one another in the fields that we're able to spend any time together during the day.

The painted dog and I really have very little in common other than the fact that we're here, and both canine. We've spoken enough by now that I've learned he came from a different caste entirely before he became indentured, and unlike myself and most of the others here, he is here because by his own admission, he got himself into legitimate debt with the clan. Chandan, as well as Tandi, (the big, older male lion I'd seen earlier who turned out to be one of Chandan's closest friends) are both addicted to the Divine. As are at least a dozen other workers here on this plantation, I've been told. It's common practice for men who build a substantial debt with the clans who grow and produce the Divine to eventually fall into the work of producing the very drug that's trapped them. The beautiful flowers we're surrounded by each and every day in these fields have an insidious hold on those foolish enough to have fallen prey to their lure.

It's an unfortunate story, but not an uncommon one. Before I'd been through my first plantation, I'd met addicts of the Divine. Even home, closer to the Hyronses where the flowers don't grow as well, the Divine is everywhere. I'd thought for a long time it was merely a distraction for the rich, but time spent in indentured servitude had taught me otherwise. Even the poorest man can procure it, often for very little… at first. The hyena clans use it like a net to drag in fish, and once you're caught you're caught forever. Chandan says he's tried to leave the drug behind many times, and his body barely survived the attempts. The Divine, much like a steel animal trap, will tear you apart before it lets you go.

"The collar," he says as he sits beside Tandi on a large flat boulder, many of the workers here have taken to using as a sitting area during our breaks, "was just the final, physical manifestation of my enslavement." He says it with dry amusement, like he's reciting dark poetry. He's probably said these exact words to many others, many times. "I'd been a servant to the Divine far before I had a contract."

He rolls his mixture of herbs and drug while we all sit to eat, he and the lion speaking lowly as they carefully prepare the cigarette. The men here who buy tobacco are rare enough, and it's far less expensive than the meager amount of the Divine Chandan is able to buy on a weekly basis. They mix it with tobacco both to make it easier to smoke, and to save themselves some expense. But he's admitted to me he almost never finishes a week without owing more to the clan than he's earned.

Which is why he's still here, six years after he became indentured. It's why he may never leave. He seems fairly resigned to the fact, and that only makes me sadder. Angrier. But it's complicated. I don't really know how much anger I should reserve for the clan, and how much I should direct at him, for allowing this to happen. I always used to judge people who let themselves become indentured, but now that I've seen how easily it can happen, even to those who think they know better…

"Have you ever even seen your contract?" I ask randomly, tearing off a piece of my bread and dipping it in the small clay bowl of soup they brought us for our midday meal today. Chicken broth, at least.

Cooked with bones, if not any actual meat.

Three heads turn to stare at me. I blink back at them, and eat my bread. "What?" I demand.

"Haven't you?" Tandi asks, his voice stereotypically lion, deep and masculine. I've learned by now not to be intimidated by the man, though. He's uncommonly mellow for one of the big cats. But then, when you're his size, you don't really need to prove yourself as much as the leaner, smaller men, who pick a fight with just about anything that moves to show everyone what a big man they are. Like Raja.

"I saw it when I signed it," I snort. "But it hardly matters. I only know what they tell me it says. And considering they told me it was a labor contract when I first signed it, I'm not inclined to believe much of anything else they say."

"A labor contract?" Ahsan speaks up.

I nod. This is a shameful subject for me, but I'm in the company of a whore and two drug addicts, so I don't feel particularly terrible about telling them the truth. "I was referred to this caravan," I recount. "Or at least, that's what I was told it was. An acquaintance of mine who'd worked for the Rochshan Clan, one of the larger clans near the Hyronses, referred me. Now that I think back on it, I remember he had a gambling problem. He was probably working for them to pay it off. Anyway, he said these people had work for me, guarding a caravan that was heading for the sea—"

"I thought you used to make bricks," Ahsan interrupts, then when I shoot him an angry glare, his dark ears tip back and he instantly looks nervous. "I—I'm sorry," he stammers, "I just— you'd said—"

"Yes, I used to be a kiln worker," I say. "You're not wrong. I came from a family of kiln workers, as far back as we can trace. It was good work."

"Hard work," Tandi says, taking a drag on his cigarette and passing it to Chandan, who continues to listen thoughtfully. As much as we've spoken over the last month, we haven't really talked much about our lives before this place. All I really know is that he was a herder, which puts him slightly over me in caste, because it means his family owned animals.

"So why did you leave it behind to be a caravan guard?" Ahsan asks carefully, quietly. "If you liked it?"

"Because I had to get somewhere," I state matter-of-factly. "I had to go very far, all the way to the coast, and I had no money, and not enough food to make the trip. Not to mention the dunes are death to anyone who doesn't go by caravan or camel. I thought by signing on to work a caravan, I'd get where I needed to go without having to pay for the travel."

"You must have suspected," Chandan says.

I nod. "I did. But it was the only way. And I was willing to risk it, and trust in my friend. It was a mistake."

I was desperate, I think to myself. But I don't say it out loud, because it will invite too many questions.

"Why did you want to go to the coast?" Tandi asks curiously, tossing his tail at a horsefly nibbling on his exposed thigh.

This is where I need to slow the conversation down. "I needed to get somewhere, to see a family member," I say, making it clear by the edge in my voice that this is getting into personal territory. "Honestly, it's been years, and it doesn't really matter anymore. It feels like another life. For a while, after I realized I'd signed my life away, I was desperate to get out, to get back to what I had before. But it's been too long." I stare down at my bowl, and watch the meager contents of my soup float through the thin broth. "I'm not sure what I'd even find if I went looking for my family, for my old life, now."

A palpable silence falls over us, and I know I've caused the other three to think on their own lost lives, their own doubts. But they pulled it from me, so they can just suffer with it same as I am.

"What they did was illegal," Chandan says at length. "Lying to you about a contract. It's forbidden. Even if you can't read, they're supposed to read it to you before you sign."

"What does it matter what's legal, when the Clans exist?" I ask, bitterly. "Who besides them is going to enforce the laws? Nothing matters except what they want, what they *say* is legal."

"The Northerners made those laws," Chandan says, blowing smoke out through his nose and gesturing to the horizon. "After the last war. Made a whole bunch of dictates about how they're supposed to treat people like us. You'd think they'd enforce them."

"How?" Tandi counters. "Another war? You don't get one without the other, you can't demand their protection if they're not here, and when they were here all they did was displace the Clans and make colonies out of us. The war was necessary, or we'd just be a part of them now."

"Who's to say that would be any worse?" Chandan replies, and I can sense he and Tandi are about to get into another of their philosophical debates. They get like this whenever they smoke. "I'd swap an overbearing canine for an overbearing hyena any day. They might tell you how to live, but at least they don't believe in owning people."

"You're just saying that because you're canine," the lion points a thick finger into the painted dog's chest ruff. "We shouldn't have to bow to anyone, *every* type of people were meant to live free."

I tip my ears away from them and focus back on my soup, drowning out their conversation with my overwhelming disinterest. I've never been one to think too hard on the state of the world. I don't really feel I should have much to say about how anyone lives their lives, and I wish other people would do the same. But apparently one of the effects the Divine has on Chandan and Tandi is to make them feel that the whole world is entitled to, and indeed should hear, their opinion.

I both hear and feel Ahsan settle down beside me at my feet, a habit of his I find disconcerting. But he seems comfortable as he settles on to the sandy ground, so I don't dislodge him. I feel his eyes on me as I finish up my soup, and when I set my bowl down he's looking squarely at me, inquisitively.

"What?" I ask with a sigh.

"Just..." he pauses for long enough that it's beginning to annoy me. "I mean, have you *never* read your contract?"

"How could I?" I reply, irritated.

"Have you never had someone read it to you?" he asks, instead.

"What would it matter if I did?" I snap. "I'd have no way of knowing I could believe them."

"I... I could read it to you," he murmurs.

I stare at him like he grew three more heads, and he begins to shrink back from me. Before he can skitter away like a sand crab, I grab him by the shoulder and lean down. "You can read?" I demand.

He nods.

We skip dinner that night, which is testament to how determined I am to make use of my newfound companion's ability. I'd spent the remaining half of the day in the fields making biting remarks at him for not telling me sooner, even though that admittedly hadn't at all been his fault, since I'd never thought to ask. But impatience makes bastards of us all, and as usual, he'd taken it all with no complaint and still smiled at me the whole way back to the lodging house. He seems incredibly pleased that one of his domestic skills can finally be of use to me.

Not that I don't enjoy having my fur brushed, or my clothing washed. I don't think I've been this clean or this well-groomed... well, ever. But that's a mere pleasantry. This, this is important. It could even be life-changing.

I don't understand numbers well, or really at all, if I'm being honest with myself, but I can memorize one if it's this important. Knowing this will finally give me a frame of reference as to how impossibly far away, or, (I dare hope) close my freedom is. It's an answer I've wanted for many years, but never believed I could trust, coming from the people who owned me.

Ahsan will tell me the truth, though. It isn't just the fact that he's a sniveling, cowering creature who bends to my, and nearly everyone else's, will at the slightest provocation that makes me believe that. He's earnestly fond of me, for some reason. And I can't help but trust him. I can't imagine him lying to me or deceiving me in any way.

We head up the hill as the sun sets, the distant stone building an easy marker to find in the otherwise colorful expanse of the fields. Usually by this point we'd have been stopped by a guard for being out so late, but the perimeter guards generally don't linger by the guardhouse, since it's the last place a runaway would be likely to head. And an unusual sound makes my ears turn as we draw nearer, explaining away where any of the other guards might be.

You don't hear it often when you've lived a life like mine, but I've seen one or two swordfights in the streets near the Hyronses. The distinctive ringing of metal moving through the air, or making punctuated strikes, sticks with you so that you remember it forever.

I can't say I'm concerned, but I'm definitely curious. By the time the yard comes in sight, it's clear it's a less life-threatening scenario than I'd imagined. Shame.

Lochan is in the yard with one of the lioness guards I've seen around, a big lady who looks like she could put me down with her sheer bulk. She's wearing old, tarnished metal armor made up of banded strips of some kind, holding a large round shield and jeering something at him in Halvashir, one of the dunes dialects I don't know. Some lions speak it and only it, which makes them confusing

to communicate with. I've never heard her speak common Huudari,
so I'm guessing she's not great at it.

They don't seem to be locked in mortal combat, especially considering she's not even using a weapon unless you count the shield,
and he's chuckling. I'm not really certain *what* they're doing—sparring, maybe? I've never seen anyone spar with a real weapon before,
but he's using the scimitar I've seen at his side since I got here, and
I'm very certain it's a real blade. And by the look of it, a well-maintained one.

He catches her in the shield, and she shouts something again
at him that almost sounded mocking, and he comes at her harder
with a less-than-threatening growl, pulling back his sword at the last
moment and bulling into her with his bulk. She puts up the shield
again to block, but he gut-checks her with enough force that she

goes toppling (no mean feat considering her size). Startlingly fast, more so than I'd ever expected of the man, he leaps over her and jabs the scimitar into her collarbone, between two strips of the banded metal. The accuracy is baffling. I'd have had trouble doing that with time and a flaying knife, let alone a weapon that large, swung that fast.

She lays there for a time gasping, catching her breath. Then at length she mutters something in Halvashir, and he chuckles again, offering her a palm. She takes it and slowly gets to her feet, dusting herself off with a long sigh.

It's at that point that we're finally noticed. Lochan's ears perk and turn towards us, and he sheathes his scimitar. He says something to the lioness I don't catch, then begins to make his way towards us. The sun's gone low in the sky at this point, and I'm certain the first thing he's going to tell us is that we can't be out after dark.

"It's getting dark," he barks at us as he approaches. I can smell that his paws are sweating, the musk that's thick in his fur and trapped beneath his leather armor, and the constant tinge of aggression I always pick up from him, amplified likely by his sparring match. "You shouldn't be this far from the lodging house this time of day."

I wait for him to make his way entirely to us, making it clear I'm not coming any farther without his say-so. I don't play around with Lochan. I've tested and prodded some of the other guards by this point, but there's an air about the Aardwolf that makes me dislike my chances. I've long suspected he's more competent even than he lets on, and today confirms at least some part of that. Besides which, the one beating aside, he's always been fairly decent to the people here, from what I've seen. Decent, but firm.

It's rare I've ever wanted to be on the good side of a guard. But in this case, it's probably in my best interest. At least for now.

His dark eyes move to Ahsan, softening some, and before I can speak he does. "Are you here for your dinner?" he asks the striped hyena. "I didn't think you were coming, but I saved a bit of lamb." His gaze falls on me, and shifts to a glare. "Only enough for one, though."

"No, sir," Ahsan says with an ease I can't imagine having around the Aardwolf. "Actually, we were hoping to see Kadar's contract."

Lochan's expression turns surprised, at that. "His contract," he repeats.

"Yes, sir," Ahsan nods, then pauses. "They *are* kept in the guard building, are they not?"

"We keep a copy, yes," Lochan replies, his eyes moving between the two of us. "For keeping track of expenses and daily pay. The original is kept up at the Manor. We update the totals at the end of each month on the master."

"I'd like to read Kadar's," Ahsan says with a smile, and a flick of his tail. "Please."

A look of understanding passes over Lochan's features, and he inclines his head towards me, snuffing out his nose. He's silent just a moment, then nods. "As you wish," he says, turning and gesturing for Ahsan to lead. "You're welcome to read your contracts at any time."

Ahsan bobs his head and begins to head up the hill, Lochan staying right where he is until I start moving ahead of him, as well. He falls in behind me, uncomfortably close, and for a few moments I think he's just doing it to unnerve me. But then he speaks, in a low voice.

"Found another use for him, have you?"

I don't look back at him, only reply, "He's more than happy to help me, I didn't force him to come up here. He enjoys helping me."

"Just like he enjoys bringing you all the food I give him?" The Aardwolf mutters back, in an acrid tone. I feel my tail bristle, but he doesn't give me a chance to respond, only continues. "You think I don't know? You must think you've got a good thing going, don't you, jackal? Another servant at your every beck and call, giving you everything he has—"

"I didn't ask for it," I snap, trying to keep my voice low even though I know Ahsan can likely hear us. He hasn't turned around though, isn't acting as though he can. He probably won't, no matter what we say. But it feels rude, talking like this about him when we both know he can hear us, like he's not even here.

Lochan seems to pick up on that, too. "Later," he growls, and shoves me unnecessarily. I feel that aggression in him spike. Like a father with his family, or something. It's hard to pin down.

We head up to the building, and he makes us stand aside while he unlocks the thick, metal-barred door. It swings open with a grinding noise and he gestures for us to head inside. The dust particles swirl through the stale air, and I'm immediately hit with a sickening sort of nostalgia, not because the place smells any worse than the lodging house, but because the scent of the air here reminds me of the weeks I spent in the cell, suffering with my injuries.

Mostly, it smells like the guards who frequent it. A lot of lion, since two of the guards here are lioness and one is the big, dark-maned male lion who's made me uncomfortable and wary during every small interaction we've had thus far, and Lochan, whose scent permeates this place the most. It's thick enough in the air that I'm certain he must live here, a jailer atop being the head guardsman. The building isn't large enough that it would be much of a home to any of the other guards. I'm guessing they have barracks somewhere else on the property.

There really is just the one hallway he'd led me down on my way out, and a few rooms off of it. One large door at the very end must lead to Lochan's quarters, since it's where his scent is the strongest, but tonight he leads us towards one of the other two rooms. It has no door, only an archway and a large enough window that it's dimly orange-lit when we step inside. The room has a worn wooden table in the center, clawed and chipped at on the corners over the years, showing its use and age. I catch the vaguest hint of old curry and alcohol, and what must have been dinner for the guards an hour or so ago, judging by how fresh the scent is. Lamb, just like Lochan said.

There's also a shelf built into the wall, with a few dozen small, square boxes. Many of them are occupied by round leather scroll cases. As Ahsan and I wait, Lochan drags a claw down the line of boxes, before stopping at one and tugging out the leather case there. After he pulls it free, he tugs at the leather cord binding it closed and places it down on the table, unrolling it carefully.

I stare down at the document, fighting back a rush of nausea. I'm suddenly glad I hadn't eaten, because I was not prepared for this wash of memories. I'm staring at the document I signed years ago. Or at least, a copy of it. My signature, which had been little more than the pawpad on my right pointer finger dipped in ink, is the only thing missing. Even without being able to read it, I remember the look of the script, the line breaks where the man who drew this damned thing up indicated were the provisions for my 'labor agreement'. He sat me down and explained what each of these lines meant, and I believed him. Or I just didn't care enough to question it. It's been so long, I can hardly remember my motivations.

But I remember the document. And I haven't seen it since that day. It's disturbing to think I've gone this long without ever understanding what it was that had enslaved me.

There's other writing on the contract, in ink that dried differently. A long list of scribblings, with figures following each that I know to be numbers. I can't make sense of any of it, but a moment later, Ahsan steps forward and leans down over the contract, looking it over.

"'Contractual obligation of labor, providing for a debt owed to the Rochshan Clan… for services to be rendered at termination of contract…" he pauses, his muzzle twitching. "Wow. They actually admitted the services you were indebted for hadn't even been rendered yet."

"They can do that," Lochan states, crossing his arms over his chest. "Especially for smaller, seasonal labor contracts with ships, for housing, caravans." He shrugs. "You can't receive the promised service until after you've paid your way. That's the mindset, at least."

"The rest of the disclosure is fairly standard," Ahsan says, his eyes moving down the page, until he gets to the area with the fresher scrawlings, the ones I didn't recognize. "And here," he points to the list, "is where they've kept track of your earnings, and expenses." He pauses, then looks to me, "You've worked on a *lot* of different plantations, Kadar."

Lochan leans down over Ahsan, resting a paw on the boy's slim shoulder and narrowing his eyes at the contract. "I'm not good with much other than numbers," he says, "but I recognize 'termination of labor.'" He turns towards me, giving a dry chuckle. "They told me you were a trouble-maker. Have you ever worked an entire season at even one of these plantations?"

"They were trapping me," I snarl back. "I know how the game works. They were charging me more for board than I could possibly make in a day."

Lochan waves a paw. "Not saying that doesn't happen," he snorts, "but not every plantation gets away with that, jackal. Did you ever bother to find someone to do your numbers for you, and find out?"

I'm silent, because I don't like to speak when I have nothing worthwhile to say. I'm starting to feel like the Aardwolf is looking down on me, in a different way than he normally does. When he pushes me around physically it's one thing, I'm weakened since my injury and he's armed, but now he's acting like he understands my life better than I do. Even watching Ahsan's eyes sweep down over my contract is making my fur bristle, all of a sudden. It's not my fault he can read, and I can't. It's not my fault I don't understand numbers.

I'm beginning to feel stupid. And I know I'm not. I may not have the kind of learning the hyenas do, or the knowledge of numbers Lochan says he has, but—

"This second plantation here charged you for the use of your tools," Ahsan speaks up, suddenly. "And with that plus your board, you were coming up short each day."

"You see!" I snap. "Exactly as I said."

"Aye, you're every bit the victim you thought you were," the Aardwolf says derisively. "Happy now?"

I'm not, of course, and his snide tone just makes me angrier. It's not like I wanted validation that I was oppressed and abused, I have the scars to prove that. It's just that I've struggled against my 'owners' all this time for good reason, fought and refused to work because what was being demanded of me was built on lies! It's not as though it's been unreasonable to expect I should have freedom. I never even *had* a debt.

"The last two plantations you were on were paying you enough to exceed a ruval a day," Ahsan says, as his claw traces towards the bottom of the contract. "Not much, but it seems like you didn't amass many other additional expenses. You're actually paid partway into your debt, despite all the charges you were docked for property damage and disorderly behavior at your previous places of employment." He looks up to me, his eyes flicking briefly to Lochan as a tentative smile crosses his muzzle. "And you're earning two ruval a day here, same as I am."

"I told him when he arrived," Lochan states, "that if he walked the line, he'd pay off his contract here. I'm very careful with the board costs."

"Why the hell would you care?" I snarl. "I've never met an Overseer who didn't squeeze every last drop of blood out of his workers."

"Then they're fools," Lochan states. "Workers who know they're making progress work harder. That hopeless, angry attitude of yours is what drives servant uprisings, and it's why I'm able to get contracts like yours for a steal. Almost every worker here was a lost case like yours, at one point. Unwilling to work, violent, without value. Your last plantation practically gave you away, they were so desperate to be rid of you. And now look at you. You're pulling your weight in the fields, and I've yet to have to lob something off of you to keep you docile. We both made out well."

I snort, disbelievingly. "If it's all that simple, I fail to see why every other plantation hasn't adopted your brilliant strategy."

"I came to an understanding with the Steward of the Sura Estate when I was first hired," he says. "About how to adjust pay and manage our board costs. It was a rare chance, and a hard sell, but she trusted my experience on the subject."

"I'll bet she did," I say, pressing a finger up beneath the edge of my collar and adjusting it, pointedly.

He doesn't miss it. He also doesn't seem phased. "Yes," he states. "I was indentured. And if you think your lot here, picking and carrying weeds all day is a hard life, I have news for you. You don't know shit."

"That isn't the point!" I growl. "I used to work the kilns, making bricks. I know what a brutal day's work really is."

"I'm weeping for you," he replies, monotonously.

"The point," I say around a snarl, "is that I was lied to. I had this... *thing*," I indicate the collar, "soldered on to me, against my will, and then some woman I'd never met told me she *owned* me. That isn't right, it isn't just, and it shouldn't happen! To anyone! To you, to me, to Ahsan," I look to the hyena, whose ears have tipped back likely due to the fact that I'm raising my voice.

The Aardwolf gives me an even, unflinching stare. "Jackal," he says, "I think you were lied to far before you were contracted. Because whoever told you that the world was supposed to be 'just' was selling you a bill of goods."

"That doesn't mean—" I begin.

"No," he cuts me off. "You need to figure this out, before you get too old, too tired or too dead to live your life in any meaningful way. The world is neither cruel nor caring. It just is. And it's a different world for all of us. There's no balance, no fairness to it. A hyena, or a dog from the north can be born with their life laid out for them, gilded in gold and royal. Everything will come to them easier and they'll receive all the more accolades for their triumphs, even when they worked half as hard as the rest of the world to achieve them. Because that's their world. And they can lose it all just as easily as they got it."

"I never wanted all of that!" I insist. "I had a humble life, and I was happy for it. I worked hard every day, and I never expected more than I was given. I didn't earn this debt because I did something foolish, it just…" I struggle with my words, my throat heavy, "…*happened*," I choke out, finally, "to me. I had no control over any of it."

It's only partially a lie.

"First off, a humble man never has to say he's humble," the Aardwolf says, his voice cold. "And secondly, no matter how much you enjoy basking in your outrage at your current situation now, you need to keep one thing in mind." I see his eyes fall briefly on Ahsan, then they turn towards the dying light streaming in through the window, and stay there. "No matter how low you think you are, there's always a bottom farther beneath you. And it's endless. Somewhere, someone is enduring suffering you've never endured. Pain you can't even imagine. And someone somewhere has it worse than them."

I can hear the tightening in the Aardwolf's usually thick, deep voice, but nothing about what he's saying feels self-serving. The sadness there is in the present, like an open wound, so it can't be for himself. Ahsan, then?

"No one's saying you're blessed," Lochan continues. "But life can be whatever you're able to take from it. And sometimes the best way to take the biggest bite is to accept that shit like this can happen and deal with it, not fight against the indignity of it until the fight itself kills you."

"That sounds like giving up," I growl. "Bowing to them, because everyone bows to them. If more people fought them, if more people were willing to stand up and say what they're doing to us isn't fucking acceptable, we'd overpower them. The only reason they're in power now, able to do this," I look to Ahsan, whose gaze shrinks away from mine, "to all of us," I continue, "is because not enough people told them they can't. It's never going to stop. Letting them herd us with their self-serving laws is like accepting we're livestock. 'Servants'. Slaves. People shouldn't own people. I don't care what they call it."

Ahsan and Lochan are both silent, and the room feels oppressively still in the wake of my words. I can see some of the sense in Lochan's argument, but he isn't the first man I've met who's felt that way. A lot of servants fall into that mindset over time. Acceptance. They stop caring why they're indentured, they just live with it, and either give up on ever being free, or work their asses off towards paying off whatever nebulous number was attached to their contract. Hell, some of them do, eventually. It's not like no servant has ever been set free, or they wouldn't need Liberators at all. They'd just bury us all in our collars.

That being said, even if I've never doubted how I've felt over the years, it's hard to find the strength to back my beliefs, sometimes.

I have stretches of time when I'm just so… tired. Living with your teeth out every second of every day is exhausting, and bucking control when you're so outmatched almost always inevitably ends in pain, if not death. I've seen others dragged to the gallows, or simply run through by the guards right on the fields. I've stepped over month-old bloodstains that sunk into caked sand, and wondered if that's all my life would amount to, some day. All my pride, all my anger, all my resolve to fight against the chains that bind me. A stain on the ground, a warning to others. If anything, wouldn't all my struggles have served the opposite goal, in that case?

If this life kills me, I'd like to at least leave it as an inspiration to others. Not an example as to why people shouldn't fight.

So I understand Lochan's words, and I can tell in this moment, as he stares at me with sunken eyes and a scarred muzzle, that he's probably suffered enough to have earned the right to give up. To bow. But I just can't do that, no matter how much sense it makes.

He seems to know, and his response is simply to frown, and look away. "You're going to live as you choose," he says, in a subdued tone. "Just try not to take others down with you." He looks to Ahsan at that, and steps closer to the striped hyena, who much to my surprise, never seems to shrink back from the Aardwolf, even when he's well inside his personal space. It's baffling. Even I don't feel comfortable around the large man, and Ahsan is literally terrified of loud insects. Why he seems to tolerate Lochan so well, I can't understand.

Lochan's hand returns to his shoulder, his thick fingers pressing into his fur. He drops his muzzle down to the striped hyena's dark ear, murmuring something quietly, but I catch most of it.

"—dinner is in my room. Go retrieve it and return to the lodge."

Ahsan turns his dark eyes on me before he shakes his head at Lochan. "I haven't finished reading—"

"I'll tell him his numbers," the Aardwolf placates, squeezing his shoulder. "Go. Before you lose your sleeping mat."

"No one's going to take Kadar's mat," the hyena insists, his ears tipping back.

I don't miss the low growl the Aardwolf barely suppresses at that. He lets his paw slide off Ahsan's shoulder, and he gives him a gentle tap on the back instead, in the direction of the door. "Go," he says more firmly.

Ahsan again looks to me, uncertainly. I give him a nod. "Do as he says, Ahsan."

The hyena seems worried, but ultimately, he listens to me. He glances back at least five times on his way out the door, and I wait long enough to hear his footsteps fade down the hallway before turning my attention back to the Aardwolf.

To say he looks angry would be an understatement. When we both hear the distant creak of his bedroom door, he lunges for me. I saw the look in his eyes, but to be honest I'm caught off-guard by the attack. I only barely manage to put an arm up, but he gets one of his large, powerful hands beneath it with ease, and soon I'm pinned to the wall by my collarbone, his thick fingers inches from getting a stranglehold around me. What's more, he's worked his thumb up beneath my collar, which tells me he might actually have *experience* strangling people wearing collars.

I almost laugh, my breath coming out in a wheeze. "What the hell kind of servant *were* you?"

"Shut your muzzle, you piece of trash," he snarls, baring at least three good fangs out of four. Strangely, I do as he says. But only because something is just now clicking into place in my mind, and I'm not certain how I feel about it. I feel the claw of his thumb against the hollow of my throat, and I don't lean back when he leans in.

"Are you fucking him?" he demands of me, in a low growl.

"Are you?" I counter. I'm not certain of the answer until the telling silence that follows. And then, I begin to know how I feel about it. Angry.

"Answer me," he says, the threat evident in his tone.

"I wouldn't do that to him," I say defiantly. "I wouldn't *use* him the way they obviously intended for him to be used."

"No, you only steal his food," he bites back, "and command him about like a slave, and force him to sleep on the cold earth—"

"He sleeps next to me on the mat now," I interrupt. "He has for the last few weeks."

He only snorts. "The guilt got to you, did it?"

"Yes," I reply, matter-of-factly. "Like a serpent, coiling in my gut, taking little bites out of me until I relented. He didn't deserve the way I treated him when we first met, but I convinced myself I had to focus on survival. It wasn't an excuse for how I treated him, and I eventually felt awful enough about it to stop." I pause at that, and lean in to his claws, to let him know I'm not afraid of him. "Can you feel the serpent inside you?"

He releases me at that, and stalks away from me, circling the table with no obvious destination in mind. I try not to show how relieved I am to be free of his iron grip, and suck in a few breaths quietly, trying to maintain my composure. I'm not honestly as fearless as I pretend to be. Nor is anyone. Like all brave men, I'm just very good at faking it.

Other than a low, frustrated growl, he hasn't responded to my words, so I press forward. "Is that why you give him food? To pay him off, to sleep with you?" My nose wrinkles in disgust, because this is worse now that I'm involved. It's enough that it's happening, continuing to happen to him now, even in the fields, but the thing that really hurts is... *I've* been benefiting from it. Unknowingly. I feel like he's involved me in it, made me a part of it.

"I started giving him food far before," he waves a paw in the air, then puts two fingers to his brow, his tone losing some of its anger. "Because he was half-starved when he first came into my care. I was worried he'd drop dead in the fields. They have his head all turned around about food, about his weight."

My fur settles a little as I listen to him, the fury gone from the air. Now the Aardwolf simply sounds upset, and the hunch in his shoulders is achingly familiar to me. There's guilt there. This isn't turning into what I'd expected it would.

"It's not just his weight, it's his height, his stature," I say, hesitantly. "I don't understand it, either. It doesn't make any sense to me, even from the perspective of an owner. Why would they want him weak?"

"Because it makes him easier to control," the Aardwolf replies, with a grim certainty. "They didn't raise him for labor."

I narrow my eyes. "You know they twisted him. You must know he chose to come out here to get *away* from what they were doing to him. How the hell can you keep doing it to him?"

"He came out here to get away from Matron Sura, and what *she* was doing to him," Lochan states, an ounce of that conviction returning to his voice. But a moment later, he's sighing, his ears flattening back. "And it wasn't… I didn't intend for it to happen, he and I. It just did."

"You don't unintentionally abuse someone," I snort.

"I wanted to protect him!" He growls. "The only worker in the lodging house who'd even acknowledge him was Raja, and the cheetah still treats him like shit, he just watches over him like a valuable. I was honestly worried he'd die out here, *that's* why I started bringing him here."

"For some reason, I doubt your 'concern' for your workers would extend to those you didn't want to bed," I reply, unimpressed.

"So, I'm not *Paropakura*," he snuffs, and I vaguely understand the reference, if only because the name is unusual. The Dhole God, a god of charity. "He's beautiful, pitiable… desperate for someone to treat him decently." He shakes his head. "I'm a battered-up old man, do you know how long it's been since someone needed me like that? My resolve gave out."

"It doesn't change the fact that you're doing exactly what they were," I say. "You hate them as much as I do. I can tell. How can you act like them?"

"Would you have kept him close if you weren't getting something out of it?" he counters. "You think I don't have eyes and ears in that lodging house? You bullied him into submission right from the start. I never demanded anything of him. Never forced him into anything. He just…"

He lowers his head, and I blow out a breath. "Relented," I fill in for him.

"He was *so* eager to please," he murmurs, his deep voice losing some of its strength.

"That's how he is," I say, averting my gaze from the man. "They made him that way. Eroded away whatever spine he had, shaped him into what he is now. Not hard to do when you start with a child."

"You sound like you have experience," he says, his eyes cast down on the contract on the table.

I blink a few times, and stare into the glare from the window, so I have an excuse to close my eyes. "I never had much of a chance to raise my son," I say, not knowing why I'm saying it as I do. Let alone to a guardsman. I haven't spoken to anyone about my child in years. "But," I say after a short moment of silence, "I was a son myself, once."

He nods. Something is happening between us, and I'm not sure what. But when he speaks again, I can sense that he's doing as I did, letting words slip out that he might not normally part with.

"The man who sired me sold his children to pay off tax debts," he says it, cold as a desert night. "He had his first and second son. My sister and I were just assets he was better off rid of."

My mouth feels dry. I'm not certain I want to talk about my father. Instead, I just say, "I'm sorry," because I am.

He leans on the table, his thick, calloused hands tensing over the table edge, the muscles in his arms gone rigid, and all at once they relax. "It's in the past." His eyes, seemingly either grey or blue depending on what light I see them in, come up to rest on mine, finally. "For me. But my sister is still indentured. The brothel they sold her to force-fed her the poison we grow here. To make her compliant. But she's like me, or... how I used to be," he snuffs. "She's a fighter. She never... stopped... fighting." He lifts his muzzle entirely. "Like you."

"Then you should be proud of her," I say.

"She's dying," he replies, stoically. "I've been sending my coin to her for years, trying to help her, but it all went to the drug. A year ago, she stopped taking my money."

"The Divine is killing her?" I ask, thinking of Chandan, fearfully.

"One of the men who paid for her," he clears his throat, "gave her a disease. Something foreign. She's lingered for the last year, but they cleared her contract recently, which means they no longer have any value for her. She's at a temple in the Piravh region, a few days north of here. She won't last much longer."

I'm not certain what to say to that, but it turns out he doesn't require a response from me, because he circles the table then, pushing the contract down towards me. He stabs a claw into one of the upper lines, next to one of the numbers.

"Do you see that?" He asks.

"Of course," I sigh. "It doesn't mean I can make sense of it."

"That number there is your initial contract amount," he says. "Four hundred ruval."

I balk. "Four *hundred?* I've never even seen—"

"Shut up," he says in a tone that doesn't invite argument. "And listen. How long have you been indentured now?"

I'm honestly not certain, so that's what I say. "Several years," I say. "Perhaps four?" It can be hard to follow the changing of seasons near the Hyronses, especially when you're nowhere near the river.

"Even at your first plantation, you could have earned that amount in a little over a year," he says. "If you'd just cowed and done your fucking work."

"They had no right to—"

"That doesn't matter!" He finally raises his voice to where it shakes the air, and I flinch back despite myself. "You've lost four years of your life to your pride! It doesn't matter what's right and what's wrong, what matters is that these are the people who have the power, and they will *kill* you if you fight them. Fast or slow, with a noose or a filthy, rotting disease. In the end you'll have your pride, and a grave, and *no one* will remember the former!"

"Why do you care?" I demand.

"Because now you're going to drag that boy down with you!" He roars back, his mane raising where it isn't braided back. "And he actually has a chance! He doesn't take the drug, he's young, his health was on the mend… he…"

I let some of my breath past my teeth, averting my eyes from the man and staring down at the old, scarred table. "He isn't your sister," I say at length.

"No," he agrees. "He isn't. I might have actually saved him. And I thought…" he shakes his head, closing his eyes. "I thought he really cared about me."

I open my muzzle, then shut it slowly. The aging Aardwolf's eyes are tense, his posture stiff, and the more I've heard him talk about Ahsan, the more I'm starting to think I may have made a mistake. "I don't know what's between the two of you," I begin to say, but he cuts me off.

"It doesn't matter anymore," he says. "He hasn't come to me in weeks. If I had to guess," he says dryly, "I'd say it probably coincides with whenever it was you started letting him sleep with you."

"I don't want him like that," I insist. "I still consider myself married. I'm not looking for a lover."

"I never wanted to use him," he says. "I wasn't trying to barter food for," he sighs, "whatever it was we had. I'm just a fool. And I'm not going to continue it, if that's all it was." He sweeps his tired gaze back towards the wall, and heads over towards it, running a clawed finger down along the line and searching for another scroll case.

I'm not certain what he's doing, but a moment later he asks, "Is he eating *any* of the food I'm giving him?"

"He tried to give it all to me," I admit. "But I make sure we split it half and half."

"Good. I'll keep saving a bowl for him, then," the Aardwolf says, and apparently finds what he was looking for, tugging it free. Another scroll case, this one far more weathered. He strides forward and carefully places it on the table, unfurling it slowly.

I peer down at it. This contract is more complex than mine. More fine print, and there are multiple pages bound into the roll.

"This is Ahsan's contract," he says, and I find myself caught off-guard. Why is he showing me this? "His contracted amount," he continues, looking up at me, "is over ten times what yours is. Do you understand what that means"?"

I don't know numbers well, but I know roughly what ten is, and ten times means it would be ten times as difficult to pay as mine is, so that puts it in some context for me. "How is that possible?" I ask, confused. "Wasn't he a child when he was indentured? What kind of debt could he possibly have had?"

"Oh, children who are sold almost always have astronomic debt amounts," Lochan replies. "Think about it. For one, children are valuable. You get more time out of a child, you get to 'shape' them, like you said before. And almost without fail, a caregiver has to be in desperate straits to sell one of their own children. That usually means a large debt. That, or they're a cold-hearted piece of shit," he says the last bit with an edge of dark humor.

"Which was it, in his case?" I ask.

"Ahsan was sold to pay off an entire clan's debt," he says. "The Sura clan loans money and resources to smaller clans all the time, and when the debts come due, it's pay up or face their mercenaries. At some point, Matron Sura was in the market for a child, and she found someone willing to pay up what she demanded to save their skin. The number attached to the contract hardly matters, she intended to have him for life."

I curl my lip at his phrasing. "'In the market for a child?'"

"The Matron can't have her own children," he says, with a meaningful look. "I'm sure by now you've noticed he refers to her in a rather... motherly way."

"You don't *buy* a child," I say venomously. "And you certainly don't make them wear a collar their whole damned life, or sell them for sex. If she wanted to raise a child, she did a piss-poor job of it. He can't even stand to live in the Manor any more, and he won't tell me why—I can't make any sense of this at all," I say, running a palm over my face. "This is sick."

Lochan only nods, dropping his voice. "Sometimes it's best if we don't understand. Different worlds, remember?"

"It's sick in *any* world," I insist.

"Well, it's the world he comes from," he says, as he begins to roll up the hyena's scroll, carefully. His eyes flick up to mine, reflecting the last fading hints of red sunlight in the room. "And if you give a damn about him at all, you'll see to it that he never returns to it. He's halfway through his debt."

My brows raise. "Half?"

He nods. "He didn't earn much as a child, but over the last few years, when he started reaching the age where he could dance and 'entertain', well… He'll earn less as a field worker, but I've been putting a few ruval a week towards his contract out of my own pay, so he's making about what he was before. It will take some time, but eventually, he could be free of this place forever. He just needs to keep working."

"Lochan…" I stammer, which I hate doing, but I'm beginning to almost feel for the man, and that's even worse. "If you care about him—"

"It doesn't matter what I feel," he says, and he finishes rolling up the second contract. Mine. He holds it out across the table to me. "He made his choice."

"I was never trying to take him away from you," I say quietly, as I take the scroll.

"You didn't," he says, firmly. "Whatever was there to begin with, I imagined it. Maybe I *was* using him, without realizing it. It doesn't matter anymore. You're right," he holds his muzzle high, and stares at me evenly. "He is not my sister. And even if I really could have helped him, it's not my job here to save just one of my workers. I've been too focused on him, when I should be keeping a closer eye on imminent disasters, like you."

I look down at my contract, and for the first time since I had the collar placed around my neck, I feel the full weight of it on me. I think of Ahsan in that moment, not myself, and imagine the collar ten times heavier. And then I imagine the impossible… spending my entire life wearing it. Never knowing what it means to be free of it. I can remember a time when life wasn't like this. He's never known anything but.

I think of the Aardwolf's sister, even though I've never met her, rotting to death of a disease given to her by one man—not *the* man, but just one of many—who raped her. I imagine her as fierce as Lochan, fighting the men violating her. Every day. For years, and years, and years.

And then I think of the future I could have had, if I'd accepted the misfortune life had given me, so many years ago. One year of service. One year, and I'd have been free. One year, and I could have renewed the search for my wife. My son. And then, after only one year, I might have stood a real chance. I might have really have found them. I might have reclaimed the life I'd lost.

I think of the future I could have, if I continue living my life the way I have been. But more than that, I think of what will happen to Ahsan, led so easily by anyone willing to show him an ounce of kindness. It seems impossible now, but I imagine him stronger, more defiant, following me down the road I've so proudly walked. Where can it possibly end?

I've been willing to throw my life away, because I felt it was increasingly becoming my only option. Or at least, the only option left to me in which I kept my dignity. But I would have sacrificed every bit of dignity I had, for my family. Or at least, that's what I'd always told myself. I suppose if I'd really felt that way, I'd have worked. I wouldn't have fought the tide. I would have thought only of my wife, my son, of reuniting with them. Somewhere, amidst the storm of outrage, I lost sight of that goal.

It was anger. It's always the anger. Anger runs through my veins, a legacy from my father, as surely as my green eyes are his. It's the same anger that caused him to make so many mistakes, and now it's ruined my family as thoroughly as it once ruined his.

Ahsan doesn't deserve to be dragged down by it, as well.

I grip my contract, and look up to the Aardwolf, who has gracefully allowed me the few moments of silence I needed to let this resolve settle in. It sinks into me and simmers, like a hot stone in a pot, but I know it must be so.

"Don't worry about me," I say, my voice rough. "And don't worry about him." I hold the scroll case back out to him, and he takes it from me. Without another word, I turn and begin to head for the door.

"Going back to the lodge?" he asks me as I reach the arched doorway.

"Yes, sir," I reply without looking back. "We have to cut tomorrow, I need to get to sleep or I'll be too worn to pull my weight."

"Go straight back to the lodging house, don't linger on the grounds," he commands. "It's gotten dark out."

"Yes, sir," I reply.

Chapter 5

Violated

I was married when I was fourteen. It wasn't a choice so much as an obligation. By that point, my family had begun to fracture. Mother's patience was near eternal, but even the most devoted woman has their breaking point.

Father was almost never home anymore. He still worked, the same as he ever had. He never stopped coming to work, never lost that strength I'd so admired, growing up. Even as he began to age and his body began to break down, he never bowed. Not physically, anyway. He was a rock. But when he wasn't working, mostly, he drank. By that age, I knew exactly where he went in the city. I knew why we never had any money remaining at the end of each day.

I don't honestly think my mother ever blamed him for his vice. I don't even think she wanted more from him, from our life. She was a good woman. Happy with very little. She made the most of what we had, no matter how meager we lived. She worked herself to the bone same as he and lived in threadbare clothing and a small, dirty hut she could only ever dream of keeping clean. But we had the best-maintained hut on our street, because she tried.

My mother wasn't perfect though, as much as I struggle now to find flaws with her. All I saw was the love she gave. All I remember was a saint. But her weakness was her timid nature, her acceptance of her position beneath my father. She wasn't an indentured servant, but she *was* a possession. And she never really thought to challenge that. I'm not really certain if it's because of how she was raised or because of her character, but either way it was a failing. She had a son to think about, and her passivity hurt us both.

My wife, the woman that was chosen for me by my father, was not like my mother. I know he met her before the wedding, if only once, so I can only assume she must have acted demure and agreeable then. Perhaps to please him. Perhaps to please her family. I don't think she wanted the match any more than I did, so there must have been some pressure involved. Whatever happened in that first meeting, I know my father did not see through to the type of woman she truly was, or he never would have chosen her.

Ishaya was born of a different caste of workers. The Vasja, the laborers with specific skills, like craftsmen. Most Vasja make something for a living, Ishaya's family had been weavers. But her family had lost their house and most of their possessions in a fire that had consumed many blocks of homes in Hyronses' Capital City, and she was only one of four daughters. Her parents couldn't afford the dowry to marry her to another tradesmen, but they also wanted to be rid of some of their daughters while they rebuilt their family's damaged fortune. Ishaya had been just barely old enough to marry, unlike her two younger sisters, so they'd been willing to give her to an unskilled tradesmen. A laborer. Really, anyone who would have had her, but my father insisted I'd been lucky to claim such a wife. There weren't as many golden jackal families in the Hyronses as there were further north, so he and my mother had long worried it would be difficult... and expensive... for me to find a wife at all.

By the time I was fourteen I was nearly as tall as I am now, if less filled out, but still very strong and able-bodied. I was, as my father insisted, an adult. Or at least, my body was. Inside, I didn't feel ready to marry. It terrified me, but I couldn't tell my father that.

Marriage meant supporting myself and a wife, and potentially a child very soon after. It meant I would need to become a provider, like my father. I'd seen what the demands of providing for a family had done to my father. He'd told me himself it was why he needed to drink. The weight he had to carry every day, worrying over me and my mother was heavier than anything he had to carry at the kilns. I couldn't even fathom what lay ahead of me. All I knew was that soon, I'd have no choice.

I'd seen Ishaya for the first time on the day we were married, when the priest had brought her to the river for the binding ceremony. I remember thinking she was beautiful and feeling some small amount of relief, because I was young at the time and that had been my first, shallow fear. If I couldn't desire my wife, we couldn't make children. And without children, we'd never be able to survive when we grew older.

But for all her beauty, Ishaya was cold, and it didn't take long for that chill to seep into every corner of our lives. Thinking back on it, I don't begrudge her the distance she put between us, even if it frustrated and angered me at the time. She was scared. We were both young, and much was expected of us. And we'd had little to no preparation for what was to come next.

We hardly knew how to speak to one another for the first few months. I was still living in my family's hut at the time, as was customary. We couldn't live together until we were fifteen. And that's when we were supposed to start making pups. I remember that uncertain year, living under my parents' roof with a wife I could barely understand. It wasn't just the emotional distance—we literally spoke different dialects, so for a long time we had trouble making any sense of one another. It couldn't have been a worse match if she'd been a tiger.

I'd never lived with anyone but my family before, and for all their failings, I knew them and understood them. So it was terribly disorienting, really. Waking next to a stranger every day. Trying to learn her, trying to make sense of her wants and needs while rationing my own. Ishaya was hard to please, and seemed perpetually ill at ease and sad.

I think she was terrified, too. But not just of being married. She was terrified of me.

It frustrated me, which made me no more pleasant to be around, I'm sure. But I was trying so hard to be a good husband, even if I didn't necessarily know what that meant. I wanted to make her happy. I wanted to impress my family.

I wanted to be better than my family.

So I made sure not to do the things my father had done that had hurt us, or made mother sad. I didn't drink. I tried to save the coin I earned, and I bought her some things I promised she'd never have to sell. I even tried not to raise my voice to her, but she made it so difficult sometimes. No matter what I did that first year, she flinched from me and distanced herself from me, like I *had* been hurting her. Like I'd been a bad husband.

Nothing stings quite so much as being treated like you're the person you want least to be in the world.

By the time we were ready to live as a married couple, I was certain things would have to get better, because the idea of them getting worse was just too much to bear. It seemed impossible.

Then we started trying for children, and it got worse.

Father told me the most basic elements before I left the family home, and by that point my body had begun to take its own interest in other bodies. I didn't have much trouble accomplishing what was necessary to make pups. At least, not the first few times. I still found it awkward, strange and not at all as relaxing as the other boys had told me it would be. The whole of it felt both natural and horridly unnatural, because even if my body seemed to know what to do, it always felt unwelcome. Ishaya was a beautiful woman, and I wanted her… but I don't think she ever wanted me.

Eventually, I stopped wanting her, as well. It became something I felt I was forced to do, like work, except it was harder to will my body to be with my wife than it was to carry an entire sack of bricks. For her part, she never really seemed to respond any different, although eventually I could tell it was at least hurting her less.

When she finally became with pup after her third heat we'd spent trying, it was honestly a relief. I left her alone after that, and I worked very hard to care for her while she carried our son. And finally, somehow, things began to change for the better. I remember the first night it began to feel right between us. Not loving, really. But at last, after so long feeling a stranger in my own house, coming home to her, eating dinner with her, lying beside her at night felt… comfortable.

I never desired to be with my wife again. I suppose for some people, sex is just never what it is for others. There's so much uncertainty and confusion tied up in my memories of being with my wife… I can't stomach the thought of taking pleasure in another's body anymore. But I can't deny that even for us, it eventually brought us the only happiness we'd ever know together.

It was Amon who changed everything between us. Our son brought us together, as our families, the priests and the Gods themselves never had.

Ahsan's cough is getting worse. It started some time ago, how many days at this point I'm honestly not certain, but it's progressed from a dry, hacking sort of thing we all have, from the dust from the over-turned fields, into something more wicked-sounding. Wetter, harsh-er. Like he's trying to heave something up.

He insists he's fine, and he *is* still capable of going about his daily work without much obvious change. And he's not the only man here with the cough. It's starting to make its way around the lodge. I've seen it pass through a few others already, and none of them were worse for the wear when they got past it. It's probably not life-threatening.

But Ahsan is fragile, not used to this harsh way of living. He still doesn't eat well, and I can't help but feel a pang in my chest when I see him cough. Some of them wrack his thin figure like a hollow reed in the wind, and damn it, I'm worried.

Over the last few months, the hyena's become like an adopted family member to me. The transformation I've undergone this sea-son, at this new plantation, seems to have brought my life full circle. It's closer to what it once was, in a way. I rise, I do as I'm told, and I retire. All beside the other indentured workers—which are as close to family as I may ever come again. The only difference is, now I check my contract every week and I watch my earnings climb, and wait for the day when that coin is mine to do with as I please.

Ahsan is with me nearly every waking moment, a reminder of why I must accept this reality. Unintentionally, the boy forced me to swallow my pride, to accept my fate and toe the line. Now and again I cringe inwardly as a voice from not so long ago—my voice—screams my doubts. But all I have to do when I begin to reel is glance to my side and see him. And remember that I'm pulling someone else down with me. I wish I'd had that foresight long ago.

I would resent that this has essentially been forced on me… but honestly, it's a truth I needed to see. Because the fact of the mat-ter is, years ago, I still had the chance to save my family. I still had the chance to find my wife and son. And because I refused to bend then, that chance has all but disappeared. I am worlds apart from them now, separated by force and time. I could blame it all on the hyenas as I have been for years now, but ultimately I know I'm just as responsible. And I've known that all along.

But I've grown silently desperate on the matter of this cough. It's been nagging at him for over a week now and it's only gotten worse. Most of the other men who picked it up passed it faster. I've asked around about what can be done, but only casually and only a few people I trust, because I don't want to let on how much I'm worried. The most I've gotten from anyone is that the guards sometimes have medicines they'll trade to the workers here. Things they're able to purchase at the market district in the city to the south. Things I'd never have access to from the few merchants who deign to come here and sell to us.

Almost invariably, when I begin to ask how one could get any of this medicine from the guards, I get a different answer every time. Bribery, begging and appealing to their sympathy, trading goods… I have little to trade and even less in the way of coin, and I can't simply ask the guards to put the charge on my contract, since the house would never repay them for fetching something for me. But there is one guard I know of who may actually have sympathy for my situation, or more specifically for Ahsan's.

I've kept my distance from Lochan since the talk we had at the guardhouse, and strangely, so has Ahsan. He hasn't even been going there at night to fetch dinner for us (which unfortunately means we haven't been eating as well, but it isn't my place to say he should go). It's not as though I think I did anything wrong, but for some strange reason I feel guilty and awkward about the whole mess. I was offended and angry when I thought the Aardwolf was taking advantage of the boy, but honestly, the more I think on it, the less I'm able to hate the man. His claims of throwing coin at the hyena and wanting to see his health improve aside, there was something in his spirit that was just too aching and familiar to me. Nothing hurts more than discovering someone you care for won't ever feel the same about you.

And aside from that, Ahsan never treated him with any fear. Ahsan might not be entirely right in the head, but he's not so placid that he'd take abuse time and again without showing fear for the man inflicting it. I saw him flinch from and attempt to escape the hyena in the gardens. He never acted that way with Lochan. Besides which, knowing what little I know about the Guard Master now, it's hard to imagine anyone who's lived the life of an indentured servant would be willing to visit the same tortures upon others that they endured.

But then again, he *is* a guard.

That's the stumbling block I keep hitting, and why I haven't gone to speak to Lochan since the last talk we had. For all his empathy for our situation, he's still made a career out of helping the hyenas keep us under their thumb. An indentured servant assisting the hyenas in keeping other servants under control. It rubs me wrong no matter how I justify it. Maybe things *are* better here because he manages the pay. Maybe he's harsh to keep us from doing stupid shit that could get us killed. Maybe he thinks what he's doing is for the best.

But he's still a guard. It could just be a power trip. The subjugated becomes the subjugator. He even admitted he used his position of power over Ahsan, and the things he could give him, to get close to him.

Although sometimes I wonder about that. Ahsan is smart. At this point, I've come to accept that he's far smarter than I am, and not even just in what you'd call 'book smarts'. The hyena is clever. I've caught him playing pathetic, tucking his ears and tail, even shivering, when I try to take the occasional night to sleep alone. I always inevitably fold, and come to wonder afterwards if he was toying with me to get his place back on the mat.

I sometimes wonder how much of his demeanor is intentionally geared to get him pity, or things he wants. He doesn't seem to care much about his severed connection with the Aardwolf, and that tells me he probably never did. But he reaped the rewards while they were together. Up until I showed up, anyway.

If my suspicions are correct, I can't exactly blame the boy. This is a horrible lot in life, and we all do what we have to. Ahsan has little to work with except his charm and his body. I use my body to intimidate and beat on people who get in my way. I can't really judge him for using his in whatever way he sees fit. But it makes it harder to dislike Lochan.

And that's why this whole thing's complicated, and why I've been avoiding the Aardwolf.

Today though, I've made up my mind. My pride isn't worth watching Ahsan suffer any more. Even if it's a disease he'll live through, it *could* get worse. I don't feel like playing the odds. Maybe it's all misplaced protection for a family I can't ever reclaim, but maybe… just maybe… I honestly care for the boy. I don't know. I'm re-learning myself in this place.

I'm staring at the guard lodging house, the sun growing low in the sky. The red of the poppies surrounds us, following the slight swells of the land, like folds in a crimson blanket. This place has never felt more ominous to me than it does now. I have a prickling at the back of my neck, my fur rigid, and I'm not sure why. Sometimes I have these instincts, but they've been wrong before and I already told myself I would do this. I've fought myself enough on it.

I've never asked a favor of a guard before, (except for the various occasions when I asked them to go fuck themselves). And I'd almost rather owe a favor to some of the guards I've attacked in the past than owe anything to Lochan.

I sigh, pausing at the door for longer than is really necessary, before steeling my nerve and lifting my fist to knock. If I wait much longer, it'll be dark and Lochan will chastise me for being out after curfew.

My knuckles are closing in on the wood when the door creaks open and I'm staring down the muzzle of a dark-furred lion, not the Aardwolf I'd expected. The man is roughly the same height as me, but leaner, his mane unkempt, clumping in places and dirty. Most of him is dirty, honestly. His leather armor smells old, worn and vaguely coppery, and it mixes with his distinct feline musk in a powerfully unsettling way.

I remember Lochan referred to him once as Vikram, and I've seen him in passing around the plantation. He's always elicited a creeping sensation down my spine, and that feeling is even worse now that I'm inches away from him, unexpectedly. Lions, specifically male lions, always have this predatory air about them. Near the Hyronses, where the hyenas have the strongest foothold in the country, their religion and their Prides aren't even permitted to exist, but I'd still see them in the city. I worked with some of them, in fact. There are a lot of lone male lions out in the world without a Pride. I've never had good dealings with them. They're the hyenas' natural enemies, something we'd share in common nowadays, but they're arrogant, specist pricks who tend to see all other predators as beneath them. And jackals aren't all that high up amongst predators as it is, not in a city full of hyenas and big cats.

His thick jowls slide up into a smirk and his pale yellow eyes sweep over me, giving me the distinct impression that I may as well be hanging on a hook. "Evening, jackal," he rumbles. "You're the new boy they brought in a few weeks back, right? I've seen you around." His eyes flick down my body. "Haven't had cause to discipline you yet, though. Come to give me a reason?"

I swallow, not taking the bait. "I'm here to speak to Master Lochan," I say instead, not wanting to start trouble with any of the guards right now, most especially him.

"The aardwolf's not here," the lion says, licking over a long, stained fang. He leans against the doorway lazily. "But I'm assuming you didn't come up here for his company. You want something?"

"Not here?" I parrot back like a fool, instantly hating myself for it. "Wh—then where is he?"

"Visiting with his kin," the lion replies, snorting. "Sister, I think. Dodging work, more like. He won't be back for a few weeks."

"Weeks," I repeat, too struck by the sudden blow to care that I'm parroting again. Lochan left? Since I'd come here, he'd been such a constant, I hadn't even considered that he might not always be around. And Ahsan is sick *now*. I need medicine *now*.

What the hell am I going to do?

Vikram is starting to look annoyed, and with a snuff, he pushes himself from the doorframe, swinging his tail as he turns. "You're wasting my time, jackal. Unless there's something else—"

"Wait," I say before I can stop myself.

And he does, slowly turning to regard me. That smirk returns, and he lifts a paw towards me. I brace myself, but all he does is gesture inside.

"Come in," he offers. "And let's talk about what you came here for."

"I need medicine," I say, preferring to get right to the point. And stay outside.

His ears perk at that, and then he gives a rough laugh. "For the ragged cough?"

I'm briefly startled. "How did you—"

"It's been making the rounds," he waves, idly. "But you're not sick," he notes, then smiles again. "Who's it for?"

151

"It's preventative," I lie. "I have weak lungs."

He doesn't entirely look like he believes me, but he also doesn't really seem to care. He just snorts, then reaches forward and closes his thick, calloused fingers around my arm, the claws extending and digging in *just* enough to hurt. His eyes measure my reaction, and I make sure to give him none.

Like I said, bravery isn't a real thing. It's just that some of us are better than others at lying about not being frightened.

"Come. Inside," he repeats, no room for argument in his tone. In a few moments I know he'll be hooking those claws around my collar if I don't budge, so I do as I'm told.

I've gotten better at that lately. Especially when it's for Ahsan.

The guardhouse feels altogether darker than it ever has before when I step inside. Maybe it's the angle of the setting sun outside, just barely not making it through the windows anymore. Maybe it's the stale quality in the air, like the place hasn't been cleaned or aired out in a while. I can vaguely smell moldering food somewhere. Lochan kept this place clean and orderly, if not inviting. That's all I can think about as I follow the lion down the hallway, towards the sitting room. The Aardwolf's going to tan the lions' hide when he gets back.

I can hear another guard in the sitting room, which is sublimely comforting. When we turn the corner, I see the big lioness, finishing up a meal at the table. She looks like she was expecting us, her round ears are up, but she doesn't follow with her eyes. Her demeanor is different than it was the occasions I saw her with Lochan. More subdued. I think she looks at me, but then her eyes go straight back down to her bowl.

"Get out, woman," the lion commands, his tone cold and disinterested.

This was the fierce guard I saw sparring with Lochan, putting her bulk into the Aardwolf's blows and nearly bulling him on to his back several times. I expect some resistance, but there is none. The woman stands, keeping her eyes down as she moves to the counter and deposits her bowl, then adjusts her belt over her wide hips and moves past us, going out of her way to do so on the other side of the table.

As she passes, and Vikram moves towards one of the cabinets, I catch her pausing in mid-step just out of the corner of my eye. I twist an ear and partially turn my muzzle, and I swear, for a moment I seem to see her shake her head at me. Her brown eyes catch on mine, and then I'm certain. But a second later, she turns the corner and is gone.

"Here we have it," the lion's gravelly voice breaks through the silence, and I look up to see him dangling something before my eyes, encased in a wax paper packet. "Medicine," he supplies. "An herbal mixture they make in the cities, for the ragged cough. We keep some on hand so we don't catch your filthy ailments."

I again say nothing. Even when I was looking to get in trouble, I wouldn't respond to the sort of immature mockery the lion seems so fond of.

"I can brew some here for you right now," he offers, a knowing look on his muzzle.

"I'm not planning on drinking it now," I say, still unwilling to part with who the medicine is actually for. The last thing Ahsan needs is for this man to take an interest in him. For any reason. I can handle him, the hyena can't.

I reach out for the packet, but he only withdraws it and chuckles. "It's all we have left," he says. "It'll be a lot of trouble for me to replace it before the boss gets back. He'll notice it's missing."

"Then I'll talk to him then," I insist. "We can settle up—"

"You'll settle up with *me*," the lion sneers. "*I'm* the one holding your precious medicine, here and now, when you need it." He shakes the packet, looking downright jolly, if it weren't for the yellowed fangs. "And you *do* need it now, don't you?"

I resist the urge to show him *my* fangs, if only barely. Instead, I growl out a, "Yes, sir."

"Ha!" He exclaims, giving a wheezing cough. "And here the boss said you'd be a troublemaker! You're docile as a lamb, aren't you?" His chuckles simmer down slowly, into his favored smirk. "Or is it just my aura, jackal? A bitch knows its place around a powerful man, after all."

I feel my temper rising up inside me, the fur along my spine growing jagged. But he's still holding that wax packet just out of reach, and if I jump him for it, I'm very likely to lose, and absolutely likely to lose the medicine.

"You haven't got money, I take it?" The lion asks.

"I wouldn't be here if I did," I state.

"You might," he shrugs. "The merchants that come here don't sell it all that often. Might be our stash is the only game in town."

"Just tell me what you want," I press, wanting to finish this as soon as possible. It's getting dark and Ahsan's going to start worrying, and I'm afraid the smell of the lion is starting to sink in to my fur.

"If you have no coin, you'll have to work it off," he says, in perhaps the most reasonable statement I've gotten from him all night.

"All right," I agree hesitantly. That's what I do here, anyway. Work off my debt. I'm not sure how I could fit more work in to a day, but maybe he means to have me work after hours. I suppose even if it means I get less sleep, I'll manage.

He's silent for a bit, clearly deciding on something. What I can't say, but I have a few suspicions about what he might plan to ask for, and I know what I'll agree to and what I won't. If we can't reach an agreement, I'll find this medicine another way. If he attacks me, I'll defend myself. This is no worse a situation than I've been in in the past. He's not even bigger than me, and even though he *is* armed, he'd be a fool to mortally wound the Matron's property.

"First thing's first," he says at length, and begins opening up the wax paper envelope. "You've got me concerned. I don't care if you aren't sick, you drink some of this with me. I'm gonna have you clean up this place, but I don't want that rotten cough."

"I'm not—"

"I don't care, you clearly know someone else who is," he says as he begins to boil water. "Drink the damned medicine. There's enough here for a dozen doses, so a few less won't matter."

He makes up two cups for us, and I take mine without further argument. The idea of cleaning up the lions' filth isn't appealing, but it's better than what I imagined. And as much as it galls me to admit it, he has a point. Ahsan could have gotten me sick by now. It's not a terrible idea.

The medicine tastes awful and strange, but then all medicine does. The lion seems to have no issue finishing his cup, so I push my way through my own, quickly. Ahsan will have to drink this eventually, and at least I'll be able to tell him I managed when he complains about the awful taste.

The lion pushes his empty cup across the table at me, then gestures to a mountain of dishes on the nearby counter. Likely where that moldering food smell is coming from. There's a wash basin nearby, so I'm fairly certain I can deduce what my first task will be.

"There's a well out back," he instructs, standing and moving across the room towards the door. "And the bucket's in that corner. Place is gonna take at least a few nights, the condition it's in. Floors, too. Don't forget the floors."

It's getting dark by the time I've gathered the bucket and made my way outside, seeking the well. I exhale into the evening air, sucking the smell of poppies through my nose. The cloying scent is oddly intoxicating at times. Even surrounded by it all day as I am in the fields, it can still get to me. Perhaps especially tonight, it makes me feel lighter.

The soles of my paws are especially sensitive as I walk across the rocky earth towards the distant silhouette of the well. I feel as though each and every grain is pressing into them, leaving an indent. But that light feeling persists, so I'm certain I can't be walking as heavily as it feels like I am.

This was the best possible outcome for tonight. That feeling of dread has entirely lifted, and is being replaced by a warm swelling in my chest. I may not sleep tonight, but I'm accomplishing what I came here to do, and Ahsan will be well again. I'm so content in that knowledge, it's almost unreal. I can't remember ever feeling this light of spirits.

Am I still walking? At some point the stars began to come out, and the well hasn't gotten any closer. My feet are too light to touch the ground anymore, so it's hard to tell if I'm still moving. I dropped the bucket some time ago.

I'm staring at the stars. I should be working, but I can't stop staring at them. I've never really taken the time to just… look at them, in the past. They're rather like the poppy fields. Endless and colorful. Forming random patterns. Is the whole world like this? It can't be that there's no order to anything, that everything is chaotic like this. But the poppies are like that. The stars are like that. Maybe we're like that. Maybe the world can't be directed or changed. It's just random, pointless chaos.

Powerful hands grip me beneath my armpits, and the last thing I remember is being grateful for them, because I'm certain my knees had struck the earth. Not so long ago, I fell right here, in this dirt, because Lochan had shoved me over. But these hands caught me.

My arms are aching when I wake, stretched high over my head. Something is cutting in to my wrists, cold and unyielding, and my back hurts viciously. There's another pain, too. Jarring and terrible and unfamiliar, and it's what woke me.

My mind is mired in a fog that feels like one I've traversed before, but so much denser than I remember. That strange, confounding feeling of warmth and well-being is persisting, even as I begin to regain some clarity and the horror of what's happening to my body pushes through into my consciousness. The two make no sense in the same moment together, and that makes it all the more disorienting.

I can smell that familiar, sickening musk, heightened by the lion's current state of arousal. The rhythmic grunting as his hips jerk into mine is unmistakable even if I can't entirely sort through the physical pain of being violated... at least, at first. After a few moments my mind begins to truly return to me, and every second I become more aware is worse.

All I can think to groan out is a stuttered, breathless, "...the med... icine..."

The lion laughs, and there's a sharp slap on my rear, my mind beginning to pick out that one of the many pains afflicting me is caused by his iron grip on my tail, held up at a painful angle, clearing the way for him to assault me. I have never experienced a pain like what lies beneath that, in the whole of my life. I feel like I'm being torn apart inside.

"Got a strong constitution, don't you?" Vikram chuckles. "I gave you enough to put most men out for an hour at least."

"You—d... drank it... too..." I weakly insist.

"I take the Divine every day," he says with a satisfied, guttural growl as he slows his pace some. "Higher tolerance." He smacks me again, but it's so secondary to the rest of my pain, I barely notice. "You slaves are all stupid as donkey shit. Haven't met a one of you I can't dose and fuck, one way or another."

I give a gurgling groan that was meant to be a scream, and try to put my all into breaking away from whatever's got my wrists held above my head. What I ultimately manage is to shake the chains, and scrape my knees against the stone floor. My body is unbelievably weak.

I'm in the cell I was in when I arrived here, I realize. Back where I began. Under the influence of the Divine. Again.

My emotions are at a fever pitch, and I can't be sure of how much of it is coming from me and how much of it is the drug, but I can't stop the sob that breaks out of my muzzle through my teeth. The lion heightens his pace, and the pain intensifies.

"Normally I like you filthy pissants asleep," he growls contently. "So much more pliant when you're limp as a corpse. But I'm liking this struggling, jackal. Tightens you up. So you keep at it."

He pushes his free hand into the small of my back at that, forcing me to arch my spine in the same way that I'd woken in, and the ache returns with it. I put up a weak resistance for only a few moments longer, before I realize through the flower's haze that I have no chance of fighting him off. He saw to that.

And I fell in to his trap like the stupid creature he thinks I am. The realization sinks in to me like a knife. He's right. I'm every bit as foolish and worthless as he said. I couldn't see through a guard's shallow treachery, didn't even think to, and now I'm suffering for my mistake.

Everything in my life seems to have led to this new low. Lochan was wrong. There is no bottom beneath this. This is my whole worth as a person, symbolized in one heinous act.

It's my fault I'm here, it's my fault this is happening to me, and the only thing worse than enduring this is the fear that somewhere in the world, this could be happening to my family, as well. And it's my fault. It's all my fault.

I know when he's done, because he pulls from me, which I take as a small mercy, but then I feel the wet streaks across my back, crawling down through my fur, and all I can do is squeeze my eyes and try not to be aware of it. Which is impossible.

Some time (I'm barely aware how much) passes after that. He's been quiet, but I know he's gotten to his feet and is standing above me. I have no desire to turn my head to see him, I have no desire to even be alive in that moment. And then, almost unbelievably, it gets worse.

I'm hit with a wet heat on my back, more of it than before and the scent is unmistakable. He's relieving himself on me, and I'm so sickened by the defilement it gives rise to the first real energy inside me. I thrash against the chains, roaring like an animal, unable to form any intelligible words except to scream my outrage against the stone wall I'm bound to.

He laughs at me, and the more I fight, the more he laughs.

The sand tossed about by the wind sticks to my fur as I limp my way back to the lodging house, barely able to keep both eyes open. I'm numb like a man who's been hit in the head, and the only thing keeping me upright is the knowledge that if I pass out here on the road, the other workers will find me in this condition tomorrow. The distant, flickering lantern light outside the lodging house door is my beacon, and I follow it, trying to think of nothing else in the world.

Clutched in my palm is a wax paper packet. A different one, which the lion tossed out the door on top of me after he dragged me out of the guardhouse. He said this one had the medicine in it, and that if I ever wanted anything again, he'd be more than willing

159

to make another trade.

I'll drink it first, before I let Ahsan drink it. But I believe Vikram. He's just the sort of man who'd expect someone he raped might be desperate enough to come back to him for another favor. And there are probably some here who have.

I can hear the sounds of the other men sleeping inside as I approach the door, but as desperately as I want to go inside and lay my head down, curl up on my straw mat and sleep, I walk past the doorway and the dim lantern that had been my goal. I make my way toward the baths.

The water's freezing and I haven't the time or energy to heat it up, but the shock, as it hits my back, is welcome, awakening. I shakily grab for one of the discarded coarse bristle brushes, my wrist panging with a deep pain that tells me I'll be bruised beneath my fur there. The manacles he had me bound in weren't tight, but struggling against them and the time I spent with my entire weight resting on them did some damage.

I rake the brush through my fur as hard as I can, again and again. When my bucket is empty I go for another one, and then another. I try to pull him, and the memory of him, from my body, but it's sunk into me. Into my fur, into… inside me. I can't get his smell out of my nose, and I'm certain I still reek of him everywhere else, as well.

I scrub until my body feels raw and there are wet clumps of my fur on the ground all around me. I can still smell him. I've gone through five buckets, and I don't know how long I've been at it, but nothing seems enough.

Eventually I give up, not because I want to but because I'm starting to lose my balance. My body is aching and unbelievably tired, the Divine still battling with my senses. I worked all day today as well, and that's normally enough that I'm tired by now, but this is… too much. I have to get back to the lodge or I'll collapse here.

I head back towards the lantern, the cold air hitting my soaked, equally cold fur, and seeping into my bones. No one bathes at night. The nights here are cold, colder even than near the Hyronses, and there's no sun to dry off in. Thankfully I'm so tired, I don't think it'll stop me from getting to sleep.

When I open the door into the lodge, only a few eyes flicker up to look at me, and most quickly turn back down. Only one pair, their normally dark discs glowing green with night shine in the dim sliver of light from the doorway, remain on me until I make my way towards my sleeping mat.

"Kadar," Ahsan says with relief evident in his tone, sitting up on his knees on our mat and making as though to get up entirely, but I wave my hand at him, and he stills. I step over the rat who sleeps near us, and it takes everything I have to kneel down slowly on the mat without outright collapsing. Ahsan's eyes follow me the whole way, and I'm suddenly hyper-sensitive of my smell, now that I'm close to him. Surely the scent is just trapped in my own nostrils. He can't know.

But, when I finally turn and slide my legs out on my side of the mat, and I look him in the eyes, I know he knows. He's quiet, but his big dark eyes are wider than usual, and he's never looked at me this way before. He opens his muzzle as if to say something, but doesn't seem able to complete the thought. And I can't bear to see him looking at me like that anymore, so I turn my back to him when I lie down.

"Kadar..." he whispers desperately, his hands slipping up over my shoulders, hesitantly.

I shove them off of me, roughly, expecting he'll probably recoil and leave the mat for the night. I'm wet and cold and angry, *and* in pain, and the last thing I want now is to sleep alone, but I want his pity even less.

He surprises me by insistently putting his hands on my shoulders again, his elbows wrapping over my side. And when I try to shove him off this time, I find him far harder to shake. Frustrated, I reach up and grab for his fingers, prying them off of me and kicking back at him when he stubbornly clings right back on to me a moment later. In response, he only wraps his arms around me completely, and I feel his muzzle against the back of my neck.

I growl out one warning, and when that doesn't work, I wrench around and shove him off of me with all the strength I have. He fights me—he *never* fights me like this—and I'm growing desperate now. Why is he fighting me now, when he's always done as I wanted in the past? Why tonight?

I'm still stronger than him, even in my current state, so it isn't very difficult to roll him on to his back. I slam him down harder than is probably necessary, and I hear the wind leave his lungs with the impact.

And then he coughs, and I'm undone.

"I'm..." I go weak over him, my arms shaking as they try in vain to hold me up. "I'm sorry. I'm sorry..." I feel my head dropping, the weight of my exhaustion crushing down on me. I drop to my elbows over him, this horrible, desperate feeling welling up inside me. It's like everything that happened back at the guardhouse just became far more real to me. Maybe the drug is starting to wear off. All I know is that I haven't felt more like sobbing in my entire life.

I don't. But I'm shaking now. It's not just the cold. It's like a visceral reaction I can't control. I feel like I've got to burn something off inside me, and this is the only way.

Ahsan stares up at me, his dark eyes seeming endlessly deep without any light to reflect in them. I can't look into them for long, so I just bend my muzzle to rest against his collarbone, and let him put his arms around me again. I can feel his heartbeat against my chest and it's so... calm. I focus on it, and only it, and it's like it bleeds in to me. My own breathing evens, the shaking begins to subside in small measures, and my body slowly loses its rigidity.

His calm becomes my calm, eventually. It takes time. But it becomes easier the more I accept it.

Miraculously, he doesn't ask me what happened. Good thing, because that's the last thing I want to talk about right now. He only moves his hands down my back to wrap more loosely around my waist, and urges me to turn on to my side. I do so, and then he settles back in against me. This time I couldn't want him there more, and I make that clear by wrapping my arms around *him*. He returns the gesture, and reaches over to pull the thin fabric we use as a blanket over us.

"I always thought you were weak," I croak out, my voice sounding unrecognizable even to my own ears. I swallow, but the hoarseness is from screaming, not a lack of water. "I'm sorry," I say at length. "I was wrong."

Ahsan's ears perk slightly and he turns his muzzle up against my fur to look up at me. "How were you wrong?" he asks.

"The things you've done," I manage, not wanting to put a name to them right now. "The work you did up at the Manor."

He frowns marginally, but the sympathy I see in his eyes isn't for himself.

"I thought you were weak, for letting it happen to you," I say, my jaw shuddering. "I pitied you," I admit, with a painfully self-aware guilt growing in me. "I thought a stronger man wouldn't—couldn't let them turn him into what they did."

He continues to look at me evenly. There should be some anger, or some sense of betrayal at my words, but I see none.

"A weak man couldn't live with this, for as long as you did," I say, swallowing around a lump in my throat. "I'm the weak one. For judging you—"

"Kadar, stop," the hyena insists, tugging my muzzle down to his, and holding me closer as I shake my head and rock against him.

"I'm sorry," I say again, because I don't know what else to do. "I'm sorry."

He sighs softly, and runs a paw up my neck scruff, his slim fingers moving down beneath my collar and rubbing gently at the abused and furless skin there. "People are many different ways," he says. The statement doesn't make much sense on its own, so I wait for him to complete it.

"I mean," he clarifies at length, "that you can't say someone is weak or strong. I could never carry you. I could never do the work you do in the fields."

"Having a strong body doesn't matter," I say, bitterly. "They find other ways."

"It's not just that," Ahsan says with a sort of hesitation, like a man who's having trouble admitting something. "I... have trouble saying no to the people around me. I follow orders because I'm afraid not to. People like you are *strong* enough to risk things, even if it might be harder for you. If people like you weren't strong like that, the Clans would own the whole world."

"For all the rotting good it's done me!" I snap, unintentionally. He doesn't flinch away, though. Not tonight. "Lochan is right. You've had the right idea all along. We need to *stop* saying no. We need to stop fighting. There's no damn point."

Ahsan lifts his head to look me in the eyes. "If I hadn't said no," he says quietly, "the one time it mattered the most, I'd still be at the Manor. Or I'd have allowed myself to be sold to that man." He moves his paw up to cup my cheek, running his thumb along my cold fur.

"I've spent so long telling myself they couldn't do this to me," I breathe, closing my eyes. "And they keep proving me wrong. And it's my fault—"

"You can't ever tell yourself that," he insists.

"You don't know me," I grit out between my teeth. "You don't really know me. You don't know the life I've lived, Ahsan. The mistakes I've made."

"It doesn't matter," he says. "No one has the right."

"How did you stomach taking up with Lochan?" I ask, the question coming so suddenly it surprises even me, in addition to Ahsan. "After everything that happened to you," I continue, desperately. "How could you choose to let it happen again, even after you escaped that place?" I don't know why I'm asking the question, I just know I need it answered.

The hyena's eyes are wide and confused for a few moments, and then he seems to understand, and answers back as though it's obvious, "The evil isn't in what happens, Kadar. It's in the person."

It sounds simple, but trying to wrap my head around it is hard. Ahsan often speaks like that. In small words, short statements, but there's always more beneath them than seems to be at the surface. It's part of why I've begun to accept that he's 'clever', not just smart. He understands things more deeply than I do, sometimes.

"A lot of things can hurt you," he says. "It's the person that's causing the hurt, though. Lochan wasn't like that. I could tell right from when I met him that he wasn't like that." He gives a slight smile. "Just like with you."

"I'm not as good a man as you think I am," I murmur.

He wraps his arms around me again, and nuzzles his nose into my neck, his breath warm against my chilled fur. "We'll talk about it tomorrow," he promises.

It's almost surreal how calm he is about all of this. My mind is still reeling and I want to make him understand. So many things. But his heartbeat, his comfort, is starting to seep into my mind again, dragging me down with him into the well of exhaustion I've been ignoring up until now.

The last thing I remember thinking is that I was supposed to protect him. How am I supposed to do that now, when things are so reversed between us?

Chapter 6

Waiting

I respected my father. I really did. But he was a man broken by a hard life, who tried to heal his pain with drink.

I grew up wanting to believe everything he said about the honor in a life as honest and humble as ours. I had to, just as he had to, because for us it was all there was and all there ever would be. You *have* to find meaning in labor when you know for a fact it's all you will ever do with the life you're given. You *have* to be proud of making bricks. You have to hold your head high, or you'll succumb to desperation. You'll think on it too hard and wonder about why you were born so low. Why you have to suffer, and repeat the same hard, back-breaking day, over and over again, for the rest of your life or, more likely, until your body breaks down.

I wanted to believe my father when he said that even if it seemed lowly, the life we led was noble. I wanted to find peace in that.

But over time, it became clear to me that he no longer believed it. The work breaks you, like I said. Not just your body. Eventually, it breaks your spirit. And men with broken spirits lose track of who they are.

My mother hid it from me for a long time. But we lived in a small shack, and eventually I grew older and more perceptive, and her lies stopped convincing me. The first injury, the first really bad one that I remember, was when one of her eyes swelled shut. We couldn't afford a physician, especially with father drinking our coin away, so we worried for a time that she'd lose it.

I hadn't seen the fight, but I'd heard it. I hesitate to call it a 'fight' because she never fought back, but I just don't know any other word for it. Any time she tried to talk to him about the drink, about where our little coin was going, I could all but dictate the series of events to follow. It was depressingly predictable. As a pup I was more able and more willing to ignore it. As I got older and more aware of what was happening… of the destructive nature of my father, and the passivity of my mother… tucking my ears back and sitting in the corner served less to chase it all away. When I was young I'd fill my mind with thoughts of what I was going to do with my friends the next day, or how many fish I could catch for dinner if I really tried. As I got older, what began to fill that space between my ears… was anger.

Being a laborer, being poor and low-caste is humbling, difficult and often painful. But it never made me feel helpless. My father taught me what it meant to feel helpless. And that fear of being helpless again pervades my every action to this day, bubbling up inside me whenever I feel threatened or talked down to, whenever someone challenges me or makes me feel like less of a person. In those moments, I'm that little boy again, sitting in the corner, unable to protect my mother. And it's the worst feeling in the world, all over again.

Any perceived slight can evoke that pang, that stab of memory. And then the anger is there again, like a wound re-opening. My chest burns, my heart rises in my throat, and all I want to do is stop that feeling. That anger is my father's legacy. I don't know if it's in our blood, but I know he gave it to me. If not through inheritance, then through his actions.

And just like him, I've done some terrible things when I was angry. Things I only hope my son will not remember.

There were benefits to the drug. What had seemed almost too clear, too bright and vivid the night before, when I was still suffering the effects of it, became a distant haze by morning. I would never not know what had happened—what had been done—to me, but the sharp images were obscured by the mask of the Divine. I'd heard that the Divine dulled minds, that it could erase a man's memory if it was abused, and Chandan had told me more than once that he used the drug to forget, but I'd always reflected on that statement with sadness. Now, I was beginning to understand.

That's not to say I wanted any more to do with it. They say the Divine takes hold in some people, but I'd been force-fed it twice now and I had no lingering desire to use it again. But then, I hate all things that are forced on me on principle. So perhaps that's why.

I drift through the field work that day like I'm still drugged, and maybe I am. I have no way of knowing how long the effects will last. All I know is the fields look like crimson waves lapping at a beach, and Ahsan and I are alone in the vast expanse of the flower sea, his body moving impossibly through the tides at waist-height. Sometimes I just stop and watch him, and his ears twist back towards me eventually, when he realizes I've stopped collecting. And then he smiles at me, his dark eyes growing slim as his cheek fur crinkles.

I'm overwhelmed then by two contrary feelings. I feel lost, adrift. I'm finally coming to the realization I should have long ago. I really *have* lost everything, and I will never get it all back. The threads I clung to so precariously and desperately for the last few years were ripped away last night when I realized I couldn't even protect myself any longer, let alone a family so long gone. Everything I once had, everything I once was, is gone. Desperate dreams and plans can't undo the past.

Ahsan is the only person in the world who cares what happens to me anymore. And he's the only person relying on me. The only person I can protect. This hyena who months ago was a stranger to me has become the only family left in my life. We're bonded through mutual misery and, I am coming to admit, mutual co-dependence. I need him and he needs me. And after last night, I'm no longer ashamed of feeling that way.

I know to him, it might be more than it is to me. Or at least... different. That's a conversation we'll have to have eventually.

I've lost track of him amidst the red again. At some point while my thoughts meandered, he got too far ahead of me and clearly hasn't realized it yet. I flick my ears about, listening for him, but even my hearing is hazy today. Damned drug.

I hear something, at last, but it's several seconds too late and not what I was listening for. The big cat must have been moving beneath the tossing sea of flowers, and he did so expertly, because I am legitimately spooked and stumbling backwards when he rises up from the stalks behind me. The noise of the flowers shifting is the only warning I have, and even that was probably allowed by him.

"Gods!" I grab at a stalk for purchase, snapping it and nearly losing my balance, falling back on my bad foot hard enough that pain lances my ankle. I grimace, and then growl. "What the hell are you doing stalking me?" I demand.

The cheetah barely regards my outburst, only stares at me evenly. It's been some time since Raja made any significant appearance in my life, save to keep vigil over me like he does the rest of the workers from across the room. He's like a self-appointed 'king', with the way he regards this place. No one cares enough to stand in his way, at least not if it means they get kicked around by him. I've taken to ignoring him, and I thought I'd be able to stay far beneath his notice, considering I don't keep company with any of the workers he seems to favor as part of his inner circle. Once he dumped Ahsan on me like unwanted baggage, he seemed done with me.

But yet, here he is, prowling up on me in the field.

"I can only assume since you didn't beat my ass," I say with a sigh, "that you just wanted to stalk me to prove you could. Well, good on you. I had my ears forward, you stayed downwind... if I were a gazelle, I'd be dead. I admit defeat," I mutter, then turn. "Now leave me alone."

"I was avoiding the attention of the guards, not you," he speaks at my back. I pause, because he just did something he almost never does. Explained himself.

I turn my head, but not my body, granting him some small measure of my attention. "What do you want?" I ask.

The cheetah doesn't respond with words. Instead, he lifts an arm from beneath the roiling flowers, and primal fear briefly takes a stab at my heart as I see the glint of a blade come up with his hand. Is he here to kill me, for some reason?

But... no. The blade is odd, and he's not holding it as though he intends to use it. He's holding it out to me. Like an offering.

I turn entirely at that, and look down at the strange weapon. Or, no. Tool? It's hard to say. I think I've seen something like it before at one of the other plantations I worked, but I've never used one. It resembles a sickle, but it's far larger and more durable-looking. I'd say it resembles a scimitar, but it has no guard. It's humble, old and worn, but the blade itself looks like it was recently worked and sharpened.

"We aren't supposed to have weapons," I say, glancing back over my shoulder for any nearby guards. Or Ahsan. Whatever this is, I don't want him involved in it.

"It was my understanding that you didn't give a damn what the rules here are," Raja states.

A few months ago, that would have been true, I say to myself silently. But Raja and I haven't conversed much since then, and he's probably still going on first impressions with me. I came in here a thug, and I'm now… well, still a thug, I suppose. But I'm trying to be smarter about choosing my battles these days.

"I'd rather not have my collar as tight as yours," I point out. That gets a reaction from the cheetah finally, a curl of one of his lips and turned-down ears. "I can get out in a few years if I just walk the line until then," I explain. "Not interested in fucking that up by hiding your contraband."

"There is no need to hide this," he says. "It is not a weapon."

"It looks—"

"It is a sickle, if anyone sees it from a distance," he says firmly. "And tools do not leave the field, so no one will have a chance to see it closer. The guards do not care what our tools look like while we work."

"Why are you giving it to me?" I ask uncertainly, glancing down at the weapon. "And what is it, actually?"

"It is called a shotel," he states, turning the old, weathered guard in his palm, the blade glinting in the sunlight. "It is built for combat, despite its appearance. It will not bend on a man's skull like the dull, fragile tools they give us. But using it should come naturally to any man who's worked a plantation before. Any worker who has reaped."

My palm itches to reach down and take it. I know this 'gift' must come with some kind of cost. Raja isn't the type to share fortune with any man. And even if this is some odd form of peace offering, it could still get me in a hell of a lot of trouble if his assessment of the guards' perception of tools versus weapons is wrong. And Lochan, for one, seems like the type of man who'd know the difference.

"No," I state flatly. "I don't want it."

Yes you do, my mind screams at me. *It's protection. It's a way to ensure that what happened last night never—*

The cheetah seems surprised, which is something to see, because I rarely get any emotion out of him other than aggression. He releases the weapon, and it falls to the earth with a dull thud, disappearing beneath the flowers. "I am disappointed by you," he says, the edge of a low growl in his voice. "I took you for a different man."

"Why are you trying to give me a weapon?" I demand again.

He's silent a few heartbeats, and his lack of a ready answer makes me nervous. But in time, he replies, in his usual cool voice, "I suppose it doesn't matter if you know, whether you have a spine or not. If you try to tell anyone, I or one of the others will kill you."

My heart jumps. I think I know what he's planning to tell me, a moment before he says it.

"We are revolting," the words come out like the growl of a lion in the seconds before he takes down his prey. "Tomorrow night. We are taking the guardhouse. The Manor. Everything."

"Are you mad?" I demand. Even in my wildest years, I never took part in a revolt. I've fought guards, I've bucked authority, I've even tried to escape. But actively fighting the Clan that holds me? Never. They have every advantage. The guards, the weapons, the armor, the knowledge of the land, the buildings themselves are all theirs, designed by them, walked by them, it is *their* domain. You don't attack hyenas in their own territory. It's suicide.

The cheetah cracks the slightest smile, more eerie than any malice I've seen on his features before. "Yes," he replies without missing a beat. And then he begins to approach me, not stopping when he's inside my personal space, forcing me to take a step back for every step he takes forward. "My kind are meant to run. To roam. To travel Mataa freely, as we always have, for generations. These miserable souls, these piteous creatures here who made their own beds, who cursed their own lives by taking up the Divine or gambling or fucking their lives away, into the Clans' pockets, *they* deserve to be here. They... made... *mistakes!*" He roars the last word, loud enough that I hear it echo across the field, and worry the guards will hear. But there is no fear in Raja's eyes.

"I did not sell myself into this life," the cheetah continues after a few silent beats, his tone now so quiet in contrast with his previous yell that I have to crane my ears to hear it. "I was set upon. Stolen, in my sleep, when I was young. For the express purpose of turning me into a *commodity*, these beasts killed my brothers... killed my mother... and sold me to a woman who wanted me... for my *pelt.*"

I stand in stunned silence. Not once has the cheetah ever spoken to me about his past, and where he came from and how he ended up here I know to be a topic of hot debate amongst some of the other workers. And here it all is, laid out plainly. I'd long wondered at his unique markings. You don't often see a cheetah with spots that bleed together. It makes him unique. Rare. Special.

Expensive.

"I'm sorry," is all I can croak out.

"I have fought the life that was forced upon me since then, every day," the cheetah growls, plucking at his tight collar with a claw. "With sheer rage and ferocity when I was young, and then as I grew, by planning, and waiting, and *striking* when I saw an opening!" he snaps the last bit. "And I have failed, and been beaten, and tortured, and sold again, and watched my debt grow and *grow.*" His voice is little but a rumbling growl now, and I've backed nearly to the end of the row we're in. "They punish us for daring to take our lives back," he says. "For yearning to live free. I will... *never...* stop fighting. Until my dying breath."

He stops finally, staring down at me with eyes the same color as the sky. "They made a madman out of me. When you first came here,

I thought I saw that madness in your eyes, as well." His gaze grows narrow. "I suppose I was wrong."

I sigh, putting my hand up. "I... understand," I say, because I do. "I've fought the Clans before. I still..." I close my eyes a moment, wondering how I can be talking someone else out of what months ago I would have embraced, "...but, a revolt is just an inevitable road to death. Revolts always fail. For one simple reason—"

"They have a Liberator," the cheetah says suddenly, with a fanged smile.

An hour later, Ahsan and I are baking in the sun in the precious last few moments of our meal break. The heat is hours away from abating, and I'm not looking forward to the last half of the day, but then, that's every day. Oh, some days it's cooler. Some days the work is easier. But every hour we spend in the fields is just misery punctuated by small bits of relief that convince us it's bearable.

The only other options, I tell myself again, are much worse.

Maybe it's my half-full belly, or the remnants of the drug, or the sun cooking my brain, but I find myself asking Ahsan something that serves no purpose to ask.

"Have you ever thought about what you would do if you could escape this?" I turn towards him.

He gives me a sleepy-eyed look, leaning back on his palms, the sun making the white fur along his chest seem far too radiant. "Of course," he replies. "Because one day, I will."

"You're so certain of that," I say, my voice monotone.

"I thought Lochan talked to you about our contracts—"

"I know now what it will take to buy my way out of mine," I assure him. "But yours... yours is much worse. You know that, right? I mean, you know numbers. You can read."

He flicks one of his ears, looking away from me. "I know," he says at length.

"So," I say uncertainly, wanting to hear him tell me about how it's going to be alright, for him. How Lochan, or someone else, is going to help him buy his way out. Some trick, to make the figures Lochan told me sound less impossible.

"So," he says, looking back to me with a wan smile, "that just means I have that much longer to figure out what I'm going to do, when I'm free."

"Ahsan—"

"Don't worry about me," he insists. "I got away from the Manor. Away from moth—" he pauses, "away from the Matron. This work, I can do. And I'll have you here with me, at least for a time."

"I could stay on," I say before I really think about it. "My contract may be up in a year, but I could stay here. As a paid worker."

He reaches up to toy at his ear, at one of the many holes in it that probably once held gold finery, from his entertaining days. When he eventually looks back towards me, his eyes are dark, plaintive, asking for an answer to something. It isn't the question he speaks aloud, but I can see it. "Why would you do that?"

I know what he wants me to say. I wish I could say it in earnest, but lying to the boy feels worse. Men have lied to him his entire life.

"Because you've taken care of me," I say instead, and I see the slight droop in his ears. "And I want to help take care of you."

"What about your family?" he asks.

I feel my ears flatten at that, and I try not to show how defensive hearing someone else speak on my responsibilities makes me. "My family," I try not to grit out between my teeth, and I can still hear my voice trembling through the words, "is gone."

Ahsan reaches out for my arm, and I don't push him away. "Are you certain of that?"

I shake my head. "They're gone from my life, Ahsan. I gave up the right to protect them, far before I was ever indentured."

"What do you mean?" he asks.

I tip my muzzle down, the crest of my brow cooling my eyes in shadow. "There are a lot of things that happened to you at the Manor," I murmur. "Things you don't talk about, even to me. I understand why, and I don't press. Some things happen to us, or we do things and we just... don't talk about them. Because it doesn't help."

He seems to understand, and falls silent. I find myself looking back out towards the fields, at the silhouettes of figures rising up from their plots, just barely visible acres away. It reminds me of stories I was told when I was young, of the dead rising from the earth. That's how these people appear. Dead on their feet. Stiff, dark, thin, like the meat's already been stripped from their bones. Even on the best of plantations, this is a hard, terrible life. Even with a man like Lochan, who knows what it means to wear the collar, looking out for us and trying to guide us towards freedom. Legal freedom.

What Raja is chasing is so much more dangerous, but it holds so much allure. All this while that I'd been letting them destroy me, convincing myself I didn't care what they did to me, so long as I didn't allow myself to be subjugated... I was accomplishing nothing. But freedom, real freedom, was what I really wanted. I just wasn't willing to make the kind of sacrifices Raja's risked, and is risking now, because I knew it more than likely meant death. And with it, no chance to return to my family.

But if I put that aside, if I accept that I've lost all chance at that, what's really left to protect? Ahsan?

I look over at him, and find he's never stopped looking at me. And when we lock eyes, he smiles. For some reason of his own, I'm sure. But it's every bit of encouragement I need in that moment.

I can still find reasons to be here. Even if all they amount to is a hyena with a kind smile, who for some reason thinks the world of me.

"Have you been drinking the tonic?" I ask him, pointing to the small gourd bottle he's carried with him to the field today.

"It's bitter," he says, sticking out his tongue. "But yes. I think it's working already. My breath's been coming easier."

"Good," I say, not allowing myself to show how relieved I really am. After what I went through to get that medicine, I need to know it was worth it. Ahsan has been good enough not to question why I did it, or to tell me it was unnecessary, and I am again glad for his empathy. He always seems to know when not to say something.

I haven't told him about my encounter with Raja in the field, yet. I probably won't, until the inevitable happens. If we even talk about a revolt, we're likely to get caught up in the whole mess, and that's the last thing I want. Raja is a man who has nothing except the promise of one last desperate grasp at freedom. I don't know how he thinks he has any chance, but as uncertain as I've been about my future over the last few months, I know that throwing my life away for such a small hope is simply not something I'm willing to do. And once again, having Ahsan's welfare on my mind is making that decision easier to abide by. I barely even think about the shotel, left there in the dirt in the middle of the field, as we get ready to go back to our work for the day. Raja left the invitation open to me, regardless how firm I was in my disinterest. He seemed to think I'd have a last-minute change of heart, for some reason.

"Kadar?" I hear the hyena call my name, and I turn to regard him just as he closes the space between us.

Before I can stop him, he's brushing his muzzle over mine in a fleeting kiss. It happens so suddenly, and passes so briefly, I'm almost not certain it happened at all. But the memory of the heat from his lips is still there, his scent still caught in my nostrils. I have very little time to think on it, because he's soon up on his feet and making for the fields, but as I push myself up to catch up with him, all I can do

is try to compare it to kissing my wife. It's like a reflex, she is after all, the only other person I've ever kissed, and maybe my memories of her have paled with time, but I just can't quite recall them enough to hold them up against the vivid afterimage of what just happened.

"Why did you do that?" I ask the hyena, as I stride up beside him, our claws crunching dirt and sand on our way down the next row.

"Because I wanted to," he states in a strangely self-assured tone, for him. "Not because I felt you wanted me to. I know how you feel about me making my own decisions."

I sigh. "About that," I say. "I do care about you Ahsan, but I think you and I feel differently."

He forces up one corner of his muzzle into half the smile he wore a few moments ago. "I know," he says.

"You do?" I ask, a little uncertainly.

"By now, most men with any interest in me... in that way... would have taken advantage," he explains, and I try not to wince at how casually he says those words.

"I don't like taking advantage of people," I say, trying to keep the growl out of my voice.

"I think that's why," he says cryptically. I wait for him to say more, but we're starting to approach the end of the row and I've still gotten nothing, so when we arrive, I put a hand on his shoulder and stop him.

"Tell me what you mean by that," I say, and it isn't a request. He looks up at me, except it isn't really up, because we're essentially the same height. It's just the way he carries himself, I have to keep reminding myself. As an afterthought, I add, "And stand up straight."

He corrects his posture some, then replies. "Why... you don't want me," he says.

"Ahsan," I blow a breath out through my nose, "it's not that—"

"Not just me," he says. "Your wife, too."

That gets my hackles up, and I utter an angry, "What?" before I can stop myself. He shrinks back a bit, and I try to correct my tone. Sometimes Ahsan *doesn't* know what not to say. "I've hardly told you anything about her," I insist.

"You told me you were married, and you are no longer," he supplies. "And that you can't go back to the life you had with her."

My ears droop. "That... is true," I say, at length.

"I know there are things we don't talk about, because talking doesn't make them better," he says, almost mimicking my words from earlier. "But you have to at least know them yourself, on the inside, or you'll never know why you do the things you do. Sometimes thinking about the dark times is what helps me get up when I hurt in the mornings, or do things differently today than I would have done then."

"Ahsan, trying to get deep with me isn't going to get me into bed," I sigh.

"We already sleep in the same bed," he points out. But before I can give him an annoyed counter, he says something that stops me dead. "There was a room, in the Manor," he says. "Mother called it 'the black room.'"

I'm silent, because what could I possibly say to that? I can tell by the expression on his muzzle that he means to say more, and I'm afraid any word from me will interrupt and forever silence him, somehow.

"When she was unhappy with me," he continues, "when I was being disobedient, or unpleasant to look at, or I wasn't making the guests happy, she'd send me there."

He seems to have trouble getting past this part of the story, so I wait patiently, watching his toes curl in the dirt, his tail twitching at flies. I wait for what seems an eternity and he's still not continuing, so I press, "What was in the room?"

"Nothing," he replies, simply. "Not even a window. That's why it was black. There were shelves on the wall, I think, but they were all bare. Once a day, someone would slide a plate under the door, and every few days they'd refill a bucket of water and open the door for a few moments to clean, but the servants who'd come to do that never spoke to me, even when I yelled at them. Even when I cried at them. Mother said when I was in the black room, I didn't exist. And that's... how it felt."

"Days?" I repeat, somehow unable to close my jaw. "How long did you spend there?"

"I tried counting once. Forty meals. Other times longer," he murmurs. "Sometimes it felt like I wouldn't ever get to leave. I can't remember much about the time I spent in there except that I thought a lot. And most of the things I thought about were terrible. Eventually I'd get out, and no one would talk about where I'd been. No one acted like I'd been gone. Mother said it was to show me that the world would keep going, without me in it."

I couldn't understand what he was describing. I'd imagined the sorts of things the hyena had probably been subjected to as a house servant, but all the things I'd pictured were within the realm of cruelties I understood. This was... I didn't know what this was.

"Talking about the black room doesn't make me feel better," he says, an edge in his voice. "But remembering it does. When I left, the Matron told me life out here would be intolerable. Worse than life with her ever was. And for a while, I was just waiting for it to be like that. But it never has been." He looks to me. "From the time we met, you always seemed worried for me, angry at me even, that I'd let someone take advantage of me. And last night, you were angry at yourself. You always have your claws out."

"The whole world will take advantage of you if you let them," I say, trying not to think on the ache in my body, the reminder of how inescapable that reality is. Claws out or no, I hadn't been able to stop Vikram. I hadn't been able to stop myself from being taken advantage of by the men who'd contracted me.

"Not the whole world," he says quietly. "There are good people, Kadar. People will care about you, your situation will and can change. You're waiting for it to get worse."

"It got worse last night," I remind him with a growl.

"And it's better today," he says. "Remember Vikram, and whatever came before, and remember how bad it can be, but be happy today. Today's different. Something could change. Someone could be good to you, today. Someone could be there for you," he says, and I know what he means to point out. I remember last night well enough. "But, not if you can't let them," he says just above a whisper.

"You're waiting for people to take advantage of you. And me. You expect it. You're always ready for it."

"And I still couldn't stop it from happening," I point out icily.

"So why agonize?" he asks in a tone that's more of a statement than a question. "At some point I stopped waiting for it to get worse. And even if it does someday, at least I'm not spending every single moment afraid of it."

"I am not afraid," I growl outright now.

"Yes you are," he replies in a rare show of defiance. Maybe it's because he's been rejected. Even if he did see it coming, as he says, maybe he was hurt by it. Maybe. His eyes look hurt.

Maybe I just want to think he looks hurt.

"I don't know what happened to you, Kadar," he says, before I can get another word out. "But you're waiting for everything to go wrong, for everyone to turn on you—"

"They will, and they have!" I bite out.

"You'll never trust anyone!" He shocks me by raising his voice, not anywhere near as loud as mine but somehow, I'm still stunned silent. "You're even afraid *you're* going to take advantage of me," he says, his posture rigid, unused to conflict. "You trust yourself less than I do, and you know yourself better than anyone."

"Maybe that should tell you something," I say.

"You're afraid to hurt people as much as you're afraid they'll hurt you. It's in everything you do. You're always on the defensive," his ears lift up from their flattened state just an inch or so, and his expression softens. "You think I don't know what that feels like? I knew it from the second I saw you. I've never said anything because... because I thought you knew, too. But if you can't honestly see it, I feel like I have to say something. Or you'll never understand why."

"Why what?" I ask, bitterly.

"Why it feels like the world's so cruel," he says quietly. "Why it always seems like you're under attack. That's how I spent every day in the Manor. Waiting for it all to go wrong. Waiting to go back to the black room."

"And your life there *was* horrible," I point out. "Your life there *was* cruel."

"Life isn't cruel," he insists, "just some of the people in it. You can't assume everyone's going to hurt you just because the people who raised you did."

My eyes widen, and I barely restrain myself from lunging forward and grabbing him. "What the hell do you know about the people who raised me?"

"I was talking about *me*," he says, an edge of suspicion in his tone. "But… Kadar… if I assumed everyone was going to be like the woman who raised me, I'd never have trusted Lochan when he told me life outside could be better. I'd never have left. I'd never have gotten to know you."

"So save your affections for Lochan," I almost snarl. "If you feel like I can't trust you as much as you want me to."

"I'm not judging you, Kadar," the hyena reaches for me, and this time I don't let him close the distance. He seems hurt for sure now, and I get a perverse sort of satisfaction out of that.

"You're talking about me like I'm some kind of coward," I roar back.

"No!" he insists.

"Like I'm afraid of the world," I say, "and everyone in it. And, what, that's why my wife and I aren't together anymore? Because I was afraid of her?"

"You never talk about her, or why you were separated," he says. "But as soon as you found out you could be free of your contract, you gave up on returning to your family. You're afraid of *something*."

I'm all too aware of the fog of anger as it rises inside me, but the haze of exhaustion from the night before, and the memory of the hyena being there for me at my side the whole while, allow me to push it down. The boy can't know how his words are resonating, the memories they're stirring up. It isn't his fault. He's trying to help, I tell myself, as I swallow down the words that want to erupt from me.

Anger is no excuse.

He's naive. I've known that since I met him. He thinks he understands, but he barely knows the world, let alone my life. He can't understand.

"I am not afraid of being close to you, Ahsan," I say, just barely managing to keep my voice even. "I do care about you. But I won't use you the way they used you. And, I think if you thought about it, you'd realize you don't want that either. You've just been taught to offer yourself to people. You don't need to do that with me."

"Listen to yourself," he sighs, softly. "You don't even believe that I know what I want. You think I'm still being taken advantage of."

"I think," I say, closing my eyes for a moment, "that Lochan might honestly care about you. Regardless how it started. If you honestly feel like you need someone to fill that role—"

"Wait," he stops me, "how do you think things between Lochan and I started?"

I pause a few moments, before saying, "I really don't need the details."

"He has *never* taken advantage of me," he says, suddenly sounding vehement. "He helped me escape the Manor."

"Because he wanted to sleep with you, Ahsan."

"Because of his *sister*," he states, in a hard tone. "Kadar, he saved me because his sister was a prostitute. He couldn't stand the way they were keeping me in that house. He wanted to help me."

"I'm sure that's what he told you," I say, trying to keep the uncertainty out of my voice.

"I came to *his* bed, Kadar," he persists. "And he was just like you, at first. He didn't want to treat me like the Clan members did. He resisted for a long time, even though I knew he was attracted to me."

I think back on that suspicion I had, the last time I spoke to Lochan. Like Ahsan might not have been the innocent victim in their arrangement. I'd wondered then, and this seems to confirm it. The conviction in Ahsan's tone was unmistakable.

"Why?" I finally ask. I find it hard to believe the young hyena was simply physically attracted to the Aardwolf. The guard had to have at least twenty years on him, and even if there was no accounting for taste...

"Part of it may have been because I couldn't think of many other ways to thank him," he admits, abashedly. "But, also, I've always genuinely liked him. I've known him since I was young, and I never really thought of him as a potential lover when I was in the Manor. Once I left, he became more of a protector, and I probably wouldn't have pushed it past that, except..."

Something about the way he trails off makes me uncomfortable, so I look at him expectantly, making it clear I want an answer.

"...well," he sighs, "Raja said I should pursue him."

"Raja?" I reel. "Why the hell would he care whether or not you were fucking a guard? Was he getting something out of it?"

"No more than you were," he shrugs. "Some of the food. But Kadar, I honestly think it's just because he knew I was fond of him. Raja believes we should take what we want when we can. That's what he told me to do."

"Raja believes in taking for himself," I snarl. "And only himself. He got something out of Lochan, mark my words. You're a fool if you think he was just being kind."

He narrows his eyes at me. "Not everyone takes advantage of other people," he repeats.

My eyes fix on something in the distance, and I point out towards the heat-hazed road down past the fields, "How about you ask Lochan, then? Whether he and Raja made some kind of deal? I guarantee you—"

"Master Lochan is back?" the hyena interrupts me, his ears twisting and his entire body turning towards where I'm pointing. There's a stab of jealousy when his attention is diverted so quickly from our conversation, from me, and I have to remind myself that I'm not supposed to care. I can't tell Ahsan one moment that if he wants a lover he should go back to the guardsman he was seeing before he met me, and then resent him for doing just that.

Besides, it's not as though it's gotten to that just yet.

The distant, distinctive figure on horseback is a few rows down, and this isn't the first time I've seen him this morning, but it must be the first Ahsan heard of his return.

"He returned this morning," I say with obvious bitterness in my tone. I'd seen him lingering near the guardhouse when I'd gone out in the morning to wash myself again, still reeking of lion, and I'd instantly hated myself for not just waiting a day to ask him for the medicine I'd needed. I'd had no way to know he was going to be back early, though. He wasn't supposed to return until the end of the month.

The way Ahsan is looking out over the fields towards the Aardwolf, his bushy tail swaying just slightly, is starting to upset me, so I grab at his shoulder and move him back towards the row. "I wasn't serious," I say. "You can go see him later if you want, we really need to get back to work."

"I want to ask him how his sister is—"

Hoofbeats suddenly break through our conversation, and now that I'm paying attention, I was probably hearing them from a distance for some time, but I was too engrossed to pay much attention.

Right now, though, it's very clear they're closing in on us, and both Ahsan and I turn to see the four horses rounding the corner in the field. They're cutting right through the poppies, and the men and women atop them are not Lochan's guards... they're far too well-armed and armored.

"Clan guards?" Ahsan asks, his voice frightened and confused. I'm at least those two things as well, but I try not to show it, and I don't push him away this time when he grabs at my arm. The guards don't have their weapons out, but they're clearly making a path towards us.

What the hell did we do?

The two women on horseback in the forefront are large, dangerous-looking hyenas, wearing the distinctive camel hide leather armor of the Manor house Guards, falchions on their hips, cold professionalism in their eyes and their demeanors. One of them holds up a hand to halt the others behind her, and looks down at us, taking a few moments to assess us silently.

"What—" is all I get out.

"That one," she says, cutting me off, and pointing at Ahsan. "The hyena. Take him."

"Huh?" Ahsan looks between the guards and me, wild-eyed. I yank him back behind me and try to demand an explanation from the woman who spoke, but I've barely gotten us back two paces before the two guards in back, a woman and a man, dismount and cross the space between us.

"Out of the way," the woman decrees, pulling what almost looks like a polearm from her back. I hadn't seen it before, but the two guards in back have weapons... shit.

"Mancatchers!" I warn Ahsan, throwing an arm up to shove one of the poles aside as she aims it for my neck. The woman's good though, she twists the pole with my arm and moves around my body with two side-steps, bringing it back up to clamp neatly around my collar, just as they were fitted for. I've been in the grips of a man-catcher too many times to count throughout my life, and it's never any less frustrating.

I snarl and thrash, grabbing at the pole and trying to wrench the hyena holding me to the side, but the weapon is made to put me at my weakest, and the woman is strong besides. I can hear Ahsan screaming from behind me, crying out for help. Another heavy metal on metal clang tells me he's been caught as well, and a thud a few moments later tells me they've gotten him down on his knees already.

"Ahsan!" I give up on wrenching at the pole, and try to twist my neck to see behind me, but the woman yanks me hard then, nearly sending me down to my knees as well. My legs quake, blood sings through my ears and it takes every ounce of my strength just to stay standing let alone fighting.

An even louder thud, and Ahsan goes silent. I scream for him again, but all I hear is the sandy scraping of a body being pulled along the ground.

"Knock this one," the hyena holding me down says impassively to another of the guards. "He's being difficult."

I open my mouth to yell for him again, and then everything goes black.

Chapter 7

No Dreams

I don't dream. I don't revisit my memories. This is a blackness I've floated through before, dark and empty. When I wake my head will ache, my perception will spin and nothing will seem right for days. They think it's so simple, striking us over the skull. That it doesn't hurt us, only puts us out of their way for a while. They're wrong.

It does damage that doesn't go away. It always does damage. It was the same when my father did it to me.

When I wake, no one is with me. The skies are darkening from blue to black, the flowers seem purple in the waning light. I'm exactly where I was when I was struck, face-down in the dirt, smelling pollen and tasting the faint coppery edge of blood from a split lip. There's sand between my teeth, and a deep ache in my bones from lying splayed out on the ground for so long.

Everyone else has left the fields by now, and several of the guards and workers would have had to pass me on their way back to the shacks. No one even cared enough to move me.

I don't bother getting up. I'm too tired, too worn down, and there isn't any damn point in it.

They took him. The last thing I had to cling to, a day after they took my dignity... the second to last thing I had to cling to.

This is it. This must be it. The bottom Lochan spoke of. The bottom beneath every other low. I don't care if I'm not some whore, suffering a wasting disease in a brothel, or flayed and beaten in a city square. For me, there is no further to fall.

I had a family, once. A mother and a father. I lost them. I tried to remake my family, with a woman I couldn't seem to get to love me. I had a son with her. I lost both of them. Then, for a while, I at least had hope I could mend that family back together. When that was extinguished, I always told myself... I still had my pride. And when I at last gave up on that, I had Ahsan.

It's fairly clear where he was taken. And the Manor may as well have been past the gates of death, as reachable as it was for me.

My claws dig into the dirt of their own accord. Why was I ever proud, I think to myself? Why have I ever imagined myself to be worth anything? I am, and have always been, nothing. My life's a testament to that very fact. Everyone around me has been trying to make it clear to me from the time I was born.

I promised to protect Ahsan, and I was barely able to lift a fist to defend him, the moment that promise was tested.

If I lie here long enough, I wonder, maybe the ground will simply swallow me up. And I'll become part of the flowers, just like every other indentured worker who's died here.

I barely notice the sound of hoof beats, until they're stopping near me. I don't care who it is, I don't care why they're here, and I haven't the strength to lift my head besides. Maybe I'm already dying.

The crunch of claws against earth nears me, and then a shadow falls over me and I smell the scent of the Aardwolf. My spine prickles as he reaches out for me, but when his paw settles on my forehead, brushing over the sticky, bloody fur, it's gentle.

"I've been searching the fields for you," he says, his normally deep voice strangely hoarse. "Put up a fight, did you, jackal?"

His tone isn't accusatory, isn't stern. He sounds more... sad.

I don't turn my muzzle towards him, and he doesn't force me to. Instead, I hear him shift to settle down beside me, and we share a long silence. I have nothing to say to the man, even if I am strangely comforted by his arrival. I'm not even certain why. Perhaps simply because I know now that someone was looking for me.

"How did we get here?" he asks, clearly not requiring a response. He's asking the question to the sky, to the pinpricks of stars beginning to appear overhead.

"I don't know if I believe in Gods," he says at length, after another long silence. "Or rather, I don't know if I want to believe in them. It's hard to accept we all came from nothing, but it's even harder to accept that anything would make a world this beautiful, and ask so many people to live such horrible lives in it. And what... be content watching the luckier peoples around us, making the most of all that beauty? Ruling, conquering, making us all suffer, and reaping the rewards of it? Life was made easier for them to begin with, so we're supposed to congratulate them on their successes, on their victories? Because they were born with the right pelt, or to the right family. The right caste. We help them defend their riches, keep their slaves, clean their homes and suck their cocks, because they already have the power. How is that right?"

"You tell me, 'Master,'" I say, my voice rough as gravel when it at last comes. I slowly turn my head, my skull aching with the minor movement. "If it galls you so much," I let out my breath in a long shudder, "you shouldn't have become one of their guards."

That genuinely sad tone creeps back into his voice. "I earnestly thought I could protect some of you," he murmurs.

There's a stab of guilt in my chest I can't ignore, so I turn my eyes away and mumble back, "You tried."

I honestly think he did.

"I tried to get work at the brothel my sister belonged to," he admits, a heaviness in his tone. "It would have killed me to see what she suffered, each and every day. To serve the people who kept her, and be part of that insidious place. But I would have done it, because it was the only way I could protect her."

"Why didn't you?" I ask.

"They wouldn't hire me," he replies simply. "They knew we were siblings. They feared we'd collaborate. I came here because this plantation is the closest place to her that I could find work. And I told myself I'd do what good I could here."

That silence descends again. I hear him open his muzzle once or twice, and I can see the shadow of his throat bob as he swallows.

"She died yesterday evening," he says at length. "I am glad… I was close enough to her that I could be with her, when it happened. For that alone, working here has been worth it."

I recognize the defiant way he's holding his head up, the stiff posture of his shoulders, the pride there. I knew what that was once. I don't commiserate with him on his loss, because I know he doesn't want it.

"They took Ahsan," I say instead. I suspect he already knows, and his lack of any response confirms it.

"That's what the Clans do," he says, an edge to his voice. "They take. They steal, and murder, and rape, and no one stops them because they don't want to lose anything to them."

"You're the one who told me to work within the system," I growl up at him. He doesn't even know the consequences his advice had on me.

His gray blue eyes finally flick down to mine. "If you want to live, you should. That fact hasn't changed."

I'm silent a beat. "What if I don't care about living, anymore?" I finally ask.

He uncrosses his arms slowly, and lowers a hand down to me. "Then you're in good company."

I only hesitate a moment longer, before I clasp his paw in mine, and the big Aardwolf slowly helps me to my unsteady feet. My vision spins and for a white hot moment, everything hurts. But Lochan is there, hooking an arm beneath my shoulder as I find my bearings.

"Maybe I do believe in the Gods," he says after we've stood there, staring at the stars for a long while. "It's hard to feel like someone, or something, hasn't conspired to bring all of these events together at once."

"You don't know the whole of it," I say. "But help me search the flowers for something, and I'll tell you more."

The guardhouse has never looked more appealing as we approach it in the starlit darkness of the early evening. I don't know why exactly, but it's probably just because I'm not going back to that damn cold building with my threadbare mat again. I have no reason to go back to the servant housing. Ever. If tonight goes wrong, I'll be dead.

I tell myself I'm at peace with that fact, but it's hard to ever be at peace with the thought of death. I think the people who live to boast about not fearing death are liars, or they'd obviously be too dead to talk about it.

My feeling of relief lasts exactly as long as it takes us to open the door, and step inside the main hallway. Because just as Lochan is quietly telling me to wait while he gets his spare armor, a shadow steps out from the dimly lit doorway into the sitting room.

I recognize his smell before I recognize his silhouette. The lion must rarely, if ever bathe, because his fur is thick with old musk. A streak of light from the wall sconce in the sitting room throws the scar on his face into stark contrast. Lochan has facial scars too, but they've never looked so ugly.

"Oh, you don't want this'n, Aardwolf," the lion gives a rasp of a chuckle, taking a few lazy steps towards us, his tail swinging behind his ankles. "I've stretched out that jackal too much for your tiny prick."

Lochan's eyes briefly flicker to mine, questioningly, but the look is blessedly short.

"What are you doing wandering the hall at night?" He asks instead, ignoring the bait. "Are the workers locked in? You should be on your rounds."

"We were missing one," he says, scratching his lower jaw. "Guess you found him." He's getting closer to us now and every fur on my body is standing on end. I can feel a growl growing in the back of my throat, and something like acid rising in my throat.

I can only describe it as something primal, and old. An instinct that tells me I need to fight, to tear him apart before he attacks first.

The lion seems to sense something is amiss, in the few seconds of silence that follow. Maybe it's just that neither of us responds. Or maybe it's that at that moment, Lochan steps back, clearing a path for me.

That empty space between us is all the beckoning I need. Vikram has a hair trigger like any other lion, and like I said, he already seems to know something is wrong. His jowls fall and his body stiffens, but by then I've snarled and charged, and he still hasn't noticed the shotel I've been holding behind my back this whole time.

The lion is unarmed at first, and maybe it's my rage, or maybe I'm just not as good a man as I thought I was, but I feel no need for fair play. I grip the handle tight and swing it in an arc in front of me, imagining the spray of blood, the resistance I'll meet when blade hits flesh, and readying myself for it.

Instead, the lion easily back-steps my admittedly wild swing. I may not have even hit him if he hadn't moved, honestly. I swung too soon, and realized it too late.

The swing has me off-balance, and Vikram seems all-too ready for it, bulling into me and sending us both teetering to a collapsed heap on the hard stone floor. And then he's on me, yellowed, enormous fangs snapping at my face as he digs his claws into my shoulders.

I'm more at home fighting a man like this, wrestling for a pin and relying on tooth and claw. I try vainly to grab for the shotel, but it came free of my hand when I fell to the floor and is lying just barely out of reach. I give up on it all but immediately when the lion's claws sink deeper into my flesh, past the barrier of my fur.

My muzzle is longer than his, and he seems wary of the fact, hesitant to close in for my neck. But it's not just that, I realize. He's also trying not to bite my collar. For the first time in my life, the damn thing is protecting me.

One of his hands releases from my shoulder, and he starts reaching for his belt. I'm certain he has at least a knife there, so I seize the moment before it's gone.

I've been letting him think he's got me pinned this whole time, because he's a lion and they always assume they're stronger, but he's a gangly, older man than I am and with one good buck of my hips, I'm able to throw him a full foot up off of me. His weight falls entirely on one knee and his arm whips back from his belt, producing the knife I knew was there. He'll use his momentum to bring it back down on me, hard. I have a few seconds to stop him.

I snap my knee up between his thighs, and though it isn't the crushing blow my rage and indignation truly want, it's enough that he reels back and unsteadily plants a foot to keep himself from falling down full-force onto my knee cap.

I lunge for him and snap my jaws around his forearm, the one holding the knife. My teeth sink in deep, penetrating muscle, filling my mouth with blood. I expect to hear the clatter of the knife any second.

Instead, the lion grits his teeth and reaches for his right hand with his left, switching the blade. My eyes follow the glint of candle-light on the blade, my jaw releases, and my mind tumbles end over end trying to figure out what to do in the next few seconds.

I thought for sure he'd release the blade.

I do the only thing I can think to—I bring my arm up, to block whatever's coming. It may have been too slow, it may not be enough, but it's all I can think to do.

The blade never comes down like I'm expecting it to. Well, it does… eventually. But only because the lion suddenly collapses over top of me, his head falling at an unnatural angle beneath the two of us when he falls, the blade finally slipping from his fingers and skittering along the ground.

I give him a hard shove, pushing myself back away from his limp form, and it's only then that I see that his head's facing down at his own chest, held on by shreds of bone and viscera, like a chicken just barely slaughtered.

I gag, despite myself. I've seen people die before, I've seen corpses of workers and some nasty injuries, but I've never seen so deep into someone's body. It's jarring to see the things that hold us together so exposed. It's not the gore that shocks me so much as the transparency of the moment.

Lochan stands over the both of us, as unaffected as I am horrified. It's clear by the blood on his wide blade that the mortal wound was his doing, and done in one cut.

The old Aardwolf gives the lion a long look, as if he's trying to decide if he warrants a second, but Vikram's head is barely attached to his body anymore, and I can't help myself from stating the obvious.

"He's dead," I snap. I can't decide if I'm angry or relieved.

"I'm only glad you gave me an excuse," the Aardwolf says, as he pulls out a cloth from his belt and begins to clean his blade. "I've wanted to kill him for years."

"Then why the hell did you wait?" I demand.

"He pre-dated my time here," Lochan states, simply. "I never would have hired a sadist."

"I meant tonight!" I'm yelling, pushing myself up onto damnably unsteady feet. I've seen death before! Why is this so different? "Why didn't you step in earlier?" I flex my shoulders, feeling the ache from the small puncture wounds his claws made. "You let me fight him alone!"

"I thought you wanted the fight," he replies, an edge of irritation in his tone, like I'm the one being unreasonable. "You were armed. I thought you stood a good chance, and that you wanted him to yourself."

"I..." Did. "I wanted to be the one to kill him!" I say instead.

"Not enough, clearly," he replies, maddeningly calm.

My body is coming down from the rage of the fight, and my anger is turning more helpless and frustrated than fierce. I hate how this makes me feel. I hate that he saved me from the man who tormented me not a day earlier. I don't even hate that it was Lochan who killed him. I just wanted so badly to do it myself.

"You're wrong," I say, my tone weakening. "I wanted it. I just... I couldn't..."

The Aardwolf's ears tip down and he's silent for a time. I force myself to stare down at the dead lion, then. I can barely look at him. Could I have had the conviction to do what Lochan did? Even if I'd had the chance?

The fact is, I've only ever killed one man, before. And it took half a lifetime of torment for me to finally gather the nerve to do it.

Even now, I'm not certain how much good it's done me.

"Kadar," the Aardwolf shocks me by using my name. I lift my gaze to his, because I can feel he's looking at me. There's nothing patronizing in the older man's eyes, nothing pitying. He looks stern as ever, but there is a certain kind of empathy in his tone when he speaks, even if the words bite at my ego.

"You aren't a warrior," he states, with such certainty it makes them hurt even more. "You're an emotional man, and I think your anger's seen you through some bad years... but anger isn't a substitute for training."

Anger isn't an excuse. My mother's words ring through my head, fitting like a patch to a broader tapestry some twenty years later with these new words, and the old Aardwolf imparting them to me.

"Vikram had more experience," he continues. "More will to kill. And to put it bluntly, a better appreciation for his blade. You *never* release your weapon. It is your lifeline. You have nothing left to lose if you lose that blade. It's worth the hand holding it, the arm attached to the hand... whatever you have to give up. You hold fast to your weapon, no matter what. Vikram understood that."

I can't even remember releasing my grip on the shotel, and I'm about to try to explain that to him when I realize how futile I'll sound. Because he's right. Excuses don't matter if you're dead.

"There's no need for all that shame," he says with a sigh, sensing my mood. "You're a laborer, not a soldier. There's only so much willpower can do before skill and experience overcome it."

"How did you learn?" I ask around a dry muzzle. "You were a servant, too."

"I was indentured to an arena," he says, with no evident pride in his tone. "A warrior for sport. I became a Gladiator at seventeen, after I'd endured the first few years of drilling and practice matches."

I'd heard of the practice, but never near the Hyronses. It had been outlawed since the age of slavery had ended because of one particular law, a law which all servants knew.

"Servants can't be ordered to die for their owners," I insist. "I thought the arenas were a thing of the past."

"Gladiators are paid better than nearly any other contract affords," he says, quietly. "I fought willingly. You either pay off your debt fast, or you die. I wanted to help my sister, and I was good with a blade. It seemed an obvious choice."

For someone willing to kill people for sport, I can't help but think. I don't say it, though. Over the last few months I've been trying to judge people less for decisions I can't understand. I've done things others wouldn't understand, unless they'd lived my life.

My eyes drop again to the dead lion, and the blood puddling into the cracks of the stone floor, nearly black in the dim light. The smell of blood almost overwhelms his musky odor. Almost.

"If you wanted to kill him before, why didn't you?" I ask, trying not to let my anger trickle down through the question. He already knows what happened to me, thanks to Vikram's taunting. I don't need him thinking I blame him for it. But it's still a question I need answered. If not for me then for everyone else here the lion must have abused.

"The same reason you've never killed a guard, I'd imagine," he replies. "I didn't feel like visiting the gallows. I had no cause to have his employment terminated. The hyenas don't care what he does to the servants here so long as it doesn't damage them or impede his ability to do his job. He wasn't incompetent. Just disgusting."

He begins to sheathe his blade, and looks to me. "He had to die tonight regardless. I don't want to have to deal with him on his rounds, where he could actually alert the Manor guards. We need to get moving, on that note. Shallya will come around this way in about an hour, and I don't actually want to harm her."

I'm having trouble tearing my eyes away from the dead lion, and the confusing stew of emotions I have over what happened to him. The Aardwolf doesn't let me think on it long, though.

"...or would you rather stand here and feel sorry for yourself some more?" He asks, in a deliberately nasty tone. I flick my ears back and glare up at him, but he seems unimpressed. "Just keep in mind," he growls, "as bad as it was for you, Ahsan endured it for most of his life. And he may very well—"

"Shut your damn mouth," I snap, shouldering past him towards his room, even though I don't know what I'm looking for. "And let's find this armor."

Even Lochan's spare leathers are a bit too sizable for me, despite the fact that he insists he was slimmer 'back then'. I get to rib him a bit for it while he adjusts the old buckles on me. His response is to over-tighten them and cut off most of the blood flowing to the lower half of my body, and then we get in a brief shoving match that ends with me splayed on the floor.

There's no denying that when the armor is properly fastened on me though, I feel... changed, somehow. It's only thin hide, and it's old and torn in places, nothing fancy like what the Manor guards wear. But it makes me feel more capable than I did before. Even if my skill with a blade was just proven to be fairly miserable, I can at least use my gods-given toughness to my advantage. And now I have real protection.

We have to step over Vikram's body on the way out, and I force myself to look at him the whole while. I briefly consider giving him a kick for good measure, but I just don't have it in me. Disrespecting the dead is a step beyond murder, in the eyes of the Jackal God... who just so happens to *be* the God of death. Best not to burn bridges with the one deity that might someday save my soul.

Lochan pauses near his body and reaches into his belt pouch, producing a silver coin and tossing it beside the lion's body with a flick of his thumb. It tinks on the ground beside one of the hollow depressions in the stone now full of the lion's blood.

And then we move on.

"Vikram said you were the only servant missing," Lochan states quietly as we move down the hill. "I'm guessing that means the others haven't gathered, yet."

"Raja's leading them," I mutter. "The cheetah is mad. I'm not even certain they have a plan. Beyond having weapons."

Lochan puts his hand on my shoulder, stopping me. "You go," he says, suddenly. "To the servant housing. They will not trust me."

"I thought you wanted to save Ahsan," I insist.

"Go find out what they have planned," he presses. "I'll wait here. We can either work with them, or work around them. I'd like to know what our options are."

I don't take the time to argue. Vikram won't be making his rounds, so I make my way down to the lodging with little fear of being caught. Most of the other guards will be closer to the Manor this time of night.

When I near the door, I can already hear the sounds of many men awake inside. That in and of itself confirms something must be happening tonight. Usually the entire lodge would be asleep by now. I push the door open slowly, and emerge into a throng of bodies.

It seems like the entire lodge is awake, voices in eight different dialects and at least three different languages trying vainly to speak over one another without speaking so loudly as to be heard from outside. They're only partially succeeding.

A hand grabs at my arm and I instinctively bristle and yank free of it, only to see Chandan's wide eyes.

"Kadar?" He whispers fiercely. "Where were—what are you

wearing? Are you a part of this madness?"

"No, I'm," I pause. "Sort of," I try hastily to explain. "What the hell is going on?"

"Raja's riling up all the men he can for some kind of ill-fated revolt," the painted dog says, his eyes sweeping up over me. "I *never* thought you'd be a part of it, too. You're smarter than this. They're all going to die, Kadar."

"They took Ahsan," I say, trying to impart on him the importance of that. He stares at me blankly, so I continue, "The Manor guards. They took him earlier today. No explanation, no nothing. They just attacked us, and took him away."

"That was… really only a matter of time, Kadar," the painted dog states, looking at me for all the world like he can't wrap his head around my desperation. "He belongs to the Clan Leader. If she wanted him back at the Manor, that's where he has to work."

"Do you know what they do to him there?"

"Do *you?*" He counters. "No, really, Kadar. Do you really know? I liked the kid, but before he came out here he clearly hadn't done a day of hard labor in his life. He's not even hooked on the Divine, so it's not like they were drugging and forcing him like some of the brothels on the coast do to their workers."

"Is that how bad it has to be before we do something about it?" I snap.

The painted dog's ears tip back and he leans away from me. "Kadar, calm down," he insists. "What the hell's gotten into you? Not for nothing, but…" he pauses, then sighs, "…he's a hyena. They already control our lives, are you really going to throw yours away for one, now? I didn't know you were so close. I thought the kid was more of a meal ticket."

"You've sat with us and talked to him," I say, aghast. "Broken bread with him. He's not just a hyena, he's a servant. Like us."

"I tolerated him for your sake, Kadar," Chandan says. "But to be honest, I was always nervous around him, knowing where he came from. You had to know they weren't going to let him slum out here for long." He hesitantly reaches out his hand again, and settles it gingerly on my bicep. "Kadar, whatever he was to you, you can find it with one of us here. Don't throw your lot in with these people, please. Revolts always fail. I've seen enough of them in my time to know. This place isn't so bad, compared to a lot of other plantations we could end up on. Really. It's good here."

A lot of things start becoming apparent to me in that moment. Like the divide that's beginning to form in the room, some of the people here will never understand the urgency I feel, or the outrage. They're accepting what's happening to them here. And I can't even blame them. I've fought against being collared since it happened to me, I know how exhausting it is, how hopeless it can feel. These people, men like Chandan, have given up. For the painted dog in particular it must feel completely inescapable. He's collared by more than just the metal around his neck. Like he once said himself, the drug is what has him truly trapped.

For them, escape might be more terrifying than an entire life serving the clan families. Here they have food and lodging, they harvest the very drug they need so badly, and they don't have to face the unknown beyond this place. Even if they could walk free with no threat of death, it's likely that many of them wouldn't choose to.

I can see Raja, standing heads over most of the crowd gathering around him. His deep voice booms in the small room, beckoning for like-minded men to follow him. I don't even need to hear most of the words, I heard his entire recruitment spiel already when he came to me today in the field.

At one point his blue eyes catch mine, and focus sharply on me. He takes but a moment to look me over, and then he slowly smiles and begins to press through the crowd of men towards me. He says something to one of the warthogs beside him, and the man nods and begins taking up where the cheetah left off, speaking to the mass of men. Now about where they've hidden their other weapons.

When he approaches me, I hold my ground, but it's amazing that even armed and armored as I am, when he wears little other than a loin cloth, the big cat still intimidates me. Tonight he seems particularly radiant with energy. The man could lead a cult. He essentially is.

"I knew the hyena would do me some good, in the end," he says, the words catching me off-guard. I expected something smug out of him, but not that.

"The hyena—you mean Ahsan?" I ask uncertainly. The cheetah's response is simply to smile, the black teardrops down his cheeks curling up into his jowls.

And then it clicks.

"This isn't a coincidence," I state, knowingly. "You set off this whole chain, somehow. You're the reason they took him, aren't you?"

"I can't take that much credit for it," he says smoothly. "I didn't bring the boy out here with us, I just knew he'd be useful when he entered our ranks. And I knew they'd take him back eventually, and his savior would rush to his aid."

"Why did they take him?" I demand.

"Because of his illness," he replies, without missing a beat. "Once word got to the Manor guards that he'd gotten ill out here, she got worried for him—"

"You son of a bitch!" I snap at the big cat, lunging for him. Much to my surprise, he doesn't stop me from grabbing him by the collar, even though I know he could. He just grins at me, the tips of his fangs visible. "You sent him back to that place just to recruit *me* for your damned revolt!"

206

"*You?*" He snuffs, and begins to laugh, the sound bubbling up deep in his chest and shaking his entire frame. "You certainly think highly of yourself, jackal!"

My snarl drops from my face as realization dawns.

"No… I hooked a much bigger fish with the hyena," the cheetah smirks. "And I'm guessing he's the one who gave you that armor."

Chapter 8

Bloodshed

I remember the first time I fought back. I was fourteen, and I'd been thinking about it since I was twelve. You can only watch the man you're supposed to love and respect beat on your mother so many times before you start to think he might not be worthy of that respect.

I'm not sure if it got worse as I got older, or if she shielded me from it more when I was younger. She used to tell me I'd been too young then to understand, but there's nothing confusing about what was happening, even to a child. I loved my mother, even if her passivity frustrated me. And over time, I'd begun to love her more than my father. At some point that unbalance reached a tipping point, and I couldn't endure it any more.

I don't even remember what they were fighting over. I think it was how much rice she'd cooked for dinner. We never would have had to ration like we did if he hadn't been drinking away half our coin, but that's beside the point.

It wasn't even that it was a bad fight, compared to some of their others. It just happened to be the last one I could stand.

Thinking back, it's hard to put it all together into one memory. I remember moments. I remember watching them yelling back and forth, then watching him grab her by the forearm. I'd seen enough of their fights to know what would follow, and by the time he had his fist back, something erupted inside me. It was like being burnt at the kilns. White hot, sudden rage. It wouldn't be the last time I'd feel that surge of anger. It's led me to make countless bad decisions since then.

But in that moment it gave me the strength to knock my father down from behind. It's all in flashes past that point, but I had no skill with my fists at the time, I just hit him until my knuckles ached, and until his momentary surprise passed long enough for him to fight back. It didn't take him long after that to subdue me, and give me the beating of my life. I didn't wake up until the next morning, to my mother treating my injuries.

And hers. He'd resumed where he'd left off with her after I'd blacked out.

But something changed, after that. It's not that I'd won, but I'd made a stand. I'd showed my father that he wasn't safe anymore. That at least one of us *would* fight back, and even if I couldn't yet overpower him, he couldn't do what he'd been doing anymore without repercussions.

I made sure to do the same the next time he raised his hand to my mother. And the next time. And each time, I gained some ground. I was growing up. Getting bigger, stronger, and heeding my father's advice from my childhood. I ate everything put in front of me and worked hard, and unlike my father, I respected my body enough that I didn't poison it. He was once and remained my greatest role-model, if only in memory of who he used to be, before the drink took hold of him. And I grew into exactly the kind of man he'd wanted me to be.

By the time I'd married, I'm fairly certain he was afraid of me. I took no joy in that, but it meant he treated my mother slightly better, and was more careful around me and my wife. Up to that point I'd still never won in our scuffles, but what mattered wasn't overpowering him. What mattered was showing him he'd have a fight on his hands, if he ever tried to hurt us again.

Sometimes just showing you're willing to fight is more important than the outcome.

"Did you know he was using you?" I demand of the Aardwolf, as I make my way up the hill towards his moonlight-paled figure.

He gives me a confused look for only a few moments, before he seems to understand. "Ahsan?" He clarifies.

"Raja!" I snap back, before really thinking it over. Then I balk, "Wait, what do you mean? Did Ahsan know what Raja was doing?"

Lochan only sighs. "It's always hard to say, with him," he says. "If you're asking if he knew he was being used, I think he had to have known that. Raja fixated on him and controlled him from the second he took up residence out here. You've been through it yourself, it's what he does. He's king out here, in his own mind. He makes sure everyone knows it, gets to know every servant in the house just about as well as he has to, figures out if they're useful to him at all, then gives them some sort of order to follow."

"That's insane!" I tip my ears back. "Why did Ahsan listen to him?"

"He did the same to you," the Aardwolf points out, "and you did exactly as he said, as well. Don't judge the boy, he's even less interested in taking a beating from the cheetah than you were."

I shut my muzzle, finding it dry all of a sudden. He was right, of course. Raja had told me to take care of Ahsan for him, and that's exactly what I'd done. He'd handed his protection duty for the hyena off to me, while still finding a way to continue using Ahsan. I'd essentially protected his interests for him.

My mother had once told me that lions were dangerous because of their power and resources, but cheetahs were dangerous because of their selfishness, and ego. They traveled great distances alone through the deserts and grasslands, and only a truly self-centered creature would choose to intentionally deny society for a life spent with only their own thoughts. At the time, I'd thought she was just specist, but Raja was the first cheetah I'd ever gotten to know well, and he was proving to be one of the most selfish men I'd ever met.

"If you're asking if he... if Ahsan... meant to use me," the Aardwolf continues, then takes a long pause. The way his posture weakens a bit and his jowls crinkle makes an uncomfortable pressure settle over my chest, like I'm watching someone be grievously injured. "I prefer to think he didn't know of Raja's plans. I think he believed what you believed. That Raja simply wanted extra rations."

"*You* knew you were being used?" I ask, that discomfort growing.

"I didn't want to know," the Aardwolf replies, trying to keep his tone neutral. "Any fool could see it from the outside. You did. I was just a willing fool." I can see how much his pride is hurt by all of this, and to add to that the fact that he earnestly seems to have cared for the boy... it would be conceited for me to say I understand how he feels right now. I couldn't possibly.

"I think," I say, trying to break up the silence, "that if he'd known of Raja's plan, he'd have told me. And he never did."

That seems to comfort the Aardwolf some, and before long, his grey-blue eyes are on mine. "Yes," he says. "Yes, you're probably right about that."

"But you must have suspected," I press. "If you knew Raja had pushed him to pursue you."

"I didn't know why," he says, "until today. And fucking hell, I most certainly didn't know the cheetah was planning a *revolt*. I knew he'd probably try to use my attachment to Ahsan eventually, but not like this."

"I don't think even Raja knew what his plan was," I shake my head, "he just seized an opportunity when it came."

"It's not much of one," Lochan snorts, reaching down to tighten one of the straps of his armor along his calf. "Any servant revolt is ill-fated, whether they've a guardsman or a dozen on their side. Do you know how many manor guards there are? And that's only the ones on patrol at night, there are a retinue they'll call upon that are asleep right now."

"Well, we should probably talk it out with him," I sigh. "Manipulative bastard or no, we may as well join forces at this point."

"Why in the hell would we do that?" Lochan retorts.

"For," I almost stammer, because it seems like the answer should be obvious but that obvious answer isn't coming out right as I try to say it. "For mutual—"

"What about Raja's behavior so far makes you think he wants this mutual?" Lochan replies, icily. "No. I'll tell you right now what he's going to do. It can go two ways. We either join up with him and he uses me as his spearhead to push up the center of whatever asinine plan he has—what is he after, anyway?"

"Huh?" I blink. "Oh. You didn't know?"

"I'm assuming he intends to do more than just run," the Aardwolf says. "Or he would have done that already. He wants something in the manor house."

"Running doesn't work," I state, with conviction. I hook a finger under the collar, popping it out from beneath my fur some. "Not so long as we have these on. We'll just be hunted down and returned."

"That fact hasn't stopped men from trying," he says. "Myself included."

"Obviously, it didn't work for you either," I snuff.

"No, it did not."

I fix my gaze on his, intently. "I just thought you would have heard," I insist. "Raja says there's a Liberator in the Manor."

The Aardwolf's eyebrows lift. "I..." he goes silent a few beats.

"Could it be true?" I ask, my hopes hinging on the answer to the question.

"I don't know," he admits. "I feel like I would have heard. But it's possible. I don't know of any servants in the fields whose contracts have been fulfilled, or anyone who's really even close to release, but the Manor servants are not under my watch. It could be for one of them."

"So it's possible he's telling the truth?" I ask again.

"Or stringing the other servants along with hope," Lochan says. "It's the perfect way to motivate them to do what he wants."

"If there isn't a Liberator inside those walls, why bother attacking them?" I push. "Why wouldn't he just take his chances, use the mob to kill a few guards and run?"

"That wouldn't sate his anger," Lochan's voice is barely above a low growl now. "That cat has a lot of rage, and anger that deep can lead you to make terrible decisions."

"I'm well aware," I murmur, my memories nipping at my heels.

"As I was saying," Lochan continues, "he either uses me to punch his way into the Manor and get what he wants, or we use him, and whatever ill-fated plans he has, as a distraction to go in there and do what we need to do."

"Get Ahsan out," I nod. Then I think a bit more deeply into what he's saying, and I frown. "Lochan, I have... I don't know if you'd call them 'friends', but... men I've worked with, who've been at least decent to me, amongst those joining Raja tonight. Not anyone I'm terribly close to, but I still feel for them, somewhat. I understand why they're trying this, even though most of them must know it won't work. I don't know how I feel about using them."

"They're going to try this regardless," the Aardwolf points out, and judging by the steadily growing clamor I can still hear in the distance from the servant house, he's about to be extremely right. There's no stopping this now. "I won't force you to come along with me," he continues, leaning down to adjust the strap of his scabbard, and check one of his knee guards. "Join your comrades, if that's where you feel your heart lies. I'm going for Ahsan, and I won't find him mired amidst a revolt, bogged down by all that mindless rage." He strides past me, wrapping his scarf once over his shoulders so it trails down his back. It's crimson red, and seems too feminine for him. Ahsan had once told me that it belonged to his sister.

It's clear to me that for him, this fight isn't just about the hyena he's trying to save. This is about what happened to his sister... what happened to him. For the men following Raja, it's much the same. This is about making a stand against the people and the power that's subjugated and controlled us, made it impossible to prosper, and trapped us in misery for no other reason than to turn a profit with people's lives.

A year ago, there would have been no question that I'd be right beside them, fighting for the same thing. Now, I'm not so sure. I learned a lot in the last few months, and swallowed a lot of truths. I may have been tricked into this life, but I've known since it began, somewhere deep in my mind, that what really put me here were my own decisions. And what's kept me here, despite the fact that I could have paid off my meager contract years ago, have also been my own decisions. I wasn't bought as a babe, like Ahsan. I wasn't sold as a child like Lochan or Raja, or forcibly drugged and hooked into the life like so many of the men here who take the Divine. I wanted to travel somewhere and I couldn't afford to pay for it, and I couldn't read the contract I signed. That's it.

I have plenty of anger, most of it righteous. But the worst of it, I reserve for myself. Not even for becoming a servant. I hate myself for who I am, and what my mistakes once did to my family. And the reason I've fought and bucked control the whole time I've been collared is not because I've ever been a freedom fighter, like Raja. Not even like Lochan, who tried and failed to fix the system from the inside.

I've been punishing myself, all these years. And I've been using the hyenas to do it.

I don't really deserve to fight beside either of these men. Raja is raw, unadulterated anger and outrage, ready to die and go down fighting simply for a chance at freedom. Lochan is a man beaten down by a terrible life and terrible circumstances, who made a lot of sacrifices to try and improve those circumstances, and in the end made little change that mattered.

So, why am I doing this? Why am I not simply ignoring it all like Chandan, and going back to sleep in the lodge tonight, so I can get up tomorrow and keep working my contract? I could pay it off in a year and be free, and alive.

The answer to that question comes immediately, and it makes my next choice very easy.

I jog up beside Lochan, catching up with his stride and falling into step beside him.

"Make up your mind?" The Aardwolf asks.

"I have," I nod. "The truth is, you're a friend to me too, Lochan."

He gives me a narrow-eyed stare at that, and I smirk.

"If you don't want to be, stop acting like one," I point out.

"I wouldn't have given two shits about you if we hadn't had a mutual interest in common," he snorts. "You're like any other simple-minded, arrogant canine who's come through here. Don't think for a second you're anything special."

"But you and I both care about *him*," I say, and his gaze on the horizon softens a bit at that. "And he needs us, and I know you'll make him your priority in all of this. Not revenge, or looting, or even freedom. You want to save him from that place. Because you didn't," I pause just a bit before I say it, and drop my tone so he knows it isn't an accusation, but empathy, "for her."

"I should have thrown caution to the wind and gone for her, long ago," he growls. "I kept talking myself out of it, convinced it would be worse for her if I tried. Nothing can be worse than what happened. I won't watch it happen again."

"That's why I'm following you," I state, with conviction.

"Don't think you're doing me too much of a favor, there," the Aardwolf sighs. "You're shit with a blade."

"My heart is in this—"

"That doesn't fucking matter," he almost laughs. "I don't care how much heart you have son, all the fire and passion in the world can't make up for years of rigorous training. You're not a warrior. You're a man who can take a hit, sort of, and brawls with the occasional underfed field worker. Even the laziest, greenest, most under-equipped guardsman wields a blade as a profession. That blade in your hand, you've held for less than a day. Don't think for a moment you'll somehow best a career soldier just because you've got more at stake. That's the stuff of stories, not life."

I sniff, trying not to be offended. "So," I sigh, "what should I do, then? I want to help. You got me this armor."

"Oh, you'll fight," he says. "But only when I need it."

"Won't you need *help* the whole time?" I ask, perplexed. "You were saying before how many guards there were, how crazy this is."

"I wouldn't attempt this unless I thought we had some reasonable chance of succeeding," Lochan says.

"Yes you would," I retort. "You love him."

He stops in his tracks, and turns slowly to look back at me over his shoulder. It only occurs to me then that I used the word one might use for their wife, not the northern Huudari term for 'care for', as in more in a family sense. He's probably from the south, so there are subtle differences between the languages, but that word must have carried over.

It wasn't entirely what I meant, but at the same time, what else would you call it? I'm not sure how to regard how two men can care about one another. Male prostitutes can be as common as female prostitutes in some brothels, (except the ones on the coast, all the foreigners prefer females) but I've almost never known two men back where I grew up along the Hyronses who were bound as 'mates'. I've heard the lions have a tradition for it, but they all but have to, considering their tradition of harems. There are a lot of lone lion men without the resources or land to keep a harem, and not enough lionesses to go around, since the ratio's all off.

But men can't marry, in any society I know of. Not even amongst lions. If two men love each other... that is, in the way a man and wife can love each other, not just as brothers or comrades... what do you call that? How do they live?

Now is not a good time to ask. Lochan is still looking at me with an expression I can't discern, but it seems caught somewhere between defensive and uncertain, like he's not sure if I meant what I said as an insult.

"The Gods say it makes us stronger," I say, weakly trying to show him I meant no offense. "Loving someone. That's why they bless husbands and wives when they marry."

"It isn't the same for two men."

"How is it different?" I ask, ears perking. He's sort of opened the door now, and we've begun walking again, so we've nothing else to do but talk.

"Have you ever known two men who lived together as a husband

and wife do?" he asks.

"No," I say after a few more moments of thought.

"That's how it's different," he says, quietly. "No one recognizes you. People may know, but they don't talk of it. They don't make words for it. There is no place for us."

I frown. "Why?" He's right, though. I can't even think of a word for what he's describing. And it seems so obvious now, but I never thought to question it before. I always knew men could buy other men at a brothel, or that two men might bed one another when their options were limited, but I never even thought for a moment they might want more from one another than that. I'm not sure why I didn't ever question that until now.

It makes me wonder, briefly, what choices I might have made differently if I'd ever thought about it. Things never worked between my wife and I, no matter how hard I tried. And I've always gotten on better with men. I just always thought when it was a man and a man, it was just...

...about sex.

"Why?" I repeat again, because he's gone silent. "Why isn't there a place for men like... for men like you?"

"I don't know," he replies, shaking his head. "But how it is here—it isn't so bad. I've heard it's much worse for men like me in other places in the world. They castrate them, or hang them in the north, in the Dog Lords' territories. A sailor I once met said they'll even burn them alive, if the offenses are repeated."

"Well, the Dog Lords are tyrants," I mutter. "They steal and make war, it's what they do."

"They also don't believe in slavery," he points out. "Every society is prone to its own evils."

"But," I pause, not sure if I want to come back to the topic or not, but now I have to know if I was right. "You *do* love him. Don't you?"

He hesitates, then answers evasively, "My feelings are my own, and possibly his. It has nothing to do with you, either way."

"I'm asking for my own reasons," I say, quietly. "I want to know what it's like."

"Between two men?"

"To be in love," I press. "I have a fairly good idea what happens between two men, I've lived in same-sex servant's barracks for several years now."

He snorts out a chuckle, then sighs. "You were married. Didn't you love her?"

"I think so," I blow out a breath through my nose. "But I've never been entirely certain. It was never good, between us. I was never happy. I could never make her happy. Can two people who don't make one another happy be in love?"

"They can think they are," the Aardwolf replies sagely. "Answer me this, then. Far easier. Would you have done what I'm doing right now for Ahsan, for her?"

I'm silent a beat, then I nod. "Yes," I say. "Absolutely. She was my wife. I made a lot of mistakes in my marriage, but I'd have died to keep her out of this life."

"Then you probably loved her," he says, his voice low, sad. "More than I loved my sister."

"You thought you could save her another way—"

He shakes his head. "Love should be reckless. I know that now."

"I made a lot of reckless choices, trying to protect my wife," I say. "Mistakes. Mistakes that chased her away, and my son with her."

"Sometimes the world doesn't give us *any* good choices," he growls. "Sometimes we're set up to fail, no matter what we do."

"Gods, I hope you're wrong."

He laughs at that, a real bark of a laugh with no actual mirth in it. It's the most tired laugh I've ever heard. A long silence follows, and tonight, considering we're a few acres away from what might be our deaths, I feel the need to fill that silence.

"She… didn't love me back," I say quietly. "Of that, I'm certain."

"Love isn't always mutual," Lochan murmurs.

I fall silent again at that, because I know what he's thinking. And worse yet, I know there's a good chance he's right. I can't even hate Ahsan for it, if he really was using the older Aardwolf all this time. My mother's family came from the coast, and she used to say, when a storm comes, you cling to the nearest strong tree and hope its roots are deep. I know exactly what Ahsan saw in Lochan when he first came to know him. A strong tree with deep roots. And he may not have survived in that place, let alone escaped it, if he hadn't clung to him.

But at some point, he must have known what I was seeing now. If I could see it from an outsider's view, it had to have been obvious to the empathetic hyena. Lochan wasn't just protecting him and feeding him anymore. He was in love—not brotherly, not the kind that they say you should have for your fellows in your neighborhood, or the men you work your ass off with every day—but the kind that mates are supposed to have. I might have been a simple jackal from the kilns, but even I knew it when I saw it.

It was like watching sand crumble, to see it in his eyes. Even if we got out of here tonight, even if we all survived, I almost didn't want to know the outcome. Because even though I've come to respect the old guard, and care for Ahsan, I…

I don't want them to be together. That's what this feeling is. It's not just the age difference, or the fact that for a long time, I'd felt one was using the other. At this point I'm honestly not sure who's been using who.

But it's not that.

I don't want to be alone. And Ahsan and Lochan are the last

people left in the world who have any real reason to give a damn about me, or remember my name if I die in a patch of red sand. I don't want to be one of their memories, and little more.

I have no legacy. I've left even less in the world than my father did. I want to matter to someone. I want to accomplish something. I've lead a nothing life, and ultimately chased away and destroyed everything my family once was, generations back and going forward. I don't want to disappear like this.

"I'm afraid to die," I blurt out, suddenly. I'm not even sure why I said it, and I'm humiliated the second the words leave my mouth.

"Every living thing is," Lochan replies, without even turning to regard me. "Fear is a good motivator. Use it to hold on to your blade, this time. Remember it's your life-line, like I was telling you."

He doesn't know any of my inner thoughts, I have to remind myself. He doesn't know all the selfish shit I've been thinking. How I'm afraid my only two comrades will find happiness together and I'll no longer matter to either of them. Lochan's mind is still on the task ahead.

And that's where mine should be. I try to clear my thoughts, try to find that resolve I had in the field, when I picked up the sho-tel. I'm overthinking this. None of my fears about what will happen after this matter now. At this moment, I'm still a collared servant and Ahsan is probably locked in that room, reliving the worst parts of his childhood. Or something even more unthinkable.

"Tell me about the Manor," I say, trying to chase away with conversation what I can't seem to stop thinking about any other way. "How are you planning to get in?"

"Quietly," he replies, in a cool tone. "Raja's attack should help distract some of the guards, whenever it comes."

"Right," I nod, "we'll go in while they're busy dealing with him."

"We can't avoid them all," he states, flatly. "Anala isn't stupid. She runs her shifts like a true professional, this isn't the first or the biggest clan hold she's protected. She has rotating perimeter guards that intentionally check in every circuit around the building, so if any of them go missing she'll know. All of the stationed door guards have a specific warning cry, so the others will know exactly which door's been attacked. And she'll never pull everyone from any one area of the perimeter, no matter how much of a mess Raja makes of the grounds."

"'Anala'?" I quirk an ear. "The… fire goddess?" My knowledge of the hyena pantheon is rudimentary, but even I know the name.

"Fire, and war," he corrects me. "And Anala is an Al'Dahia, a priestess of the goddess of fire. They all take her name, to represent the swords held in her many hands."

"You sound worried," I notice.

"She's a devout, professional warrior from a sect who believes they are literally charged with their duties by a goddess whose most infamous act was setting her own husband afire while he was still alive," Lochan says, glaring back at me.

"I am now worried," I mutter.

"Pray we don't run afoul of her personally," he lets out a long breath. "Most any guard in the manor house, I have over a decade's experience on, and I'm fairly certain of my abilities in one-on-one with them. Provided it's only one at a time, I think I can get us past most of them to the inner walls."

"What happens if it's more than one at a time?" I ask, uncertainly.

"Then things get complicated, and I may need your help."

"What happens if it's her?" I press, and he stops. I nearly run into the back of him. I back up a step or two, and blink. "That bad?"

"I have experience on her," he says, resting his palm lightly over the hilt of his scimitar, before turning to regard me. "But the Al'Dahia are easily as well-trained as gladiators, and she's far younger than I am. She refuses to spar with anyone other than her fellow priestess-es—I don't honestly know how I'd fare." He turns back around after that to stare off towards the horizon. "And I'd rather not ever find out, to be honest with you."

The Manor looms enormous and dark across the rice fields, its wrought iron gates and intimidating fences a reminder to me how truly impenetrable this place would be to me were it not for the rogue Guardmaster on my right. He's gone over the general layout of the grounds, and which route we'll be taking to get inside—a gardener's path to the servant staff's housing in the kitchens, where they bring in fruits and vegetables. From there we can make our way through servant's stairs and passageways, there are apparently a whole network of them through the house meant to be out of the way and invisible to the clan hyenas and their guests. They don't like to have to see us as we work for them. For women like the Matron, it's probably just because we're disgusting to her, but for some of them I'd like to think it might just make them feel a bit guilty. It's easier to reap the rewards of slave labor when you don't have to stare them in the eyes every day.

"I'm curious what Raja's plan would have been if we'd accompanied him," I question. "It doesn't sound like we could get many people through the route you're planning."

"I'm certain he didn't think it through much," Lochan snorts. "If all he'd wanted was information about the inside of the Manor, he could have asked Ahsan. He probably just wanted the muscle, and access to my weapons."

"They're doomed," I murmur. "I'm starting to feel even worse about abandoning them all."

"Don't be. He gets what he wants either way," Lochan tells me. "We can wait here all night for that mob to make it here and tear down the gates, but that's just a game of chicken. And it's one we'll lose."

"What?" I glance his way.

"Raja can afford to wait for us to make the first move," Lochan sighs. "He might have a little trouble keeping the men in check, but he will. He's not going to make himself the first target. He's going to wait for us to inevitably alert the guards. Then he'll come at the place from whatever side we're *not* on."

"Why aren't we waiting *him* out?" I ask, incredulously. It seemed to me like Lochan and I could muster a lot more patience than the cheetah.

"Because Ahsan is in there," he replies evenly, "and we don't know what's happening to him."

I take a deep breath, then narrow my eyes. "Right."

"We do this quiet, for as long as we can manage," he says, standing up from our crouching position behind a long row of scrub grass. I hear his knee pop, and he winces, then gives a rough chuckle. "I'm too old for this shit."

"How do we do this quietly?" I ask, my eyes searching the perimeter of the gates. Even from here, I can see at least five silhouettes of guards moving around the fences. And those are just the ones on walking rotations. Lochan's already assured me there are guards at every entrance, and nearly every single door and threshold within. The Sura family is one of the richest in the area, and servant revolts are the least of their concerns. This manor is meant to defend against groups of well-armed raiders, assassins, even other clan attacks.

"Follow me," he commands lowly, and starts making his way down a row, towards the eastern side of the estate. I follow, mindful of everything he's told me so far, going over everything in my head.

Stay behind Lochan on his left side, it's his weak side. Stay back unless I see an opening he isn't defending, and if I feel it's time to step in, keep my blade at least five feet clear of him. Do not swing at any opponent locking swords with him, and if he tells me to stay back, no matter what, stay back. I'm willing to trust that the man knows what he's talking about, and I hate feeling like the weak link, but I also know my pride can't fill in for my lack of skills. Right now, I need to listen to him, and do as he says.

I'm surprised by how brazenly we're approaching one of the many back gates. Lochan isn't attempting to hide or obscure himself in any way as we near the grounds. I'd expected we'd at least attempt to sneak in close before charging whoever's there.

Something occurs to me then, and in retrospect it seems obvious. Lochan is a guard. Of course we don't have to hide.

"Is your blade still tied to your hip?" He asks me quietly, as we approach.

We hadn't had anything designed for the shotel, so we'd simply lashed a small twine loop to my belt, to fit the handle through. I could feel it there still, a pressure against my hip, and a reminder of the one fight I'd had already tonight that I'd failed to triumph in.

"I have it," I assure him.

"Move it to the small of your back," he commands me.

"They'll see it when they let us through the door," I point out.

"They're not going to let anyone through that door," he says. "Past sunset, no one comes in or out, unless they retrieve permission from inside the house to let them through. We can't bluff our way in."

"Shit," I sigh. "For a moment there I thought this was actually going to be easy."

"I told you," Lochan says. "They're wary of assassins. The fennecs in particular favor night attacks."

"So how are we doing this?" I ask, as I see a guard take notice of us in the distance. He begins making his way towards us, taking his time, but every step he takes makes my heart race just a bit faster. This is happening.

"Shhht," he shushes me sharply, and stops along the path, as the spotted hyena closes the distance between us. He looks like any other nondescript Manor guard I've seen, thankfully... not a warrior priestess.

"Oh," is what the hyena ultimately says when he finally sees us up close. His eyes shine just vaguely red in the moonlight, as they flick between the two of us. "I thought the lanky bitch there was Vikram, seeing'm from a distance. Who's the jackal, Aardwolf?"

I'm thankful at that moment that Lochan's spare armor includes a hood, because right now it's bunched around my neck, obscuring my collar. As servants, we're forbidden from wearing anything that covers our collars from view, so he must have gotten even this armor after he won his freedom.

"New in from the pits," Lochan says. "Field guard. Anala said she wanted to look him over before we hired him official."

"I'll have to confirm that," the hyena mutters, sounding annoyed. "Can't we just do this in the morning?"

"*She* wanted it done tonight," Lochan states firmly.

The guard shrinks back a bit, his ears flicking behind him to the Manor. "Well... I'll still have to confirm it."

"That's fine," Lochan nods.

We start approaching the gate, and as we close in, the first of my fears tonight is realized. There's another guard at the gate, a female this time. She also doesn't look like a warrior priestess, let alone one who's supposed to be younger than Lochan, so there's that, but she's another guard. Lochan said two at a time could be tough, and it looks like that's how we're starting off.

"Krisna, we've got two to the barracks," the male guard says as we approach, and she gives us a once-over, before yawning.

"The Guardmaster's dealing with a disturbance in the Manor right now," she says around a set of particularly fat jowls. "Can't it wait?"

"That's what I said."

My ears perk at what she said. A disturbance in the Manor? Inside... could it be...

"Krisna," Lochan speaks up, and steps up to her, within her personal space. She momentarily seems put-off, but then he lowers his voice and leans in close, whispering something so quietly near her ear that even I can't hear it. The male guard takes a slight step towards them, craning his ears towards the conversation, too.

I'm curious what the hell he could be saying to her, when I catch the glint of steel slipping from a small sheath on his right side, blocked from sight of the other guard by his own body. The woman he's talking to catches it a moment too late, her eyes widening.

He brings the blade up just underneath her chin in a snapping motion, sinking the whole of it to the hilt up through her throat. The blade is barely half a foot long and thin, but her throat isn't armored, and all that escapes her mouth in the seconds following is a surprised gurgle.

The male guard hasn't even seen it yet. He's about to though, and I know I have to do something. Lochan's released the hilt of the dagger, leaving it in her, and he's going for his sword, but all that guard has to do is send up a warning cry and we've blown it right out of the gate.

I'm about to go for a tackle from behind, hoping to get my hands over his muzzle or at least knock him down and knock the wind out of him, when Lochan takes a step towards the man and draws his scimitar in the same movement. I've seen it before, when he was sparring with the lioness. He's going to swing for the man in the same motion he uses to pull his weapon from its sheath.

And he connects. The hyena had a few seconds to do something, anything, and all he ultimately did was open his mouth and put up a hand. The scimitar leaves a spray of blood in its wake, although not as much as I expected for a neck wound, and the hyena vainly thrashes at the air with one hand and tries to go for his weapon with the other. When he does make a noise, it's as wet and useless as the woman's, and empties more blood from the enormous gash through his neck.

He falls to the ground clutching at the wound and Lochan steps over him, planting a foot on either side of his body and reaching down to grab him by his head scruff, before bringing the blade down on the opposite side of his neck… several more times. Until I hear a crack.

A few seconds later, he does the same to the woman.

I force back a wave of nausea and fight a dry throat, at last managing a quiet, "Why always the neck?" to him. I'm not even sure why I'm asking. Does it matter how you kill someone?

"I don't like to hear what people say when they're dying," the Aardwolf replies, his tone seemingly cold, but I can tell something about all of this still bothers him, no matter how long he's been doing it. "And right now, it benefits us if we kill quietly, regardless."

"Did you…" I swallow, making my way around the man's body, "…know… them?"

"I know every man and woman who works on the guard force," he says, kneeling down to inspect the fallen woman, specifically around her belt. "And I'll kill every one of them if I have to." He produces something from her belt with a few metallic notes in each movement—a set of keys. He then reaches down to her side and tugs her shield free of her stiffening hand, before standing again and staring my way, evenly.

"They're paid to die," he says. "Just like I once was. This is how they earn their wage, and they accepted the risks when they took the work."

"It's just…" I can't find the right word. Cold?

He turns and starts sorting through the keys, trying out one after another. "I learned long ago you can't examine killing too closely, or you'll go mad," he murmurs. "There's never a good enough excuse to take a life, if you bring morality into it. Just accept that sometimes to live, you have to kill." The lock clicks as he turns it slowly, the metal gate creaking open.

He steps back and leans down to pluck his dagger from the woman's neck, wiping it on his thigh before re-sheathing it, then turning back to look at me. "Someday, it will be our turns. And I doubt it will come as quickly or mercifully, for us."

I follow him into the gardens, paranoid and bracing for whatever's to come next.

"Why take the shield?" I ask him quietly, as we walk along a row where they're growing these big red vegetables dangling nearly in the dirt. I've seen them in the market before but I never had the money to eat things like this.

"Better to have it than not," he states simply.

"I've just never seen you fight with one before."

"I used to sword and board in the arena whenever I was up against multiple opponents," he says. "You can only fight from one side—or at least, that's the best I can manage—best to cover your other, if you possibly can. I'll admit it's not my strong suit."

"I can cover your other side," I insist.

"You can do that, too," he says, then opens his muzzle to say something else, and just as quickly shuts it, grabbing for my shoulder and forcing me down behind a mass of gnarled vegetable bushes. A moment later, a small group of men round the corner just past us. Judging by the buckets and the shabby clothing, they're likely workers. We wait a time to let them pass, then slowly rise and start making our way into the orchard.

I vaguely remember some of this from the one time I visited, and when we see the stables on the other side of the tree line I begin to get my bearings. I twist my ears as we move, mostly hearing the horses in the stalls beyond, stirring in their sleep or moving about, still awake. I can hear what are definitely paws moving around in the hay, but judging by the lightness of their footsteps it's probably a servant, some kind of smaller species, tending to the animals.

We skirt the barn, hugging the side, and I'm about to mention the servant inside to Lochan just so he's aware and we don't surprise anyone, when someone surprises us.

Rounding the corner, we nearly run headlong into a wandering guard, a striped hyena with a falchion slung over his back. Unlike the gate guard, this one takes those few crucial steps back when he sees us, rather than panicking. He begins to go for his blade and lifts his head to bay, a short bark making it past his teeth before Lochan is on him, smashing his shield up into the side of his muzzle and cutting short the noise into a sharp yelp, instead. The hyena is knocked off-balance and shakes his head dizzily, bringing out his falchion with enough time to block Lochan's next swing.

I begin to circle around the man, cutting off his escape and pulling out my shotel, ready to step in if need be. But the fight moves faster than I expected—all of these fights have been over in seconds, which makes me wonder how anyone gets any pleasure out of blood sport.

Lochan presses in close with the man and easily deflects his next swing, and before the hyena can open his muzzle again, there's a scimitar through it, cleaving through flesh and bone. The first wound is hideous enough that I can barely watch, but the Aardwolf follows up with two more cleaving blows in succession once he's got the man reeling.

I'm amazed and somewhat horrified by how unyielding he is

when he presses his advantage. He has what I lacked—resolve. Each first blow is followed by a series of faster, more certain, more devastating blows. Killing blows.

I watch, and commit everything to memory. Even if it's hard.

The yelp got the attention of another guard nearby, and Lochan wastes no time, gesturing for me to follow as we hurry across the manicured yard towards the ornamental gardens. A woman steps from between two of the statues. This time I know we can't stop her. Her warning cry, a distinct multi-toned cackle, carries out across the yard, and it's not long before it's answered in the darkness by several others.

"Come on!" Lochan snaps, charging forward for the woman.

This one puts up more of a fight, likely because she had more time to ready herself, but it isn't long before she's down in the dirt, leaking her life out into the cracks in the cobbled ground. An enraged shriek comes from around the nearby hedge. We have very little reprieve this time, immediately beset upon by the other guard who must have been on rotation with her. Lochan blocks her charge with his shield and gives her a hard enough shove that she nearly topples, skipping back on one foot in a desperate attempt to catch her balance.

He shouts my name, and since he gave her a firm shove in my direction, I figure that's my cue to step in. Steeling myself, I squeeze my fingers tightly around the shotel's hilt and repeat again and again the two things I've been told in the last day about the weapon. Use it like I would if I were reaping a field, and *don't let go*.

I try to aim for her neck, but my swing catches her lower, hooking beneath and behind her right arm as she raises it. I encounter far more resistance than I thought I would, jerk it up across her back and snag it on her armor, and though I smell blood, the wound is probably superficial at best.

She makes the mistake of turning to see who else is attacking her though, and that's all the opening the Aardwolf needs. He bulls into her and knocks her down before bringing the blade down just over her gut, beneath the seam of the armor that runs across her chest. She screams and wretches up blood. I begin to close in to finish her off, when I remember what he told me about swinging at someone locked in combat with him.

Considering my accuracy, there's a pretty good chance I'd catch him in the arc of my swing if I even try. So I catch myself, taking a step back.

He wrenches himself to his feet, apparently not bothering to put this one out of her pain. I'm not sure if it's a personal grievance or if he's just in more of a hurry now, but I don't argue when we take off sprinting again.

"She was Al'Dahia," Lochan explains, panting as we run, "if Anala finds her she might take a moment to put her out of her misery. They have an oath about that. Buys us just that much more time. Damn it, where is the—there," he suddenly stops, and gestures towards the back wall of the main house, a few hundred yards away. "Near where those fancy windows are. Around that wall is the servant's entrance."

A chorus of distant hyena cries goes up, piercing the night air. But these sound much too far away to be the guards in the garden. They're further out, near the wall. And over the sharp smell of blood in the air I've begun to sense something else on the wind. Panic, and fear.

"Raja is attacking," Lochan states with certainty. "Sounds like they're at the main gate."

"Stupid," I snarl.

"It's what I would have done, in his position," he shakes his head. "Anywhere else and a mob that size would be bottle necked. They could pick them off with crossbows or those revolting powder weapons."

"I vaguely remember Ahsan mentioning something about those," I say offhandedly. He talked about a lot of things that happen inside the Manor that I didn't really understand, though. I have no idea how powder could be a weapon, it all sounds exotic and strange to me. We had some Amur traders sell their wares along the Hyronses, but I know little about their goods, seeing as we could barely afford the bare necessities.

"They buy them mostly to resell, but I wouldn't be surprised if some of the clansmen decided to dishonor themselves by carrying one." He snuffs, and shakes his blade free of some of the blood on it. "Come on."

We take off along the wall of windows, which look to lead into a hallway in the main manor. I have no idea what area of the house we're near, but I'm sure Lochan does, so I let him lead. Soon enough, we've rounded the corner and come to a far less opulent, plain back wall of the estate. It's clear this isn't the side the Clan's guests are meant to see, considering the chipped paint and lack of landscaping. There's a distant well pump, a few lines strung up with limp, tattered clothing drying in the cold night air, and a lot of worn dirt trails that are obviously well-traveled. This is what amounts to the servant's housing here inside the Manor.

The doorways here have no actual doors on them, and there aren't any guards I can see. Lochan takes a moment, scanning the yard to make sure, before we round the corner. The sky is just starting to lighten in the distance, thin bands of gold criss-crossing against an otherwise washed blue slate where the meager rays have begun to fall. If we were in the servant housing in the fields, we'd be waking up in an hour or so, but the servants here must be on an earlier schedule because I can already hear the sounds of some of them milling around inside.

A horrible thought occurs to me.

"We're not going to kill any of the servants, are we?" I ask Lochan.

"Not unless any of them get stupid on us," he mutters. "But don't worry, they won't. These people are used to staying out of the way."

As it turns out, when you wave around a scimitar at most people, they do in fact get out of the way. Lochan and I make our way through the small doorway and emerge into a crowded, cluttered, dingy room, one of the kitchens by the look of it. I'm guessing by the stink of familiar porridge being prepared in their pots that this is a kitchen *for* the servant's food, not the one for the Clan member's meals. An older female rat drops a pot as we enter, and the squirrel plucking a chicken near the doorway screams.

It takes me a minute to realize why. At first I thought Lochan might go about this as he did at the gate, and just pretend to be a guard on duty. These people have every reason to listen to the guards here and they probably don't know them all from one another all that well.

But we're covered in blood. Even I am, I realize, from being caught in the spray of my own shotel and Lochan's repeated near-beheadings.

"All of you, take refuge somewhere," Lochan calls out, loud enough that I can already see a few others peering around from the next doorway, more rats by the look of it. "There's a revolt at the main gate, and we don't know how far into the grounds they'll be able to make it."

The old rat wastes no time, bolting into the next room and grabbing at two of the younger rats who were poking their heads around the corner. The squirrel, however, twists her ears towards the yard and seems to consider her options.

Lochan barely pauses, he's already making his way towards the next room and I have no choice but to follow. I wish I could stop and see if the squirrel wanted to come with us, though. If she joins in

the revolt, odds are, she'll die. I turn to look over my shoulder as we make our way through the next doorway, and I see her looking down towards a knife block, and the large butcher's blade there.

We move through three other small rooms, one of which is a sleeping area and still houses quite a few occupied beds. Lochan gives the same warning to all of them, but it's almost unnecessary by now. I can hear the hyenas baying in the distance, and so must they. It's clear the place is under attack.

When we shoulder through a slim hallway towards what looks to be a more lantern-lit, golden area, I can tell by the scent of incense that we must be nearing the inner walls. Lochan's ears twist, and he takes a sharp turn into a small supply closet suddenly, grabbing at my armor to force me in there with him. A moment later, what look to be the silhouettes of three guards run past, in the hallway we were about to enter.

"These are the inner walls," he whispers fiercely. "I'm going to take us the most direct route I can think of to the sleeping rooms, because I'm guessing that's where he is. But from here on out it gets a lot worse. Some of the guards here never leave their posts, even in an attack." He turns towards me, baring his fangs. "If I'm injured too badly to move, you keep going on your own. I can try and give you directions."

"That's not going to happen," I insist.

"Just do as I say," he snaps, then turns and listens again for a few beats, before nodding at me and slowly making his way towards the golden hallway beyond.

When we reach it, I realize it's that long expanse we saw from outside, with the intricate windows. The lantern light isn't the only reason it's brighter in here. These windows face the sunrise, and it's just starting to crawl its way in. It's surreal to walk down such a beautiful corridor. I feel intensely out-of-place, my paws tracking in the dust from the fields, and the blood from Lochan's many kills. This place really is like a different world, crafted by the Clans. It's no wonder they feel so above all of us that live in the dirt. To someone like me, this place may as well have been built by Gods. I can't imagine how much wealth, how much manpower, how much sheer brutality must be necessary to live like this.

A guard's shadow steps out into the arched doorway at the end of the long hallway, and unlike many of the others, this one doesn't call out right away when she sees us. She doesn't do much of anything for a long moment, actually, simply stands there in the doorway.

Lochan stops as well, and I hear him hiss between his teeth. The two take a few moments to regard one another. Then she steps past the threshold, and my heart jumps into my throat.

The woman is a spotted hyena like many of the others, with a regal bearing and similar armor to most of the other guards we've encountered, save more intricate burnt patterns in the camel hide, but less finery adorning it. I vaguely recall seeing her once long ago, and she stood out then strictly because of her unique armor. But it's not that which truly sets her apart. It's the shaved fur around her eyes, and the tattooed red skin beneath. I've seen it before, the red mask on the statues of the goddess Anala.

"Guard Master," she greets him, in an even tone.

"Guard Master," he greets back, between his teeth.

"You're part of this foolishness at the gates, then?" She queries.

"No," he states. "But I am still your enemy."

She tilts her head at him a moment, then lifts her nose. "Every living thing is my enemy," she replies coolly, pulling her own scimitar from her side. The blade and its ornate hilt gleam with fresh polish in the dim sunlight. I know little about weapons, but I can tell even from a glance that her weapon is better made than his. I can also tell from his labored breaths that he's already tired. She, on the other hand, looks fresh.

"You are just my enemy today," she says, as she advances slowly towards us.

"I just want Ahsan," he says, bringing his blade and his shield up. "Go deal with the disturbance at the gates, and protect your Matron. Just let me have the boy. That's all I came for."

"That is unfortunate," she says, "because he is *with* my Matron. So, I am where I am most needed, right now. You're a greater threat to her than a few ragged field workers ever will be."

I step back a pace or two from him, giving him his distance. Giving the both of them distance. I'm not sure what I should do here. Will he want my assistance fighting her? I feel like I should at least try, given what he told me about her.

"When we lock blades," he whispers roughly to me, "get around to the other side of her."

I'm thankful he seems to have sensed my indecision, and I give him a wide arc. When she's about five feet from him, she pushes off on one foot and charges the Aardwolf. She's not bothering to use a shield, but I see immediately what Lochan was so afraid of as she closes in.

The woman is fast. Her blade is at least as large as his, and she swings it near effortlessly, coming down on him hard. He barely manages to get his shield up in time to block the first blow, then swings his own sword out in an arc to try and catch her while she's close. It's easy to see, now that they're next to one another, the discrepancy in their swings. What had seemed so quick and precise outside against the less skilled guards, now seems far slower in comparison to her.

She side-steps his swing easily and moves in a V, back-stepping then lunging in at him again, forcing him to pivot his body to face her. His shield arm doesn't come up fast enough this time, and for a moment I'm afraid I'm about to see her bisect him, but he catches her blade with his own.

In a contest of strength, he seems to have her beaten, pushing her slowly back, the blades shrieking against one another. I remember what he said and use the chance to move around the two of them, getting in behind her.

He glances over her shoulder, waiting until I'm safely around them, then gives her a monumental shove, forcing her to hop back lest she get clubbed by his shield arm. He's using it almost like a weapon, like I saw the big lioness doing when she was fighting him. I have to wonder if he learned that from her, or if he's the one who taught her how to do it.

"Kadar!" He shouts, and I wait for my command to attack.

Instead, he takes a wild, wide swing at her, which even to me looks like it wasn't meant to connect. It does force her to step even further back though, snarling at him in a way that looks far too much to me like she's enjoying this.

When she tries to press back in, rather than blocking or parrying her like he's prone to, he instead tries to dodge her, putting his shield up to cover his flight out of her path. He catches the edge of her first swing, but she twirls as he ducks past her. Suddenly he's got his back to her, and I can feel the hit before it lands.

He winces as the scimitar connects with his back, somewhere on his right side. I stand my ground, staring at him slack-jawed as he rushes towards me, not turning around to face her again.

"What the hell are y—" I begin.

He shoves me with his shield, barking a quick, "RUN!" and pushing me ahead of him.

"What?" I ask incredulously. He isn't giving me much option though, and even the hyena, who also seemed dumbfounded by his sudden flight, is recovering from her moment of shock and starting towards us again.

We take off down the hallway towards the distant open doorway she came through. I jog up beside him and easily pull ahead, having to check myself to keep up with the older man.

"She is *faster* than us!" I point out the obvious.

"Shut up and run!" He shouts, and shoves me through the doorway when we reach it. I can hear the woman hot on our tails.

Once Lochan moves in behind me, he grabs for something near the wall... a brass handle... and slams the thick wooden door shut. A second later the door shudders as the hyena bulls into it from the other side, and I shoulder up alongside him, digging my claws into the grout between the tiles of the floor, helping the older man shove it closed with all our might.

Once the latch clicks, the Aardwolf drops his shield and goes to his belt, grabbing at the set of keys he stole earlier, and fishing through them for a moment. There's another shudder as the hyena on the other side makes a second attempt, and my heart is racing. "Sooner would be better," I grit out.

"I thought you were strong, jackal," Lochan taunts. He finally pulls up one of the keys, looking it over just to be sure, then shoves it into the lock and turns.

The door shudders again, the handle twisting, but this time nothing gives. I slowly stand back from it, disbelievingly.

"I… thought…" I utter, breathlessly.

"That I was going to fight her?" Lochan snorts, reaching back to run his palm along his back and side, where I can see a thin line of blood seeping out from beneath his armor. "Why the hell would I do that if I could avoid it?"

"Are you alright?" I ask.

"Graze," he assures me, reaching down with a wince and grabbing up his shield again. "Now let's go. She's not omnipotent. She can't break down a hardwood door, but she'll find another way around."

He frees the rest of the key ring from the key in the door, and we move.

Chapter 9

Rage

There's a stark difference between anger, and rage. And that difference is unmistakable, if you've ever felt it. Anger can be repressed, controlled, hidden away and unspoken of. Anger can exist in your mind without ever surfacing and affecting those around you. If you're strong. If you have self-control. If you're smart enough to think through the consequences, most of the time, it isn't the best choice.

Rage is not a choice. Rage cannot be controlled, it cannot be reasoned with, and there is no keeping it from the world.

Men like my father, men who lose themselves to drink or drug, or simply lose control because they had no discipline to begin with, are not in a rage, they're just weak-willed. They're angry and they *let* that anger take hold of them. They *can* control themselves, if they really have to. They just don't, because they don't care enough.

Rage is primal, something from the time before we had speech and culture and respect for one another. It's what happens when we fall to that feral side and fight on sheer instinct, with all the wrath we once lived by. It's a desperate state, and in my opinion, you have to earn the right to be pushed over that edge with a lot of pain and suffering. A lifetime's worth.

I remember falling over that edge, but I don't remember much about the fall, and I think that's for the best. I remember the moments that led up to it. The fight with my father, about nothing more important than what we'd always fought over in the past. His earnings, and where he was spending them. His harsh words to my mother for spending too much at the market, when he was drinking away half of what we made. I'd been married for a few months then, and maybe that's why I was so quick to fight. Things with my new wife were going poorly.

My mother was one of the best women I'd ever known, and she was wasted on my father. I came to feel that way even more once I married. She'd given him everything my wife would not give me—respect, understanding, love. She deserved a husband who would give her just as much. And I'd deserved a father who was respectable and strong, man enough to face his life without the crutch of the drink to lean on.

Questioning his manhood was one sure way to start a fight, and I knew it. I wanted one, that day. He hadn't even used his fists on us in some time, I was just itching for it. I just had so much anger brewing inside me, like a pot with the lid on tight, waiting to bubble out. I was frustrated with my marriage, offended every waking day by the way our world was, hurt inside and out from years and years and *years* of abuse I couldn't escape, even at home.

I wanted to hurt someone back.

Every time we'd fought in the past, he'd beaten me into the ground. He was always bigger, stronger, or so drunk he couldn't feel anything. But I was older, taller even than him by then, and this time our argument was in the morning, when we were standing at the bank of the Hyronses getting water. He was sober, and I was a grown man. He'd finally lost his edge.

The monster I'd both respected and feared my entire life was mortal at last. And this time, he wasn't going to put me in the dirt. This time, I was going to make him afraid of *me*.

He seemed to realize a few blows in that he'd finally been overcome. And honestly, had he simply done what he should have rightly done and given me the chance to fight him and beat him at last, that's as far as it ever would have gone. But instead, the man crumbled before my eyes, and took all my remaining respect for him away.

He threw his arms up and began begging for me to stop, yielding to me, denying me the victory he'd had over me so many times. The very first time he ever faced defeat by my hands, he backed down like a coward.

And that was the last thing I can remember, before the rage took over. For all his shortcomings, and all the pain the man had inflicted on my mother and me, I'd never before seen him for the weak man he truly was... until that moment. And it made everything I'd endured over the years come to the surface, all at once, like a wave crashing ashore.

He wasn't going to deny me the right to overpower him and have that catharsis. I deserved to beat him. I deserved to beat him until he was down on the ground, his vision gone black, like he'd done to me so many times. He'd endure what I'd endured, at least once.

At some point, he'd fallen. My mind was back in our hut, awash in memories from the dozens of times he'd done this to me. But we weren't in my hut, with the straw mats on the soft earth. We were on the riverbank of the Hyronses, the jagged rocks from the quarry making up most of the shoreline near the slums.

He must have hit his head.

I honestly, even to this day, cannot remember those last few blows. I just know that when I came back to myself, I was sitting beside his crumpled body, my feet in the water, watching the slow curls of blood floating atop the gently-swirling eddies at the edge of the river.

My father never woke up again. And I never told a soul what

happened there that morning.

No one ever looked for him. The only people in the world who cared about him were my mother and I. My mother assumed he'd finally left us, or gotten himself in trouble drinking in the city. And I spent the next few days trying to forget that I knew exactly where he was.

I don't mourn that he's gone. But I mourn what I became that day, because it left me forever changed.

I can tell when we've entered the Clan family's main quarters, by the sheer level of opulence. The floors shine like the surface of water, with elegant natural patterns through the stone—marble, I think. Working at the kilns, sometimes I'd see some of the stone from the quarries in the mountains come in. The walls are covered in ornate henna patterning, painted by hand on to nearly every surface. Some of the colorful borders and molding look like they're made of gold. Equally-elegant vases adorn the thick windowsills we occasionally pass, full of exotic flowers from the gardens outside. The place smells like poppies and incense, and beneath it all, the distinctive musk of hyenas.

Our feet pound down the immaculate hallways, tracking blood and sand in our wake. We haven't stopped running since we escaped Anala, and I can tell Lochan is tiring, but he doesn't let up. I'm beginning to wonder how large this place could possibly be, before he finally slows to a stop near the end of a hallway, pressing his back against the wall and putting an arm out for me, grabbing at my chest to stop me before I overtake him.

"Silent a moment," he snaps in a harsh whisper. "I hear something."

I press my back against the wall with him and wait, craning my ears towards the hallway beyond. My shoulder presses against his, and as I lean to try to look over his mane, I get a strong scent of blood. My gaze falls to the gash in his side, which for the most part he seems to be ignoring, and I grimace. Graze or no, he's bleeding a lot. I can hear my own blood pumping in my ears from the run, so it's no wonder why.

A shout echoes down the hallway, sharp and sudden, and thanks to the echo it's hard to tell from how far away it came. It didn't sound like the warning bark of one of the guards, though. It's hard to tell what it was, except a surprised noise. And female? Higher-pitched, but with hyenas it can be hard to tell sometimes.

I can tell by the way Lochan scrunches up his brow that he's equally confused, trying to pick through the sounds and discern what's going on. There's another of those shouts, even shorter and more clipped this time, like someone in a struggle. Scuffling, claws on floors, rumbles that could be growling.

I bump his shoulder impatiently, and his gaze briefly flits back to mine, then he nods and pulls his weapon. I do the same.

He charges around the corner, and I in his wake. The hallway beyond is more narrow, with no windows, and there are cabinets along the walls and doors every few feet. The corridor dead-ends, so the noise has to be coming from...

The last door at the very end of the hallway is open, a lantern dimly flickering from a wall sconce the only light illuminating the corner. As we race towards it, two figures suddenly stumble out and slam into the door, bashing it back against the wall adjacent. A third figure follows in their wake, grabbing at the second.

Two of them must be guards, based on the armor. And they're both struggling in vain to tackle the third, thrashing and bucking at them like a feral beast. I can hear chains amidst the cacophony, and then one of the guards shrieks and reels back, or at least tries to, if it weren't for the jaws clamped on her arm.

"To hell with this!" The other shouts, reaching desperately for her belt to pull her blade. It's just then that her ears twist and she looks up to see us, though.

"The revol—" she gets out, before her distraction costs her a kick to the gut from her prisoner, and I see my chance as she buckles.

Up until now, every time I've swung my shotel, it feels like I've been doing so blindly. This time, I keep my eyes wide open, fixed on the spot I want to swing. There's a weak spot where the camel hide isn't layered, along their lower backs. I've seen Lochan target it several times. If I had his accuracy I'd aim for their necks, but right now I just want to make absolutely certain I connect.

I grip the hilt of my shotel with more certainty than I've been able to muster thus far, knowing as I close that I'm going to hit where I intended, with real strength behind it this time. I remember Lochan's words. Hang on to the blade like it's your lifeline, because it is. This time I keep my eyes wide open, and force myself to watch it connect. This is a life I'm trying to take, and I need to own that.

The blade catches her right where I intended and sinks in deep until it's lodged, and then I yank on it to be sure, hooking her flesh in the crook of the weapon. She doesn't scream—more gurgles, and coughs suddenly in shock, dropping her scimitar on the ground with a clatter. Her rust-colored eyes flick over her shoulder as she tries to crane her neck back, but it's too little too late, and we both seem to know it.

She manages a wet-sounding rasp of, "Please…" and for the first time tonight, I feel a pang of extraordinary guilt, before I re-grip my weapon and finish what I started, yanking the blade out of her with all my might.

Pieces of her… that's all I know what to call them… come out with my blade, and she's barely able to clutch at herself before falling over. Lochan has already dispatched the other as I'm shaking off my blade, my whole body shuddering like the last leaf on a tree. She's crying now, and the hilt of my shotel feels slippery in my palm. I stare down at her crumpled, bloody form for a few beats, readying myself.

Lochan spares me, bringing his own blade down on the woman's neck. At that, I do glance away. I'm not certain I'll ever get used to seeing someone's head separated from their body. But I do understand now what he said earlier. I don't want to hear what dying people have to say before they die, ever again. Quicker is better.

The shifting of chains breaks me out of my dark reverie, and once again, I'm beaten to the moment by Lochan, who's already stepped over the two dead women to the other crumpled figure on the floor. He's shaking as badly or worse than I am, his fur matted with blood, mostly around his wrists and his muzzle, and he looks more terrified and frayed than I'd ever even seen him out in the fields, but it's definitely Ahsan.

For a few moments he doesn't even seem to recognize us, pressing his back against the wall and digging his claws into the ornate paint. His eyes are wild like I've never seen them, pupils blown so wide he looks feral, his teeth out and bared.

Lochan stops a few feet from him and slowly lowers himself to a crouch, reaching out for him with an offered paw, dropping his usually deep, commanding voice to something far less intimidating. I feel oddly out-of-place watching the moment, like I've intruded on something intimate.

"Ahsan," he coaxes, moving just a bit closer to the hyena, hand still out. "You're here with me. You're not in the black room anymore. Please. Come back."

Clarity slowly returns to the young man's eyes, and then they begin to tear up, and he chokes on a sob. Hesitantly at first, he inches away from the wall, then all at once throws himself forward. The Aardwolf catches him easily and wraps his arms around him, then slowly stands with him.

Ahsan turns his head against Lochan's shoulder and notices me, finally. He drags a thick breath through his nose and blinks a few times, rasping a quiet, "Kadar? Is that you?"

"Yeah," I reply, rolling a shoulder a bit uncomfortably beneath the unfamiliar armor. I force a half-smile. "Don't let the leather fool you."

Lochan brushes a rough palm over the hyena's mane, smoothing some of the jagged edges back. "Fought like hell, did you?" He asks him, a hint of pride evident in his tone.

Ahsan's whole body begins to shake anew, enough that I can see it even from where I stand in the dimly-lit hallway. His voice is equally shaking when he speaks again, punctuated by a sobbing breath every now and then. "She had them... put me there... when they took me from the field," he says. "I woke up and just... just... darkness, and I was alone, and then when they finally came for me she was *so* angry at me," he hisses between his teeth at that, terror in every word.

He grips Lochan's biceps and stares up at him, eyes wide and intense. "She's angry... I left her," he cries, something in his normally weak, strangled voice shifting to sound more... outraged. "She said if I wanted to leave her, she would sell me. She knows I don't want to go to him. She *wants* him to hurt me!"

Lochan shakes his head, ears tipped back, his grip on Ahsan still tight. He pulls the hyena in just a bit closer for a moment, then slowly releases him, looking him in the eyes. When he speaks again, his voice is that low, deep tone I've come to know. Intense as an oath, in every word. "You're not being sold to anyone," he promises.

"Especially not that bastard. And you're not staying here any longer."

Ahsan looks between the two of us, suddenly seeming to realize what's going on. "Where are we going, then?" He asks, uncertainly.

"Away from here," he replies, as if that's enough. And honestly for right now, it is. I haven't put much thought to where we're going when we leave here, either. I assumed Lochan might have a plan, but if the extent of his plan is to run from here as far and as fast as we can, that's good enough for me.

I wipe off the hilt of my shotel on a rag I'd stuffed into my belt earlier, and glance down the hallway. "We should get going then," I say. "While we still have a chance. We can talk more later."

"Ahsan," Lochan says, catching the hyena's attention once more. "Do you know where she is?"

I'm momentarily uncertain who he means, before it dawns on me. The Matron would be well-guarded. Wherever she is. Which means we need to avoid her at all costs.

"She... was in the parlor, last I knew," he says, his eyes going blank for a moment at the memory. "She had them bring me to her, then after she... talked to me... she had them bring me back here." His shoulders hunch, and he winces as if in pain, casting one fleeting look over his shoulder, at the open doorway behind us. For the first time, I take stock of the room itself. It seems like the two guards were struggling to get him inside, when we arrived.

It looks so normal, from what little I can see from here. Just a closet, essentially. With nothing in it.

Except claw marks marring every possible surface.

"Who was with her?" Lochan presses.

"She was alone, except for two guards," Ahsan answers quickly. "One was the priestess."

"We already ran into her," I mutter, glancing worriedly down the hallway. "We're in a dead-end here," I point out, "we need to move."

"There is no way out of this area of the house that doesn't go through either the parlor, or the main entrance hallway where we ran into Anala before," Lochan growls thoughtfully, looking down the corridor. "We're essentially in the center of the Manor."

We're all silent a few moments, before Ahsan speaks up, his ears perking. "What about the courtyard?" he asks.

"The courtyard's even more central," the Aardwolf states, confused.

"There's a servant's entrance," Ahsan presses. "For the gardeners. There's an access hallway that heads right out the gardens, to the water pump. I used it sometimes to tend Moth—" he stops himself for a moment, then murmurs, "the Matron's personal poppies."

"Lead," Lochan nods, then as Ahsan steps forward, grabs his shoulder and pushes him back behind him, "I meant tell me where to go, don't actually take point. Let me handle that."

"Left at the end of the hallway," Ahsan says, and we start to move.

We run into one more guard who thinks the better of fighting us and tries to escape, but Lochan insists we can't let her, and I end up being the one to chase her down and tackle her, being the fastest one amongst us. This time, with my comrades behind me, I have the conviction to bring my blade down in an arc that catches her in the chin. One swing doesn't do it, but I tear out most of her throat at least, so she isn't able to say much of anything before I deliver the final blow.

Lochan gives me a nod as I stand and join them again, and then it's one elegant room and hallway after another as we make our way towards the central courtyard. I can smell it in the distance before long, fresh air and pollen, an escape from this opulent prison and the choking incense and stale herbs in the air. I know it's not, at least not yet, but it feels like the promise of freedom. Whatever lays beyond this, at least we'll be free of this place. Ahsan will be free of the Matron, and the confusing life he lived here.

The pale gold of the morning light filters between pillars on a stone patio beyond us, at the end of one more long corridor. My spirits lift, and even Ahsan begins to hurry his pace. But Lochan, strangely, stops.

I stumble a bit and halt my own pace as well, staring back at the guard as his ears flick from side to side. "What is it?" I ask.

"Something…" He's silent for just a second, then with a flare of his nostrils, his eyes go wide and he lunges forward, grabbing for Ahsan around the waist.

She moves like a lioness in the brush, pouncing between the two men from just behind one of the pillars. I'm mortified I never saw or smelled her there, but the woman is like a specter, fast and nearly scentless, something she must do intentionally.

I go for my blade, my heart leaping to my throat as Lochan, for the first time since we've come in here, fails to pull his blade in time. The fumble could cost him everything.

Anala doesn't have her blade drawn though, I suddenly realize. Instead, she wedges an arm between the two men, and easily wrenches the hyena away from Lochan, who'd only intended on moving him away from her, not holding on to him. Ahsan is easily flung to the ground by her, and soon she's atop him, pulling a knife from her hip and drawing it against his throat, pulling him back up to his feet screaming.

I'm not able to act fast enough to stop the whole chain of events from unfolding, and by then I can hear the pounding footsteps of two more guards behind us, or rather to the side of us, from the wall along the inside of the courtyard. Two big males, with man-catchers.

Lochan viciously swears, finally pulling his scimitar and starting towards Ahsan, before Anala barks a warning. "Back!" She bares teeth, pushing the small blade in her hand up beneath Ahsan's collar.

To his credit, the hyena is kicking and fighting her, but the woman is dense and muscled, and I know he can't overpower her. Lochan glances behind him, then back to Ahsan, his gaze going from angry to helpless over the course of a few seconds. I look to him, uncertain what to do.

"We can't let them—" I begin.

"No matter what, you get him out of here," he snarls at me, beneath his breath. "Remember what I said."

"How?" I insist. "She's got him."

"This isn't like her," he growls in frustration. "She's under orders." He stares back out into the courtyard, to where she's pulled Ahsan back against a row of flowering bushes. He bucks against her and they crash into the leaves, shaking petals free in a maelstrom around them.

I notice something then, behind them in the center of the courtyard. One of the many statues on the estate.

"Look," I point it out to Lochan.

He notices too, his eyes widening. And then he raises his voice to Anala, shouting at her across the field. "Your goddess looks down on you, Al'Dahia! Will you disgrace yourself under her very gaze, by using an innocent as a shield?"

The woman's red gaze fixes on us, and then she slowly lifts her head, looking behind her and above her. The statue of the hyena warrior goddess looms in the very center of the courtyard, tall and imposing, cast in stark relief in the morning light. I can see her expression shift slowly as she stares at the chipped, worn red paint beneath the sandstone eyes, mirroring her own markings.

"No!" A shout echoes across the garden, a new voice from a distant doorway, barely visible through the shrubs and trees. I don't need to know her voice from memory to know who it is, by the way Ahsan suddenly stiffens and shrinks back, his tail quaking.

The woman steps out from another pillar in the ringed courtyard, on the far side. There's no mistaking her, even in a simpler saree and wrap than when she was expecting guests the last time I beheld her. She's tall, stately and sharp-featured, and I can feel her hate from where I stand.

"Bring him to me!" She demands. "Do not let him goad you!"

The two guards I heard are behind us now, blocking our only other way out. They seem hesitant to approach us even with the man-catchers, probably because they've already seen the trail of blood and bodies we've left in our wake. Lochan's full attention is on Anala, though. And honestly, so is mine.

The woman seems caught in indecision for far too long, although it might honestly have only been a few seconds. At last, she narrows her eyes and stands to her full height, grabbing Ahsan by the collar and retracting her knife from beneath his throat, before shoving him in the direction of the Matron.

"Let the men restrain him," she says coldly to the Clan leader, who snarls at her, then snaps her fingers at the two men behind us.

Anala turns her gaze back towards Lochan. "We have unfinished combat, Aardwolf." She pulls her blade, and steps towards him. "No running, this time."

"No running," he agrees, then looks to me silently.

I know what he intends without needing it explained. There are two remaining guards, and one unarmed woman. It's more than I think I can handle, but there isn't a choice. It's the only chance we have.

The two men circle wide around us to get to Ahsan, who's only now recovering and trying to get to his feet, gripping at his neck where the blade was pressed. I narrow my eyes and split from Lochan to follow them, giving the two warriors just as wide a berth.

When they clash, even with my back turned, I can hear it. There's no mistaking the slide of steel against steel. I force myself to look away, knowing I have my own task. I try to focus on Ahsan, stumbling up with the help of a tree as the men close in on him.

The first is easy to catch by surprise, since he's got his back to me. The other notices me at the last moment and tries to bark a warning, but too late. I go direct this time, jamming my shotel, point first like a dagger into his kidney. His armor is thicker than the woman's, but it's easier to puncture when I'm stabbing, rather than slashing.

My blade doesn't sink as deep as I want it to before he pulls away from me, but the end of the shotel is hooked, and that proves to be fatal for him. He screams as it tears away a hunk of bloody flesh and camel hide in its wake, and stumbles forward, giving me the chance to drop my knee down on his lower back, and raise my blade high, swinging it down towards his thick neck with all the force I can manage.

Either Lochan is far stronger than I am or his weapon's just much better at this, but I don't nearly manage as deep a cut as he always seems to. It's enough that I tear a bloody gash through the back of the guard's neck muscles though, and that seems enough to, if not kill him, knock him out of the fight.

I hear the other's man-catcher before I see it, the hook descending on me with all the precision of the guards in the field. This time though… this time, I'm not going to let it happen.

I put my shotel up to catch it, hooking it in the curve and trying to push it aside. My weapon's size works against me though, he's got a lot of leverage once we're locked, and he uses it to fling the blade out of my hand.

I curse, angry at myself once again. This time I'd held on as tightly as I could, there was just no escaping being disarmed. The man knows what he's doing.

He begins to close with me, and then much to my shock, sags backwards as a pair of arms lock around his neck, pulling him down from behind. Ahsan snarls and clings to his back, fighting desperately despite the sheer bulk the far larger hyena guardsman has on him. It's all the chance I need.

His knees are shaking trying to keep from being pulled backwards, so I level a kick at the side of one of them. He buckles, tumbling over, losing his own weapon in the process. And then Ahsan is on him, balling both fists and bringing them down hard on the man's nose, blood spraying out as he connects. The guard snarls and snaps at him, proving his grit.

I circle around, and in the process, catch sight of what's happening in the clearing. Lochan's abandoned his shield for speed and the two warriors are dancing around one another, circling and cutting through the air at the space they leave behind, in a way that makes me dizzy. If it wasn't so terrifying to watch, it would be stunning.

It isn't like when he sparred with the lioness. They could kill one another with any swing, with any mistake made. They're fighting for their lives, with every fiber of skill they possess.

I glare back down at the hyena guard, who by now has managed to shove Ahsan off of him. He has a knife on his belt like most of them do, and I can tell his hand is inching down towards it, so I level another kick at his wrist, pinning it. I'm about to grab for it myself, when something out of the corner of my eye catches my attention.

She's slunk around the edge of the courtyard, I'd lost track of her a while ago, assuming she wasn't much of a threat. But Matron Sura has made her way closer to the fray, her thin figure silhouetted between two of the pillars. She stands there for a moment, gaze moving from Ahsan and me to the two warriors fighting nearer to where she is now. And then, for some reason, her shoulders straighten and she begins to stride towards the fighting.

She lifts one arm straight in front of her, gripping something that glints silver and strange. It looks like she's pointing at them...

A crack like thunder splits through the courtyard, echoing off the walls and momentarily deafening me. I wince and tip my ears back, a scent permeating the air like the world is burning. It smells like a forge.

I hear Ahsan cry out before I've registered what's happened. Anala steps back from where she'd been standing, staring at the Matron in shock, her blade frozen in the air.

Lochan drops his scimitar, and sinks to his knees.

"No!" Ahsan screams raggedly from beside me. I can't stop him when he bulls past me, rushing right past the priestess, who doesn't bother to stop him either. Ahsan skids down onto his knees beside the Aardwolf, gripping him by the shoulders as Lochan shakily reaches around to clutch at his stomach... and his back.

He has two holes in him, like he was run through from behind. And I have no idea how she did it to him. But I barely have time to process it all before the woman is looking towards me, and lifting that thing in her hand again.

Her expression is like the twisted demon masks they wear at the lunar carnivals along the Hyronses. I literally feel for that moment in time as though I am staring into something so empty, so dark, I could fall into her eyes and never be seen again.

There is nothing I can do against this kind of power. I stand my ground, and wait to die.

And... nothing. There's a metallic click, but little more. At that, her expression falls, twisting into one of frustration and she stares down at the thing like it's betrayed her.

The guard behind me is gone, probably fled for his life. For a moment, everything is silent save Ahsan's quiet sobbing words to Lochan. The Aardwolf still appears to be drawing breath, but blood is thick in the air and I can smell worse, leaking from inside him. He's barely even able to stay up on his knees, even with Ahsan's help.

"Kill them!" The Matron shrieks at Anala, who for her part has done nothing since the weapon fired. She looks back to the older woman with an expression of disbelief still painted on her features.

I step over to where my blade fell and pick it up in shaking hands, my thoughts a tangle of panic and uncertainty. I have to get to Ahsan.

"I *hate you!*" Ahsan suddenly shrieks, his words cutting through the clearing and catching everyone, even the Matron off-guard. She takes a step back at the ferocity of his roared declaration. My own fur stands on end. The way he slowly stands from where Lochan is slumped is... wrong, somehow. Everything about the way he's moving is wrong, for him.

"I loved you!" He screams, frothing between his canines, his mane standing high on his shoulders, every fur on end. The next words he gives are more growl than anything else, growing from a low place in his chest to a full-throated shriek by the time they escape him.

"You never loved *me!*" She's shaking her head, taking a step back, but he's advancing on her now. "I... *deserved... better than... you!*"

He crosses the space between them in a few seconds, far too fast for her to react, other than to throw her arms up. He runs at her like a feral, his lean form moving with a fluidity I didn't know he possessed. When he slams into her, he topples her to the hard stone pavement, and she manages only one cut-off scream before he's pummeling and tearing at her with his fists in equal measure, ripping her fine garments and battering her muzzle bloody.

She cries out his name several times, skittering back, her clawed feet kicking uselessly at his legs. At some point she manages to roll free of him in the midst of the frenzy, and I feel compelled to follow them when she takes off running towards the threshold we came through.

I round the corner in time to see him catch her, bashing her into a wall, and grabbing for her throat with both hands. She gags and claws at his hands as they tighten around her windpipe, legs thrashing futilely. He's got her lifted full up against the wall now, and I'm at a loss as to whether I should stop all of this.

The option is taken away from me when, after one last agonized look into his eyes, something cracks inside her, and her gaze goes dead.

Ahsan stands there for a few silent moments, looking at her. There is nothing of the hyena I know in his eyes. They're wild, lost in rage. I remember what it felt like in the moments before it all went black, and I can only wonder if he'll remember any of this, later.

What ultimately brings him to his senses is a sound from outside. Lochan, giving a rasping cough. He drops her in a heap on the floor, hunkered there for just long enough to assure she's dead. And then understanding passes back over his gaze, and he blinks slowly, looking up at me.

"Ahsan?" I take a tentative step forward, and remembering earlier, offer him my hand. It takes longer this time, but slowly, shakily, he takes it.

When we make our way out into the courtyard, I'm shocked to see Lochan is standing, albeit not without the support of one of the nearby pillars. He's left a trail of blood in his wake from where he fell, making his way towards us. His armor below his wound is almost entirely stained red, and I can tell from the weakness in his eyes that he's in a terrible amount of pain.

"Lochan," I move to support him, but when I get close, he puts a palm out, rebuffing me. Ahsan will not be dissuaded so easily, and pushes past me to go to him.

Lochan lifts the hand from over one side of his injury, slick with blood though neither of them seem to care, and takes Ahsan's. "You have to go," he says in a tone laden with pain, "with Kadar. Right now."

"No," Ahsan shakes his head vehemently, his voice nearly gone.

"Ahsan," I say pointedly, gripping my shotel as I stare over his shoulder. Anala is still there, standing in the center of the courtyard, weapon still drawn. Oddly, she hasn't renewed her attack yet, even though now would be the perfect time. I have no idea what she plans to do, but she's armed and uninjured, which is more than most of us can say.

"You have to," the Aardwolf says, in a tone more pleading now, betraying some of his weakness. "I need you… to do something for me."

Ahsan only shakes his head, but I look to Lochan, setting my jaw. "Anything," I assure him.

"The brothel where they kept her," he says, wincing and closing one eye entirely. "Near the Faariz outpost. Help… the women left there. And," he narrows his grey blue eyes, "do what I should have done, years ago. Burn it to the ground."

"You're coming—" Ahsan starts to say, but Lochan interrupts him.

"Kadar," he growls, "I'm holding you to your word."

I nod, and before Ahsan can say anything more, I grab one of his arms, wrapping my other arm around his midsection. He shouts in surprise and weakly pulls against me, his body clearly exhausted as he struggles against my grip.

I feel the need to look back at Lochan once more as I step past him. I drop my muzzle to my chest, then turn to him, speaking quietly. "Master Lochan," I murmur. "Stand up straight."

He gives me an indignant snuff, but there's also the barest hint of a smile there, beneath all the pain. "You too, jackal," he replies.

I have to pull Ahsan away, fighting and screaming, and force him across the courtyard towards the servant's entrance. I can see the simple doorway plainly from where we stand, and I know I have to just keep staring forward, or even I'll lose my resolve to leave here.

Ahsan doesn't. He looks behind us the whole way, and I know when Anala's made her move by the ferocity with which he starts fighting me.

When we make it to the doorway, even I have to turn to look. The hyena is closing in on Lochan, who's managed to make his way back towards his scimitar, lifting it in one shaking hand. When he stands again, he forces his shoulders up, raising his blade.

When he dies, he dies hearing Ahsan call his name.

Chapter 10

Resting Place

The day I buried my mother, I felt real loss for the first time. It wasn't just grief over losing a loved one, though. I felt, for the first time, like *I* was lost.

Nothing I'd imagined my adult life would be like as a child had come to pass, and I'd had very humble expectations. At least, they felt that way at the time. Laborers make up the bulk of Huudari society, even amongst the powerful peoples, like the hyenas and the lions. I suppose it's arrogant to assume that wanting what most of the rest of the population are all striving for is 'humble'. Odds are, if everyone else is competing for that kind of life, some of us will lose, but the point was, my failures weren't because of anything I could have controlled.

I wasn't lazy, I wasn't a troublemaker in the city at night, I didn't drink or take the Divine, and I tried to live up to my family's expectations. I maintain to this day that I *did* become the man my father wanted me to be, back before the drink changed him. Everything I've ever said about him is true—he *was* proud, he *was* strong, he *was* a role model for me. The creature he became when alcohol consumed him was not the man I'd once idolized. I prefer to remember the jackal he was when I was young. The man I killed was a corpse walking around in my father's clothes. My real father died years before.

I wanted what everyone else wanted, sure. But was it really

so much? I wanted a place to lay my head at night, secure work I could feed myself and my family with, and a wife who loved me and worked as hard for our family as I did. My father had all of that and ultimately squandered it, and I was ready to be the man he couldn't be, and live the life of a laborer, proud and shameless. An honest life if nothing else, and more than enough for me. It had been enough for my mother.

Until she died.

The kilns have a cost that some pay more dearly than others. For my mother, it was a lung ailment. She'd had it for years and we couldn't afford the herbs to treat it. She might have lived longer if she'd gotten away from the fires, the medicine man in our village said the illness came from the smoke itself, but she refused to stop working. Especially after Amon came.

My mother lived with us for the last month of her life, and we did what we could for her. Watching her struggle to breathe for so long, wondering at night if she'd wake the next day, was like watching someone drown in the shallows of the Hyronses. She was right there, the whole time, lingering and clawing for life, but there wasn't a thing I could do for her. When we found her on the final morning, her eyes were wide open and her body was frozen, thin fingers clutched at her blankets. She looked terrified.

Everything between my wife and I changed the day we put my mother in the ground. They'd never even been especially close, but that didn't matter. Ishaya was frightened by what she'd seen. What had always been a given to me was not a future she wanted, and if she'd disliked the way we made our living before, from that point on she loathed it.

Ishaya was from a higher caste than my family, and she never let my mother or I forget it. In the first few years it was simply evident in her dislike of... well, everything about our lives. Our living conditions, our few possessions, our meals. She held her tongue most of the time in the beginning, but as she grew from a young girl to a young woman, she became bolder. And once my father 'disappeared', she no longer feared to speak her mind. And that was a problem, because she had a lot to say.

My mother, gentle as she was, dealt with Ishaya's demanding ways by placating her and comforting her to the best of her abilities. But I began to resent her, no matter how hard I tried not to. It wasn't that she was bitter or angry like some women can be with their husbands, more that she was just never really... happy. With anything in our lives.

She wanted more. Not just more things—I tried to give her those. I worked hard and provided for her and for our pup, and we did well. Far better than my family had growing up, because all of my coin came home. But good water jugs, warm blankets, even better food couldn't make her happy. She wanted us to live closer to the Hyronses so we didn't have to carry the water. She wanted a house with less drafts, so we didn't need better blankets. She wanted to find work that paid well enough to eat well all the time.

She wanted a different life. And after my mother died, she became even more frantic with her demands. Worse yet, she had a grave to point her finger at when we argued about our son. She used my mother's death as an example as to why our life wasn't good enough for him.

She wanted Amon to learn how to read. She wanted us to leave the village my family had lived in for generations, and chase the ridiculous dreams she had in her head. She wanted to fly away from our lives, and ascend. She wouldn't, or couldn't open her eyes to the truth around us.

If I'd had wings, I'd have flown from my life years before. But wanting doesn't make it so. I'd wanted far less out of life, and I still hadn't gotten it. I'd tried to find happiness instead with what I had, and I'd mostly managed. My family may not have been everything I'd ever hoped for, but I had my son.

But Ishaya refused to accept things as they were. She wouldn't rest. She wanted us to be more, and that was the beginning of the end.

Our flight from the Manor was a blur, after we lost Lochan. Ahsan could barely stand, let alone move his legs. By the time we made it out to the gardens, I was nearly carrying him, his whole body slumped against me and wracked with sobbing. I said everything I could think of to him, trying to pull him back, but he wasn't making much sense anymore. It was more than just grief and outrage, I think he was also simply physically exhausted. It was easy to forget it had been a day since they'd taken him, and not only had we worked an entire day in the fields before that, none of us had slept.

My own paws were dragging, my lungs rasping with each breath, body aching in the aftershocks of the combat I'd endured. I'd gotten off easy, I know that. Other than a snapped claw on my right hand and a few areas that felt bruised, and of course the wounds I was still nursing from the fight with Vikram, I'd managed to avoid major injury. But I was losing strength fast, and my willpower would only carry me so far until my body gave out the same way Ahsan's had.

So it's a testament to how desperate I'm feeling, that when I see the blurred spots of Raja's hide stalking his way through one of the open walkways inside the compound, I'm honestly glad to see him.

"Raja!" I call out, my voice coming out weaker than even I expected.

The big cat turns once to regard me, and I'm almost afraid my eyes led me astray. His face is dark like a panther's, the darkness smeared down from his jaw across what should be a normally white chest. It takes me a few moments to realize it's just... a lot of blood. Very dark blood.

His shoulders are hunched in that predatory way cats have when they prowl, the fur down his back, mane-like as it stands on end. He makes his way towards us, and the closer he comes, the more I brace myself. I can feel the anger coming off of him in waves.

But when he eventually speaks, he actually sounds as tired and ragged as I am. "I can't... find it," he snarls, the menace in his tone tinged with desperation.

Then he lunges forward and grabs at my collar, and my reflexes, honed by the horrors of the day, finally avail me against him. I bark out a warning at him and shove my arm up beneath his chin before he can grab for me, pushing him back with enough force that even he seems stunned.

"I don't have the goddamn time or the patience to get shoved around by an ally right now, Raja!" I snap. "Neither of us do! We need to get the hell out of here! What are you even doing inside the gates? The guards are rallying, can't you hear? You should've been gone by now!"

"You're not listening to me," he insists, vehemently. "I can't find it!"

"Just take what you can!"

"I can't find the Liberator!" He roars.

I set my teeth at that, uncertain what to say. I'd suspected since he'd told me that it was an unlikely coincidence. Fate has never conspired in my favor. He'd been waiting for this chance for some time, and the events involving Ahsan and Lochan that had made this day the ripest time for his attack hadn't even really been planned by him, he'd just seized an opportunity. To think that all of that would come together during the same days in which a Liberator was somewhere within these walls, right in his grasp, was beyond unlikely. In fact, he may have never had any good information regarding that at all. He could have been lying to us—and possibly himself—about the chance this whole time.

"What made you think there'd be one here?" I ask, as calmly as I can. My gaze moves towards the horizon I can see past the wall, to the rising sun. The hyenas are baying and it's not going to be long before they rally. Even with the Matron dead, there are others along the chain of command in this stronghold who will assume control before long. The chaos is our ally for as long as it lasts, but hyenas are good at reigning in chaos.

I'm not sure what I'm expecting, but I'm not prepared for his response.

"I *saw* him," he utters, his voice laden with what must be a lifetime's collection of powerful emotions. Desperation, hope, fear, sadness, yearning. His ears are tipped back, his blue eyes wide like a child's, and there's no guile there. I believe him.

"I saw them leading him down the lane, three days ago," he insists vehemently, his whole body shaking.

"How did you—" I begin.

"The broken circle," he says. "Burnt into the flesh on his brow. I know a Liberator when I see one, I've seen them before." His eyes fall to the earth. "Never for me. Never for me."

I swallow, unsure what I can say that will ease the devastated cheetah. Or my own disappointment, for that matter. If there really was a Liberator here, and we either killed him, or missed him by a day or two…

Much to my shock, it's Ahsan that breaks the silence.

"There was a woman amongst the serving staff," he says, his voice thin and fading, "when I still worked there. A cook. She was a few months from paying off her contract, when I left. He may have been here for her."

My heart lodges somewhere in my throat. I wish Ahsan had said nothing, because it confirms what Raja believed, and I know as well as he knows that if the determined cheetah hasn't found the man by now, he's either one of the nameless casualties strewn in the hallways inside, fled from the attack by now, or was never here at all. The last is the worst option, because that means we just barely missed him.

"No!" The cheetah suddenly screams, raggedly. "No!"

"Raja," I put out a hand, slowly. "We need to go while we can—"

"Where?" He howls, wrapping his fingers around the unyielding metal collar around his neck, and yanking it up beneath his jaw, his fur bunching up around it as he struggles to rip it from his head, to no avail. His voice is becoming more frantic, almost crazed now, and his eyes are wild.

"There is no freedom in the world with this binding on me!" He snarls. "I'll always belong to them! A possession to be reclaimed!"

"We can go somewhere…" I grasp at nothingness for ideas, "… somewhere… where they can't find us. Where no one knows us. Maybe… we'll flee somewhere foreign—"

"Mataa is my home!" The cheetah cries out, and he's literally crying, I realize. The tall, strong cat doesn't even seem ashamed, just exhausted and angry. "These lands are where I was born! Where my family, the family these people took away from me, has always walked! Why should I give up who I am, who I was meant to be, disgrace my ancestors and flee? Why must I let them win? I want to be free! I want their claim on me," he pulls at the collar until it's biting into his flesh, "gone! I want to die with my dignity, with my neck bare! Why must I continue to endure this! Have I not suffered long enough?"

"I'm sorry, Raja," Ahsan says quietly, where he's resting against my shoulder. His dark eyes open to thin slits, and the cheetah looks down at him for the first time. "What happened to you… is wrong. I wish… I wish we could take it away."

Perhaps it's simply hearing the hyena, whose life has been filled with the sort of horrors men like Raja and I can't even make sense of, apologize to him, but Raja begins to lose his anger. Ahsan has a way of doing that. He takes the blame for something needlessly, like he's taking away some of the pain by assuming responsibility for it. As though anything that's happened here is at all his fault, just because he's a hyena.

That had been my mindset a few months ago, I realize. It's hideous now in retrospect. And maybe Raja is having that same realization, because his posture slowly slackens as he stares down at the exhausted hyena.

"Where is the Aardwolf?" He asks at length. His eyes say he knows already.

Ahsan just slowly squeezes his eyes shut and presses his muzzle in against my shoulder, sobbing quietly.

"We need to go," I repeat again, trying to put some authority in my tone. I'm not smart like Ahsan, or skilled like Lochan, or even as recklessly brave as Raja, but I've always been good at setting my mind to a task and getting it done. And right now, with Lochan gone and our world quite literally falling apart around us, I feel I've assumed some kind of responsibility. I swore to the Aardwolf that I would get Ahsan out of here alive, and I intend to do at least that. Past that, I don't know yet. When the time comes, I'll have to give my own orders to myself to follow.

Raja rubs his arm along his bloody muzzle and pulls his own shotel from where it was slung at his side, then looks to me. "Alright, Jackal," he nods. "We move."

"We should gather as many of the others as we can on our way out," I say, steadying Ahsan over my shoulder once more.

"Most of them scattered the moment the first wave of guards came," Raja says bitterly, and much to my surprise, leans down to take Ahsan's other arm, assisting me in lifting him back to his feet. "You must have been making a mess inside, because we honestly didn't run into many defenders on our way into the grounds. And once we got inside, I couldn't keep the men together no matter how much I bellowed. It became... well, you'll see."

And we do, once we're inside the entrance grounds, where the first of the gardens and the stables are. There isn't much left that hasn't been destroyed or stripped somehow, two of the out buildings are on fire, and there are dark mounds leaking even darker trails that snake and settle their way between the paving stones here and there that, even in the dim light, I can tell are all bodies. Some of them wear the distinct glint of metal around their necks, others don't.

No one is moving. It occurs to me now that we must have been inside the Manor for quite some time, even if it all seemed to be happening too fast while we were living it, but this... this was over quickly. The revolt swept through here like a flash flood, and left little behind. I can hear guards in the distance, but not many near the gate, since it's already compromised. They're probably off chasing down and picking off stragglers.

"How long were you in the Manor looking for the Liberator?" I ask Raja, as we make our way towards the distant, torn-open gates.

"I don't know," he mutters tiredly. "Long enough to kill half a dozen guards. It got to where I couldn't even find any more when I was looking for them."

"We did more damage than I thought we'd do," I admit, glancing back across the courtyard, which is more a battlefield at the moment. This place looks like it endured a war. I would imagine, anyway...

I've never actually seen a war.

"At least we left a scar," Raja snarls.

My eyes narrow, but I don't bother fighting his victorious statement. What happened here is far worse for us than he realizes. I'd thought the revolt might take down a guard or two, and that some of the servants might loot and damage the place, but perhaps because it became a two-pronged attack, Raja's followers were able to tear this place to its seams. Even if they never really got into the Manor proper, we did, and so did he. And we—

That's it, I realize. We broke their chain of leadership. The clans are renowned for their strength as a group, but they have a very distinct pecking order, and we had their Guard Master distracted for most of the fight.

Still alive, though. And she'll organize them once more, and another hyena in the clan will step up to a leadership position in the Sura Clan. And Raja's right, we left a scar. One they won't forget, or forgive.

When we pass through the gates, I don't feel as uplifted as I'd hoped. I'm leaving the plantation with two companions, a weapon and armor I didn't possess before, and no one is standing in my way. But Raja is also right about our future. So long as the steel around our necks remains unbroken, we're marked.

And they'll come for us. They'll exact what we owe, and it's greater now than it ever was before.

It's burning hot, the sun high in the sky, by the time we've made it far enough that I feel safe. Or at least, safe enough that we can stop for a time. We settle, (in my case collapse) beside a grove of boulders and dead scrub grass, and I shut my eyes against the sun as my head settles down into the crushed brush. No bed of dead weeds has ever felt so inviting.

I can feel Ahsan's heat settle beside me, and without so much as considering it, I weakly put out an arm for him. The hyena moves into my hold a moment later, and I tug him up against me, squeezing his nose in tight against my chest. I hear Raja moving past us, his footsteps distinctive by how little noise they make, even amidst the weeds.

"We should have gathered water on our flight out," I mutter, irritably. "I'm angry at myself for forgetting it."

"Other priorities at the time," Raja says, back to the calm baritone I came to expect from him, on the plantation. It's comforting at least to know he's settling, somewhat.

"The heat will kill us before the hyenas do," I point out.

"We aren't far from a trade post," he replies. "The one the merchants that sell on the estate camp at is barely four miles from the plantation, and so long as we stay in sight of the camel road, we shouldn't have any trouble finding it."

"We can't just walk into a trade post run by hyenas and expect a warm welcome," I say. "Even if word of the revolt hasn't made it here by now, we're still marked men, unescorted—"

"You have armor," he reminds me. "And a hood. You can cover your collar. We'll wait behind while you get provisions."

"With what coin?"

The cheetah gives the first hint of a smile since the day began, and produces something from gods-know-where, tucked into the waistline of his loin cloth, where his shotel is still dangling from a bunched, long strip of rag fabric.

He tosses the small bundle to me, and I just barely catch it, hearing the distinct clink within the thin leather coin bag. I arch an eyebrow up at him.

"I wasn't *just* looking for the Liberator," he smirks.

"Anything else useful you may have looted that you've got shoved in there?" I ask wryly.

"Nothing else I looted," he replies. "But we could make use of it later if you wanted. I know you both prefer guards, but—"

I throw the purse at him, and he just barely dodges it, chuckling lowly at me, flashing his long feline fangs.

"While I'm glad you're clearly feeling better," I snarl, "that's not fucking funny right now. Nor will it *ever* be," I try to put menace into my tone to make my point. I feel Ahsan shift from beside me, and try to tug him back in, but he's already shakily getting to his feet.

"The air out here is clearing my mind to the possibilities," Raja says, dragging a long breath through his nose and closing his eyes for a moment.

Ahsan's managed to get up and is staggering off, away from the cheetah. I growl and force my own aching body up, my knees threatening to buckle when I put my weight back onto them and finally manage to stand.

"You're a fucking asshole, you know that?" I inform the cheetah. He seems nonplussed. "You manipulated him just like everyone else in his life, manipulated Lochan, and now you don't even care enough to spare his feelings. The kid's lover died a few hours ago, dammit! Ahsan had to see it, had to—" I grit my teeth, slicing a hand through the air, "—watch him die! I had to drag him from that place, from everything he's ever known—"

"I'd say that's a good change, considering his previous circumstances," Raja says.

"What the hell do you know?" I curl a lip. "In the whole time you've known him, have you ever bothered to *really* know him? He was a means to an end for you."

"Without the Aardwolf's aid, you never would have gotten him out of there," Raja points out, narrowing his sky blue eyes at me. "So you should be grateful I pushed the boy at that man. *He* should be grateful." Before I can come up with another outraged argument, he interrupts me, "In any case, it's not as though I had specific plans for either of them. The Aardwolf took male lovers from the servant ranks for years before you even arrived here, everyone knew it. And he was watchful over the boy from the moment he came out here, I simply encouraged what was likely inevitable, anyway."

"For your own means!"

The cheetah shrugs. "The entire world only exists in our perception of it," he says. "It is natural to be selfish. If I spent my life worrying over how others experience it, I'd never see my own journey to its fullest."

"I assure you," I growl, "the world will still exist once you die."

"Not for me," he replies evenly. "And the world I can see is the only one I know."

"Are all cheetahs this self-absorbed?" I ask, flatly. "Or are you just the worst example of your people?"

"For better or worse," he says, turning to stare off at the horizon, deliberately avoiding looking at me any longer, "it makes sense at this point to travel together. And I would rather not clash the whole way. You don't cow easily. I don't have the energy to keep putting you in your place, so I'd suggest a peace between us, for now. We'd do better to save our aggression for our enemies."

"My 'place' is wherever I want it to be, now," I say, my hackles raised. "I'm not some half-starved new recruit in your miserable little kingdom anymore, you can't and won't tell me what to do!"

He chuckles, still not turning to face me. "Indeed. I knew you were defiant when we first met, but you still stood down in the end. You grew a spine, jackal. You're welcome."

"Don't you dare take credit for anything!" I snap. "You don't know me, you don't know what I've been through, and if anyone pushed me to this point, it was Lochan! The man you just dishonored. I wish he was still here with us and you were lying in that courtyard with your neck severed, but the gods always seem to kill men like him and reward assholes like you."

I walk around him so he has no choice but to face me. Maybe it's the uneven terrain, but when I finally make eye-contact with him again, he seems less imposing than I remember. I might even be taller than him, it's hard to tell.

He holds my stare, but his ears are flattened defensively, and his posture's rigid. I've got him on edge. I wouldn't go so far as to say he's afraid of me, but something between us seems to have leveled out.

"You want peace?" I demand, and when he doesn't reply after a few moments, I stomp one foot towards him and put out my chest, making as if to charge him. He takes a step backwards and growls, but catches himself before he gives more ground to me.

"You treat Ahsan and I with respect," I snap. "You stop acting like you own us. I don't give a shit about who's top dog, here. We can talk out what we're going to do as a group, and make our decisions together. No one's in charge. Let's just get that out in the open, first. I don't want to be dealing with your constant challenges any more than you want to deal with mine. We're equal, free men right now, alright? Isn't that the whole goddamn point?"

His expression is unreadable for a few moments, caught somewhere between taking offense and contemplation. He's thinking this through, and he's afraid that even agreeing with me means he's somehow giving in.

"That idea you had about my stopping in at the trade post, because of my armor," I point out. "That was good. It should work. We need more ideas like that, and we'll do better out here if we're all listening to one another. Alright?"

The compliment seems to win him over, and eventually, he nods. "Right. That's all I was saying. We work together."

278

"That includes Ahsan," I point out. "Stop taking advantage of him. It's all anyone's ever done to him, except for Lochan, and he just *lost* him. Show some fucking respect."

Raja averts his eyes for just a moment and drops his voice when he speaks again. "I honestly didn't realize either of you gave a damn about the guardsman. Especially not you."

"I... haven't given the impression of being a man who respects authority, I'll give you that," I admit.

"Not that," the cheetah snorts.

I tip an ear. "Then what?"

He narrows his eyes at me, as though he's annoyed. "Obviously. You want the hyena for yourself."

His words stick in my skull, reverberating inside the whole short walk it takes me to find Ahsan. I can't help but question myself, despite the fact that on the surface, it seems ludicrous.

I never wanted Ahsan, at least not in the way Lochan wanted him. I just wanted him near, so I could protect him, and have a companion, someone to talk to and sleep beside, someone to take comfort in, because...

It's my own mind, so lying to myself is pointless. I was lonely. Losing my family left an enormous void, and filling it with nothing but anger and outrage for the last few years has made me a miserable, hateful man whose only comfort has been the thought of returning to a life long-gone. My time on the Sura plantation, with Lochan and Ahsan in particular, forced me to face the reality that I'd made for myself. That this is my life, now. Even if at some point in the future, I'm able to somehow find them again, everything will be changed. And it's my doing, in the end. Blaming the hyenas throughout the years was a way to ease my conscience.

And maybe there was a time when I felt I needed to separate Ahsan from Lochan, but that was when I thought the guardsman was taking advantage of him. I'm pretty certain none of it was jealousy.

There was… damn it, I can't lie to myself. There was a moment, after I'd spoken to Ahsan about how he and Lochan came together, and I knew the hyena had actually begun the whole thing himself, but we were fighting and… just for a moment, right before he'd been taken, he'd rejoiced in the thought of seeing Lochan again. And then he'd been taken to the Manor, and everything had become chaotic.

But for a brief second in time, I'd felt that stab of fear. I'd just essentially rejected Ahsan's feelings for me, whatever they were, outright. I hadn't even taken a moment to listen to them, because I'd arrogantly assumed he didn't know his own mind. That he was simply throwing himself at every available man for protection, because it's what he'd been raised to do. But that was shit of me, and after seeing him turn on his own mother, I'd never again question that the boy could have his own mind.

But when I saw him, so happy to see Lochan returned, I'd felt suddenly like I'd made an enormous mistake. I'd spent the whole of our time together essentially pushing him away, because I'd assumed on the surface that we didn't want the same thing from one another. It wasn't even that he was a man. It was just that he… in some way, embodied every fear I'd ever had in my marriage. That I would somehow inevitably take advantage of him and hurt him. Like I'd done to my wife.

It had been so pervasive a fear, I'd even assumed another man was doing it to him.

Why the hell was this all so complicated? It had seemed so simple when I was young. You find someone, you marry, you live together, you're happy. I'd always assumed the only reason it hadn't worked well for my parents was because my father started drinking. And I didn't drink. I was even a good man, once.

Was it sex? Was that what complicated it for me? It's what made my wife hate me, it's what made me feel like I had to hurt her to be with her. It's why I'd assumed Ahsan was being hurt. Because it's how he'd been hurt in the Manor... how I'd been hurt by Vikram.

If you took that part away though, it all made sense. I'd been afraid if Ahsan began going to Lochan again, I'd lose everything else we had. The comfort, the companionship, even having him beside me at night. It had been a long time since I'd felt... needed. Or that someone might be there for me, when I came home from a particularly hard day. The way he'd been there for me after Vikram.

It's how I should have felt in my marriage, and never did. And somehow, impossibly, I'd found it with a hyena in mutual slavery, on a drug plantation in the middle of the desert. And it must have been what Lochan had hoped to find with him.

My eyes sting, and I swallow heavily. How the hell do I handle this? I don't know what to say to Ahsan. I don't even know, in the end, how the hyena felt about it all. It's never been clear. But he's certainly acting like someone he loved died.

Gods, my feelings don't matter right now. This is the worst possible time for me to realize I've changed my mind. There couldn't be anything more manipulative or terrible than seizing on Ahsan's sadness now to take from him what he lost with Lochan. But I... I also don't want to act distant with him, or push him away again. What the hell am I supposed to do?

I find him sitting beside a large boulder, as far from Raja as he can. He's leaning against a jutting slab of sandstone, staring out across the dusty scrub land. It's drier the further inland you go towards the Hyronses, and this sort of land would be considered lush back where I came from, but for three men with little to their names other than the clothing on their backs, it's too barren to survive in for long.

He's quiet now, his head resting against his own shoulder, elbows over his knees. I slowly sit down beside him, unsure how best to comfort him. He seemed to accept my hand before, so I offer it again, tentatively.

He takes it again, without hesitation. And he leans against me, dispelling all my concerns at once. Of course Ahsan still wants to be near me. He always has, that's not going to change now.

I envy how certain he always is about his feelings. I wish I knew my own as well.

We sit in silence for a time, until I notice something. Jutting out from a shaded crevasse of rocks, there's a particularly green patch of earth. It probably traps rainwater well. And growing out through the center of it are a cluster of very familiar red flowers.

I growl and go for my shotel, intent on removing the reminder of where we came from. They probably drifted here on the wind from the Sura estate, and they're the last thing I want to see right now.

"No, don't," Ahsan says hoarsely, squeezing my free hand. I glance down at him questioningly, and he keeps his gaze on the flowers. "I like them. I want to look at them for a little longer."

"Why?" I ask curiously, putting my shotel away.

He lowers his eyelids slowly, and for a moment I'm afraid he's going to fall asleep, but then he speaks. "I know you worked at a number of plantations," he says, "but for me, the fields were... they were the first place I was ever really happy. They were a place I could be, where she felt miles away. No parties, no dancing, no one to entertain. Just flowers, and work, and," he pauses, then looks up at me, "you."

I want to ask him if he remembers anything of what happened in the estate, if he's come to grips yet with what he did to her. But there will be time for that later.

Instead, I lean in closer against him and finish what I know he wanted to say. "And Lochan," I murmur, softly.

"I met him inside, first," he says, his muzzle quivering. "I never would have left, without him there to strengthen my resolve."

I can tell he's trying not to cry, so I shake my head. "You can mourn him, Ahsan," I assure him quietly. "No one will think you weaker for it."

"You thought," he says, swallowing, "that I was just with him because Raja told me to."

"I didn't understand," I insist, guilt-stricken. "I'm sorry, Ahsan, I didn't—"

"Do you think he thought that?" He asks, turning towards me.

I feel my ears fall, and my mouth goes dry. I saw the doubt in Lochan's eyes on our way towards the Manor. I saw the pain. The questions he had, questions that Ahsan never got the chance to answer. He died never knowing if what he'd had with the hyena was real.

"He knew you loved him," I lie. "He knew."

"We never really... said it," Ahsan chokes out, softly. "I wasn't sure. For a long time, I didn't really... I thought the... Matron loved me. I wasn't sure what it was, to love someone. But this has to be it." His head falls to his chest, his eyes closing fully, finally. His ears are tucked back and I want so badly to take hold of him and stroke them with my palms, like my mother would do for me after my father beat on me.

"I wish I'd said it," he whispers, giving a long sniff.

My resolve crumbles at that, and I lean down, wrapping both arms around him and pulling him in as close as he'll allow me. He not only allows it, he clings to me, returning the gesture twofold.

And then all at once, he pulls back just enough that he can look me in the eyes, and he grips my arms, hard.

"Kadar," he says, "I love you, too. Please... please don't ever wonder."

I stare down at him in shock. The declaration seems to have come so easily to him. I should say something in return, but I can't seem to find the bravery to make my mouth move. How is this all so easy for him?

He's opened the door, and I'm still not sure what's right. Is it wrong of me to seize on this time, when he's at his weakest? What kind of love does he mean?

Does it matter?

"I'm," I manage the one word with no idea how to follow it up, except to stare down into his expectant eyes. "I'll always be here for you, Ahsan," I say, finally. "I'm not going to let them take you back to that place. Wherever we go from this point forward, we go together."

It's so much less than I wanted to say, but it seems to make him happy. He smiles softly and moves back in against me. I weakly lean back against the sandstone and reach up to stroke his ears.

"Where *do* we go from here?" he asks, after a time.

"I get us some supplies, first off," I reply. "And then, we have a promise to keep."

After everything we went through at the Manor, the distant brothel, squeezed in between two equally-downtrodden, ramshackle shops, looks like a bad joke. There is one guard at the entranceway and no door, just a dingy red saree cloth, the color indicating what's inside. The place has no windows that aren't boarded up or covered somehow, and no sign or markings as to what it is, but places like this don't have to.

"This is it?" Raja asks, and for once I'm in agreement with the mockery in his tone. "This is the place our almighty Guard Master was so afraid to break into? His sister must be rolling in her grave."

"I don't doubt he was capable of laying this place to waste if he really wanted to," I growl at him, peering once again past the brick building—one of the few in this miserable little trade town—we're currently taking shelter behind.

"He talked to me about her a lot," Ahsan says softly, his hand gripping my bicep lightly as he leans past me to look at the place as well. "She was the one who didn't want him to make trouble with her owners. This place is also owned by the Sura clan, they have nearly all the holdings in these parts."

"Right, and they're hyenas," I sigh. "You make trouble with one of them, you've got trouble with all of them."

Raja chuckles lowly. "Well, we're already in deep, there. What's one more conquest?"

I sigh, and look back towards Ahsan. "Did you hide the provisions?" I'd managed to get us some basics at the trade post, thanks to Raja's plan. Really, with the armor on, none of the merchants there had batted an eye at me. And the cloak covered my collar entirely when I bunched the hood around my neck.

He nods. "I dug them in back by the hitching post. Do you want camels or horses?"

"That depends," I say. "I know you can ride a horse. Can you ride a camel?"

"Not... well."

"Horses, then," I say. "And be safe. If you don't think you can snatch any without getting mobbed on, don't. We'll find another way."

"I almost hope we have to," Raja smirks, showing his fangs. "To hell with running. We can take the guards in this village. They aren't even armored."

"One mistake," I hold up a finger, showing my own fangs to the cheetah. "That's all it takes, Raja. One wrong move, one missed moment, and one or all of us dies. They have weapons, and even piss-poor village guards are better trained than we are. Don't get stupid."

I lean past the brick wall again, eyeing the harem guard at the door. He looks bored. A Dhole, so probably not a eunuch. Hired help. Not even a hyena, so probably not trained by the clan. The hyenas inside might fight back as well, and we don't know how many of them there are. Judging by the size of the building, not many. But it's an unknown.

"Enough waiting," Raja says from beside me, impatiently. I glare at him briefly, but say nothing. I'm glad enough that he was willing to come along for this, seeing as it's really just trouble we don't need. But I made a promise to Lochan, and I intend to keep it. Raja just enjoys the thought of further violence against the clan. And in his own words, 'the gratitude of some desperate women.'

"We need to see if we can get inside," I remind him. "I don't want the women inside caught up in the violence."

"Well you'll pass for a traveling mercenary, or something of the like," Raja says, plucking at his collar. "But there isn't much I can do about this."

I sigh. "We should have stolen some clothing. I'm not sure how we can get you ins…" I trail off as I catch the cheetah's shifting golden hide in a stray ray of sunlight, the beautiful patterns rippling with the movement of his lean, muscular shoulders.

He eventually glances back and catches me looking at him, and narrows his eyes. "What?"

"You're an awful pretty man, Raja," I smirk.

He just gives me a confused look, and then Ahsan starts laughing from behind me. I see realization dawn in the cheetah's eyes, and then he growls, "Hell no."

Raja, as it turns out, makes a pretty enough would-be male prostitute that when I bring him to the brothel, I barely have to lie my way through the front door. All it takes is getting halfway through my opening line about him being a new acquisition, and the Dhole waves us right on through.

We emerge into a smoky, dimly-lit, cramped entrance room, with little more than a table and one chair, and another curtain leading to the main lounge. The smoke reeks of the Divine, unsurprisingly, and there's the distinct smell of musk and sex from many different creatures beneath it all. Not a pleasant combination, in my opinion.

I try my best not to show my distaste when a female hyena emerges from behind the curtain and starts making her way towards us. She looks thin and ragged, but she's not wearing a collar. Her eyes are bloodshot and when she gives a rattling cough, I recognize the sound. Chandan had a similar cough, as did most of the other workers who were hopelessly hooked on the Divine.

She gives us a curious look when she finally takes stock of us, then just makes her way to the table and pulls out a drawer, sorting through an unfolded stack of parchments. I hate to admit it, but the guardhouse where they kept our papers at the plantation was far more organized.

"I didn't know they were sending us a boy," she mutters, irritably. "We've little need here. Business is slow enough for the women. And we probably can't afford him. Where are his papers?"

I glance to Raja, whose shoulders are shifting enough that I know he's slipped free of the loosely-tied 'restraints' I'd put on him by now, (little more than the same strip of cloth he'd been using to tie his shotel to his waist). He gives me a curt nod.

I lunge forward and grab for the woman's throat with one outstretched hand. She hardly seems lucid to begin with, so it's no surprise to me when she puts up little to no resistance. Her eyes widen and she begins to open her mouth, but by then I've got my shotel out and cupped around the other side of her neck.

"Don't try my patience," I warn her. "Not a sound. Just lead us to the women, and your coin."

"Do you have any idea who you're robbing?" she whispers fierce-ly, flashing yellowed teeth.

Raja removes his own shotel from where I'd hung it on the other side of my belt, and gives it a test swing through the air, glancing back out towards the thin curtain separating us from the outside, and the guard. "Let's move this into the next room," he cautions.

We do. As we head towards the smell of smoke and sex, I drop my voice and demand of her, "How many others are here, save you? Clan members?"

"Just," she hisses, as I yank her arms behind her back and begin to shove her forward, "two… men. Here for the girls. They're in the back rooms."

"You'd better not be lying," I warn her. "Because the second I find out you miscounted, this blade rips you a new hole to breathe through."

We scare the shit out of a few women in the main sitting room, and I get my first look at some of the workers here. Some kind of squirrel and a pair of meerkats. I've never had a lot of experience with prostitutes save those I'd see on the streets in the city grow-ing up, but they resemble many of the women from my memories. Underfed, superficially well-groomed and dressed in brightly-col-ored but cheaply-made clothing. They all wear collars and jewelry that I'm certain they don't own, and the two meerkats are obviously very young. The squirrel looks closer to my age, and bears scarring along the edges of her ears that suggest she's led a hard life, either here or elsewhere before here.

Before they can scream, Raja hisses a warning at all of them, striding forward. The meerkats huddle together on an over-sized, torn cushion in the corner of the room, and the squirrel regards him warily, clinging to a curtain near one of the hookahs.

"Here's what's happening," I tell them all, still keeping my blade to the hyena's throat. "We're tearing this place apart and taking whatever we damn well please in the process. Now, that doesn't include any of you—"

"It could," Raja purrs, his tail thrashing behind him.

"—but if any of you want to leave, now's the time," I finish, glaring at the cheetah. "We're willing to take any of you with us when we go, if that's what you want."

There's a brief pause of silence in the room, until the squirrel finally speaks up. "Where?" she asks.

I consider that for a few seconds, then reply, "Away from here."

"They'll hunt you all down like game!" the hyena I'm holding spits, and I tighten my grip on her, the blade pressing into her fur.

"Cut her throat already," Raja growls.

"She's right, though," one of the meerkats says, shakily. "We can't leave. We have contracts, they'll send their hunters to collect us. I don't want any part of this!"

"That's your choice," I reply, trying to keep my tone even and calm, and keep this whole scene from spiraling out of control. I hadn't thought for a moment we'd come in here like these womens' personal saviors, I'd been owned long enough to know that some people wouldn't or couldn't imagine running from their contracts. Hell, some of these women may have been like Chandan themselves, working to pay off their addiction.

"You're not giving us a choice," the squirrel says, boldly. "Whatever you do here, they're going to take out on us. You know that, right?"

My jaw opens at that, but I'm not sure what to tell her. She might be right. But, is letting this place continue to operate really any better? I'm getting a small taste of what Lochan must have endured throughout the years his sister was here, and now I'm not certain what to do.

"I want to leave," the other meerkat says, speaking for the first time. She stands, and tugs away from her friend, making her way shakily towards us.

"Davika!" Her friend, (or sister, I can't be sure) cries out. "Don't be a fool! They'll find you!"

"I don't care," she insists, showing her small incisors. "This place is so much worse than the one we grew up in, and nothing they promised is true. We were supposed to be dyeing cloth, Kanti. They lied to us, and I can't spend another day here." Then she looks to Raja, and points towards an alcove that must lead to another hallway. "There's two doors down that way. One leads to her quarters," she points to the hyena. "All the coin's kept there, in a lock box. She takes it from us at the end of the day. They won't even read us our contracts, I don't think any of our earnings matter."

"At least here we have a guard to protect us from the men on the street," the other meerkat insists.

"They *sell* us to the men on the street!"

"Speaking of the guard," Raja mutters, glancing past me, then back to the small meerkat. "We're going to need one of you girls to lure him in here."

"Wh—why?" The meerkat named Davika asks, suddenly sounding less certain. Raja's next words certainly don't put her any more at ease.

"Well, we can't just kill him in the street," he says with a smirk. "Too much noise."

"You see, they're just murderers!" the squirrel cries out. "Don't trust them!"

"We're not going to kill him," I interject, glaring daggers at Raja. "He's only a hired soldier, we're just going to take him out of commission for a bit."

"You should kill him," a new voice—sedate, deep, yet feminine in tone—emanates from a corner of the room I hadn't even realized was occupied. Raja stiffens about the same time I do, proving he also didn't realize we'd missed someone.

She pushes herself up from one of the large collections of ratty old cushions, partially obscured behind a curtain in the corner of the room. When she steps out from the shadows and reveals herself to be a lioness, I feel slightly less embarrassed. They have a knack for being near invisible when they're sitting still.

She looks rough around the edges like the other women here, but built stronger, like she had considerably more muscle-tone at some point in her life. She's topless and doesn't seem concerned by the fact, and unlike the other women, wears little in the way of colorful attire. The wrap around her lower half is faded blue and hiked up to her knees, and she's easily the least feminine woman here. It's little wonder she wasn't one of the workers kept in the main area for the clientele to see.

"That man takes his payment in drug and time with us," she says, lifting her muzzle. "He's a miserable, brutal cur, and every woman here knows it."

The other women are silent at that, which only confirms her claims, as far as I'm concerned.

"Gut him," she says, the deep furrows beneath her eyes crinkling as she narrows them. "If you need help, I will help you."

"You, come with me," I motion to her, then look to the meerkat. "Davika, was it? You go with Raja. Take him to the strongbox, then wait out here."

"The men in the back—" she begins.

"Raja will handle them," I assure her. "They're with a few of the girls, right?" She nods, then I look to Raja. "They won't be armed, then. Don't kill them if you don't have to, and for gods' sake, don't hurt the women. Give them the same offer."

The lioness crosses the room towards me, shoulders held high, her stare impassive as she comes to stand beside me. She doesn't seem intimidated by either Raja or I. I'm not sure if that's a good thing or a bad thing yet.

I slowly remove the shotel from against the hyena's neck, and she begins to open her muzzle to ask me something, when I bring the pommel down hard on her skull. The first hit doesn't knock her cold, but it puts her on the ground senseless, and a kick to the side of her skull does the rest. I'm a bit concerned I may have overdone it, but I'm not exactly an expert at rendering people unconscious. Most of the time if it happened when I fought people with my fists in the past, it was just a side-effect.

"Lead me to the coin," Raja purrs at the young meerkat, who seems more terrified than charmed by his manner. She scurries off towards the hallway, the cheetah in tow.

"Are you certain you shouldn't accompany him?" The lioness surprises me by asking, her golden eyes following his departing tail. "He seems… unhinged. If any harm comes to the other women—"

"He can handle two unarmed men," I assure her, glancing back towards the curtain out. "And anyway, we need to do this thing with the guard quietly, or he'll alert the whole damn village. Do you think you can—"

She bumps her shoulder into mine as she pushes past me, calmly making her way out through the curtain to the small entrance room. I follow her after a second's pause, and wait in the shadows behind the threshold as she heads outside into the waning dusk light.

There's a brief conversation between her and the dhole, and a moment or two later, she lifts the saree cloth that serves as a curtain to the outside with one arm and steps back inside, the shadow of the male canine following behind her. I step back behind the threadbare curtain separating the entrance room from the main parlor, and wait to see what he does.

"The rooms are all occupied," I hear her say.

"Where, then?" He asks, and now all I can see are their silhouettes beyond the curtain, cast into stark relief by the light from the road outside.

Her figure tips over the edge of the desk, her elbows leaning over it, tail curling up against her back. "Here is fine," she says. "The madame's sleeping."

My ears easily catch the distinct clink of a belt being undone, and with it the heavy thud of a scabbard hitting the stone floor. It's all I need to hear.

I do my best to push the curtain back quietly, and walk softly up behind the man. Luckily, he's distracted and facing away from me. His ear twists at the last moment, but by then it's too late.

I clap my paw over his muzzle and hook the shotel around his neck. I'd been prepared to give him the same chance as the hyena, but in a snap decision I decide it's not worth the risk he'll yell, and the lioness's words make that decision all the more easier.

The hesitation I feel in my chest is less this time when I drag the blade across his throat, the jerk of my arm more certain. My confidence makes it go faster, and within a few seconds, he's a gurgling mess on the floor, his pants undone around his ankles.

The lioness straightens up slowly from where she was bent over the desk and gives the man an impassive stare, fixing her wrap. When I lean down over the man to level the shotel at his neck to finish the job, she speaks.

"He deserves to suffer," she informs me, in that same dead tone. "Let him bleed out."

"Sorry," I mutter, "but no."

It takes more than one chop, for me. I don't have the strength or training Lochan had, and the shotel's not ideal for it, either. I don't manage to sever much, but eventually something cracks, and he stops twitching.

When I stand, the lioness is sitting on the edge of the desk, looking at me expectantly. "You never did say where we were going," she says. "Do you even know? You're about to make a lot of powerful people very angry."

"Trust me, we've already done that," I assure her. "And... no, we're not entirely certain where we're going, just yet. Away from here, like I said. With whatever we can take."

"The girls in there are right, you know," she says. "They'll hire hunters. They do nothing but track down collared people for the clans. You need a way out of the country to escape them entirely, or at least a safe haven to take refuge in while you find a way out."

"You've given this some thought," I arch an eyebrow at her.

"This isn't the first place I've run from," she replies, slowly shifting up from the desk.

"You know a place we can go," I guess, after a few silent beats.

She nods. "Not far from here. A few days through the desert. Do you have camels? Food, water?"

"We have provisions," I say. "And one of us is... acquiring some horses now, as we speak."

"You didn't plan this out much, did you?"

"We didn't have much time to," I sigh. "What do you want? And how do I know I can trust you?"

"I'm indebted to you," she admits, flattening her ears and looking a bit vulnerable, for the first time since I've met her. "I couldn't get out of this place on my own. I tried more than once. The location of the oasis is a gift, if you'll just get me there."

"An oasis?" My ears perk. "They're usually owned by the clans."

"Not this one," she assures me. "I promise you. I'm as desperate to get away from them as you are."

"Alright," I agree, only a bit uncertainly. What she's saying makes sense. We have mutual enemies.

"Lavanya," she says. I tilt my head, and she explains, "My name."

"Oh. Kadar," I say. "The cheetah in there is—"

As if on cue, the lanky man pushes through the curtain and steps into the room in a brisk walk, followed by a string of women. "We should go," he says curtly, making for the door.

I sniff, my hackles raising. "Raja, what the hell—"

"The crazy cat killed all the hyenas and tipped the lanterns!" The squirrel cries out, rushing past us all. "The place is going up like a brush fire!"

"Raja!" I snarl.

"'Burn it to the ground,'" he pauses just long enough to smirk at me. "Were those not his exact words?"

"I would have, after we were all outside!" I snap at him, grabbing the curtain and opening it for just long enough to get a mouthful of smoke, and glimpse into the parlor beyond. The fire is clearly deeper into the brothel, probably in one or all of the rooms in the back. Two more women follow in Raja's wake, a fennec fox and a rat, and they at least seem unharmed.

The hyena I'd knocked out in the parlor has a knife I don't recognize jammed into her back, though. I'm not certain if it was one of the girls or Raja, and I'm not even certain if she's dead yet, but we don't have time to check.

"Shit," is all I can say. I give Raja a shove, and we make our escape.

I leave the place feeling like a robber and a murderer, and I'm not even certain we did what was right for the women here. But it's done now and it can't be undone. And at least I kept my word.

Chapter 11

Oasis

To say my marriage was loveless almost sounds too charitable. 'Loveless' could mean there's no regard for one another in a romantic sense, but at least there's mutual respect.

My wife and I fought more than my own parents had. We said things to one another that make me sick to think about, and if our son had ever grown old enough to understand what was happening in our house before we'd all been separated, it would've been hell for him.

Some people are not meant to be together, no matter how much circumstances try to force them to be. Just because Ishaya and I were capable of making a pup together doesn't mean we were ever meant to. Amon was a consequence of the fact that at the beginning of our marriage, I thought we needed to try to be parents. I loved him, but he didn't change the problems between Ishaya and me. If anything, he became the new focus of all of our anger towards one another, and the source of most of our arguments.

We were so fucked, from the start. People shouldn't be chosen for one another by their parents, and their criteria for spending their lives with someone certainly shouldn't be dependent on pelt color. There were other jackals near the Hyronses that just weren't golden jackals, hell, even a few wolves and other canines. I'm not sure who can make pups with who, or even if that really matters in the end—

there were orphans on every corner of the city that we could have raised if I'd married just about anyone. But Ishaya and I brought out the worst in one another, and I can love my son and still admit that the marriage that created him was a mistake.

Only one other woman aside from the lioness chooses to come with us in the end, and it's the meerkat. I'm not sure what awaits the others, but I know they're likely to be caught if they don't just turn themselves in on their own. I try not to think about it much.

Ahsan managed to get us two horses in the end, not enough to keep us all mounted, but enough to carry our provisions. Our escape from the village went relatively unnoticed, the blazing fire that used to be the brothel was quite the distraction. That, or no one in the small village thinks they're up to taking us on. The second seems more likely. They've probably sent a messenger for help already, though.

If we're lucky, they've sent for help to the Sura plantation, and they've got their hands full already. We might have a little lead time.

The lioness insists we take a circuitous path through the dunes west of the village, because the shifting sands there will cover our tracks relatively quickly. Raja doesn't trust her, but I suspect that's because he doesn't like listening to a prostitute. Or a woman, for that matter.

We travel for as long as we can manage, but once it starts getting dark and the scrub land begins to lose its heat, my body won't avail me any longer. Ahsan and the meerkat had gotten up on the horses hours ago, and they're slumping in the saddle. Even Raja's feet are dragging. We'd taken a short rest after we'd gotten provisions, but we haven't had any proper sleep for almost two days now.

We make 'camp' in the wind-sheltered lee of a large rocky ridge, ringed by small, tough little trees and scrub grass. Raja starts us a fire while I pass the water skin around, cautioning everyone to ration.

"About how long?" I ask Lavanya, taking stock of our limited supplies.

"A little less than two days from here, I think," she says, narrowing her eyes and looking to the dark horizon.

"If the clans don't run the roost at this place, who does?" Raja asks, leaning back against the boulder and stretching out his long legs. For some reason, he felt the need to remove his loin cloth when we settled down for the night. He insisted he just couldn't tolerate the feel of the thing any more, until we can find some place to wash. To be fair, most of our clothing *is* filthy. But I think it might have a lot more to do with the fact that we have female guests. I can't imagine the kind of ego it takes to believe you'll impress a prostitute, but he's getting more looks from Ahsan than any of the women. And that might just be because the hyena's as befuddled by his display as I am.

The lioness doesn't even look his way. She's made a point of ignoring him almost from the moment we met. But Raja's question was actually a good one.

"Lavanya?" I ask, tilting my head to force her to look me in the eyes.

She eventually does, then replies, "Women."

I blink, uncertain what the vague response means. Raja anticipates me, sounding irritated now. "What kind of women?" he asks. "Clan women? Do they have warriors, or is it just more of your fellow whores"

She slowly turns to regard him, narrowing her gold eyes. "Those are the only two types of women you know, aren't they? The women who subjugate you, and whores."

"I speak as I find," the cheetah growls back.

"Surely you had a mother at some point. Which was she?"

I ready my body to stand, to get between them as the cheetah's hackles raise and he flashes his teeth, but the lioness speaks again before things escalate.

"You asked me who ran this oasis, and I answered you," she states calmly. "It is run by women. Of all sorts. If that isn't enough of an answer for you, then I'll be clearer. They aren't clan women, although some of them are hyenas. They aren't all servants like us, but some of them are. They are enemies to no one, except those who wish them harm. They simply live out their lives there." She narrows her eyes. "And absolutely *none* of them are whores."

"How welcome are we going to be there?" I ask pointedly, looking between myself, Ahsan and Raja.

"They'll protect anyone in dire need for a short time," she says, then looks again to Raja. "Although men like him will not be tolerated long."

"What exactly have I ever done to you?" Raja snarls. "I haven't so much as laid a hand on any of you."

"All you've done since you walked into our brothel is posture and intimidate," Lavanya replies, evenly. "I've known many men like you, and you don't intimidate me. That's the thing about us *whores*," she emphasizes the last word. "I've seen enough men in my time that I can figure them out in their first few words. You know what strong men, *truly* strong men all have in common?"

She looks back towards me for a moment, then to Raja again. "They don't want anyone to know how strong they are. They don't need to posture, because they know that when the time comes for them to prove their worth, they can and will."

"Alright, enough," I cut them both off before this can escalate.

"Lavanya, you're as damned as we are if the hunters catch us, so I'm going to trust that you're taking us some place safe. We should have a few days on them, considering their nearest stronghold is the plantation, and they're a mess right now. Hopefully, they'll have no idea where we went. Is this oasis well-known?"

"It's location is a well-guarded secret," she assures me. "I only knew of it because I've sheltered there before, and I was led there by one of the women who lived there at the time."

"I hope you're right," is all I have to say to that.

Things begin to calm down after that, mostly because everyone's exhausted. I spent the small amount of coin we had on water and food, so we don't have anything in the way of bedrolls, but Ahsan's busied himself grabbing and pulling up grass to make a small 'bed' of crumpled weeds, and it's looking pretty inviting by the time I make my way over to him with the water skin.

"Here," I offer it to him.

He takes it, then before I can even ask, moves to the right edge of his little grass bed to make room for me. I'm more than willing to take him up on the offer, moving in beside him and slowly settling down onto my side. As soon as my body comes to rest, I'm more comfortable than I think I've ever been in my life.

Ahsan drinks carefully, then stoppers it and hands it back to me. He gingerly reaches out for me, and I reach back and wrap an arm around his waist, to let him know he's welcome to get close. Before long, his body's pressed up against mine and I'm too tired to contemplate any more whether or not this is right. It feels right.

I slide my palm up his arm and bring it around to cup one of his ears, stroking the soft velvet there. He closes his eyes and leans into the touch, and just seeing the smallest hint of peace come over his features melts away the rest of the world.

"How are you feeling?" I ask softly. He hasn't said much since the plantation, and I have no idea what's in his mind. I know that just because he's been quiet doesn't mean he's not roiling inside. I know, because that's how I've felt.

"Terrible," he replies honestly. "But," he pauses for a moment there, "I'm… trying to feel better."

"We've had a shit day," I say with a pained smile. "It's alright to feel bad about it. You don't need to put on a brave face."

"I'm not brave," he says, sighing quietly. "I'd never pretend to be. It's not that."

"You stood up to them, at the Manor," I say, choosing my wording carefully. I don't want to remind him about his 'mother' while trying to comfort him. "You didn't go quietly into that room, you fought back. That took nerve. You're not the terrified kid you were when we first met. I'm… really proud of you, Ahsan."

He opens his eyes a sliver, and gives a fragile smile. Then it falls away, just as fast. "I shouldn't be this sad, though."

"Ahsan, it *just* happened—"

"And *we* got out," he emphasizes, his voice cracking a bit. "We're free, Kadar. I can't… squander that… by being weak and bringing everyone else down. I don't want to mourn everything that happened, I want to…" he's silent a few beats, as though considering. Then he looks up at me. "I want to *honor* what Lochan and all the other servants who fought at the Manor did for us. Like they do when they celebrate the souls lost in the last war. They wouldn't want us to remember what they did in misery. Right? I know Lochan wouldn't."

I stroke my fingers through his mane. "I guess that's a good way to look at it."

He sniffs, burying his nose against my collarbone, his voice coming out somewhat muffled. "I can't be as strong as you, Kadar. But I'll try."

I sigh, holding my tongue. I can't explain to him how weak I feel.

It's a rare moment in my life that I allow anyone to see inside that deep. After Vikram, I… couldn't hide it from him. Maybe that's why we're closer now. Because for just one night, I didn't have to be the strong one.

There are so many things in my head that I've never shared, never told anyone about. Even now, the hyena lying next to me, probably the closest person in the world to me right now, doesn't know the worst of me. My mother never knew, my wife knew more than I ever wanted her to, but not entirely the truth.

What the lioness said resonates inside me. Strong men don't need to appear as though they're strong, they just are. I've spent my entire life appearing to be stronger than I am. And most of the world is fooled.

The reality is, I'm so weak inside, I can't even admit to it. I've never known how to be any other way. And this is why.

The people in my life who've always needed me have needed that sturdy, unwavering man. The tree with the deepest roots, to cling to in every storm. Ahsan needs that man right now, and I can continue to pretend to be him. So I will.

The desert grows flatter and more barren the more inland we head. I'm beginning to wonder if we've been following a madwoman when finally, on the third day, we see a wavering distortion in the distance that vaguely resembles a grove of trees. A large grove.

The land around it is more fertile than we've seen nearly anywhere else, the grasses growing to several feet in places, with the occasional gnarled, wind-swept tree bravely jutting out.

Lavanya comes to stand beside me, sniffing the wind. Her ears flick back and she silently eyes the horizon for a time, before murmuring, "We've been spotted."

My hand instinctively goes to my shotel, but she grabs my arm to caution me before I can pull it, shaking her head. "Do not produce weapons," she warns. "Or they'll kill us where we stand."

"Who?" My eyes dart across the grassland. "Where?"

"Just follow me," she instructs and steps past me into the tall grasses, making her way towards the distant grove. Ahsan and Raja look to me uncertainly, Ahsan in particular seems on-edge. His big, broad ears flick from side to side, and he must have smelled what Lavanya did, because he keeps sniffing at the wind, presumably trying to discern where it came from.

My own nose isn't availing me. All I can smell are the date palms in the distance. They remind me of the Hyronses, and with that comes a wash of memories that's making it hard to focus on anything else.

"I smell smoke," Raja comments quietly as we move. "Cooking fires. Olive oil."

Ahsan nods. "There's definitely a community ahead."

"I'm curious why the hyenas or the lions have never claimed this place," I mutter quietly.

"They have," Lavanya says, coming to a stop without any warning. I nearly bump into her, feeling foolish for keeping my eyes on the grassland rather than right in front of me, when the first of the women appears.

There's no saving your dignity when a lion, or in this case lioness, prowls up on you. I argue I should be forgiven in this case though, because after the first, nearly a dozen more rise up from the churning grassy sea, all of them within barely ten feet of us. And they all have spears trained on us.

I manage not to make a complete ass of myself, and only jump a foot or so back. Raja loses his composure completely, flashing fangs and hissing like a cornered feral animal. I suppose it's far more humiliating to be surprised by cats when you're a cat yourself.

The women are all lionesses of varying ages and origins, judging by their differing pelts. Some of them are marked or painted, some of them wear the large hoops through their ears that are distinctive of lions from the far south, and some of them even wear patchwork armor. The one thing they all have in common is their gender.

My hands itch to go to my shotel. Many of these women are at my back, and more disturbingly, behind Ahsan. And the historic relations between clans of hyenas and prides of lions are, to say the least, usually violent. 'Ancient enemies' wouldn't be much of a stretch. The lion prides are the only groups in Mataa who've ever successfully rallied enough numbers to fight the hyena clans for control of the country. Unsuccessfully, but even still, they're nothing to be trifled with.

One of them near the front lowers her spear hesitantly for a moment, taking a step forward. Her face is painted in dark mud, her figure lean and a bit crooked, and her eyes look somewhat sunken-in and yellowed with age. She's wearing a headdress that almost resembles a mane, made of horse hair, and she's one of the women wearing patched camel armor. I eye her warily as she approaches us. I learned my lesson with Lochan. Age does not equal weakness.

"Little Lavanya," she says at last, straightening her spear to more of a walking stick, and putting up a hand to the others.

"Dela Eden," Lavanya says, stepping past me and approaching the older lioness, embracing her like they're kin to one another. That sets me a bit more at ease, but sweeping my gaze across the other hunters surrounding us, I'm still getting a lot of hard stares, and most of them haven't put down their spears yet.

The older lioness pulls back and puts a hand over her muzzle, gasping quietly as she picks at Lavanya's collar. "Child," she says in a mournful whisper, "what manner of trouble came your way?"

"We can speak over the fire this evening," she replies, gently taking the older woman's hand and lowering it.

The lioness finally catches my gaze and narrows her eyes at all of us, taking us in. I feel like she's staring through me.

"Who are the men?" she asks flatly.

"Refugees, the same as I am," Lavanya answers. "I wouldn't have made it here without their help, Dela. Please be kind to them."

I blow out a breath, hoping they won't hear or see my relief. I'm extremely glad my faith in Lavanya was not misplaced. She comes off so cold, so dispassionate, I honestly don't know what to make of her just yet. But she seems to have kept her word so far.

The older lioness—Dela, I think she called her?—begins to circle us, reaching out with the blunt end of her spear at one point to push it against my shoulder. "This one's big." She looks back to Lavanya. "They're all very large men, Lavanya. We have young, and some fled from the territory skirmishes to the southwest. Some with child. They will make everyone uncomfortable."

"Don't talk about us like we can't understand you, damn it," Raja speaks up, and I fight the urge to roll my eyes. I could have counted down the seconds until he said something impulsive and stupid.

"Be polite," I say to him instead, glancing about at the hunting party still surrounding us pointedly. "This is their territory, Raja. Their home."

The lioness smiles up at me, although just barely. She was probably even taller when she was young. "Ought to get a leash for that one, hmnh?" she says, waving the tip of her spear in Raja's direction idly.

"Don't talk about me like I'm some beast of burden, woman!"

Dela laughs at that, as do several of the women surrounding us. I'm seeing spears go down though, so I'm fine with them getting a chuckle at Raja's behalf, if it means none of us get impaled.

"I like the cheetah," one of the younger women says from my

right. "Any man who can argue with a spear in their face is a man worth having!"

"Let them in, Dela!" another calls out, and soon a few more voices go up from the hunting party in favor of… apparently… allowing us to live.

"Mmmnnhh," Dela continues circling us, smiling now, but still apparently drawing out the deciding process. "I'm not certain we can take them. The cheetah says he does not wish to be a beast of burden."

Another round of amused laughter and a few shouts of mockery come from the gathering of hunters, and I'm getting the feeling it all has to do with some kind of private joke I'm not privy to.

One of the young lionesses, the one who spoke up on Raja's behalf before, yells again, cupping her hands over her muzzle. "The cheetah can share my rations if he comes home with me tonight!"

I arch an eyebrow, glancing back at Raja, who looks at once confused and intrigued by the literal cat calls coming from the hunters now. "You seem popular with these ladies," I point out, smirking.

He begins to say something, before the older lioness smacks him on the shoulder with the butt of her spear repeatedly, punctuating her next statement and actually managing to cow the cheetah. "No. Men. Who will not. *Work!*"

"Oh!" I exclaim suddenly, "Yes! I mean, no, that's fine! We'll work. Is that what you meant?"

"This is not a patriarchal Pride," Dela says, holding up her fingers to count down the rules. "Everyone here works… even the men. No free-loaders. No touching a woman unless she invites you to touch her. No trouble, or you will *have* trouble. The last man who we were gracious enough to shelter who crossed us was buried up to his head in the sand and left for the scorpions."

"Understood, ma'am," I assure her, putting my hands up. "We

really only need a place to rest for a short time, anyway—"

"You will work!" she repeats. "Or you won't eat."

"Um," Ahsan finally manages to speak up. "If I could... what kind of work?"

The lioness looks at him like she's noticing him for the first time, and her gaze softens quite suddenly. She approaches him, putting a thin hand up and gingerly brushing it over his cheek and up to his ear. I feel a brief stab of protective jealousy.

"This one is a gentle boy," she says. Then after a short silence, in a quieter tone, she murmurs, "Someone has been hurting you for a long time."

Ahsan's eyes widen, but before he can ask her another thing she lets her hand slide away and steps back from all of us, giving us one last look before turning to her hunters. "They may join us."

There's a raucous chorus of cheers from the women, and quite suddenly we're all descended upon by the throng of lionesses. It's a little overwhelming. They quite literally group around us as we walk and many of them are speaking at once, asking too many questions for me to answer. At least three of them ask if they can touch my fur or my armor, and I'm not really certain what to say to that.

At some point Lavanya begins walking beside me, and she gives me a sidelong glance. "I apologize for their manner," she says. "They don't see many men here."

"What is this place?" I ask, eyeing the trees of the oasis as we draw closer. I was right, date palms. And definitely olive trees, as well. I'm beginning to smell the olive oil, and some kind of flat bread cooking. We've had little over the last day save some salted camel meat, and it was tough and tasteless. Whatever they're cooking in the olive oil smells amazing.

"A refuge," she says.

"For women?"

"Not *just* for women," she says. "But Dela Eden and her 'Pride' have been taking in refugees from the territory skirmishes to the south for some time. Women who were spoiled by soldiers, and shamed."

It takes me a moment to make sense of what she's saying, but when I do it leaves a bad taste in my mouth. "Shamed?" I ask. "Like the untouchables?"

"Amongst lions it is different," she says. "We do not keep to castes. But, a lioness who has been despoiled before she is married may as well be untouchable. The violation is a shame she must bear for the rest of her life. Men may have her but she can never marry. And if she has a child, her father or her brothers are honor-bound to destroy it." She's silent a beat, her eyes on the ground. "Or her, if they cannot bear the shame of having her in their Pride any longer."

I almost don't want to ask, but I do. "Is that how... you..."

"No," she shakes her head. "I was married."

She doesn't explain any more than that, so I leave it alone.

"Eventually she began to take others in, including myself," she continues. "A medicine woman named Uri decided to make this place her home nearly a decade ago, so they take care of ailing and pregnant women now, as well. And their children. These women have no other place to go, no place in the world in which they'd be welcomed, or even tolerated. Their own families have turned on them."

She looks to me. "It is not that Dela dislikes all men. But, most men have other options, when their lives do not turn out as they'd hoped. This place is a last option for the most desperate. Do not expect it to be a paradise. The oasis gives very little, it must be cultivated and cared for with extreme patience and devotion. You will likely be put to work at the well."

"Carrying water?" I guess. It certainly won't be a new task for me. I've been carrying buckets of water since I could walk.

"Or pulling up water," she says. "The well is very deep. Only the strongest pull up the buckets. We had an ox, last I was here, but it was very old. That is why she laughed at you."

"'Beasts of burden,'" I sigh. "I get it. So we get to be your grunt labor for a while. I can handle that."

"The cheetah seems to be getting on better already."

I glance over my shoulder at Raja, who seems to have had no issue with allowing the lionesses to touch him. He's basking in being the center of attention.

"At least he'll be in better spirits," I mutter. "Raja's happiest when he's being appreciated in some way."

"They'll tire of him eventually," Lavanya snorts. "He had better work."

"Raja isn't lazy," I insist. "He's just an asshole. If anything, he'll try to impress them all, and throw out his back over-doing it. He worked hard on the plantation we came from, it was another way he made it clear he ruled the roost. He's fiercely competitive, no matter what he's doing. Even if it's pulling up water, he'll make sure everyone knows he's the best at it."

"You don't seem to share the same affliction," she notes, with some evident respect in her tone.

"I've never really cared what people think of me, so long as I'm respected enough to be left alone," I reply. "Men who think themselves important bring a lot of trouble down on their heads. I've never really wanted to stand out. I just wanted to make fucking bricks," I kick at a small stone in my path, out of spite. "But even that's too much to ask for, apparently."

"Don't get bitter," she warns me. "The people you're about to break bread with have suffered in ways you can't imagine. They won't want to hear your sob stories."

I sigh. "That's fine. I don't like talking about myself, anyway."

"I appreciate a quiet man," she says. "You and the hyena will do well here. Just stick with the strong, silent routine."

"You've got it," I mutter.

"And don't be afraid, you don't need to hide it here," she says, cryptically. "No one will judge either of you. And if they do, they'll do it silently."

After that she moves off, and I'm left confused and alone, since Ahsan's already somehow managed to endear himself to the lionesses. A few chat amiably with him about brushing out and braiding back his unruly mane while we complete the short walk to the oasis. I'm glad to see him attempting to be social and more himself again, but when one of them offers to take him to her hut, I decide it's time to interject.

"Actually," I speak up, trying to keep my tone polite. "We could all use some water, if that's alright? We ran out this morning. Lavanya said you needed some help over at the well, so…"

"We're not so cruel that we'd make you work immediately," Dela assures me, still walking ahead of us. She chuckles, "No, come. We will feed you all, and you may rest the night. Tomorrow, I will show you some tasks you can put those broad backs into."

The first night we spend at the oasis is relatively subdued, but pleasant. They bring us food and water and ask us to stay at a palm-thatched clay hut near the outskirts of the oasis. I get the feeling the isolation is part of our induction, to assure we won't make trouble inside the community on our first night. And to watch us.

But they bring us some kind of flat bread drizzled in olive oil and spices, and two bowls, one full of steaming rice, and the other a vegetable curry that may as well be meat, it's so hearty. They say hunger is the best spice, but in all honesty, it might be some of the best food I've ever eaten, regardless.

There's also some kind of alcohol they drink here, that tastes enough like the bread they make in liquid form that I'm fairly certain it's made with the same ingredients. It's not the worst alcohol I've ever had, but it's definitely meant to be drunk like medicine, not enjoyed. It puts us all in a content stupor though, and I'm pretty sure that's the point. We all sleep like the dead, on some of the best-woven straw mats I've ever had the pleasure of sleeping on, in a dry, cool hut. With real, actual *blankets*.

When I wake the next morning, I am the best-rested I've felt in years. Which is good, because we're joined before long by Lavanya, who was allowed to stay at the main camp, and two other very large women. A tiger and a warthog. They're introduced as our working companions for the day, and finally, we're escorted into the center of the oasis.

I'm not sure what I was expecting, but the inner sanctum of the lush, carefully-layered and cultivated land is every bit as lively and busy as any street back home near the Hyronses ever was. There aren't roads or brick buildings, just huts like the one we stayed in and pathways criss-crossing between groves of foliage. Chickens dart about between brush and people, goats and other small animals roam or are led about, and what consists of their 'market' square is dominated by carts or crates of goods, being traded or bartered, (or as far as I know, given freely). It's as vibrant and diverse a community as any well-established village I've ever visited. With one notable exception.

Nearly every adult here is female. There are a lot of children as well, and they're a more even mix, but everyone near to my age is a woman. Many of them are lions, but not overwhelmingly so. I see several rodents, smaller brush animals like the meerkat woman we brought here from the brothel, a mother cheetah with two cubs in tow, even a few other jackals. No golden, but we're more of a rarity in these parts.

Even hyenas. They move about here like everyone else, and no one seems to be taking exception to them. One of them is selling eggs to a small crowd of women, in fact. She looks to be trading them for vegetables.

And most importantly, we aren't the only people here wearing collars. I'd taken my armor off last night, and I was concerned I might need to have it on for some reason to cover my neck, but no one else here is covering theirs.

We *are* getting a lot of stares, but I'm certain that has more to do with our gender. And most of them seem more intrigued than put off by us. The fact that we're walking alongside two very large women whom I'm sure double as guards or hunters when they aren't working the well probably helps.

"It's beautiful here," Ahsan comments as we head through the 'village' square.

"We have to cultivate wherever we can irrigate," the tigress explains, giving me a surprisingly pleasant smile. "So the plots are… everywhere," she chuckles. "We more built our homes and pathways around the oasis than shaped it to our needs."

"Seems a little tricky to navigate," I say.

"You'll learn the paths and where each of the plots are eventually," she promises. "We move in teams, anyway. Usually one group of two will pull up water while the others carry it to the women working the land that day. That way the first team can fill up buckets while the others are out, and there's no waiting when they come for more water."

"Sounds simple enough."

"The land is endlessly thirsty," she says. "Only the palms would really survive here if we weren't bringing the water up all the time. It's a constant task."

"Where does the water come from?" Ahsan asks.

"Underground," Lavanya says. "No one is completely sure why."

"When the first settlers of the oasis came here many generations ago," the tiger says, "it bubbled up in a small pool. But the pool was very small, and they struggled to grow much of anything here. When they dug the well, the deeper they went, the harder and more unyielding the rock became. Dela believes the hard rock trapped all the water down there, somehow. From ancient monsoons, or perhaps a lake."

"The sands covered an entire lake?" Ahsan looks mystified.

"The sands shift constantly," the tiger says. "They say they can cover entire cities. All of this could be buried someday, and our lives will be a subject of curiosity for the people who live here then."

"That's a little... depressing," Ahsan chuckles.

"I don't think so," she says, looking back to us with the black stripes down her cheeks crinkling near the corner of her eyes. "We won't be here to mourn our own passing, and even if no one alive then remembers our name or knows us, whatever we do here in this place may matter to them."

For some reason, her statement makes complete sense to me. Usually when people talk like this I tend to assume it's 'big talk' and it will go completely over my head. But the tigress seems pretty simple, and she's saying things in a way that I can understand.

"The past is like a well spring," she says. "It can be buried and forgotten, but sometimes it can change the lives of future generations. This place is only what it is because a long time ago, water was lost and forgotten here, somehow. And now, we bring it back to the surface, back to give life again."

I smile just a bit, despite myself. "You sound like you love your work," I say, remembering what that once felt like.

"You'll come to love it, too," she promises. "I'll show you."

As it turns out, she's right.

That night, we're invited to eat around the community fire pit with the women. A goat's been slaughtered, there's rice, curry and bread, and the general atmosphere is content and comfortable. Many of the women are gathered around one of the huts near the well, and eventually, I come to learn it's because one of the lionesses gave birth in the afternoon. The goat was killed in the child's honor. A boy, apparently.

I find myself wondering what kind of future most of these children will have, as I sit and finish the last of my dinner. Right now, this place is a safe haven for them. A spot of green in a vast expanse of arid desert, and a rare place of peace and equality in an otherwise vastly unjust and unfair world. Even here, I can see the scars of hard living written across the womens' faces and bodies. Some of them came from the war-torn areas to the south, where the hyena clans and the lions still push for territory. Many of them bear torn ears, missing eyes or burnt faces, intentional scarring by families displeased by their dowries or their inability to have children. Some of the scars, I'm sure I simply can't see.

This place can only support so many people, though. Most of these women have to know it's a temporary reprieve, a place to recover and lay their heads for a while. These children can't all grow up here, and even if some of them do, their opportunities are slim in such a small community. Most of them will have to leave, some day. Especially the young boys.

We'll have to leave in time, as well. That's especially hard to accept, watching Ahsan smiling and speaking with the tigress we worked with all day, as well as Dela and some of the other women. He's eating a hearty meal and he doesn't even seem afraid to clear his plate, for once.

He's happy here. And I could be, too. If I thought for a second we could actually stay.

Raja is... delirious. Even after a long day working at the well, which proved to be just as exhausting as Lavanya promised, (although immensely more satisfying than plantation labor) he's brimming with energy. He's a favorite amongst the women here, not even just the cats, and earlier in the evening while the goat was cooking, he even danced with several of them around the fire. Despite not knowing the various different tribal chants and dances the women seem to favor in this place, the big cat has a natural grace about him that makes his unique golden and black-patterned body mesmerizing no matter what he does with it. I'd hate the smug son of a bitch for it, but I'm not really trying to compete with him for female attention.

I'm glad he's happy, honestly. Raja's been an enormous, overbearing thorn in my side since we met, but at his heart I think he's just a big, lost child. He never had a chance to grow up, and the world he was raised in fosters exactly the kind of behavior that defines him now. I think, although I can hardly prove it, that children raised as servants probably turn out one of two ways. One of them is Raja, constantly bucking at the chains that bind him and seeking to assert himself over a world that's crushed him since he can remember.

The other is Ahsan, who at this point, I'd argue is beginning to escape the confines of who they raised him to be. So maybe there's hope for Raja someday, too. If he can ever accept that not everyone is out to use him or put him down.

I'm so lost in thought, I barely notice when Ahsan kneels down beside me. When he puts a hand on my shoulder, it startles me a little.

"Oh," I blink up at him. "I'm sorry. Just..."

"Miles away?" He smiles.

I smile, too. "No. I'm very much enjoying being here, at the moment." I reach a hand up to his, gripping his fingers loosely just for some contact. "How are you feeling?"

"You've been asking me that a lot lately," he points out.

"It's been a hard few days."

He leans down on his knees, tipping his muzzle down to lock eyes with me. "How are *you* feeling, Kadar?"

I stare at him, strangely uncertain how to answer the question at first. I don't know why, it's a simple question.

"I'm fine," I say at length.

"Just fine?" he asks, his fingers squeezing mine.

"I'm better than fine," I amend. "Very glad we found this place."

"Kadar," he's still looking me in the eyes, and I'm having trouble looking away. "It's been a hard few days for you, too. And I've barely seen you blink. You've spent the whole time worrying about us. Me, the women at the brothel... even Raja."

I have an excuse to look away at that, so I do, fixing my stare on the cheetah. He's made himself comfortable on an old, weathered cushion, one of many discarded from someone's hut and now relegated as seating for the fire pit. He's got at least three women in physical contact with him, including the one lioness that seemed so fond of him in the field. I have no idea what he's talking to them about from here, but he seems to be enjoying having an audience. And the women are paying more attention to the way the light dances off his fur than whatever's coming out of his mouth.

"I'm less worried about him now," I assure Ahsan, wryly. "He seems to be doing fine here."

"Do you think he realizes what he is to them?" The hyena asks, with a sly smirk.

"What, a plaything?" I snort. "Honestly? I don't think he cares. Raja objectifies *himself*, I'm pretty sure that so long as he's getting what he wants, and the women are getting what they want, it'd be wrong of me to intrude on their fun."

There's something longing in Ahsan's gaze as he looks across the fire at the cheetah, but I can't quite place it. I don't even get the chance really, before Ahsan seizes my hand and stands suddenly, tugging at me to do the same.

"I want to show you something," he says.

"Hm?" I look up at him.

He tugs my hand again. "I can't explain it. Just come with me."

I stand stiffly and let him tug me away from the warm atmosphere of the fire pit. We're soon making our way down one of the twisting paths that leads through the oasis, and it isn't long before I realize where we're going.

I chuckle. "Ahsan, we spent all day making trips to the well. Can't I just rest my bones for a bit?"

"It's just a bit farther," he promises. "She told me they'd be out—look!"

I peer past him into the clearing beyond, where the well we spent all day working in and around sits. They've kept the area clear for ease of access, save a carpet of grasses and other weeds. In the moonlight, everything's cast in shades of pale blue, except for some notable exceptions dancing about the clearing.

"Fireflies?" I ask, dumbfounded. "In the desert?"

"Only near the well," he says, slowly stepping into the clearing. "They said they only live near where it's wettest. The grasses here are always wet from all the well water."

"They certainly came a long way," I say, mystified as I step into the clearing. The little creatures are bumbling about in the air just as lazily and clumsily as they did over the banks of the Hyronses back home. I put out a hand, not really intending to catch one, just wanting to chase it a bit and watch it zip away.

"I've only ever seen them once before," Ahsan says, eyes wide as he watches them. "When I was really little, we traveled to another plantation, closer to the monsoon lands. Things were... things were better then. I was still small."

He doesn't mention his 'mother', and I don't want to completely ruin his night, so neither do I. I hate hearing about how he was treated, though. Like some kind of doll she never wanted to grow up.

Well, she's dead now. There's some justice in the world, at least.

Compelled to return him to the present and stop his thoughts from wandering backwards, I step up to him from behind and, a bit uncertain if I'm crossing a line, move my arm beneath one of his and settle a hand on his hip.

When he leans back against me, I feel like I'm a kid figuring this out all over again. I won't lie, it is odd to be this physical all the time with another man, but that's only a small part of it. We sleep next to one another and often touch, and that stopped being strange many, many nights ago.

It's more that everything between us is so undefined. When I was introduced to my wife, I knew before I'd even met her that we'd be married, eventually. Once we were, I knew exactly what would be expected of me. I had a lot of examples all around me to look to, a definition to attach to what we were supposed to be to one another. It didn't work out that way, but at the start it all seemed a lot simpler.

With Ahsan I have no map to follow. I don't even know myself well enough to know what I want with him. He has little guile—I've known from the beginning what he would want with me, if I was willing to give it. Even now, even after everything that happened at the plantation, he is unashamed and unafraid of showing or returning affection to me. And it's becoming very clear to me that if even now, when we've endured the most frantic, tumultuous circumstances, we can't go a day without touching one another in some way... it's going to keep happening.

My resolve to resist all of this is crumbling. Ahsan clearly feels no guilt, no obligation to his misery. There's no denying that something as simple as feeling his back resting against my chest makes me feel... better, somehow. Not just about my fucked-up life right now. I was waiting for this feeling long before I had a collar around my neck. Before I was even married. I never found it with her.

I don't think it would matter to me what kind of species Ahsan was, or what kind of appearance or gender he had. It wasn't a type of person I was looking for. It was a feeling.

"Ahsan," I manage to make my mouth move, finding every word hard to push out of my throat. "I really... care about you."

He turns just enough that he can look at me, his muzzle open just a bit, eyes moving to mine.

"But I don't know what to do with you," I say, the words coming out all at once. "I don't know if I'm just simple, or stunted, or twisted up still from my marriage. I'm not sure why this is so hard for me, but I... I don't know... what I'm supposed to do, here."

He gives me a long, silent look, then asks, "What do you *want* to do, Kadar?"

I give a shuddering sigh, running a hand up over my brow. "I honestly don't know," I admit. "I know it sounds stupid as hell, but I have no idea what I want any more."

"It... sounds familiar, actually," Ahsan says softly. "I didn't know what I wanted for a long time."

"I want to be closer to you," I say, verging on certainty with that statement. "But I don't know if I want... what a lot of the other men wanted from you." I intentionally don't mention Lochan's name.

"We can be close in other ways," the hyena says, and he does an enviable job of covering up the hint of disappointment there. He forces a slim smile. "Is it because I'm a man?"

"No," I say, and of that I'm entirely certain.

"Kadar, it's alright—"

"I'm not going to say it's something I always imagined," I say, honestly. "But Ahsan, your body has never been the problem. Even if I gave a damn about that sort of thing, you're just as beautiful as my wife ever was."

The compliment seems to catch him off-guard, and he flushes in his ears.

"I think she's why this is all so hard for me," I admit, hesitantly. It's so hard to push through this part, this whole... laying myself open. Looking at it as something he's earned from me though, as something I *owe* it to him to explain, makes it a bit easier.

He waits, silent but expectant. I've told him so little about my marriage, about my life before. I know he's always wanted to ask me more, but I've shut him down time after time.

"You were partially right," I murmur. "A long time ago, when you told me my marriage was why I'm always waiting for everything to go wrong. But it's not that I don't trust you, or that I'm afraid you'll hurt me somehow."

I drag in a long breath, and my eyes un-focus, his silhouette in the dark outlined by the fireflies flickering around us. I feel like I'm learning new words. I've gone years without saying this aloud.

"I hurt my wife," I say, my throat threatening to seize up on every word. Ahsan keeps listening in silence, waiting for me to continue.

"I got angry," I say. "I get... so angry sometimes, and... I try to remember what my mother used to tell me. My father used to get angry... and drunk... and he'd beat on us. My mother and I. And she'd always say afterwards that no matter who had been right or wrong about whatever the hell they'd been arguing about, anger was no excuse."

Ahsan's ears have wilted, and he tries to reach out for my cheek, but I turn my head away from him, not wanting to look him in the eyes any more.

"I remember her saying that... so many times," I say through grit

321

teeth. "And I always listened. I was so intent on being a better man than he was. But it just went on so long, and… I was so angry at him, and so helpless. It just never went away, even after he was gone. I'd get this… *burning* in my chest whenever I got angry at someone, and this panic, like I had to lash out. *Had* to. I felt that way all the time. I still do."

I shake my head. "I can't put it all on my father. I was my own man when I was married to Ishaya. I *told* myself I'd never be like him."

"You're not," Ahsan insists.

"I struck her, Ahsan," I say, in a fierce whisper. "We were arguing… about Amon, and… I hit her so hard there was blood on the wall."

He falls dead silent at that. I can feel that I might be ruining everything with him, but it's too late now and I don't want to stop. I need to own up to my goddamn mistakes, finally, and suffer the consequences. If anyone in my life right now deserves to know what kind of man I really am, it's him.

At least he'll finally understand.

"She wanted to take him away," I say quietly, "and she was threatening to go whether I'd come with her or not. She'd been wanting to leave the Hyronses for years, and she thought she had this… opportunity… to find work far away, in a port town somewhere. Some man with a trading company was looking to hire on. There would have been a contract…"

Understanding dawns in Ahsan's gaze, and he drops his muzzle.

"She was smart," I say bitterly. "She knew what it was. She didn't care. She said it was a chance at a better life than the one we had, and I was just angry that the life I was giving her wasn't enough. Angry and… scared. It would have been one thing to put *our* lives on the line for a chance at something better, but we had a pup. I was terrified of what could happen to him. You know what can happen to children who are sold."

Ahsan's muzzle trembles. "Kadar…"

"I lost myself," I say, my own voice wavering, my eyes stinging. "She just kept fighting me and fighting me, and," my words finally crack at that, "I just *lost control*. Amon was the only part of my life that made sense any more, and she wanted to take him away." I swipe my palm over my eyes, dragging a breath through my nose. "She never said another word to me after I hit her. She just picked herself up and walked away, into our sleeping room. I was mortified. I left and walked the city for nearly an hour, trying to calm down, and when I came back she was just… gone. With our son. I can't even be angry at her. It's what my mother should have done."

Ahsan's trying to take my hands in his again, trying to force me to look at him, but all I can do is shake my head and squeeze my eyes shut tight. "I destroyed my family," I say through what I know are tears, now. "I hated my father for being the way he was and I became him. Everything that's happened since then is my fault. I deserve everything that's happened to me."

"That's bullshit!" Ahsan says suddenly, cutting me off in a remarkably deep, barking voice for him. When I open my eyes again, he's looking straight into mine, his brows drawn low.

"Ahsan—"

"No," he snaps, "you can't give them that right, Kadar! No one deserves what they did to us!"

I swallow, unsure how to respond to that.

"We… killed people, Kadar," he says, his voice thinning out near the end of the statement. "A lot of people. Just a few days ago. A lot of them probably weren't even bad people, they were just trying to do their jobs. They had families. They had their own troubles, their own lives. We killed them because we had to. Because that place was full of people that were hurting us, and they wouldn't let us leave. What did we do all of that for, if what was happening to us was justified, somehow?"

He tips his ears back, his eyes dropping. "Don't you think I feel terrible about everything that happened there? I... killed... my mother."

"Ahsan, she wasn't—"

"She was the only mother I've ever known!" he bites back at me. "My real mother sold me before I could remember her face, to pay off a family debt. Matron Sura raised me like her own, and even if things got twisted up and strange when I got older, there was a time when she was kind to me. I can't forget how I used to feel about her. But I can't forgive her, either. It rips me up inside. I don't know if I'll ever know how to feel about any of it, except that it really hurts."

"You were a victim," I say quietly.

"So were you!" he retorts, then closes his eyes a moment and forces a soft sigh out. "Kadar, I..."

Now I'm the one waiting for him to speak. I give him all the time he needs.

"I can't forgive you for anything that happened between you and your wife," he finally says. "Only she can do that."

"I don't think I'm ever going to have the chance to ask her," I murmur.

"You're free now," he points out. "Your chances are higher now than they ever were before. Kadar, you made a mistake. A really bad one, and maybe for her, it was unforgivable. That's her choice. But you have to get past it, somehow. You're torturing yourself."

"I can't forgive *myself*," I emphasize, my voice rough.

"Maybe you aren't supposed to," he says quietly. "I think... I think we're supposed to feel terrible about these things. Forever, maybe. My mother... your family... all the people we've had to hurt.

If I ever stop feeling awful about it, I think… *that's* when something is wrong with me."

He puts his hands out to my slumped shoulders, gingerly pressing his fingers into my fur and leaning his muzzle forward until our foreheads are resting against one another, and I physically can't look away from him.

"Answer me this," he asks softly. "Have you ever hurt anyone you've cared about since?"

"I almost hurt you, several times," I say.

"But you didn't."

"I still feel that anger sometimes," I insist with a whuff of breath. "It's so hard to control."

"But you do," he moves one of his palms up to cup the scruff along my cheek, chasing my gaze with his own. "We make mistakes, and we learn. If you'd hit her and justified it somehow, *then* you'd become your father. You have to live with the hurt. Good people regret their bad choices."

"I don't think of myself as a good person anymore," I say softly.

"It's been a hard few days," he says, with a pained smile. Despite myself, I give him a grimacing smile in return, but it trembles away into a sob after a moment, and I crush my cheek down into his shoulder, squeezing my eyes shut. His arms encircle me and pull me in, and I eventually do the same, needing him as close as I can possibly bring him. I feel simultaneously as though I can't need him enough, and that I don't deserve him.

All I can feel, smell and see is him. Even the fireflies fade away, even the beauty of this place doesn't mean a thing. We could be standing in a wasteland. He's here and he's accepting me, even the worst parts of me, and I don't know why or how, but I finally just don't care anymore. I don't feel any better about myself, or the things I've done, I just feel… accepted. The shame I've been living with for so long is heavier and more restraining than any metal collar. It's not gone. But I feel less alone in bearing it.

His nose presses up beneath my jaw and I lift my muzzle to brush over his, and he grips me tightly, pulling me down into a kiss. I'm so far from fighting him now. I feel boneless and strangely weak, in a way that feels liberating. I let him move one of his paws up to press his fingers through the scruff of fur along the back of my neck, pulling me deeper in against his muzzle. It's profoundly relieving to surrender to him like this. Like I couldn't control this if I wanted to.

We're moving our hands over each other's fur, grasping for more purchase at one another. It seems impossible to be closer to him, but that's all I can think about. My feet feel unsteady, my body shaking and weak, and when he pushes against me, I give way and we end up in the grass, the fall knocking the wind out of me. When I gasp, he deepens the kiss. I never knew two people could kiss like this.

He moves over me, his tall, slender figure fitting against mine in ways I never thought two men's bodies could. My mind is a tumult of uncertainty, punctuated by pops of crackling fire, as feelings I haven't had in years begin to spark back to life. The confusion and the contrary, terrible feelings of the evening begin to get a bit muddy, like I've been drinking. But I'd intentionally not had any alcohol tonight.

We could just kiss and lie there in the grass together, enjoying one another's presence, like we do when we sleep next to one another at night. That would be simple. That would be enough for now, maybe forever. If you'd asked me this morning, or even just an hour ago, that's all I ever would have said I'd wanted.

But something about the way he kissed me, the way *he* pushed me down into the grass, about the way his body feels over mine, feels so much different than it ever has before. There's none of that fear that I'll hurt him or overwhelm him somehow. There's no question that he's the one leading things between us, and if he's the one taking control, it's… alright to let go.

It feels like something releasing inside me. I give a bodily shudder and gasp into his muzzle, and I allow myself to feel that aching need grow. It's been so long, I've almost forgotten how overwhelming it can be.

He's flush against me, so he feels it almost as soon as I do. His muzzle pulls up from mine and his eyes are hazy, his body tense. I can feel his own arousal against mine. He's trying so dutifully to stop himself from rubbing against it in any way, but even the smallest movements are making me dizzy.

"Kadar…" he utters in a soft, strained, pleading voice.

"Can you please," I gasp quietly, "just make the decisions from this point on? When it comes to… this… I—I just don't want to feel like I forced you."

To his credit, he only looks briefly surprised. Then, far more sedately, his voice gone a bit husky, he asks, "Are you sure?"

"Yes," I insist in another gasp, as our hips slide together. I try very hard not to sound like I'm begging, but even that thought doesn't bother me as much as it should.

He kisses me again then, and I'm very glad to have the option for any more talk taken away, because he's lifted his body up off of mine enough to move a hand down between us. When it wraps gently around my now very prominent manhood and slowly begins to stroke me free of my loincloth, everything in my head burns away. All I can think about is how it feels to have someone touching me again, let alone so eagerly. When I feel the heat of his own cock against mine and he rubs our hips together, I buck against him without meaning to. He doesn't even stop kissing me, he just wraps his soft paw around the both of us, and begins to stroke us together.

His experience balanced with my inexperience make it sloppy and uncoordinated, but we're both so hard and wanting it almost

doesn't matter. Every touch is too much, but not enough. We're gasping into one another's muzzles and straining against one another, the claws of my footpads digging furrows in the dirt and grass, his tongue sliding over mine.

When he starts to give these little gasps with each stroke of his paw, I'm undone. Hearing him find pleasure in what he's doing with me is all I ever wanted from any lover. I surrender before he does, my teeth digging furrows into my lower lip as I struggle to be quiet. When his own release comes a short while later, he's much less concerned about being loud.

The one thing I'd never considered about taking a male lover was how much messier it could be. Thankfully, we're right next to the well to clean up.

"Tonight has been confusing," I say in a subdued voice, sometime later while we're lying nude in the grass, staring up at the stars and letting fireflies land on us.

Ahsan briefly looks concerned, turning on his side to look at me questioningly, before I lazily reach out to take his hand. "Don't worry," I murmur. "I don't mean... bad. Just... I never thought that... telling you about my family would bring us closer. I keep feeling like I should feel wrong about it."

"Why?" He asks.

"So many reasons," I say with a huff of a laugh. "Gods, where do I start?"

"Kadar?"

I look over to him.

"Do you feel any better?" he asks.

I let my head roll back so that I can stare up at the stars, my ears twitching whenever an insect flits past. "I do," I say after a time. And I really do.

He moves over and curls up against my side, looping an arm around me loosely. "I'm feeling better, too."

OASIS

Chapter 12

Shifting Sands

I come to groggily, my mind blissfully clear, the night free of dreams. Most every night has been like that for me lately. In this place, the past seems to fade away into the recesses of my mind. To have that tapestry of guilt, shame and anger as a backdrop to my life, rather than a dogging, every day source of pain is a liberation in and of itself. Collar or no, I haven't felt this free in years.

A lot of that has to do with the hyena pressed up close against my chest. His muzzle's in the hollow of my throat, his breath even and slow, one of his long arms wrapped around my hip. I can feel his toes against mine, our legs awkwardly tangled, as they tend to end up most mornings.

I'm not sure when this all became normal to me, but I'm even less sure when it was I began to rely on him to be there for me to sleep soundly. Unlike on the plantation, we have an abundance of sleeping mats here—three, and three blankets, one for each of us in the hut they sequestered us in. Raja almost never spends the night here unless he's drunk or between lionesses, and Ahsan and I have slept together since we arrived, nearly a month ago. I don't think I've ever even considered spending a night away from him, so two of the mats remain completely unused.

This is what it's supposed to be like. This is how it should have been for my mother and father, how it should have been for my wife and I. We've never even talked about what it is we have. It's unspoken, but still understood. A mutual need we're both filling. It's not that I can't be apart from him, we often work separately and Ahsan's made a lot of friends amongst the women in the village, but we always come back to one another at the end of the day.

It's really not all that different from the way we'd begun to rely on one another on the plantation. The only big changes are the... physical ones.

Until the plantation, the only lover I'd ever had was my wife. And I can't call what we had 'love', it was just two scared kids going through the motions. We often didn't even accomplish what we were trying to do, and I always felt like I was hurting her, or forcing it on her somehow. Some of the other boys I talked to at the kilns said women could enjoy it, but Ishaya was either incapable, or she just didn't want me.

I wanted her. I wanted everything to be right between us, but it just never was. And eventually I lost any interest I'd ever had in her body, because every time I'd touched her, I'd been made to feel like it was a violation. Some of that is still with me to this day, I'm sure. The thing that happened with Vikram didn't help, either. It's hard for me to enjoy what's only ever been bad for me, in the past. Regardless of what my body has to say about it.

I never grew up thinking I'd be with a man, either. The oddity and the nuances of that have been an adjustment, but not one I'd say was overly difficult. Just different. I'm sure it helps that Ahsan is undeniably good at all of it.

Well, most of it. There are things I've done with Ahsan in the past month that I'd never done with my wife, but sex... the sort of thing Vikram did to me, that is... has not been one of them. We haven't even talked about trying it, and I'm honestly glad he hasn't pushed me. The thought of it still feels wrong to me, and I'm not sure if it's because of my experience with the lion, or just the fact that it would mean I'd have to take a less passive role than I have so far. I get twisted up inside whenever I think about the possibility of hurting him. Especially considering what he went through at the Manor. I feel better about all of it when it's his decision, when he's the one leading, as it were. I don't want to mount him like all those other men did, even though I know he'd let me if I asked.

A few months ago I would never have imagined we'd be lovers, though. So who's to say how I'll feel in a few more.

My whiskers prickle and I glance down, only noticing now that he's shifted a bit and his eyes are just barely open to slits, looking up at me. They're so dark when he's half asleep, his pupils blown wide. I used to think the rust-colored, dark eyes most hyenas had were merciless and greedy. But looking down at him now with the first hints of morning light streaming in through the threshold, casting a halo along the tips of his mane and lining his body in silver... I'm not sure how I couldn't see the unique beauty in his people.

I smile a bit, slipping a hand down to lazily cup and stroke one of his ears. He leans his head into my touch and gives a pleased, soft noise.

"You're gorgeous when you're half asleep," I tell him, my voice still husky with morning roughness.

I don't miss the way his ears color up, and he glances away, shyly. "You're surprising, Kadar," he replies.

"Oh?"

His eyes find mine again, and he smiles. "You're sort of... romantic? I thought..." he trails off, as if finding his thoughts, then shifts his body to move over mine. My hands find his hips and tug him against me once we've found just the right angle where every part of us fits together. We've gotten very good at finding that angle over the last month.

Once he's over me and we're more nose to nose, he continues. "I don't know," he huffs, his tail flicking over my hands as they move around his hips to his lower back. "I thought you'd be more... reserved."

I arch an eyebrow at him. "Are you suggesting I've been noisy? Because really, if we're going to compare—"

"No," he chuckles. "No, I meant more that... that I thought you would be... not unaffectionate, but more distant? No, that sounds insulting. I'm sorry, I'm having trouble putting it into words."

"I put up a hard front," I say. "That's what you meant?"

He nods. "But you say things sometimes," he says, "like just now. And you do things, small things, but I know what they mean. Like the comb."

I flick my ears back, abashedly. "I told you, that wasn't that much trouble to trade for."

"You watched that woman's swarm of children for nearly a week, Kadar," he laughs.

"They liked spending time at the well anyway," I insist. "And I like children. I'm a simple man, so I get on well with them. It wasn't much trouble."

"See, even now you're not willing to admit it," he leans in, pressing his nose against mine. "But you are. You're a romantic."

"Gods, I'm never complimenting you again."

He laughs at that and kisses me, and I tug him in a little closer, entangling our legs once more. At length, he pulls back and looks down at me, his tail flicking against my thighs. A lingering scent in our fur, specifically our two scents co-mingled, reminds me of the night before. My sheath feels restricting, but I'm still too lethargic to consider doing much about it.

"I guess," I murmur, "I always wanted someone I could make feel safe. Happy. I like that it matters to you when I do something for you. Even if it's just a damn comb."

"I got a lot of gifts when I was at the Manor," he says, laying his head on my chest. "Expensive trinkets, jewelry, things I could wear. I wasn't ungrateful, it's just… I was always reminded how I'd be earning it, either right after I received it, or right before. So eventually, I realized I was just being bought, and I didn't even get a choice in what was being offered. But they always wanted the same thing."

I frown, but I don't reply other than to stroke his back. He talks about his time at the Manor sometimes, when he's comfortable enough to do so. I've only gotten bits and pieces, and I've found the best thing to do is just to let him talk. I don't know if I'll ever know everything that happened to him there, but he seems to want to impart it all at his own pace.

"It's not that they were evil men," he says. "Not all of them, anyway. Most of them would be civil, even kind. But they were being kind because they were afraid of upsetting my 'mother'. It was always a trade, or part of some agreement they'd made with her. Nothing was freely given." He strokes a hand through my chest fur, slowly. "You're kind to me and then you deny it. You don't even want gratitude. You don't seem to want anything."

"I can't think of anything more I'd want," I shrug against the blankets.

"Really?" He smirks, leaning up on his elbows over me. "I could think of a few things I know you'd enjoy."

"See?" I smirk. "I never need to ask for the things I want."

"You could," he says lowly, his hips rocking forward in my loose grip, so that my paws settle lower on his rear. "Ask, I mean," he clarifies, as if that needed clarification.

I squeeze my fingers into the tight, yet soft musculature of his rear, and his eyes slip closed for a moment, his sheath rubbing up between mine and the hollow of my thigh. He's harder than I am already, and he gives this sharp, short gasp when he feels the first hint of my own tip rubbing against his.

"I prefer things the way they are," I assure him quietly. "I like it when you lead. I never have to wonder if my affections are wanted."

"I'll always want you, Kadar," he promises, his voice always threaded with the hint of a growl when we're like this. It's odd, because he's usually so soft-spoken. But I know from the incident in the Manor that somewhere inside the boy they raised there to be docile and subdued, lies another fiercer man he's only just begun to uncover.

As if to make his point, he bows his head and begins to nuzzle his way down my chest, his broad nose pressing up into my fur so he can nibble at my skin. I never would have considered myself to have sensitive skin until him. I didn't even know men's chests *could* be made to feel this way.

My breath hisses between my teeth when he nips at me, and I instinctively suck in my stomach when he noses his way down lower. I can feel that I'm lying more heavily out of my sheath now by the weight resting on my lower stomach, and I know what he has in mind. One of those things my wife never did for me. It's been a struggle for me to enjoy it without my mind wandering to the likely reasons he's so skilled at things like this, but… I've managed, some-how. Likely because, as aforementioned, he's really good at it.

One of his paws, finally roughening up from a few months of hard living, grips me gently by the sheath, and I watch his muzzle part over my tip, but shut my eyes before his tongue makes contact with me. For some reason, I'm still a bit embarrassed about watch-ing him do this. Even though I really should, if I ever want to be any good at it, myself.

Which I am not, as it turns out. The one time I tried, I mostly made a fool of myself, and he was good enough not to laugh at me until afterwards.

Like I said, it's been an adjustment.

His muzzle's unbelievably hot as it encompasses my length. I have to fight myself not to arch up into his mouth, even though every instinct in me is telling me to do just that. My hands need somewhere to go, and I know from previous experience that he'll not only allow me to hold him by the mane, but that he actually enjoys it, so that's where they end up.

He takes me into his muzzle from root to tip, cupping my sheath and rubbing at it softly in time with his motions, coaxing the rest of my length free. I run my thumb and forefinger down the ragged edge of one of his ears, and he hums appreciatively as I do so. I can feel the low, thrumming growl, almost like a purr, through every inch of skin he has in his mouth, and I don't bother fighting the groan that escapes me then.

I'm not really sure how long this goes on, because time gets a little fuzzy when he does these things to me, but I'm drunk on bliss and approaching a state of complete contentment when, as he has a tendency to do, Raja ruins everything.

More specifically, he stalks through the doorway, stares at us for a moment, and then gives a disgusted growl and prowls off to his corner of the hut.

He can't be half as disgusted as I am, though. Ahsan doesn't exactly like the cheetah to begin with, but he especially doesn't like him being around as an audience, so the second we're no longer alone together, he groans unhappily and stops what he was doing, planting his nose in my belly fur and hiding his face away as well as he can.

"Raja," I growl out. "Knock."

"On *what?*" The cheetah gestures roughly with both of his hands at the open threshold, and the thin hide we have covering the opening.

"Alright, I'll give you that," I mutter, letting my head thud back into the blankets, giving a long sigh.

"You two are completely disgusting, by the way," he mutters.

"I saw you trade plenty of 'favors' with the men on the plantation," I snort. "Up to and including with the rats. So you've got no leg to stand on."

"I don't mean because he's a man," the cheetah says, throwing down a satchel of what I'm guessing are his few possessions onto his empty sleeping mat. "I mean you're disgusting because you're always all over one another."

"What's this now for you?" I grate out. "Lioness number six? Seven?"

He briefly gives a fanged grin. "Eight," he corrects me.

"Yeah, and this one tossed you out, too," I point out. "You're making your way through a very limited population, Raja. It looks like the word's getting out on you."

"What 'word'?" He looks up, confused.

"That you're a dick."

"Says the man who sucks dick," Raja snarls.

"Not well," Ahsan comments mournfully, his voice muffled by my fur.

Raja gives a full-throated laugh at my expense, and I'm honestly too frustrated to get up and deck him. Not to mention still hard. My humiliation is furthered when even Ahsan starts laughing eventually, chuckling against my stomach. I grumble and shove him off, all enthusiasm for continuing where we left off now officially gone.

"Aren't you supposed to be out roaming the world, making other people's lives miserable by now?" I inquire of the cheetah, not really angry, but feeling the need to vent my bodily frustration in any way I can think of.

"I'm out of lionesses," he says with a smirk, "but there are a pair of vixens that might still be willing to take me in for a time. And plenty of work and food, for however long I decide to stay."

"I just never thought any place would hold your interest this long," I say, being honest. "Or... tolerate you this long."

"Dela tells me they've never had a man more capable at the well, actually," he crows. "She is very happy to have me here."

"Mmh," I give a noncommittal noise, not wanting to show how exasperated I am. I had literally predicted he'd take his job hauling up water as some kind of challenge, and he did, insisting on out-performing me every day. I don't actually care, and neither does anyone else, but it's just a little sad how predictable the cat can be.

"Speaking of," he stands, stretching out his long legs. "It's dawn. Get your asses up, or we'll be late. And Dela won't accept... what you're doing... as an excuse."

"You've changed since we left the plantation," I point out to him. "You used to be an asshole with a presence about you. It was honestly a little intimidating. Now you're just an asshole."

"I'm happier here," he says, his statement surprising me because of how forthright it sounded. I glance up at him as he heads for the door, in time to see him level one last look at me. "And I trust you two. I know you don't want to get one over on me, or mess with me. We're comrades out here, not just slaves to the same master."

I'm almost touched by the rare admission, and then he smirks. "Besides. I don't need to impress men like you. An entire oasis full of women, and you're still fucking each other? The hyena, I could see, but I thought you were more of a man, jackal."

I *do* get to my feet at that, and he makes as if to accept my challenge. Then his eyes travel downwards, to where I'm still poking out of my sheath, and he cringes, "Ugh. I'm not fighting you like that."

"Fight nothing," I reach out for him, and he skips back away from me. "C'mon, Raja. Let's share a manly embrace."

"Go fuck yourself," he shoves me back, snarling but still smirking. "Or better yet, let the hyena do it."

I all but chase him out of the hut with his tail between his legs, a rare victory in the battle against Raja's ego.

By mid-afternoon, when the heat is so bad that even Dela won't make us work through it, I am extremely ready to find some way to be alone with Ahsan. But not nearly as impatient about it as he's being.

"Where?" He asks, following me to the outskirts of the date palm grove. "We could go back to the hut, I guess—"

"Do you want a repeat of this morning?" I ask him plainly. The hyena's flattened ears and cringing expression are answer enough.

"It's a small oasis," he sighs. "So long as he's staying at the hut with us, we might not be able to find many moments alone."

"Let's just get some food," I sigh.

He's silent for a bit, and he doesn't say as much, but I can tell he's dissatisfied by how quickly I let the matter drop.

"We can still sleep beside one another," I say, spreading my hands. "It won't be that bad."

"Is this about that comment Raja made?" he asks. "Because you know I'd never—I mean, unless you wanted me to—"

"What?" I blink, confused. "No, I... look, I'm just not certain where or how we'll find any privacy until he moves out again. That dhole nearly caught us at the well the last time, and I don't want to anger Dela or the other lionesses. And there aren't really many sheltered areas in this place," I gesture to the grove, and the thin palm trunks and occasional olive trees.

"Gods, I never thought I'd miss the fields," the hyena mutters.

"Don't tempt fate," I warn him.

"They were just such a great place to disappear," he smiles a little, then suddenly stares past me, his eyes going distant.

"What?" I ask, then curiously peer over my shoulder.

At the wind-swept grassland beyond.

I look back to him. Then he looks to me. Then we're both taking off to the outer edge of the oasis, into the tossing sea of high grasses. Some of the oasis water must seep into the land around it, because the grasses for half a mile in every direction grow far taller and lusher than they do anywhere else in this expanse of scrub land. It's all golden and drying, of course—still scrub grass, not fit for even rats to eat. The women know of some weeds that grow in the shade of the nearly waist-high grasses that are good for eating or medicine, but for the most part it's just a buffer around the oasis for the lionesses to stalk through and keep guard. And a beautiful sight in the midst of the day, when the sun shimmers and ripples across the surface of the tossing, tall blades.

We manage to find a small dip in the land that's probably sitting over some of the bedrock that the well springs from, and crash down into the weeds together. Ahsan can actually get a little rough when he's this enthusiastic, but I can take a pin here or there. For the first few minutes that's really all we end up doing—wrestling like pups. I'm stronger than he is, but that may not be the case for much longer. Hyenas are powerful, and Ahsan's not lacking the frame, he was just terribly malnourished back at the plantation. That's begun to change, ever since we left. Not only is the food good and plentiful here, he's finally begun to feel less self-conscious about his height and weight. He eats full meals, he carries himself with less of a slump, and we're all working very physically demanding jobs, so he's begun to put on some muscle, as well.

He gives me quite a challenge today, but ultimately, as I always do, I let him have his way. I think he knows I succumb on purpose, but it never dims that triumphant grin he gets when he moves over me. I give a playful snarl and lean up to brush our muzzles together, and it isn't long before we're kissing and picking up where we left off this morning.

This time, thank the gods, we're left alone long enough to thoroughly enjoy one another. I forgo another attempt at using my muzzle on him, since we don't have *that* much time and I know for a fact how long the last attempt took to… ultimately accomplish nothing. Ahsan loves my paw anyway, and I'm much more certain of my skill there. The reprieve ends with him lying against my chest, my arms wrapped around him, stroking him until he's bucking into my palm and spilling himself into the crushed grass around us.

We lie there for a time afterwards, staring upwards at the cloudless, endless blue desert sky. We're both panting in the heat, a lazy fog creeping into my head and threatening me with a mid-afternoon nap, if I don't force myself to move soon. The insects thrum in a lulling chorus, making it all the harder to consider going back to work.

"I wish we could stay here," Ahsan murmurs wistfully.

I frown silently and shift my arm a bit from where he's been lying atop it, moving it to wrap around his shoulders instead. He leans his head against my chest, and I sigh. "We can't," I eventually say. "This place isn't meant for us. It's not a haven for wanted men, it's a watering hole for the desperate, for people who need the help they can offer here. We were lucky to find it, but… we're able-bodied, and we can't keep being a drain on their resources."

"We work—"

"We could never live this well anywhere else, as laborers," I say with a grimace. "Trust me. What we do could be replaced by one camel, or an oxen. And they could feed it grass, not meat and rice. We're here because Dela is a kind woman, and she has yet to force us out. We shouldn't take advantage of her Pride much longer."

"I'm afraid to go back out there," he murmurs, quietly. I squeeze his shoulders closer to mine. "Where can we go, Kadar?"

"I don't know," I reply honestly. "Somewhere foreign, maybe. Somewhere the clans have no influence."

"The north?" he questions. "The Amur lands?"

"I'm not sure," I say, uncertainly. "Moving north would be a very long journey. Following the Hyronses would be the best idea, but it's completely controlled by the Clans."

"I used to look at some of the maps in the estate," Ahsan says quietly. "Mataa is our country. It was orange on the map, and there were markers inked across it, with dotted lines and symbols. One of the men I used to see explained to me once that those were all different Clan territories. There were a *lot* of them. And we're really far down, near the bottom. We'd have to go through so many..."

"The land itself is a problem, too," I flick an insect off my ear. "There's the Great Expanse to the north. This old lion I used to talk to at the kilns said the Expanse is so hot, and so dry, the sands turn to glass in places. He said it's why the Dog Lords have never conquered the Clans."

"What about the ocean?" the hyena asks, turning towards me.

"The coast?" I turn my gaze back to the sky, considering. "It's all controlled by the Clans as well. But there *are* a lot of foreigners there. I hear, anyway. This is actually the farthest west I've ever been."

"Kadar," he says suddenly, more urgency in his tone.

I lean up on my elbows, because he just did. His ears are turned up, the fur of his mane bristling. He always seems to hear things before I do, and I'm not sure if it's his species or just that his hearing's better than mine, but by now I've come to trust his instincts.

"What is it?" I ask, sniffing the wind, but it's very still right now, and the aroma of the grasses is all I'm getting.

"Someone's moving through the grass," he says, his own nose twitching. "Or... was. I don't hear them anymore."

"Probably one of the lionesses," I sigh. "We should head back."

"We wouldn't have *heard* one of them," he insists, a snap in his tone.

As much as I'm concerned he's overreacting, he's probably right about that. "Is it an animal?" I ask, uncertainly.

Something... no, someone, they sound two-legged... shifts in the grasses then, and this time I hear it too. He jerks and stiffens, his body going still. Then the wind kicks up.

"I still can't smell anything," I murmur, confused. It sounded large, and if it was a feral animal of some sort out here, I'd certainly be smelling it by now. The lionesses have mentioned that on occasion, Atlas lions will come through here looking for game, but they usually know to avoid the oasis and the Eden Pride. And anyway, this really sounded like a person, the way it walked.

I glance back to Ahsan to ask him if he's heard anything I haven't, and that's when I notice he's shaking. His muzzle's just barely open, and his gaze looks miles away. "Ahsan?" I reach out for him, concerned.

"It's her," he says, with startling certainty.

"Who?" I blink, glancing back out towards where we heard the grasses move. I can't hear a thing any more, and I still can't smell anything.

"The priestess of Anala," he whispers. "The woman who killed Lochan."

"*What?*" I snuff, completely bemused by his guess. Of all the things I thought he'd say, that wasn't even in the spectrum. "Wh... what the hell makes you think that?"

"She had no scent," he says, his jaw shaking slightly. "When she attacked us in the courtyard. She smelled like clay, and sand. I think she rubs it into her fur."

"Ahsan," I say evenly, "I know that was a terrible day. I know it's hard to shake the memories, but we've put a lot of distance between ourselves and that place. They don't know we're here. They can't know."

"It's her," he says, still staring into the gently tossing grasses like he's seen a ghost. "Kadar, I know it's her."

"Because you *didn't* smell something?"

He finally looks back to me again, his whole body shaking now. "They've found us."

As unlikely as it all seems, by the time we've made it back to the oasis, Ahsan's demeanor coupled with a strange uneasiness in the air has me on edge. Something definitely doesn't feel right.

One of the first people we come across as we head towards the village square is Davika. The little meerkat woman's managed to settle in well enough here, from what little I've gleaned from the few interactions I've had with her since. She and Lavanya apparently stay in a hut with one of the older lionesses and work in one of the olive groves. I see Lavanya far more often, since she spends more time with the lionesses and the other large species, but I'm not on bad terms with the meerkat.

She looks nervous when she sees us from one of the footpaths that lead towards the groves, and I'm hoping that's nothing unusual. She often looks nervous. But when she rushes up to us, clutching a basket of olives in her small paws, I can tell something's really bothering her.

"They sent out Lavanya to find you two," she says, hurriedly. "I'm glad you're safe."

"Safe?" I ask, narrowing my eyes.

"Dela's calling everyone away from the fields," she explains. "One of the lionesses was hurt. I don't know much. She's with the healer."

"Thank you," I tell her hurriedly, and then I double my pace to the village square. Ahsan follows me, dread in his eyes. It's far too early to assume he's right about his wild guess, but it's certainly coincidental that this is all happening at the same time. *Someone* must be out there.

The women are massed in the center of the village around the doused cooking fires, and there's an especially large group near the healer's hut. I start pressing my way through the crowd when someone grabs at my shoulder from behind, startling me.

"Where were you?" Lavanya demands, her yellow eyes wide. "Someone told me they saw you heading for the fields, I've been out there looking for you for half an hour now."

"I'm sorry," I put up my hands. "We were just—"

"Never mind," she cuts me off, "did you see anything while you were out there?"

"We didn't see anything," I begin, "but—"

"It's the Sura clan," Ahsan says, shakily. "I know it is."

Lavanya's ears tip back at that and she looks suddenly far more worried. I shake my head, "We don't know that," I insist. "Anyone could be out there. Vagabonds, criminals like us, maybe even a lost caravan."

"I know it was her," Ahsan insists, vehemently.

"'Her'?" Lavanya repeats.

"Ahsan's convinced it was a Guard Master from our plantation," I sigh. "A priestess of Anala."

Lavanya shakes her head, looking to Ahsan. "Well, you're wrong there."

"We can't rule anyone out, I suppose," I say. "However unlikely."

"No, I mean it can't be her," Lavanya insists. "The lioness who made it back said she saw men. Foreign men."

"She saw them?" Ahsan asks, ears twisting towards the healer's hut. That gets my rapt attention too, and without another moment to spare, we all make our way there.

When we draw near, I can hear Dela addressing some of the

women's concerns. My impatience threatens to overwhelm me, but I stand back and don't interrupt for now. Our presence hasn't gone unnoticed, though. Many of the women who live here have never been fond of the fact that we're here, even if the lionesses tolerate us. They usually keep quiet about it, it's just a sense of not belonging I pick up on sometimes when I come to dinner. I can't blame the women, considering what many of them went through. But right now, that sense of not belonging is growing steadily with each passing moment.

Finally, one of them speaks up.

"It's the men," the woman, a cheetah with a baby on her hip says bitterly. "They're criminals, aren't they?"

One of the rats in the crowd hears her, and is less afraid to be rude to Dela apparently, because she raises her voice. "She's right, what if they're here for the men!" she cries out. "They're the only ones we've taken in this season! They're owned—"

"So are you, Lakshmee," a squirrel says from beside her, plucking at her own collar. "Many of us are owned. They could be here for anyone."

"We were fine until the men showed up!" another voice calls from the crowd.

Other voices begin to join the fray, and amidst the throng of bodies, I see Raja in the distance, emerging from one of the paths with an empty bucket slung over his shoulder. He stands out almost entirely because he's heads over most of the women here. He looks confused, especially when the crowd begins to turn against us. He gives me a long look from across the crowd, and I grind my teeth, considering taking Ahsan right now and joining him, just for safety in numbers.

As if that would matter. We're three men in a sea of women, and for the first time, that feels dangerous.

The scene begins to grow chaotic, every voice trying to be heard at once. I can tell the moment Dela's lost her patience, because her ears flatten back and she opens her muzzle to bay out a roar. It's nowhere near as shaking as a male lion's, but the old lioness still manages to quiet the clearing and make tails tuck, all the same.

"Enough," she growls, showing her yellowed fangs. "You will all listen for now. Speaking is pointless when your words are lost in a roar of ignorance." She waits a further few moments to assure she has everyone's attention, and then begins talking again. She doesn't seem to have to raise her voice to be heard.

"We are not living on some other world," she says, sternly. "We live in Mataa, and so long as we live in these lands, we will have to contend with the clans, the Prides, and all the troubles that plague the Huudari people. This is not the first time this place has been attacked, nor will it be the last. We are fortunate enough here to have what many others want, and so long as that is the case, we will have enemies." She raises her hand, sweeping it over the crowd. "Almost all of you came here, fleeing your own troubles. We took these men in just the same as we did all of you. It does not matter who these strange men who attack us are here for. We stand together, as cast-offs and unwanted people."

"The Eden tribe has no harem lord," one of the other lionesses, a younger hunter by her side, speaks up. "We chose not to, not because we hate men, but because we wanted to be equals... and no woman in a Pride is the equal of her husband. If we treat them as lessers now, we are not elevating our gender. We are only putting theirs beneath us, as our husbands once did."

"It's my fault," Lavanya suddenly speaks up. Slowly, all eyes turn towards her, including Dela's. She takes a deep breath. "Dela Eden, I'm... I'm sorry. It's my fault we were found."

"Child, we're not even certain who found us," Dela assures her, calmly. She lifts an aging hand and gestures to us. "Come. Please. Come and speak."

Lavanya moves past me through the crowd, and I decide to follow, trailed eventually by Ahsan. Dela's hunters part for us and let us through, and we join the older lioness as she heads into the healer's hut.

The second we're inside, I smell blood, herbs and desperation. I don't even need to look at the fallen huntress to know her condition is dire. She's on her side, a compress over what must be a terrible wound on her hip. It's bled through, and there are several others like it boiling in a pot nearby. The aging medicine woman looks up at us from where she's grinding something in a mortar and pestle. Dela kneels beside the injured lioness and then looks up to us.

"I have never seen a wound like this," she admits. "She was speaking for a time when we first found her, collapsed and bleeding in the grass. She'd been out hunting, I'm not sure where or how far she went, but... she said she saw a group of men. Canines, in strange clothing."

"Are you sure they weren't hyenas?" Ahsan asks.

She shakes her head. "I don't know, but she insisted the ones she saw were not clan hunters. She said they were dressed strange, and didn't look like any men she'd ever seen before. Their ears were turned over."

"Turned over?" I repeat uncertainly.

"Northerners," Ahsan says, suddenly. "Men from the Dog Lord lands. They look like jackals and wolves sometimes, but different. And they have weapons—can I see her wound?"

Dela nods sagely, and gingerly reaches forward, removing the compress. The moment the herb-soaked bandage is removed from her matted fur, I suck in a breath. And Ahsan wilts.

"I've seen that kind of wound before," I say darkly. "Once before."

"It's from a powder weapon," Ahsan says, his voice gone thin. "The men from the north come and trade them for spices and drugs, sometimes."

"They're loud," I point out. "Very loud. Like thunder. Which tells us at least that she must have been attacked far off in the scrub lands. We would have heard it if they were any closer."

"That's something," Dela's muzzle twitches. "Although they could be upon us at any time. If she was able to make it back wounded, they could easily have us surrounded by now. And we still don't know why they're here."

"I think I do," Lavanya speaks up again, knitting her hands in her lap. We all go silent, and the lioness straightens her back, but keeps her eyes down. "I'm sorry, Dela Eden. I told others where this place was."

Dela gets a stern expression at that. "Who, child?" she asks, her voice reminding me of my mother's when I was being scolded.

"Another woman at the brothel," she says with a soft exhale. "She chose not to leave with us when we fled the place. She wanted to leave as badly as Davika, until they got her started on the Divine. She was afraid that if we fled somehow, we'd have no place to go. I just wanted to assure her I knew somewhere safe. I didn't tell her exactly where, just… that it was to the west."

The older lioness exhales slowly. "Our oasis is not entirely hidden away. It is known to some of the traders and travelers in this area. It wouldn't take a good hunter long to discern where you may have gone."

"I'm so sorry, Dela," Lavanya says, her body slumping over, head bowed. "She was a different woman before the drug. I thought she would leave with us, if we ever liberated ourselves."

"It doesn't matter how it happened," Dela says. "Were you not listening to me out there? Every person here is under the protection of my Pride."

"Will you fight, or flee?" I ask.

She gives me an offended glare.

"...right," I shrink back. "But, these weapons..."

"I know of them," she says. "I've met travelers who carry them. I've just never seen what they can do, before." She straightens her back, looking out towards the light streaming in from the one window in this room. "But no weapon makes the warrior. They aren't gods, just because they have these things. We know these grasslands, we know how to defend this place. They are strangers here."

"Let me fight beside you and your hunters," I press. "Even if we didn't lead them here, we're part of why they came."

"I know a little bit about the weapons," Ahsan says. "They used to test fire them in the back acre of the estate. I hated them, but... it was hard to ignore them." He looks to me. "I don't think they can fire them quickly. There would be a lot of time between shots, sometimes."

"Matron Sura seemed unable to make it fire twice in a row," I agree, remembering the courtyard. "Maybe they're hard to use."

"These men were foreigners, though," Lavanya points out. "If they're from the north, they'll know how to use their own weapons better than your Matron did."

"Mercenaries," Dela concludes, quietly. "They must not want you alive any more. They would have sent their own hunters if this was solely about collecting you."

"They have ample reason to be angry at us," I admit quietly.

"I'm certain there are hunters amidst them, regardless," she says. "We'll try to make sure we capture one alive, and find out what this is all about."

"What do you think their plan is?" I ask.

She shakes her head. "They won't attack us at night. The foreign-

ers know we can see better in the dark than they can. They'll probably come for us early in the morning, when our guards are tired."

"What can we do until then?" Ahsan asks, his voice trembling.

Dela looks to all of us, narrowing her eyes. "Sharpen your claws,"
she says quietly. "And try to rest. Tomorrow we will force the attack,
one way or another. They don't get to sit out there and terrorize my
Pride. This place is ours. We will fight for it."

Chapter 13

Dawn

When I became a father, something about my perception of the world shifted. The dangers, the pitfalls, the filth and crime around us, the destitute poverty we lived in—I'd stood strong in the face of all of it. I was proud of how resilient and fearless I could be. I was almost proud to be at the bottom, but knew that I'd survived it all. I could live my life covered in brick dust, battered and scuffed, beaten down by everything around me, including my family... and know that I was tough.

It was everything I'd once thought my father to be, and had aspired to. A proud laborer, with humble ambitions and an honest way of living. I had a few dark secrets, but I was still damned impressed with myself. Which I suppose meant I wasn't actually being all that humble.

But the thought of seeing my son have to endure this life scared the hell out of me. I never told Ishaya that. I held up the front I was supposed to, because it was the foundation of my entire life, and shaking it was too terrifying. I pretended, even after Amon had been born, that I was proud of being a kiln worker. That I was intent on carrying on the tradition into the next generation. Because the alternative, a life without any kind of security or way to feed ourselves, seemed so unfathomable. Ishaya wasn't wrong to want more for our son. She was just braver than I was.

Amon was so small. So fragile. He was born early, and for the first month, we were afraid we'd lose him. He wouldn't nurse regularly, he barely ever cried, and the medicine man we brought him to said he might be blind if he survived. His eyes were always a concern for us, even as he grew and we knew his vision was fine.

To imagine my small, quiet, gentle son being subjected to the kind of life I'd lived was absolutely terrifying. And suddenly, the world looked so much worse to me than it ever had before. I could work day and night and I'd never be able to give him enough to protect him from the simple, condemning fate he'd been born into—we were poor. We would always be poor. I'd missed my chance at education, and even if we lived threadbare and saved our coin, we'd never really be able to afford to give him the chances in life he deserved.

He was going to grow up to be like me. Even if I was better to him than my father had been to me, it wouldn't be enough. He would have to start working the kilns when he was old enough, just so we could feed him. He might want for more, but he'd inevitably go back to it time and again, because it's the only skill my family can pass down. We don't have the luxury of searching for more out of life—hunger gets the better of us all eventually, and we come back to the one kind of work that we know, strictly so we don't starve.

Many people in Mataa wear collars. Some of them are just more visible than others. Laborers are just as trapped in their lives as the servants I used to think were beneath me. Men like my father, and Chandan, are trapped by their addictions. Women are constantly trapped in marriages they had no choice in, and even the upper rungs, like the hyenas and lions, are trapped in a cycle of war that will never end so long as there is land to walk on.

I don't know where my son is now. I may never know. I just hope that someday, he knows what it means to be liberated from the forces that hold us down. If I could give him anything in the world, it would be freedom.

Raja, Ahsan and I join some of the lionesses in Dela's large hut later that night, to ready our weapons and drink a tea the medicine woman has cooked up for us. It's bitter and acidic, and I'm not really certain what it's meant to do except burn my throat. She insists it will fill our veins with fire, and make us fierce. Mostly, it makes me cough.

The mood is surprisingly calm and congenial. Dela's Pride, that is to say, her own group of huntresses, are all seasoned warriors. Many of them are from war-torn areas to the south where fighting for one's life is a daily struggle, and they're preparing for the morning like it's any other well-practiced ritual.

This is what my life is becoming. I'm an escaped servant. Until I'm either dead, or re-captured, I'll have to live knowing that I'm hunted.

Dela herself was probably hunted, at some point. By her Pride, or her husband, or whoever it was that she fled to this place to escape. Maybe she took the oasis from her husband or another Pride. It really doesn't matter how it is they came to live here—the fact is, they're surviving because they've made a family of others like themselves.

I lost my family, just like many of these women did. But, I've begun to rebuild something like it, in Ahsan... and I suppose Raja. Maybe in time, I could find more escaped servants, join forces and do as Dela's done. Claim some piece of land where we can all live, or live on the road in a band, moving from place to place so we're never cornered. Maybe there's life for us in our own country if we're willing to fight for it like she is.

The Eden Pride is nowhere near as well-equipped as the guards of the Sura clan were, but each woman has at least one well-kept weapon. Most of them use spears and bows, but two of them carry scimitars and Dela herself carries a shotel, much like mine. Hers looks better maintained and more menacing than mine, though. When I asked her about it a few weeks back, she told me she'd had it made for her by a traveling smith who comes through here now and again. She let me hold it and try it out on some dying palm stalks, and the difference was pretty striking. I'd thought the power of my swings was impaired mostly because of my lack of experience, but some of it is definitely owing to the weapon itself.

"You're a large man, Kadar," she tells me with a wry smile, reaching up to squeeze my bicep, like she's admiring fruit at a market. "You should use a larger weapon. Put your gods-given mass to use."

"I'm no lion," I chuckle. "But I have to admit, the shotel feels a little lackluster sometimes. Not that I have much experience to compare it to."

"You can use a spear tomorrow," she offers. "We have many."

"I'm not sure a fight like this is a good time to try a new weapon," I reason. "And anyway, considering our enemies are using ranged weapons, it might be best to rely on the element of surprise. I'll prowl better without something that long catching or dragging on anything."

"An experienced hand can glide through the grasses with a spear," she says. "But I see your point. Use what is most familiar to you, for now." She reaches forward to adjust my hand. "And turn your blade against the whetstone at a sharper angle."

She guides me for a few moments, long enough that I get the hang of it, and then simply watches me from her cross-legged seat. "Are you afraid?" she asks me, after a long companionable silence.

"Of?" I ask, not looking up.

"Death," she says simply.

I stop sharpening my blade and lean back, uncertain how to answer that at first. At length, I say, "I don't want to die, obviously. There's probably some fear there."

"Mmmm," she hums thoughtfully.

"Why do you ask?" I question, looking her in the eyes.

Her muzzle turns up in a slight smile. "Because I have never seen you fight before," she says. "But I have seen defiance in your eyes. That indomitable... outrage... is there, in each of my huntresses, as well. If you were a lioness, I would take you in. I would ask you to stay here in this place, and defend it."

"I'm nowhere near as experienced as a Pride woman," I chuckle. "You'll find that out tomorrow."

She shakes her head. "It does not matter. Skill with a weapon can be learned. The will to use it, and the ferocity to defend your right to breathe free air, cannot. Given the choice, most people would rather bow than fight to the death."

"Everyone's afraid to die on some level," I sigh. "I'm just not . . . I don't think it's death itself that terrifies me. It's the consequences of it."

"Death is the end of consequence," she smiles. "At least, for you. It is the ultimate freedom."

"That's exactly it," I murmur. "I'm afraid that I'll leave nothing behind. No trace I was even here, no legacy for the people I leave behind." I hang my head, tipping my ears back. "Except for the mistakes I've made. I've done nothing worthwhile with my life. So yeah, I'm afraid to die. I could die tomorrow, pointlessly, because I don't bring my blade up in time or I trip over a rock. I could accomplish nothing even in my final moments."

"You think you need to survive a fight to win it?" she asks, cryptically.

"Well..." I pause, uncertain if the question's even meant to be answered.

"Do you think anything I've done here," she gestures out towards the distant camp fires flickering in the village square beyond the hut door, "will end the wars in the south? Or protect other young children from being forced to marry, or bear children?"

"You're at least protecting the women here," I reason.

"One determined group of hunters could shatter all that," she says, slicing her hand through the air. "And I will have gathered all of these people here in one place, to be slaughtered like lambs. I could fall tomorrow, we all could. This place could be razed and conquered, re-taken by the clans or the lion Prides. It *will* be, some day."

I knit my brows. "How do you go on, knowing that?" I ask, bitterly. "I had a son once. The only way I could make peace with the world without living in terror was to turn my eyes away from his future. Not think about it. It all seemed so insurmountable."

"I hold my head high," she says, "by accepting that even though I can't see the light at the end of these dark days, someday, someone else will. Change comes about slowly, sometimes so slowly, we'll never see the victories we've won within our own lifetimes."

"That's comforting," I mutter.

"That doesn't mean the fight is not worth throwing ourselves into," she says with a calm passion. "This generation, perhaps even the next generation, may not be set free of these evils. But every step, every increment, every small gain we make now is our legacy to the generations to come. I know in my heart that someday, these terrible things we have been forced to endure will be a horror of the past. And part of that, a very small part of that, will be because of me. That's why I keep fighting."

"I'm sure you've given this speech to your girls before, but I don't know if that makes me feel any less helpless," I say with a wry smile. "How do you think that far ahead?"

"By looking to the past," she says, simply. "You know… a long time ago, half of the people in this country were slaves."

"Servitude is just slavery with a different name," I snuff.

"Is it?" She arches an eyebrow. "Slaves had no rights, at all. They could be starved, raped, beaten to death, murdered for sport."

"All of those things still happen," I point out.

"I know it's hard to see it, because you were part of it," she says, "but your life, for all of its pain and difficulty, is nowhere near as terrible as it could have been, centuries ago. The ancient people fought for this land against feral animals and unrelenting disease and droughts. They lived huddled in fear. They hadn't yet learned how to harness the rains and the monsoons to grow crops, they were entirely at the mercy of nature. Then there were the wars with Amuresca—the Dog Lords. And even then, in the midst of strife, we advanced. We learned things from them, and they from us. There were sweeping slave rebellions that joined the Dog Lords' forces, and we forged the treaty that ended slavery."

She points to my neck, "That collar around your neck may seem like it binds you, but what it stands for is a change. A change that took centuries, endless lives and blood spilled, and even now, the clans struggle to work around. Slavery was not sustainable. You cannot build a society on inequality and subjugation. People will fight and strain and push back against what they know in their hearts is wrong. Hundreds of thousands of those people died, to get us where we are now."

She reaches for me with her thin, aging paw and runs her thumb over the edge of my collar. "They died for this. So that you would have a chance. It is not a symbol of binding—it is a symbol of desperation. The clans' desperation. It is a last resort, to cling on to an aging labor system that they can barely uphold any more. They have laws, and contracts, and hunters, and they live in constant fear that the Amurescans will return if they violate their treaty."

I listen to her, considering her words. I'd never really taken the time to think about indentured servitude as a system, from the hyena clans' perspective. I suppose with all the laws and restrictions, and all the trouble it takes to enforce them, it's probably very difficult to uphold. It was hard not to think of them as our overlords, controlling every aspect of life in these lands... but the system that bound me was not of their making, it was the work-around for a treaty they'd been forced to sign with a foreign power. And that, I suppose, must have been a hard pill to swallow.

"We are living in an incredible time," Dela says. "This age will see the death throes of slavery. We have a chance to be a part of that, simply by being part of the fight. The world could be entirely changed by the time your son is your age."

"I'm afraid that I'll never find him again," I admit. "I'm afraid that somewhere, he's suffering. Without a father to shelter and love him."

"If he is," she says, "he has your indomitable spirit to see him through it. You can't protect him from all the pain in the world. But, you can fight it. Change it."

"Even in my most defiant moments," I sigh, looking down at the weapon in my hands, "I've never felt like I could change the world. For a long time, I couldn't even change my own situation."

"You are changing the world, simply by resisting," she says, her golden eyes drawing mine into her gaze and holding me there. "You are part of something larger. Whatever you give towards it, even if it's a death no one remembers in a grassy field... it is worth doing. Fighting a losing battle takes much more courage. Freedom is not enjoying a life that is already liberated. Do you know what freedom means?"

"I don't think I ever have," I murmur.

She narrows her eyes. "It means that whenever someone tries to put you beneath their heel... you say 'no.'"

Dawn comes slowly, in the scrub lands. The oasis is ringed by rolling dunes of patchy grass and sand, and the sky's begun to seep from black to blue before we actually see the first rays of light. But we don't need a warning from the sentries to know when the attack's begun.

The foreigners aren't hiding their presence. They can't, and they don't have to. Their silhouettes ring the oasis along the highest rolls in the land, keeping their distance at first. And for nearly an hour, their shots split the peace of this tranquil place, like a terrifying thunderstorm.

I stay hunkered down in the grasses with Lavanya, watching as occasionally, all around us, the grass and dirt tear up like lightning's struck it. Whenever we hear one of those cracks, I jump inside my skin, waiting for the errant shot that will hit us.

"What are they doing?" I ask with a jolt, as another patch near us explodes in a shower of grass and sand. The shots leave a deep gouge in the earth wherever they land, and seeing what they can do to earth makes me feel even worse, knowing what they must have done to Lochan's body. I can't even imagine the pain.

She shakes her head. "Keeping us pinned down, for one," she growls. "Other than that, I don't know. Maybe they're hoping to get lucky."

"They may have already, and we'd never know," I say, glancing out across the grassland without raising my head too much. "They've been firing for a while now, they could have hit one of the lionesses. They're bound to, eventually."

"Maybe this is just sport to them," she says angrily. "Are those things like bows? Can they run out of ammunition?"

"I don't know," I admit. "But Ahsan insisted they aren't magic, they're just very powerful weapons... so probably?"

"There," she says sharply, grabbing at my shoulder. I try to follow her line of sight through the grasses, and vaguely make out a few distant, bobbing dark blots that might be silhouettes, moving towards the edge of the field. They're either moving on all fours, or crouching as they move, because no creature other than a feral would be that short, otherwise.

"They're making their move," Lavanya says, her whiskers shivering with anticipation. "I hope Dela's seen them."

"I'm certain she has," I say, confidently.

"They're cutting through the footpath we thought they'd use," she says with a fanged smile. "The huntresses must be hiding well, I can't even see them and I know where they're supposed to be."

"They think we'll keep our attention on the men on the hill," I snort. "It's… a plan, I suppose. But I wouldn't have bet my life on it."

"Let's move closer."

I nod. "Stay low. They're still firing. Seems like they slowed down, though."

"Maybe they're finally running out," she says hopefully.

We cut our way through the field, towards where it seems like the attack will come to a head. The main footpath into the oasis cuts through the most uneven, rocky terrain and grass mounds, and seeing as walking through the other areas can trip and slow you down quite a lot, we guessed that for an attack they couldn't really conceal, the direct route would probably be their first choice.

Raja chose to be with the lionesses near the footpath, since he's better at prowling and concealing himself than I am. Also, the man's more than a little bloodthirsty, and he wouldn't take no for an answer. But considering what we're potentially up against, his ferocity might be just what the front line needs.

I chose to take the west field, since it's ringed by a sharp rock ridge farther out towards the dunes, and it was an unlikely attack angle for them… but it's an excellent place to corner them. The lionesses plan to push them my way once they clash, and Lavanya and I are to cut off their escape. I'd rather be out here with someone I know better, but Lavanya and I are, in Dela's words, at about the same level of combat experience. So we're not front-line material, we're just the crew that mops up the stragglers. Dela wants none of these men to escape and bring word to anyone else, and I can't blame her for that, cold-blooded though it might sound to cut down fleeing men.

Ahsan is in the interior, with a few of the other huntresses, guarding the women and children who can't fight. I know what's at stake if they get through us here.

Another shot whizzes past, clipping the grassland right in front of us and coming closer than any others have yet. We both stop dead in our tracks and hunch, knowing we've been seen. Unfortunately, that's when the shout goes up amongst the lionesses, and the attack begins.

"Damn it!" Lavanya snarls, raising her head just slightly. After a hesitant wave of her hand, I follow suit. We aren't that far from the footpath now, so we should be able to—

I'm dumbstruck when I finally get a look at our 'attackers.' The lionesses have made their move, springing upon the group that was making its way through the grassland… but they aren't what we thought. The people the women are wrestling down in the scrub grass, and pulling their spears out of, are… collared. And very poorly organized.

They're armed, but only with knives and shoddy spears, some of them with shields, and they're wearing frayed and stained clothing. Many of them look starved or sick, or both, and they're all wearing unchained manacles

It's a scene of pure chaos and confusion, the strange servants either fighting back ineffectively against the lionesses, or cowing, or trying to run. For our part, the lionesses seem just as confused, but determined to put the invaders down all the same.

And then all at once, the quiet grassland erupts into a cacophony of thunderous noise, and three of the lionesses are struck, crumpling where they stand.

"They baited us!" I hear Dela shout above the din, and then she tries to yell another command to her hunters, likely to scatter, but not before there's another volley from the ridge. Another lioness falls, and Dela herself staggers back, blood erupting from her shoulder in a spray. Then she falls beneath the grasses, either under her own control or because she can't stand anymore, I don't know.

Lavanya screams something in a southern dialect I don't know and springs past me before I can grab at her, making for Dela. The two volleys that tore through her ranks were clearly from two different groups of gunners, but I heard many, many firearms going off at once each time, so I have to assume they've all fired by now. I take the chance that we'll have a brief reprieve and finally stand so I can get a better look at what's happening.

I can smell blood everywhere in the air, and the acrid stench of those weapons, bringing back a terrible ache in my gut from the last time I saw one of them used. I can actually see the men on the ridge, or at least some of them. They're moving in closer now, still just silhouettes, but I can make out at least that they're canine.

There are two lionesses on the ground in the footpath that I can see, and I know at least two more were struck. That's half their hunting party that's out here, and even if they're not all dead they're not going to be able to get back to their feet and fight.

There are twice as many bodies of the servants that were sent in… whoever they were. Most are run through by spears, but some of them look like they were caught in the hail of fire, same as the lionesses. I'm not even certain if I should pity them, because we never got a chance to find out who they were.

"Sacrificial lambs," a familiar, deep voice rumbles from nearby, and suddenly I'm being grabbed at by my belt and yanked back down into cover. Another crack sounds across the clearing, this one clearly coming from near the edge of the grassland. It doesn't come anywhere near as close as the others to hitting me, though.

"Some of them have two of those weapons," Raja says in a growling tone. "I caught sight of a few of the ones coming closer, before Dela ordered us back into the brush."

"Is she alright?" I ask in a sharp whisper.

"Bleeding a lot, last I saw," he says. "Other than that, I don't know."

"Shit," I growl, my knuckles tensing around the hilt of my shotel.

Raja cranes his neck up just enough to peer to the ridge, then flattens his ears. "They're lining up again, and some of them are breaking off."

"They're going to make a real push down the path this time, and take out anyone who tries to get in their way," I guess, quietly. "We should—"

I'm interrupted by another sound piercing the night air, but this one isn't a weapon… it's a howl. A strange, baying howl unlike one I've ever heard from a wolf before. And it's coming from the other side of the oasis. A moment later, it's returned by one of the men in the group of attackers on our side, and then there are muffled voices from his group, in a language I can't understand.

"It's a two-pronged attack," I snarl, whirling around to look towards the oasis. "Gods, there are only a few huntresses on that side."

"And they're probably on their way here to Dela, since she sounded the attack," Raja says grimly.

"You need to go to them," I say quickly, "reinforce them. You're the only one fast enough."

He looks past me, uncertainly. "They're coming from this side, too. And the lionesses are scattered—"

"Run!" I snap, gripping my shotel tightly and rising onto my haunches. "If they get into the interior they can take hostages! We'll hold the footpath."

He narrows his sky blue eyes at that and gives a curt nod, then turns on his heel and with a coiled spring of his lean, strong body, he takes off into the grasses. I've seen cheetahs run before, but it still always leaves me awestruck.

Someone fires off a shot at him and misses by a mile, cutting through the grasses in his wake. That shot sounded *incredibly* close, and my suspicion is confirmed when I turn to see the first of the attackers wading through the edge of the grassland near the start of the footpath. There's a large group of them, probably a dozen in all that have broken off from the line of gunmen on the ridge. The light's just starting to edge its way over the dunes and spill its golden hue down towards the oasis, and in it I catch sight of the foreigners for the first time.

What the lioness said is true. They look vaguely like canines, but with strange muzzles and ears, and very foreign clothing. Most of them are armed with blades in addition to the firearms they've been using, and they have them out as they cut their way through the grasslands towards our settlement. There are several hyenas with them as well, although it's impossible to tell if they're Sura guards yet.

There are too many of them coming, and more on the hill. And they're obviously soldiers for hire. Whatever experience they have, it's probably more than mine. It's the plantation all over again, except this time, there are no doors to lock them behind, and I have no Guard Master to fight beside.

I look across the grasses from my position and see several of the lionesses hunkered down, readying themselves to spring, including Lavanya. I know what they're feeling. We have to make a stand here, but there's no way we're getting through this without most of us falling to the mercenaries' blades, or failing that, the men on the hill.

But it doesn't matter. We have to fight.

I know my chances of surprising anyone are slim now that the grass is lit up. My dark armor gives me away. But the lionesses still have a chance, and I can give them more of one if I make an obvious threat of myself.

I stalk forward, trying to feed on my fear, since I know I can't just stop feeling it somehow. If there is such a thing as being 'fearless', I've never known it. I try to remember what Dela said to me. It's hard to find any comfort in the thought that dying here in this field somehow serves some greater purpose, but there's a more immediate purpose right at my back… and that's the community we're all pledged to protect.

And the hyena I'm afraid to admit I love.

Except I did just admit it to myself, I realize. And that thought emboldens me. If I can finally come to terms with it in my mind, maybe I'll have the nerve to say it to him, eventually. It's just one more reason to survive this, somehow.

One of the men sees me and shouts to the others with him. Their thin blades glint in the brimming sunlight. On the ridge, I can tell the men in reserve are readying those weapons again. I'll have to take the chance that they won't fire into combat with their own men amongst us.

I wait until they're just within range of the lionesses, whom I'm certain they're expecting judging by how cautiously they're cutting their way through the foot path. Two very large foreigners lead the pack, with pushed-in muzzles and thick jowls, and black fur that must bake in the sun during the day. They aren't wearing armor at all, but they both have those thin swords out. One of them is holding a small firearm in one hand, beginning to train it on me.

I wait until he's raised it, just as Matron Sura did, and then I dash as fast as I can back into the grasses and cut a sharp right away from where I'd been standing. I hear the crack of thunder, but feel no pain. So he either missed, or that tea is working and I'm invincible. Either way, I charge.

The man meets me with a readied sword, blocking my first wild swing. Using my weapon's shape to its best advantage, I try to hook his blade and yank it away from him, but he turns his sword into the twist of my arm and easily frees it from me. And then the other man up front with him, who looks similar enough that they may be kin, tries to move in and flank me from behind. I whirl on him and slice my shotel through the air in a wide arc, letting him know he hasn't gone unnoticed.

The remaining lionesses spring from the grasses then and one of them manages to catch the man at my back off-guard, driving a spear into his torso. The other man I'm fighting bellows something in their language, and his group begins to mob around us. I can see Lavanya clash with one of the hyenas amongst the mercenaries on my left side, standing her ground even as her spear splinters from a blocked scimitar swing. Unlike the others, she's not moving, and I soon see why. Dela is kneeling behind her, her right side covered in blood and her arm hanging limply, gripping her shotel in the other.

I can't get past this big canine's guard. He blocks each of my swings with a practiced ease, waiting for his opportunity. And eventually, he finds it.

He moves his sword under my guard with a quick stab, leveling it for my side under my armpit, where my armor's at its weakest. I curse and try to twist away, but not in time. Pain lances through my body as he catches me in the ribs, how deep I don't know, but the armor took some of it. I try to step back, only to find they've begun to surround us. Blood leaks down the inside of my armor, and I hear one of the lionesses scream as two of the men mob up on her.

They say you see the ones you love and the life you've lived flash before your eyes before you die. I don't know if that's true, but I definitely think of my son in that moment. And, selfish though it may sound, the one thing going through my mind is—I'd been hoping that at least if I died fighting for freedom, he'd know.

Surrounded though I am, the men are still giving me a wide berth, likely because of my inexperience. I try to keep my swings wild and unpredictable, and that's seemed to have them all off-guard. But the loose group of men surrounding us doesn't entirely block my view of the grassland beyond, and that's why I see what's coming before they do.

It looks for all the world like the sands themselves are rising up, dead grasses and earth falling away, as this shape looms up behind the mercenaries and begins to advance on their back ranks. A cowl of earth and clay pulls back slowly as it raises its arms and the sands fall away, revealing a blood red muzzle. The arms shift out from under the cloak, holding blades that flicker in the sun as they catch it. The mercenary closest to the terrifying visage realizes too late that it's upon him, turning his head and shifting as though he intends to bring up his sword.

He never gets the chance. The figure brings its first scimitar down cleanly across his neck, and severs it nearly completely, his body stiffening and crumpling in place almost after the fact, as though he doesn't yet realize he's dead. And then it shoves past another man into their back ranks, and steel shrieks as it clashes into the next opponent.

The foreigner I'm fighting turns in shock, shouting at his men.

I seize the opportunity, gripping my shotel hard and punching it upwards like one would a short sword. It's not strictly meant for it, but it's still sharp enough to do the trick… especially when the man's bared his throat to me like he has.

I ram it up underneath his chin and his shout turns into a gurgle, which I cut off seconds later by twisting the hook at the tip of my blade and yanking it back out through. He falls away from me, and suddenly the men surrounding me are giving me even more space.

I snarl, leaping at another one of them, catching mostly air in my first swing. The second, he's forced to parry. I can hear the screams and shouts of confusion from the outer edge of the mob, and see the flurry of melee surrounding the cloaked figure who came to our aid. The first thing I can think of is that it must be Lochan, somehow. As impossible as I know that is. I saw Anala behead him.

Ahsan's words come back to me then, in a big way.

"Priestess!" I scream over the roar of combat, shoving back the smaller canine I'm locked with. These foreigners are smaller than me for the most part, so at the very least I can usually overpower them when we lock blades.

The figure cuts down another man in her way, and tears free her earth-caked hood. Her face is painted in red clay and spattered with blood from the two—no, three now—men she's killed, but I'm certain I'm right. She gives a baying scream and drives down another of the mercenaries, who literally stumbles over the tangled grasses in his frantic hurry to escape her.

"Your left!" she shouts at me, and I hurriedly bring my blade up just in time, as one of the hyenas seizes on my distraction to find an opening. I actually manage to dodge him rather than block him, which is good considering he's using a large talwar, which he could probably easily work past my guard. I lunge in and swing at him, but he recovers fast and he has far more reach than I do with my small weapon, so I'm soon on the defensive again.

He gives a cackling shriek suddenly and buckles a bit, grabbing at his thigh and pulling out a now blood-tipped spear. I search the field trying to figure out where it came from, then catch sight of Lavanya, now unarmed. I begin to call out to her, but the hyena in front of me isn't taking the injury lying down. Snarling, he advances on me again, shouting a, "Take care of that one!" to one of the other men near him. I actually understand him, because he speaks in Huudari.

I try to make my way to her, but I'm desperately fending off another of the hyena's brutal attacks, my wrist twisting painfully as I block the enormous weapon. My shotel is nearly torn from my hand with the force of the blow, but I hold on for dear life, even as something inside me feels like it's tearing.

"Moza!" the Priestess Anala shouts, catching the attention of my opponent, whose muzzle twists into a snarl when he sees her. He abandons his attack on me to duck one of her swings and comes up frothing with one of his own, his wide blade cutting an arc of grass around him.

"Traitor!" he roars at her.

"Coward!" she screams right back, fangs bared. "Hiding behind pistols and slaves!"

"They'll gut you and leave you for the vultures!" he promises, clamping a hand over his leg as blood streams down it. I see an opening when he turns to charge for her again. I take a run for him, dropping to skid down at his feet under his guard. The sands here are loose enough that I just barely make it, ignoring the pain in my wrist and hooking my weapon around his weakened leg.

I pull away flesh and blood with a jerk of my shotel, and it's not much, but it's enough on an already injured leg. He buckles on one side and Anala drives her scimitar into his gut, armor be-damned.

I whirl my head around in fear for Lavanya, but by the time I've caught sight of her again she's got another spear in her hands and is easily keeping one of the more skittish mercenaries at bay. It's then I remember that Dela also had a spear, and she probably had it in the brush nearby.

"Your girls can handle the remnants," Anala's voice says impatiently, as she steps up beside me. She's holding something out to me. "We need to get to the ridge, before they open fire again."

I look down at the scimitar in her hands, held out to me hilt-first. The hand-grip is wrapped in red cloth that looks achingly familiar, and I remember the distinctive pommel.

I take it from her with an acidic glare, which she returns with a far more even-tempered stare. "Save it for them," she says. "We're not done here."

We take to the hill as the lionesses chase down the few remaining mercenaries, who at this point are mostly trying to escape. Shots begin to sound as we prowl our way up the rocky rise to the slightly elevated ground that overlooks the grasslands. You'd never think, walking over this beautiful terrain, that something as simple as a four-foot lift in the earth and a few rocks could make for such a deadly area for our enemies to use. But the Dog Lords have always been good at making war.

Anala moves with a grace I can't match, even though she's also wearing leather armor and her fur's covered in crumbling earth and clay. But by the time the gunmen see me, it's really too late for them. None of them have blades out when we arrive, and even outnumbered four-to-one, Anala barely needs my help.

The last man manages to raise a loaded pistol while she's locked swords with him, and I have a moment where I realize I could simply do… nothing. She hasn't seen that he had a smaller firearm on him yet—most of the men up here had longer ones which they abandoned when we showed up. I could stand back and watch him put the thing to her midsection and fire, and be spared a very difficult decision later.

But I can't. Even after what she did at the plantation, I can't shake the memory of how terrible Lochan's injury was. The agony I saw in his face as he was dying. No one deserves to die that way, not even one of our enemies.

And I'm not even sure she's that anymore.

I've got the scimitar at my side, but I've also still got my shotel. I lunge in with the weapon and briefly see alarm on Anala's face as I wedge it between them, but then I jerk the hook around the pistol in his hand and turn it. I'm not sure if it's a last-ditch effort to hit someone or if he just reacts, but it goes off, deafening us all and burning my nose with that acrid stench from the weapon, and the smell of singed fur. Mine. He just barely missed me.

She puts him down a second later with one swift, decisive chop to the neck. I step back, my ears ringing, my whole body shaking. Everything goes incredibly quiet, or at least it seems that way in comparison to the frenzy of battle. In the distance, I can hear the lionesses roaring, and judging by the return calls from the other side of the oasis, whatever attack took place there has been put down as well. It was probably only ever meant to split our forces... the only real path of attack that could have worked was the one we knew they'd use. The footpath.

It's over, I realize with an intense wave of relief. They never made it into the oasis. Ahsan is safe.

And I'm alive.

That, more than anything, is hard to believe. I shouldn't be standing here. I'm no warrior. I'm a poorly-equipped laborer with little to no combat experience, save the occasional fistfight over the years. But I've survived a revolt, breaking into a clan manor, fleeing into the desert and now fighting a well-armed group of hunters and mercenaries. The odds that I would have come through all of this breathing seem so slim… yet here I stand.

So when I raise my weapon to the warrior priestess beside me, I'm less afraid than I've been in a long time. She gives me a long, even stare, the blood spray across her face breaking up the caked clay into choppy patches. She's sustained a number of small injuries herself, torn places in her leather and hide alike, and I can't know what the extent of them are beneath all the red. Which is probably one of the points of it, in retrospect.

Yet still, I advance on her.

"What are you doing here?" I demand of Anala, putting as much power as I can into my voice. I raise the scimitar in her direction, the very weapon she gave me.

Lochan's weapon.

She slowly lifts a hand and points to the sword. "I came to bring you that."

"You're the one who killed him!" I snap. "You work for the Sura clan!"

"Not any longer," she states, lifting her muzzle defiantly. "They were not worthy of my blade any more. Perhaps they never were." Her ears fall for a moment and she drops her jaw, blowing out a long sigh through her nose. "And I didn't kill your Guard Master. Not as I should have. Ours would have been a beautiful battle, were it not for the Matron's interference. That man had a warrior's soul. He never showed it. We worked together for years, and I had no idea. I would have challenged him long ago if I'd known… but I doubt he would have given me his best, as he did in that courtyard, unless he was fighting for you."

"He wasn't fighting for me," I murmur.

"I slew him because he asked me to," she says, her words cutting deep into me. Because I think on some level, I knew. "He wanted to die by the blade... not the agony he was facing."

"I'm not the one you need to answer to for what you did," I say stonily. "But you're coming with me right now, to answer a whole lot of other questions."

Her muzzle splits into a crooked grin. "A threat? You've gotten bold, jackal. Do you think you could take me if I didn't allow it?"

"Probably not," I admit. "But I doubt you'd still be here if you thought you could flee through the desert on your own. You came with those men, didn't you? And their supplies and horses, I'd wager. Which I guarantee you, the lionesses will find before you can get to them."

Her grin doesn't disappear, but it levels out somewhat, as understanding passes between the two of us. "Very good, jackal," she admits.

"It's Kadar," I say firmly.

"Kadar," she nods. "I did not come here to fight you. But I'll also not be butchered, so do not give me reason to defend myself."

"You're severely outnumbered," I point out.

"Do you want to find out how many of you I could take down before I'm overwhelmed?"

"No," I sigh. "But it's going to be hard to convince him not to want you dead."

"We *all* would have gotten out alive if it weren't for her!" Ahsan screams, the ferocity in his words and the growl in his voice reminding me of that night, of the creature he briefly became. I'm honestly scared he might attack her, so I put myself between the two of them, wary of her promise about defending herself. None of us have been able to separate her from her weapon yet, and I've warned quite a few of the lionesses against trying.

"The Guard Master himself asked me to end his life," she says calmly. "He was suffering. I took several oaths in my service to Anala, and one of them was to give mercy to the mortally wounded."

"He could have survived!" he cries, shaking his head vehemently.

"Ahsan..." I sigh, reaching out for his shoulder.

He throws off my hand. "She's not a healer, none of us are!"

There have been tears in his eyes since she arrived in the oasis. I know where his mind is, and it isn't here in the present. "We could have *tried!*" His voice goes weak on the last word, and he drags a breath through his wet nose, squeezing his eyes shut.

I'm less concerned now that he'll get violent, so I try again to touch him. This time I'm not rebuked. He allows me in close and seems to wilt, slumping against my shoulder and pushing his muzzle into my collarbone. I tug him in against my chest, heedless of the injury to my ribs. He notices it once he's against me though, when some of my blood rubs off on his chest fur.

His eyes widen and he pulls back quickly, looking down at the wound. "Kadar," he swallows back a sob, "wh—"

"I'm fine," I insist. "It's not deep."

"That actually looks fairly serious," the Priestess speaks up.

"I'm *fine,*" I reiterate in a growl.

"You need to be careful with deeper punctures," she argues, tipping her ears back. "It could become infected."

"I don't need *your* advice," I snap, still holding Ahsan close to me. He was *just* starting to calm down.

"Maybe you should listen to the woman, Kadar," Lavanya speaks up, from where she's crouching beside Dela and two of the other injured lionesses. We've cleared out the village square save the warriors and a few of the essential people, like the medicine woman. Dela doesn't want our 'prisoner' anywhere near the non-combatants and children. "Seems like she might know a bit more about swordplay than you do," she says with an arched eyebrow.

"Which begs the question why we're not killing her where she stands," Raja hisses, voicing his opinion about murdering Anala for about the fifth time since we brought her in. He sustained a pretty nasty gash mark across his chest, taking on the few mercenaries who'd been trying to sneak in the back, and I have a suspicion he's not as good at handling pain as I am, because he's been loud about it.

"All of you, quiet yourselves a moment," Dela speaks up, her voice frail with pain. Despite that, everyone falls silent as she slowly shifts up from where she's reclining on a straw mat. She's bandaged and the medicine woman's already seen to her, but her injury is major. She could lose the use of her arm if it doesn't heal properly.

She manages to sit upright, but that's all for now. It's enough for her to level her gold-eyed gaze at Anala, though.

"I was on the ground for most of that fight," she says regrettably. "But my huntresses tell me that this woman is the only reason we triumphed against those foreigners. It is certain at least that you turned the tide for us. Why?"

"Personal reasons," Anala replies, flatly. "I did not come here to spare you or your people. It was simply more efficient to fight beside you. There were too many of them for me to take alone."

"She serves the clan that organized this raid," I say, because I feel it bears saying.

"Served," she corrects me with a glare.

"Regardless," I say. "That means you traveled out here with them. You knew what their orders were. We lost a lot of lives out there because we didn't know about that bluff with the manacled servants they forced out into the field ahead of them."

"Those were fodder the foreigners picked up from one of the gladiator camps in the scrub lands," she says derisively. "They were actually free, once they bought them... they *chose* to sign on with the mercenaries for a chance at coin. The Amurescans put together legions of them sometimes, promising freedom and pay for service to the merc outfit."

"They sent them out there as a decoy, then fired on them," I say. "A plan I'm sure they weren't informed of."

"I take it you haven't met many Amur," Anala says dryly. "The whole of their people could be summed up with the words 'false promises.'"

"You're avoiding the point," I press. "If you knew what they were planning, you could have warned us. You could have attacked them sooner. Something."

"First off, I did *not* know their plan," she states. "I split from the raiding party two days ago and took up position in the grasslands."

Ahsan gives me a look. I reach over and stroke his mane, whispering, "I'll never doubt your nose again."

"I needed to make sure you were the ones from the plantation," she continues. "Although when I discovered that brothel once housed the Guard Master's kin, I knew it was likely you were the ones who attacked it. Also, Lord Sachsen's source had a good description of the jackal."

"Lord Sachsen?" Ahsan jolts at the mention of the man's name. I vaguely remember it from somewhere, but it's hard to put my finger on exactly where.

"He is determined to find you all," she says, her eyes narrowing. "As the Sura Clan's Spymaster, it's his duty. You wreaked havoc on their stronghold plantation, that's *extremely* embarrassing. If he doesn't get things cleaned up soon, the other clans will think the Sura weak. But his fervor goes beyond that. I think he has a personal interest in one of you."

"This is my fault," Ahsan slumps beside me, "Oh gods…"

My memory jogs, finally. "Oh, hell," I sigh. "Was he the asshole I punched in the garden?"

Ahsan nods, mutely.

"The one who wanted to buy you?" My hackles raise at the mere memory. I hated the idea before, but given the changes between he and I over the last month, it's especially sickening for me to think about it now.

"I'm not even certain if he wants you re-captured or dead," Anala says. "His orders to us were to bring you in alive if we *could*. I think he's under a lot of pressure from the clan, in addition to whatever his personal grievance with you is. He's doing what he does best—putting money towards handling a problem. He hired the mercenaries because he couldn't get together enough of the remaining clan hunters fast enough. I knew joining the raiding party was the only way I'd find my way to you." She gives a fanged smile at that. "And I knew you would fight like demons, as you did on the plantation. I was not disappointed."

"Why are you here?" Ahsan asks again, in a more demanding tone.

"You've become the center of a maelstrom," the Priestess replies, still vaguely smiling. "I joined the Sura clan's ranks because they are a large, powerful clan, with many enemies. But I went years there without seeing serious combat... until you all attacked the Manor. Were it not for the Matron's cowardly interference, I would have enjoyed one of the most difficult battles of my short life. I may have even *lost*."

The intensity and the... excitement... with which she makes that statement makes me feel extremely uncomfortable, like when you've suddenly realized the person you're talking to isn't entirely right in the head.

"She stole that from me," she says, her good humor dropping all at once. "I would have sought vengeance, but you butchered her before I had the chance." She doesn't sound the least bit upset when she says that, just vaguely disappointed. "So I have decided the cowardice and the disrespect they've shown Anala must be repaid by the clan as a whole."

More than a few ears go up at her statement, including Ahsan's. Raja is the one to speak up first, though. "Wait, you…" he leans forward from where he's sitting, "…you're going to take down the entire clan?"

"I'm no fool," she says, "and I'm no goddess. I am but one of her arms. Anala gives me strength, but she also gave me a mind. I know I cannot do it alone."

"You're insane," I state, flatly. "The plantation was *one* stronghold. They must have dozens, spread across the desert. Not to mention other clans they're allied with. We have enough trouble with them, without intentionally antagonizing them further."

"They'll never stop coming after you," she says darkly. "I saw the way you fought at the Manor. You're inexperienced, but focused and cunning," she says to me, then looks to Ahsan and flashes her canines. "And you are fierce. You fight like a feral, like the children of Bahadur. You've not realized your potential, and you never will if they hunt you down and silence your storm now. I want to see you rage. I want to help you fight them. I want the battle I was denied!"

"I want you all to leave."

The words are softly-spoken, but firm, and come from Dela Eden. All heads turn towards her. She sighs softly, pain in her every feature. "I am sorry, Kadar. Ahsan, Raja… you as well, little Lavanya." She looks to the lioness, whose ears tip back. "I almost never reject those in need, but… this goes beyond angry husbands and clan hunters. It is more than we can handle. Today made that abundantly clear."

"I understand," I tell her softly. "You've protected us long enough."

"If it were merely my hunters and I whose lives are at stake…" she trails off. "But, I must think of the others here. I lost nearly half of my Pride today," her voice is tinged with sadness. They're still bringing in all the bodies from the grassland. "We have done all we can for you. We fought, many fell, and we made a stand. But I cannot put my people at the center of your maelstrom. I urge you to continue your fight... but take it far away from here."

The clearing falls silent. I can tell by the look in her eyes that she came to this decision with a lot of difficulty. Knowing how she feels about fighting back against tyranny, I'm sure she feels terrible that she's unable to do more for us. But the people here need their defenders. They don't need a war.

"If we can just take a few rations," I ask, "we'll be gone by morning." She nods. "Of course."

I look to Anala. "And you can... join us, if you really wish to. Strictly because I want to be certain you leave here. I don't think we owe each other anything at this point. Let's part on neutral terms, while we're still all alive to do so."

"I know which stronghold they've hidden him away in," Anala says, lifting her muzzle and sweeping her eyes across us.

I pause, and feel Ahsan stiffen from beside me, and Raja stir from my left. I feel a wave of bad nostalgia wash over me, the memories from the plantation fresh enough to chill me, even now. Still, I ask, "Who?"

"The Sura Clan's Liberator," she says. "He is who you were looking for in the Manor, wasn't he?"

She's partially right, but I don't want to tell her that. Unfortunately, Raja has no stopper on his mouth. "Where the hell is he?" he demands, standing up and bristling.

She puts up a hand. "Before you try to beat it out of me, consider what you'd be losing."

"I'm not frightened of you," Raja sneers.

"An ally, fool," she replies evenly. "Is your rage more important to you than your freedom? Ask yourself: what is it you want most in the world right now? How hard would you be willing to fight for it? Do you really want to give up on your only chance?"

"You don't care about our freedom," Ahsan says. "You're just a fanatic."

Her eyes find mine at that, and bore into me. "What about you, Jackal?" she asks. "What is most important to you? What do you wish to do with your life now that it is yours to direct?"

My breath hitches, and I know the answer at once.

"I want to find my son," I say. "And if he's been sold into this life… I want to cut the collar from his neck. No matter what it takes."

About the Author

Rukis lives on a farm, where she spends most of her time working on art, caring for her animals, and hanging out doing tabletop gaming with her friends. She is a huge fan of old school D&D, White Wolf, and Warhammer, as well as studying and collecting exotic fish (Cichlids, mostly) and drinking a lot of Dr. Pepper. Her menagerie includes a rabbit, some fish, two wonderful dogs, and a whole mess of chickens.

She is the author of *Heretic* and the *Off the Beaten Path* trilogy, which also take place in the world of *Red Lantern*.

About the Publisher

We are a small press publisher serving the niche market that is furry fiction. We sell furry-themed books and comics published by us and most major publishers in the community. If you can't get to a furry convention where we are selling in the dealers room, visit our online stores: FurPlanet.com for print books and BadDogBooks.com for eBooks.